20

MW01025487

Zeineb,

You're one of the smartest, strongest women I know and I'm so glad I have your influence in my life. I know you'll do great things and I wish nothing but the best for your life after highschool!!

[illegible signature]

Don't Hold Your Breath

Book 1: The Pessimistic Series

Morgan Fields

RAINGATOR
PRESS

Don't Hold Your Breath

2014 Raingator Press Trade Paperback

This book is a work of fiction. Names, characters, places and incidents are products of the author's imagination or are used fictitiously. Any resemblance to actual persons, living or dead, or to actual places or events is entirely coincidental.

ISBN 978-0-9829920-4-3

ISBN/SKU 098292041

Library of Congress Control Number: 2014943397

1. Pre-teen – Fiction. 2. Young adult - Fiction. 3. Adventure – Fiction. 4. Thrillers/Suspense – Fiction. 5. Mystery – Fiction. 6. Ghosts – Fiction. 7. Time Travel – Science Fiction. 8. Fantasy/Paranormal – Fiction. 9. Girl's Friendships – Fiction.

I. Title.

First Edition

Published in the United States by Raingator Press, Abiquiu, New Mexico. Raingator Press and colophon are registered trademarks.

To Meredith Chase,

Trescege Ramirez-Diaz,

Zoe Venters-Tsai,

and Randall Fields

ACKNOWLEDGEMENTS

First of all, I'd like to acknowledge my family for being supportive, especially my dad and my Aunt Jackie for constantly wondering about the book and helping out. In no particular order, thank you Flynn Gilmore, Ce'Mari Sherrod, Meredith Chase, and Trescege Ramirez-Diaz for supporting me, I'd especially like to point the authors that inspired me: John Green, Veronica Roth, Suzanne Collins, Ransom Riggs, Rachel Caine, and Christina Farley are just a few of the many. Of course, thanks to the people who gave me my flash drive to begin writing - my grandparents. I would also like to point out my gecko, Squirmy, who stars as Fessed Big Tail in the book, and my very first personal pet, although that has nothing to do with anything.

ABOUT THE AUTHOR

Morgan Fields was born on December 27th, 2001 and lives in Seattle, Washington with her dogs, gecko, cat, brother, and switches days between her mom and dad's house. For college, she wants to go to New York University or École Nationale Vétérinaire d'Alfort. In her spare time, she learns French, plays piano, procrastinates, runs movie marathons, reads, and of course, writes. She has yet to complete middle school. This is her first published novel.

Foreword from a Very-Surprised Old Publisher

Morgan Fields wrote this amazing novel when she was 10 years old. Then entitled ***Un Peu Non Meurs*** (in fractured French) it translated as: ***A Few Don't Die***, the title I still prefer, but as you will see, this is totally her book.

On first receiving the manuscript from her father (my son's old college roommate), I had written her this:

"Morgan:

"You are a natural writer with an excellent ear for dialogue. That is a great gift. And you capture a nice scene. Sometimes your scenes flow with a natural rhythm. Sometimes they jump around with staccato non sequiturs. All of that can be just fine. Un Peu Non Meurs is surreal and funny, a stream of consciousness that leaps from surprisingly mature observations to child-like absurdity. Your style is endearingly non-self-conscious as you plunge boldly into the tale. Great artists have labored to achieve the voices that you come by naturally. James Joyce might envy your ear." (Yes, I actually wrote that, feeling sure that she would look up "non sequiturs," "surreal" and "James Joyce," as well as "stream of consciousness.")

"I look forward to publishing a book of yours as you continue to write, mature and develop.

"That's the good news. Now comes the fine print.

"As you already know this is a first draft of a novel that still needs editing. It is not yet ready to be published."

I followed this with three pages of advice and tips on writing, and told her that I didn't read fantasy novels, but I knew they were big with her age group and that we would certainly buy and publish one if we thought we could sell it.

I copied the Email to her dad and then wrote him a separate note, promising to copy him on all of our correspondence, and added: ***"She is so precocious I may have been a little ahead of her with my reply, which is why I urged her to print the letter and look at it from time to time. I forget that she is still a little girl."***

So Morgan set to work editing. The first edits she sent me were little improved; she was still learning many basics of English grammar and punctuation. Soon she turned 11 and spent that year writing the next two books and trying to edit this first book with another 11-year-old friend.

The friend convinced her that titling the book in French was a mistake, so she re-titled it ***Don't Hold Your Breath***. I told her that was a loss because an English-language "new novel" by a 10-year-old American girl, bearing a title in fractured French would surely find an on-line cult-following in France. But I let her run with it, and promised her a $100 advance on her royalties if she sent me a book I could print.

The cover design is also totally hers. If she really wanted a swan, I suggested, it should at least be a black swan. Not only her heroine, Amy Rae, but even more so the baby sister in the story, are both black swans (as is Morgan herself, the 10-year-old author of a hard-boiled, naïve, 280-page pseudo-realistic fantasy novel). But wondering what a really creative child author might produce if she were freed of adult nannying, I told our designer to try it her way, typeface, color and all. He did. She loves it. It's different.

Morgan did get some help with punctuation and spelling from a teacher and a school librarian, but neither got all the way through it. Nor has this hop-skipping adventure had much advice on context and contiguity. Her grandmother helped her format it. I had an editor sweep up some of the remaining "grammaticals," (leaving a few that brought smiles) but otherwise we left the text as she wrote it, a raw and un-perfumed tale.

So here is the dream-book of a 10-year old author, with a strange title chosen when she was 11, and a cover designed by her more mature, 12-year-old self. Just dive in.

And a note: *Unlike her assertive nine-and-a half year old heroine, Morgan Fields is a bright and sunny pre-teen girl who is serious about her school work. She is also deeply into her friends and animals.*

Her parents can make her available for limited interviews by accredited media. Contact Jim Horne Minter, Raingator Press. Write to: theminter@hotmail.com.

Don't Hold Your Breath

Every deceased friend is a magnet drawing us to another world.

- *Eliza Cook*

PROLOGUE

Everything in fairy tales came true. I didn't imagine this possibility, but there it was. Had people known about this? Why wasn't it on the news, years and years ago? I never thought it was true, and I definitely didn't think I would be the one experiencing it.

Hadn't enough happened? Finding out someone I loved and would trust with my life was just a fake? Wasn't real? And someone who seemed completely ordinary at first was really someone much more horrid than could be imagined?

Some people say that being in a fairy tale would be great and they'd always find a happy ending but, unfortunately, that's not always the case. It may be a dark secret, something that if shared would put you in a mental institution or maybe get you killed if things go to the extremes. That's what happened to me.

Now, let's say you ached to get away from that person, to have something real in your life, but that one little experience of reality hurt you. Badly.

Let's say a killer was on the loose, and you just happened to be in the same town while the killer is on a spree. If the killer came up to you and said, 'Give me your car or else,' and you refused, saying, 'or else what?' that would be pretty stupid of you. Now, some of you are filled with curiosity, but as they say, curiosity killed the cat, and it did. Everybody's happier when no questions are asked.

So if you ever come to my situation, when nightmares becomes reality, don't run from it, don't hide. Don't spare your life. Cooperate with it, and there will be a very slight chance of you living. Very slight.

One day, I decided to run away from all of the fantasy. I was too confused. Never, ever run away. That will only lead you on to more fantasy. When nightmares becomes reality, don't run, don't try to hide. Try to cooperate. Become what they want you to become.

When I got home, somebody new was there. She wasn't fantasy. As solid as a rock, but she was much worse. She wasn't a dragon or an evil prince or a mad scientist.

Her job was to find someone to kill, and I was in her path.

So when nightmares becomes reality, don't run from it, don't hide. Cooperate with it.

And don't hold your breath.

Part One:

Until Then

Chapter One – Pain

My fingers swept over the black and white keys on the piano. I closed my eyes and listened.

I couldn't believe it was me playing Swan Lake. "Okay, that's great! I'll see you next week?" my piano teacher interrupted my trance.

I flinched and looked up at her from the piano. I muttered something unintelligible like a *'yeah'* and walked out of the hall of arts which was a place that was literally just a hall. I quietly walked home in the darkness with the city lighting up about a fourth of a mile away. I stepped into our apartment and opened the creaky door.

"Amy, you're just in time. The doors lock after nine if you don't have the key," our desk clerk, Faith, said.

"Yeah, I know," I muttered and stomped upstairs to my room.

"Hon', you need to take a bath. Look at you!" Mom said as I threw my stuff onto the couch. "So what'd you learn today?" Mom tried to make small talk. I ignored her. What was the point of talking about something so useless?

When I looked up at the ceiling, under the bathtub water, I knew something was wrong. Why hadn't Poch come back from his business trip? It had been almost a month, and he said two weeks at most he'd be gone. I burst out of the silent water in the little bathtub. My eyes ached from opening them under water. I got out of the tub and got a towel to dry myself off.

On my way back to the bedroom, my cell phone started to ring. I quickly turned off the radio. I didn't bother looking at the caller ID. "Hello?" I said glumly into the receiver. I didn't feel like talking today.

"Hello, this is Martha Jones, may I speak to Amelia Johnson, Jay Johnson, or Nicole Shea-Johnson?" a female voice asked.

"Yeah, this is Amelia, what's the matter?" The woman sounded worried. Something bad must have happened.

"Amelia, your father has been in a car accident. He has died. I'm so sorry for you. I hope you don't have too many troubles. After all, it can't be that bad, can it?" It took me a minute to understand. I've always called dad Poch so at first nothing registered. Then I got it.

I was already dealing with Mom cheating on Poch. Some low life named Terence, bringing his kids to our apartment to stay while Poch was out of town. *Terence.* I had learned to shudder at his name.

"Mom!" I yelled and raced downstairs, astonished.

"What is it sweetie?" she asked. She always had one of those smiles on her face, where you can't tell if it's a smile or a frown.

"I just got a call," I began but she interrupted me.

"Honey, what did I say about answering those calls? And no, we aren't going to get a free iPad," she snapped, busily clattering things around for a late dinner.

"It's not that," I whined. *Why did everybody think I wanted stuff?* "Martha Jones just called. Poch just died in a car crash."

"Oh, yeah, sweetie I was going to tell you, but I thought it'd break your heart. I know that everything isn't going so well with you in school, and I didn't want to bring it up and make it worse. You know, with me, divorcing your dad," she said.

"You, cheating on him," I pitched in.

"Shut up!" she snapped with an intense glare and an oh-no-you-don't look. I gave her an icy glare in return.

I ran up to my room and took out my little red cell phone. I pressed a button to speed dial my brother. It rang four times and went to voice mail. "Jay, this is Amy," I started to cry. "J-Jay, something's happened to Poch," I stuttered. Mom came up and knocked on my door. It scared me so I dropped the phone. It shut off when it hit the floor.

I quickly swiped away the tears and sat on my bed. “Honey, I know it’s hard for you, since Daddy died, but things will be okay. And you need to go to bed. I have some very important guests coming over.” She smiled like she meant it and left. Were things already getting worse?

"Jay, Amelia, come down here!" Mom yelled the next day. We both raced down the stairs.

"We're moving,” she said, checking our expressions with great eagerness, expecting us to be upset.

"What? No! We can't move! This is the place I will remember Poch the best. We can't!" I wailed, my throat getting thick.

"Amy – Amelia,” Mom corrected herself in a serious tone. "That's why we're moving,” she smiled at her success to make at least one of us mad.

"Where to?" my brother asked.

"Tukwila, Washington,” Mom answered, picking the most unknown place in the world.

"Tukblagoobala what?" I asked, ruder than I intended.

"Tukwila, it's about twenty minutes away from Seattle,” she explained.

"No, what about Juno and Ashley and Hailey and, and, and, everybody else that you don’t care about?" I swallowed and wiped my eyes. Who would move from New York to Washington? Normal people don’t do that!

"You'll make new friends. Go pack. We're leaving tomorrow.”

That night went by in a breeze. Next thing I knew, we were at the airport boarding the plane. But it hit me that it was like Mom knew Poch would be gone. Who buys plane tickets the night before a flight?

Even worse, the house we moved into looked like it was just waiting for someone to go into it and then die a slow and painful death. "Mom, this house is stupid. I want to go back to New York with all of my friends," I complained.

"Why? This is a great house! It just sucks life out of you!" she squealed.

Normally, it's 'breath-taking,' not 'sucking the life out of you,' I thought.

Mom unlocked the door and everything, I mean *everything,* was covered in dust.

"Amy, go dust, I can barely breathe," Terence snapped.

I hadn't realized he'd come. "When did you get here?" I blurted. I'm normally on better behavior with him.

"I got here the same time you got here. I will *always* be here," he taunted, leaning into my face, breathing his stale breath into me.

"Shut up. Nobody likes you. I hope you die obese."

Mom had just walked in the room when I said that. "Amy – Amelia! Don't be rude. Terence is your father now," Mom said.

"No he's not. Check the blood relation," I muttered.

"I heard that. And yes. In that case a lot of your friends are parentless. Now dust. I can barely breathe in here," she ordered. Terence smiled.

"I kept telling her but she wouldn't do anything," he said in a sweet voice.

"Is it actually possible for you to shut up for a minute?" I asked him and ran up to my room. I don't know why I knew where it was, but I just went with it.

Mom came up into the room. "You shouldn't be mean to Terence like that. He's your father now. He doesn't deserve it," she said, sitting down onto the bed next to me, rubbing my leg.

"Maybe I don't deserve it. Maybe Poch didn't deserve it. Maybe everybody doesn't deserve anything. But there is one thing that someone does deserve. Terence deserves to get out of my life. No one else deserves anything. I can't think of anyone. Oh! Wait, I just did. Poch deserved to know. He should have. You never tell anybody anything!" I snapped and rolled over on my bed, having my back facing her.

"I only tell people things they absolutely need to hear," Mom whispered innocently like a child.

"No, Poch deserved to know," I grudged.

"Fine," she sighed. "He probably did. I would do anything for him not to know. Terence and I wanted all you four kids, but I knew Poch would without doubt take you and Jay. Let's get real. He's a lawyer. But doing that to him wasn't right. I know I shouldn't have..." She stopped and covered her mouth with both hands.

"What?" I asked, sitting up on the old springy bed. Had she really killed him?

"No, no, no. Don't say it like that. I didn't kill him," she whimpered, covering her ears with her hands.

"You did? Didn't you?" I asked, standing up, edging toward the door. I'm not going to be in the same room as a blood-red killer.

"Stop! Stop! Stop!" Mom ran downstairs, going outside.

Then, the worst thing imaginable happened. Walking slowly down the hall, Terence yelled "What did you do to her?" "What did you do to her?" he repeated. Terence pushed me down on the ground and I hit my head on a couple of boxes and dust bunnies. "What did you do to her?" he screamed with clenched teeth.

My head hurt. But his breath! Yuck!

Then he stomped on my wrist. There was a loud cracking sound coming from my arm. I heard screaming and realized it was me. Jay came down the hall, wondering what the scream was.

"What? " my brother asked, pushing Terence away, seeing me stunned on the ground.

"We've got to take you to the doctors," he muttered and looked at my right arm.

"But you don't have your driver's license," I pointed out as he took me down the stairs.

"It's good then that we blend in. Do you think a cop is gonna pull a random driver over and ask for their license?" Jay asked.

"No," I mumbled, embarrassed that I didn't think of that.

"You're small enough to fit under the seats. I'm not supposed to be driving with someone else in the car," Jay muttered.

"You're not supposed to drive at all," I whispered.

"But people won't notice! For cryin' out loud, Amy!" he shouted, frustrated with me like always.

"Humph," I glared at him with ice cold eyes.

"Just get into my bag."

"Why?"

"They'll wonder why you're with me. Now get in the bag," he explained and held out a duffle bag.

"Yes, master," I bowed down to him, but it hurt my arm so I stopped.

He moaned. "Just go."

When we got into the hospital, the lady at the desk gave us the stink eye while biting her lip. I dragged myself over to a chair.

"It's gonna be at least half an hour before you get a room," Jay told me after he talked to the strange woman. I groaned. Half an hour! That was thirty minutes! How was I supposed to keep my calm for that long?

Finally, the lady said in a sour tone, "You two punks – children's room is ready."

I just glared at her as we walked over to our room. My jaw dropped when I saw it.

"You have fun now!" she sneered sarcastically.

"What's your name?" I asked. Getting doctors mad was funny.

"Dr. Tepp!" she said proudly.

"No, first name?!" I said still glaring at her.

"No way, you little parasite! I mean, um, child," she hissed. I glared at her once again.

"Listen lady –" I began.

"Dr. Tepp," she growled.

"Lady," I confirmed with cold eyes. "When I was six, I wrestled a Rottweiler with a broken leg. All the dog was doing was going for my leg. I can easily take you down if you don't give me your name. Also, I have him," I glanced at Jay.

"You can't do anything to me, little girl. Especially with that broken arm of yours," she smiled, but not as sure of herself this time.

"Name!" This time, Jay demanded. He agreed that annoying doctors was funny.

"Oh, uh, um," she cleared her throat. "Emma," she said weakly.

"Better," Jay whispered. He was quiet after that.

"Enjoy your room," Emma murmured and walked out.

"Hey, lady," I yelled. She turned around quickly. "You're pretty," I grinned.

"Why thank you. But I still hate you." She patted her head and put a beret back in place.

"Yeah, you're pretty ugly," I finished. I started to crack up and point at her frustrated expression.

"Oh! What is wrong with you? I hate kids." She walked out and didn't come back.

I didn't even know her. How could she *hate* me? That's a little harsh.

Then, a new lady walked in. "Hi! What's your name? I'll be your nurse for the day," she said enthusiastically with raised eyebrows.

"Amy," I muttered, not sounding like the unicorns and rainbows coming from the nurse.

"Okay," her voice dropped when she saw me. "I'm Dr. Greene but you can call me um, uh, Regina. Yeah. Don't hesitate if you want something!" She ran out.

I turned and looked at Jay. "Why are they scared of us?" I asked. He laughed.

"Amy, really? Look at yourself. Black hair, green eyes, pale skin, you're wearing a spike necklace and spike bracelets all down your arm. Hate to burst your little Goth bubble, but you're a creepy little dude." He boomed out another laugh. I groaned.

"You aren't a beauty yourself," I muttered.

"Heard that!" Jay said, suddenly serious.

"You were supposed to!" I snapped back.

"Yeah, right," he punched me in the shoulder softly and he started laughing.

"Hem, hem," Regina cleared her throat, much too loudly to be natural.

"How long will you want to be staying here?" she asked. My eyebrows rose. I didn't think she'd give me a choice.

"A night or two," I answered, hoping she'd grant my wish.

"Alright, um, Amy, get in bed and we'll check you out in the morning. I'm expecting you are her brother?" she asked Jay.

"Sure."

"Okay. Take a seat, Amy. And if anyone, *anyone,* comes in here tonight, do not follow her... I mean, uh, them," Regina said, giving me a serious look. I nodded, a little scared of someone coming in, and the fact that I was already huddled on the bed.

"No promises," I whispered to myself.

"Sorry, Amy, gotta' go. Nicole wants me home," Jay said. "I'll pick you up around three o'clock tomorrow."

"Okay," I sighed, sad to see him go. "See ya' tomorrow."

"Bye," he muttered and walked out of the dark green room.

Lights went out at nine, which really sucked. I wandered over to the bookshelf, wondering what to do. Then, it struck me.

I would wait for 'the anyone' Regina mentioned. At first, I waited very patiently. I thought I would lose it after fifteen minutes, and gave up after about thirty minutes.

Finally, a girl with pitch-black hair, one side of it cut to her shoulder and the other to her chest, came in the room. She had white skin with coal-black eyes and a few little light brown freckles under her eyes and on her nose. She was wearing holey gray sweats and a white t-shirt.

"Hello Amy!" she whispered.

"How do you know my name?" I whispered back.

"I heard you talking to Dr. Greene," she replied.

"Who?" I asked.

"That fat woman with the short curly hair," she explained.

"Oh! You mean Regina," I said, remembering.

"Yeah, how did you get her to tell you her first name? She is the meanest doctor besides Buttface. I mean, uh, Dr. Tepp. Never mind. My aunt always says I talk too much. You didn't seem too surprised when I came. It seemed like you knew me," she said.

"Regina told me someone would come here in the middle of the night," I replied.

"So now she's a tattletale," she muttered under her breath.

"What's your name?"

"I'm Anastasia Hacker, but my Aunt Clara and Uncle Paul call me Scout because I'm not so girly like the name."

"Who are your parents?"

"Oh," her voice dropped. "I've heard about my mom a little bit and my dad left when I was born. There was a big fight where I was born, in Italy, and my mom got shot or stabbed. I'm not sure if Aunt Clara and Uncle Paul are my real aunt and uncle, but my older brother Alex took me somewhere when I was a baby... Then, we stopped at this huge house with lots of other kids. I don't remember anything after that except I woke up and I was at Aunt Clara and Uncle Paul's house. I've heard stories from my brother about my parents. He was only seven so he doesn't remember much either," she said.

I instantly regretted asking her the moment she said she'd only heard about her mom a little bit.

"Oh," was all I could say, and that just made it awkward.

"Okay, let's go back to the room where I stay. You probably don't want to stay in a room full of Barbie dolls, letter magnets and baby toys," Scout said. I looked around the room.

"Yeah, that'd be great," I said nodding my head.

We went on the elevator up one floor and in the door on the left. There were two other kids there.

"Amy, this is Mack," she pointed to the boy with light skin and brown hair. "And this is Veronica." Veronica was probably African American and had black wavy hair down to the middle of her back. She sat on the bed glaring at the wall and wouldn't talk. "You grow on her," Scout whispered.

"Mack has scarlet fever, and Veronica and I have pneumonia. Why are you here again?" Scout asked.

"I, um, broke my wrist," I held my right arm up.

"Hurry, get under the covers fast!" Scout whispered. We all pretended like we were sleeping and I hid in the blankets, trying to be really flat. It reminded me of children hiding from their parents when it was time for their friend to leave or time to brush teeth and go to bed. Then, the lights went out. Next thing I knew, it was eight in the morning.

"Where is Amy Johnson?" I heard nurses scream. "Amy! *Amy!* Where are you? Amy Johnson! Where are you?"

"We are going to have to call the police! She's missing!" another one said. They called for about five minutes, at least from my impatient perspective.

Finally, I gave up and walked out. "There you are!" Regina said. "Where were you, little girl?" she asked.

"Jeez, Louise. I was just in the bathroom. It takes me a while to get up!" I yawned.

"We found her! Every one, she's right here! Calm down. Everything is O.K." That kept going on for about ten minutes, or what seemed like it, again from my perspective.

"Regina, they get it!" I snapped.

"I just wanted them to know," she murmured shyly like I could actually hurt her.

"I think the whole world knows by now," I snapped. Regina made a sad looking face. Then, she brightened up.

"Hey, since your brother isn't here, I can be as mean to you as I want," she smiled. I held up my good arm with the spiky bracelets.

"I've killed somebody before, I can easily kill you," I smiled at my joke but Regina took it seriously, with a concerned look on her face.

"Amy Johnson. Amy Johnson, please go to the main office immediately. Amy Johnson." An intercom broke the awkward moment, thankfully. I took my time with walking to the main office and found Mom and Terence with his twins sitting on some fold-out chairs.

"Why are you here? You had me worried sick! I thought you had run off!" Mom scolded me.

"Since when did you care?" I muttered so quietly that I could barely hear. We were going home, I just knew it. "We are going home. Yeah, yeah, yeah," I grumbled and rolled my eyes. I started to turn away.

"That's right, we are! Young lady, get in the car," Terence ordered.

"Wait, let me pack my stuff," I lied. I ran up the stairs to Scout. I'd only known her for five minutes from last night, but, hey – what harm would it do to get to know her more?

"Scout, what's your phone number?" I asked. She scrawled out ten numbers on a ripped piece of lined paper with little games of tic-tac-toe on it.

"Hey, maybe you could just come home with me and we could call your parents... I mean aunt and uncle... and they could pick you up at my house!" I said, rushing to get her information down. Something about her attracted people like a magnet, and it wasn't awkward, strangely enough. But there was just... something strange about her.

She nodded and pulled out a large red suitcase under the bed.

When we were running out, a doctor stopped us.

"What?" I groaned.

"Miss Johnson, you need your cast on. Come with me," he said.

"C'mon," I whispered to Scout. "Is this guy new? Have you seen him before?"

"He is new. I've seen him before but he doesn't know anything about anybody. I can come in," Scout whispered.

"Alright, let's go," I whispered back. When we were going into the x-ray room the doctor stopped.

"No one but family is allowed in right now and she isn't family," he said, holding his hand out to block Scout, pushing her away with his palm on her chest.

"Um, yeah, she is. We're twins," I lied. That was maybe pushing it. We could be half-sisters, definitely not twins.

"You don't look like twins," he said, narrowing his eyes.

"Just because I have shorter hair and look creepier doesn't mean we aren't twins," I say, crossing my fingers, hoping he believes me. I stutter with my words. I hope he didn't catch it.

"Fine, I'm Dr. White. Please take a seat, um, sorry, what's your name?" he said after a long pause and his eyes widened again.

"Scout," Scout said.

"Hmm. You look a lot like a girl named Anastasia who's about your age." We both giggled.

"What? What's so funny?" he asked.

"First off, people call me Scout but my real name is Anastasia. Second off, it's funny when guys like you are confused." We laughed again.

"I hate kids and I always have! How did they convince me to become a pediatrician? Unbelievable," Dr. White muttered to himself.

"No offense, but you talk to yourself a lot," I said. That wasn't the smartest idea. Dr. White looked furious with us.

He finished the cast and forced us out, literally kicking us out of the room.

"Excuse me?" I asked the man at the front desk when we got to the lobby.

"Yes?" he responded looking up from his computer.

"I wanted to make a little comment about your employees. They suck! Fire Dr. White or whatever his name is. He was being mean to us," I snapped.

"I'm sorry, little one, but that's not my job," he answered, giving no sign of interest, returning to his computer screen.

"Don't do that. I might be skinny and a little short, but do not call me little one," I said. He was lighting my wick and it was burning down faster than normal.

"Well, I'm sorry but that's not my problem. Where's your Mommy and Daddy?" he asked and looked up from his computer, but quickly scanning the screen.

I whacked my spiky bracelet across his face. "Daddy died, Mommy cried, inky binky bonky," I snapped.

"Where did you get your influence?" he mumbled, touching his shocked face. He didn't think I just hit him with soft spikes of rubber.

"None of your beeswax, bubs!" I snapped. People started to stare. Yep. There blows my dynamite.

Scout was staring at me wide eyed.

"Any second thoughts about being my friend?" I asked, smiling like it was a joke... but she obviously didn't get it.

"Um..." she thought for a moment.

"Of course, the first impression is the true one, it is for me anyway. And this is rubber," I said holding up the bracelet.

"Have you killed anyone doing that?" she asked, not hearing the part about how that was rubber. I didn't answer, thinking she was joking. "Will you kill me if I'm not your friend?" she asked, scared to death.

"No, I only do that to people I hate or get on my nerves," I said sarcastically. "No, I won't kill you. But I have before," I lied, seeing how long she'd go until she found out I was kidding.

We were walking to the van.

"Really, who?" she asked, excited but full of fear.

"And this is exactly why I don't tell people. They get all, well, in my face. Back in New York, I didn't have any friends except the ones who knew my secret and they did it too," I lied, biting my lip so I didn't laugh, but I cracked a smile. I was a bad liar, especially at times like these. Could she tell that I was acting like a kid in a Disney Channel movie from 2005? "

So all your friends are murderers?" she asked, amazed.

Absolutely. Don't tell anybody, Scout. Nobody," I said, trying not to crack up. She looked as if she was about to cry.

I needed friends with a sense of humor.

Chapter Two - Meeting the Strange

Honestly, I think I scare people too much when I meet them.

"Hey Scout, do you want to see if you can come over to my house when we get back? I need to talk to you," I whispered once we were driving in the van.

"Uh, I don't know," Scout whispered back.

It was weird. Scout was like, *pretending* to be scared of me. There was just something off about her.

"I was just kidding. I won't kill you," I laughed. She smiled. "I need to tell you about something. It will be quick."

We pulled into my driveway.

"Oh, you live... here? I live right across the street!" Scout announced, the last part cheerfully.

"Yeah, is there something wrong?" I asked because of the expression on her face as we were walking to the porch step.

"No, just that there's a rumor that it's haunted."

"Well, I don't believe in that crap," I shrugged. She looked shocked. "What?" I asked as we unlocked the door.

"Nothing. Never mind."

Scout walked around looking at everything, but not daring to touch anything.

"Hey, let's go upstairs to my room," I suggested. She flinched back like I was a ghost.

"Oh, um, yeah." She followed cautiously.

"I'm just as surprised as you are. I moved here yesterday," I said.

"Really? I would have thought you moved in before," Scout said, staring off at other things in the old-fashioned-smelling room.

"So, this is my room," I opened the door. Scout looked disgusted by my brick red walls and untidy bed.

"You have a... great room," she said sarcastically.

"Thanks," I faked a grin. "I have to redesign it and paint it myself. Or at least that's what to expect."

Then, Scout saw my Doberman pinschers, Phoenix and Tracker. She froze with wide eyes.

"They won't bite," I said. "Okay, maybe they will, but only if you get on their nerves. They're super sweet." Phoenix, the girl, whimpered.

"Aw, what's wrong, girl?" I went forward to pet her. Tracker jumped up on his feet and growled at me.

"Tracker, No! Don't growl at me!" I yelled. He was going to back down but changed his mind. He ripped another snarl at me. I whacked him on the head. "No!" I yelled again. Tracker almost gave up again, but decided not to, once again. He barked. "I give up. What do you want?" I asked Tracker, acting like he would reply.

Scout had crouched down into a corner, as far away from the dogs as possible. This didn't seem like an act like the rest of her.

"You don't need to be scared of them. Tracker has never acted like this. It isn't normal," I comforted Scout. She slowly began to get out of her corner. I don't really understand how that's comforting, but – hey, it worked.

"So... this is isn't normal?" Scout asked.

"No, it isn't," I confirmed. She gave a sigh of relief.

"Okay. Well, I have a problem, with... big dogs," she admitted.

"Okay, I'll keep them locked up when you're here, then." There, problem fixed.

"I should probably make sure my uncle and aunt know I'm home," she changed the subject.

"Oh, yeah, let's go over."

Her house was dark green on the outside with a shiny red car parked in the driveway. I bit my lip before we went in. Scout seemed like the very well behaved and organized type. Nothing like me.

Inside, the house smelled like sausage, pancakes, eggs, but mostly of cinnamon.

A woman who was around forty or so greeted us from the small kitchen with a plate of cookies. She had light brown hair and wore oval glasses. It was probably Scout's Aunt Clara.

"Scout! I can't believe you're back. I missed you!" she said enthusiastically. Then she turned to me. "Hello, I'm Clara. Would you like a cookie?"

"No... thank you," I remembered my manners. "I'm Amy. It's nice to meet you."

"Well, Amy, make yourself at home," she grinned.

While Clara and Scout talked about why she was back and how things were going, I looked around the warm house. Two flower-patterned chairs were up against the same wall as the door we came in with a table in between of them. There was a wood stove on the right wall and a white sofa. Next to the sofa (making a square with all of the furniture) was a white grand piano with all eighty-eight keys. My jaw dropped and my eyes froze on the piano.

"Do you play?" Clara asked. I nodded. "Feel free to. We don't use it around here much. It's brand new, never used. It was a gift for me to start playing piano but I never followed through."

I slowly walked over to the piano and pulled out the bench. I sat down and put my hands on the keys. I started to play "Fur Elise."

Suddenly, everything around me disappeared. I was on the beach with Jay, Poch and some lady with blondish-red hair who looked as freaky as I did, the same green eyes and pale skin. I was the same age I am now and Jay was the same. There was a baby too, which was kind of strange.

The baby was about two years old. But before I got to observe the rest of the place and enjoy it, I heard, "Amy! Amy! C'mon! Let's go back to my room!"

I got up and followed Scout back to her room. I saw Clara shaking her head in disapproval of Scout's behavior but ignored it.

Scout's room had bright green walls and a hot pink bed on the right wall. The left wall had a white desk with lots of papers and trophies. On the wall in front of us, there was a small cage with lots of rocks and leaves and tunnels in it.

"What's in there?" I asked.

"My gecko, he's probably hiding behind a rock or something," Scout replied.

"What's his name?" I asked, wandering toward the cage.

"Fessed Big-tail."

"Hmm, that's a strange name," I said, observing him more closely.

Just then, a gigantic lizard came out of the miniature tunnel. I squeaked and jumped back.

"Calm down! It's just a gecko. You're scaring him!" Scout said.

"That thing is huge!" I declared.

"It's not bigger than your dogs," she mumbled.

"Yeah, but it's a lizard, for cryin' out loud!"

"I bet you weren't that big when you were two years old," Scout snapped.

"I was probably a few inches bigger. Oh my gosh. You don't get it. Never mind," I said, giving up on conversations.

After that, Scout came over every day for the rest of the summer until I would fake sicknesses, I got so sick of her.

About two months later, Scout came to my door and said, "Let's go meet the kids in the neighborhood."

I don't know why she did this now and not earlier, but I just shrugged my shoulders, glad she finally picked up on my mental request. We headed out the door to our left and followed the road down to a dead end.

"Julie lives here. You can't miss her house. It has all these different colors on it. When she was about four, she got into the spray paint and her parents never cleaned it up. They're really young, like around twenty-five, but it's not her real dad," Scout explained.

When we walked to the dead end, I saw her house at once. It was originally white, spray painted purples, greens, yellows, oranges, reds and blues. There was a giant gate around the house with a code on the inside, and on the outside was a little phone to call the people in the house.

"Wow. Does Julie try to get out... a lot?" I asked.

"Yeah, they don't tell her the code so she can't get out. I guess they take it pretty seriously."

She picked up the phone but didn't dial. It went straight to the person. It was kind of loud so I heard most of their conversation.

"Hello?" a female voice said.

"Hi Mrs. Tola, I'm back from the hospital and there was another kid who moved in down the street. I wanted Julie to meet her," Scout said.

"Oh Scout! I haven't seen your face around here in months! What have you been doing lately?" Mrs. Tola asked, obviously very young from her voice, much too young to be a 'Mrs.'

"I was in the hospital with Veronica. When we fell into the river, we got pneumonia. I just got back today," Scout said.

"Oh, that's too bad. Come inside. It must be freezing out there!" Mrs. Tola squealed with excitement and then there was a buzz to open the gate.

"I'll see you inside," Scout said. She opened the gate and we went into the tiny house.

A short, skinny woman with blondish-red hair came to meet us. She was wearing a striped green shirt with a white tank top under it and skinny jeans. "Oh Scout, I missed you so much!" She ran over and hugged Scout.

"Who's this?" she asked, facing me.

"I'm Amy. I live down the street in the house by the river," I introduced myself.

"Oh. That house. I understand why you would want to get out of it," Mrs. Tola shrugged.

"No, I just came to meet Julie. Why would I want to get out of it?" I wondered.

"You don't know? Oh, well, I don't want to tell you if you don't know." She looked down.

"Really, what's so creepy about that house?" I asked.

"Well, parents aren't supposed to encourage the kids' stories, but I really do think there is a g-" Julie's mom stopped herself.

Scout coughed to get our attention. "Mrs. Tola, can we see Julie?" Scout asked.

"Of course, let me go get her," Mrs. Tola said and ran up the stairs. When she came back down, a miniature copy of her walked down with her wearing a blue tank top and jeans. She looked glum, her back slouching. When she saw Scout, her face lit up.

"Scout, you're finally here!" She ran downstairs and squeezed Scout.

"Hey Julie," Scout said, hugging her back awkwardly.

"Who are you?" Julie asked me very straight forward, not like a normal kid our age.

"I'm Amy. Are you Julie?" I asked, already knowing the answer.

"Yes. When did you get here?" she asked, not having any manners.

"I moved in to the house by the river yesterday," I replied. Julie gasped.

"You live in the Baggins house?" She was bewildered. "Mama, Mama, did you hear that? She lives in the ghos –" Mrs. Tola cupped her hand over Julie's mouth.

"Don't frighten her," Mrs. Tola murmured.

"But did you hear?"

"Yes, Julie. I heard where she lives. Now go play," Mrs. Tola's voice was not quite scolding like.

We walked out and crossed a field behind their house to a little blue house. It had gardens, cats, and looked like somewhere a grandma would live.

"This is Benny's house. He prefers to stay inside," Scout said.

"Why doesn't he like to go outside?" I asked.

"He gets scared a lot. You know loud noises, fire, giraffes," she said. I giggled.

"Why is he scared of *giraffes?*"

"He had a very bad accident with them, and elephants. I don't exactly know what happened but he was too embarrassed to tell anyone."

When we knocked on the door, nobody answered.

"Too bad. I really wanted to meet Benny. Next time remind me to bring a toy giraffe," I teased.

"Yeah," Scout laughed along.

"Hey, where did Julie go?" I asked slowly, realizing she was gone. Scout froze.

"We were supposed to take care of her," Scout said. We started to call Julie's name over and over.

I finally found her under some bushes. She kept muttering, "She's watching, she's watching."

"Who's watching?" I kept asking her and trying to calm her down but she waved her arms around like a crazy person to get me off her.

"She has schizophrenia. It's fine. Julie, stop saying that," Scout said. We took Julie back home and continued our tour of the neighborhood.

"Okay, this is Veronica's house," Scout said as we stepped up to a huge pink house.

"Um, wow," I managed to mumble. This wasn't a house. This was a mansion.

"I know. Veronica's rich and gets everything she wants. I mean, look at her house. It's pink because she wanted it to be! True cheese." Scout and I just stared for a minute.

Then, a tall, skinny teenager walked out onto the lowest balcony. "Go away," she snapped. She looked around fifteen.

"No," Scout refused.

"G-" she started. A heavyset woman walked out.

"Mary Alyce Christine! How many times have I told you to be nice to guests?" she shrieked.

"But, Mom,-" the girl complained.

"No ifs, ands or buts. It's rude!" The heavyset woman looked over the balcony and the girl pouted. "What are you still doing here? Go away!" The woman ordered the girl. She stalked off.

"Hi Scout! I haven't seen you in forever. Did you see Veronica when you left the hospital?" the woman greeted her.

"Hello Mrs. Beploe. It's nice to see you again, too. And yes, I did see Veronica. I heard she won't be back until October," Scout said politely.

"Oh that's right! Who's your friend?" Mrs. Beploe asked.

"I'm Amy."

"Do you live in this neighborhood?"

"Yes, the dark blue house by the river with large field."

Mrs. Beploe made that same face Mrs. Tola had made when she found out where I lived.

"Are you serious?" I asked.

"What? What's wrong, honey?" Mrs. Beploe asked.

"What is wrong with my house? Everybody has the same stupid expression! Is there a ghost in the house? Is there a body hidden under the floor boards? I'm sick of it! Why can't people just tell me what's going –"

"Amy!" Mrs. Beploe screamed. "Stop, stop, stop. You don't know the history of your house and we'll leave it at that. Now, you guys should get moving on."

"I'm sorry, Mrs. Beploe. She gets mad a lot," Scout apologized.

"Oh shut up," I whispered. "You barely know who I am."

"Amy, go," Mrs. Beploe ordered. I glared at her and stalked off.

"Scout, you can stay if you want," I heard Mrs. Beploe in the distance. I was at the end of the street now, running.

"No, I have to catch up with her," Scout said and ran up to me.

"She's kind of rude. You grow on her," Scout said, panting by my side. She agreed with Mrs. Beploe. I could tell.

"Yeah, sure I will," I muttered sarcastically. "I hate that big, fat, burned, overgrown potato," I grumbled. Scout tried to hold in a laugh but giggled.

"Well, I guess you have your own saying: 'The first impression is the true one.'"

"Who's next?" I asked.

"Herbert. He lives in a dark green house at the end of the neighborhood. Somebody has to be home at his house. He has like a million brothers and sisters."

When we rang the doorbell, a tall girl like Veronica's sister answered the door. "Herbert!" she yelled.

"Sorry, Benny, I'm not feeling so well," a boy's voice called back.

"It's not Benny! It's Scout!" the girl who answered the door yelled up at him.

"Scout! I'll be right there!" There was a large tripping sound up the stairs.

"So, Scout, you're finally back," the girl said, turning towards us. "Herbert's been going crazy. He's in lo-"

"Lee! Shut up!" Herbert wailed. He had skin that matched soil and black hair braided down to his waist.

"Who is this?" Herbert asked when he saw me.

"I'm Amy," I introduced myself, once again.

"Well, welcome to the neighborhood," he said with a grin.

"Thanks. I think my mom's home. I've gotta' go, bye Scout," I turned to jog back to my house after Scout muttered a farewell.

I heard Herbert gasp and say, "She lives in the Baggins house?"

I didn't want to listen anymore.

A couple minutes later, they came knocking on my door and Herbert looked too scared to come in.

"What's wrong? Is it too scary for you? And I *thought* I said I needed to go," I glowered at them.

"No, it's just I've never been here. This place is cre-"

"Shut your pie hole!" Scout whispered.

"I was just gonna say creepy."

I got mad and when I turned around, I accidently pushed over a bottle of wine that was on the table and it shattered into pieces. Scout gasped at the loud sound and I stalked up to my room.

"I told you to shut up!" I heard Scout whispering to Herbert.

"Well I didn't know it would make her explode like that! If I'd known, I wouldn't have done it."

"What do you not understand about 'shut you pie hole!?'"

"I'm sorry!"

"Who are you?" A deep, scary voice said. Terence. I ran downstairs.

"They're, um, just some friends that live around the block. We were just heading out," I said.

"But we just got here," Herbert said.

"No, we didn't. Now let's go," I pushed them out the back door.

"What's your problem?! You do *not* talk to Terence like that!" I screamed. I was getting mad and they were looking annoyed. Like all the time. *How were they supposed to know?* I heard Jay's voice in my head, mocking me.

"But you did," Herbert said.

"Yeah, because I don't care if I get in trouble or shredded into cubes of cheese. But you can't. Don't do that!" I shrieked.

After I settled down and Herbert and Scout got my point, Mom's van pulled into the driveway.

"Mom, hi, what are you doing?" I said nervously when she got out of the van.

"I'm coming home early to see if Terence is cheating on me like they do in movies," she whispered and put her finger to her lips, tiptoeing across the yard.

"He isn't. He is the only one home besides me, the twins and the dogs."

"Well then who are they?" Mom pointed to Scout and Herbert.

"Mom, you're losing your mind. I don't know who you're talking about," I shoved her a little too hard toward the back door.

"Them," Mom pointed, looking like a young child.

"You know, when you point fingers there's always three pointing back right at you! Besides, there's no one there, Mom. You must be going crazy. Oh!" I gasped. "I think I heard someone just go in the door. Terence might be cheating, go," I said way too fast and shoved her toward the back door.

"I must be losing my hearing too! Don't be late for dinner," she said and ran into the house.

"You guys need to stay away from my house," I told Scout and Herbert. "Try to ignore them at all costs. Even if they ask a question, act like you didn't hear it. So, let's go into my bedroom before they get suspicious." They followed me into the house.

"See! There they are!" my mom yelled when we got in. She was my mom and all, and I was supposed to love her, but she was an idiot.

"Hide," I whispered quickly. They jumped in two dusty boxes behind them. Terence walked in.

"Nicole, there is no kids. Stop complainin'," Terence snapped.

"They were really there! I swear, Terence. They were there. Please believe me," she winked at him.

"Amelia," Terence said really slowly. "Get your friends out of here, before I get them myself!" He was yelling now. I smiled. "Wipe that smile off your face or I'll do it for you!" I bit my lip, trying not to laugh.

"I hope I can see you soon!" I said, pretending to walk people to the door and opening it for them, waving to the nothingness.

"See, Nicole? They're gone. Let's go back to our room now," Terence says, pulling her by the waist to the stairs.

"No, they're still here. Check in those boxes over there." She nodded her head in the direction of the boxes Scout and Herbert were in. I panicked and jumped in front of the boxes.

"Wait!" I cried out. I was in huge trouble now.

"The wine bottle," Herbert whispered deadly quiet.

"Guys, did you hear a crash?" I asked Mom and Terence. It was silent for a minute.

"Now that I think about it, I did. Come on Nicole. Let's go check it out," Terence said. When they were out of the living room, we made a run for it up into my room.

"Shh!" I shushed Scout and Herbert who were as quiet as mice.

I heard screaming downstairs. "Terence! Why did you do this? Nina or Cash or Jay or Amy could have stepped on this and gotten hurt!" Mom yelled, trying to sound like she cared. *Sure. Acting is out of your career choice,* I thought.

"Nicole! I didn't do this. I won't lie to you. Amelia did it! She's the only one here who could have, anyways," Terence shouted.

"Hide!" I whispered. Scout and Herbert hid in the lower cabinet of my half bathroom. Terence walked into my room with Mom trailing a foot behind him.

"Why'd you do this?" Terence asked in a deep, scary voice. Very menacing.

"I didn't. I swear to God." I crossed my fingers behind my back.

"Ames, that's cheating," Mom said quietly, clearly as afraid of Terence as I was. At least she acted like it. And acting was *out* of her career choice.

"What am I doing?" I asked.

"Crossing your fingers behind your back," Mom said, walking up to me a little more confident.

"Why did you knock over the wine bottle?"

"Where's your evidence?" I asked.

"You were the only one who could have done it," Terence interjected.

"Think twice about that. I was in the room with you when the scene happened, your honor," I said stepping up to Terence and smiling like a princess.

"We aren't playing court, Amy – Amelia," Mom snapped.

"Really? Darn. I was having fun," I said sarcastically. It was suddenly quiet. I looked down, expecting Terence to hit me and lock me into my room or do something illegal involving child abuse.

"She has a point," Mom risked a glance at Terence.

"No, she doesn't. Amelia, you're grounded for a month," Terence snapped and started to leave like I'd be fine with the undeserved punishment.

"What? That's not fair!" I said but paused because he turned around slowly to stare at me. Being a drama-queen all the time with a tough-guy attitude didn't help Terence's ego, at all.

"It's not," Mom whispered to me under her breath and squeezed her eyes shut, wishing she hadn't said that. Terence had fire flame in his eyes as he locked his glare at her.

"Yes, it is," Terence said and it sounded like a ten year old complaining.

Then, he slapped Mom across the face. For a moment all I could do was to sit and gawk like an idiot. I gasped and ran over to her but Terence pushed me away.

"Go away," he ordered.

"It's my room smart-one!" I said and waved him off, trying to push him away. I couldn't help but snap back at him. I needed to work on that.

"Get out of here! I hate you!" Mom screamed at Terence, holding her pink jaw with tears streaming down her face.

"Ah, ah, ah, remember our little rule, Nicole. Oops. I meant *your* rule. Just you and me, no matter how bad it gets. Now let's go back to our room..." Terence said, pulling her towards the door by her wrist. I winced and rubbed the cast on my right arm, just remembering how much it hurt.

"My room." Mom pulled away and tried wiping her tear-streaked face.

"No, *our* room," Terence said, raising his hand again. He was about to slap Mom if she disagreed again. She put her arms in front of her face, blocking him.

"*Our* room," Mom corrected herself in a scared whisper.

"Terence, you should leave," I said and quickly bit my tongue. Why did I say that? Why, Amy, why?

"Amelia, I can beat you up any time. Shut up," Terence snarled. I was thinking about picking up the knife that I hid under the bed. I didn't, but I hid it there for times like these.

"I have a weapon," I said, smiling. *Amy, stop! Get ahold of yourself! He will hurt you! Stranger danger! He can and will kill you and Mom! Remember Scout and Herbert in the bathroom. Don't go any further!*

I was thinking all of the right things, just not doing them. What was wrong with me?

"No you don't. Give me all of your weapons," Terence said.

"Sure, here! I'm going to give you everything just because I love you!" I said sarcastically, then frowned at him and rolled my eyes. "No can do. They are permanently stuck with me. Actually, I can lose them but you have to hit me hard in the right place. But I doubt you have the brains to do it," I said. I flashed another grin. *Oh my God, Amy! Just shut up already! What is wrong with you?*

"Amy. In case you haven't noticed, I don't like games."

"What kind of loser doesn't like Yahtzee?" My mind was telling me to shut up again.

Terence walked up to me to snatch me but I crawled through his legs. He growled and tried to get me again but missed.

He started to go for my right arm. The arm that was already in a cast. Scout and Herbert both gasped. They were probably looking through the crack of the cabinet or a hole a rat chewed out.

While I was trying to tell Herbert and Scout to shut up, Terence grabbed me.

"What's your weapon?" he snarled. I spit in his eye and bit his finger so he'd drop me to the floor. Finally, he was the one silently screaming in pain and grossness.

I backed up and took the knife out from under my bed.

"What? Are you going to kill me? Oh, I'm so scared!" he said sarcastically as he wiped the spit off his eye.

"Actually, I will." I took the knife out and pushed in on his stomach, not enough to make him bleed. I pushed further and a drop of blood started to stain his shirt.

He put his hand on the back of my head like he was petting me. What? But he took me by my hair and slammed my head into the wall. I fell unconscious before I even hit the ground.

"Amy! Amy! Wake up! Come on," someone's voice was saying. It was light and soft and worried. They were shaking me really hard too. My eyes snapped opened.

"Amy. You've been out for a few hours. Man, it was hard to sneak out and tell our parents we'd be over here for a while," another voice was saying this. It was hard and solid and cracking.

"Amy? Amy! Amy! Wake up!" The first voice was saying again. My eyes must have closed again. I sat up and rubbed my eyes.

"What happened?" I asked.

"Terence slammed you against the wall and you, and you fell unconscious," the first voice said. I realized it was Scout.

I went over to my bathroom to look in the mirror.

I had a huge black and blue mark on the side of my forehead. No more broken bones, though. That was good. But my head pounded and hurt like crazy.

"Do you want to go outside and do something?" I yawned, turning away.

"Amy, it's a little late for that. Look outside," Scout said. I walked over to the miniature window. It was dark out already.

"Oh, Amy?" Herbert started.

"What?" I yawned again.

"I have to be back at my house. It's already ten," Herbert said.

"Really? Wow. What time was I knocked out?" I asked, looking around for my alarm clock.

"6:45," Scout said.

"I've been out for four hours and fifteen minutes?" I guessed.

"Yeah, pretty much. Okay. Um, see you tomorrow?" Herbert said.

"I think. I'm grounded so, maybe," I shrugged. Mom and Terence were already in bed so it was no problem getting him out.

"Hey! Want to see if you can spend the night tonight?" Scout asked.

"Uh, sure?" I replied, wondering why someone I barely knew wanted a sleep over. I guess she was the social type.

"Wait! But won't your mom recognize me?" Scout asked.

"No, just go home, change clothes, put your hair in a ponytail and be all serious. That will do it. And say your name is Anastasia because she might have heard me talking to you. Just to be safe," I said.

"Okay. I'll go ask," Scout said and was off.

"Mom, Mom, Mom!" I yelled.

"Oh, great," I heard Terence mutter.

"Honey, you're awake! How long have you been up?" my mom asked, concerned as she opened the bedroom door.

"Um, I woke up at ten," I said, wondering why she was asking. I cringed when Terence looked at me.

"Oh, ok. What is it?" she asked, less concerned.

"Um, there's a girl in the neighborhood and I was wondering if I can spend the night at her house. She rode home with us," I said, trying not to mention who it was.

"Oh. Was her name Scarlet?" Mom asked, giving a "random" guess to act like she didn't care.

"No, Anastasia."

"Hmm, I wonder how I got her name so off track," Mom wondered.

"Yeah, I wonder," I said, playing along.

"If it's not too late for them," she answered as the doorbell rang.

"I'll get it!" I yelled.

"Amy – I, mean, uh, Amelia, no shouting! It really hurts my ears," Mom complained.

"Fine!" I yelled back. "Whoops! Sorry! I keep yelling. I can't stop," I shouted, laughing. I opened the door.

"Anastasia, you came! I was just about to go over to your house. Ha! That's so funny," I babbled on.

"Amy, shut up now. She's getting suspicious," Scout whispered.

She was wearing her hair up in ponytail on the top of her head, a bright green tank top with a little petticoat over it, white jeans, and black sneakers.

"Well, hi, Anastasia. I'm Ms. Shea," Mom said. Whew. She wasn't going to marry Terence... yet.

"Hi Ms. Shea, I'm Anastasia and it's very nice to meet you! I was wondering if Amy could spend the night tonight," Scout said like an innocent child.

That's when I realized that Scout was a horrible liar.

"Oh, um, yes, let me talk to your parents first," Mom said like she cared.

I jabbed Mom in the stomach. "Ow, Amelia," she complained. "Don't do that," she whispered.

"Shush up!" I shushed her. I didn't want her talking to Scout's aunt and uncle.

"Oh, Anastasia, if you please would, would you call her Amelia? Amy was her father's pet name for her...he died and we don't want any memories of him," Mom said. "It makes us sad."

"Really? Because Amy won't answer to Amelia," Scout said, starting to wander around a little bit, getting bored.

"Well then she'll just have to suck it up," Mom glared at me.

"What? What did I do, *Nicole*?" I asked.

"Don't call me Nicole," Mom snarled.

"Why not? It's your name and everyone else calls you Nicole," I say in a bratty voice.

"Because you're my daughter, that's why. The twins have to suck it up. So can you," she said, straightening up her back, getting ready to scold me.

"Ugh. I'm barely related to the twins. And they can't talk," I said, glaring.

"Hey just because they're Terence's kids too, that doesn't mean you aren't related to them. You're related as much to them as you are to Jay," she said, her tone getting lighter. "Oh go have fun." She pushed me out the door.

"I need to pack," I reminded her. She ran upstairs and was back with a bag.

"See ya' in the morning!" Mom said and we were out.

"So what do you want to do?" Scout asked.

"I don't know. Watch a movie?" I suggested.

"No, hmm, play with the gecko?" Scout shrugged.

"Nah, what about learning how to play the piano?"

When we had been practicing for about half an hour, Mom came pounding on the door. "Amy, now. Nina got hurt, we're leaving. Anastasia, come too. Hurry!" Mom left us hanging, so we left.

"Clara?" I asked.

"Yes, dear?" her wheezy voice chirped as she was making a batch of cookies.

"Can we take Scout with us to the hospital? My baby sister got hurt," I mumbled shyly.

"Of course, when will you be back?" she asked and put the cookies in the oven.

"I don't know. We'll call you when we do," I said, leaning against the kitchen counter.

"Okay. B-bye!" She started humming and I grabbed my stuff and ran back to my house.

"Are you ready?" Mom asked.

"Yeah, let me put my stuff in the house."

"No time for that! We're leaving." We all hopped in the van and drove off.

We went to the same hospital where I had my arm put in a cast. Emma was working at the front desk. "Oh! You and your family are here... again. Is there a problem with your cast?" she asked, trying to sound enthusiastic, but without luck.

"No. We need to get a room right now. My daughter fell down the stairs and she got hurt badly," Mom said. Emma looked at me.

"She doesn't look hurt," Emma said and did her funny stink eye.

"Not Amelia. Nina," Terence said and pulled Nina out of the blanket she was in.

"Oh, of course. Hold on for a minute," Emma picked up the phone and dialed a number. I wandered off and took Scout with me.

"Do you want to see if Mack and Veronica are still here?" I asked Scout.

"What? No, your mom and Terence won't know where we are," Scout said.

"Just come here," I took her to Mom.

"Hey, Mom," I said, as enthusiastically as I could.

"What? We're in a rush," Mom said.

For some reason, it seemed like she didn't care at all what happened to Nina, or anybody.

"I know. Me and Anastasia have to go to the bathroom. We'll be back in a bit," I lied and was edging toward the elevator.

"Okay. We're in room 344 in the baby section," Mom replied, still acting like she didn't really care.

"Alright, come on, Anastasia," I said. We ran up to the elevator and pressed the button.

After a long moment of stillness, Scout was looking at the ground really hard, and spoke up. “Amy?”

“Yes?” I replied, alert as ever.

“Do you know *how* your dad died?” she wondered. I didn’t answer for a few long seconds.

“No, not really, just an idea,” I said after thinking about it.

“What do you mean, ‘not really’?” Scout muttered. We kept looking at the ground, not daring to even glance at each other.

“I have a clue. He didn’t die from getting sick or anything natural. Mom said he died of getting run over by a car. Then again, she also said he got eaten by a whale,” I said, trying to be funny, but it didn’t work.

“So wait, wait, wait. Your mom had kids with Terence when she was married to your dad?” she asked, still looking at the floor.

“Yep, pretty much,” I answered and rolled on the balls of my feet.

“How did she keep him from noticing?” Scout asked. I was about to give up on the conversation, but I finally looked up at her and studied her eyes. There was true curiosity.

“’Said she was going on a business trip for a year,” I replied simply.

“Didn’t she bring the kids around the house?” she asked, her eyes ripping apart from their locked grip on the ground.

“No, Terence kept them. He lived alone in a huge mansion on the side of a river. Wow, was that house nice. He still owns it, just in case,” I shrugged, getting off topic.

“In case what?” Scout asked.

“In case my mom breaks up with him.”

The elevator doors finally opened and we got out. That seemed like forever. Luckily we were the only ones there. We slowly walked to the second door on the left.

“Hi! Scout I’ve missed you so much!” Veronica said jumping up and down. “Amy,” She looked at me. “I’m so sorry for the way I acted. But um, can you take me home?” Veronica asked.

"Wait a second, where's Mack?" Scout asked.

"Oh," Veronica looked down. "Mack, sorta' well, things happened and well, he's dead," she said slowly.

"What? Mack died?" Scout asked, straightening her back, looking at his empty bed.

"Yeah, he was having surgery and they did something wrong that made him get even more sick," Veronica explained.

"When did he die?" I asked.

"Yesterday morning," Veronica answered.

"That's too bad," Scout said, looking down, trying not to show the sadness she was experiencing.

"Why are you here anyway?" Veronica asked, changing the subject in a bright tone.

"My little half-sister fell down the stairs," I answered. "We have to be leaving. Sorry," I wanted to leave the room. The fact that somebody I knew in this room had died... I don't know. It just freaked me out.

"Bye! I hope you can visit again," Veronica said.

"Yeah, come on, Scout. We're supposed to be going to the bathroom. Remember?" I muttered with clenched teeth.

"But," Scout began, just like a small child.

"We're leaving," I grabbed her arm and tugged her out.

"Amelia! Amelia! Come on!" Mom was pounding on the girls' bathroom door.

"What?" I asked.

"I thought you were in there," Mom said.

"No, I went back to the baby section. Room 344," I lied simply.

"No you weren't. I was just in there," Mom scowled.

"Well then I came when you left," I sassed back. Then somebody opened the bathroom door.

"What's your problem lady? I just wanted to go to the bathroom. And my name isn't Amelia," she snapped and walked away.

"Sheesh, what's her problem?" Mom wondered loud enough so the woman could hear.

Back in the room, Nina was still crying.

"Come on! Shut up!" I complained. "I'm out of here," I said and walked out.

There was a girl standing there, with blondish wavy hair, light black and gray eyes. She just stared at me.

"Hey, can I help you?" I asked rudely.

"Yes," She grinned.

"What do you want?" I snapped.

"I need a ride." She glanced gracefully into the baby room.

"No can do. We don't let strangers in our car," I shrugged.

"Not under any conditions?" she asked like I hadn't said no.

"There might be some conditions," I warned.

"That's fine," she shrugged.

After a long pause, I finally said, "What's your name?"

"I can't tell you that," the girl quickly said, like me knowing her name was like a stranger giving you candy.

"Well, that's one condition for giving you a ride," I said.

"Maybe later. Next condition," she growled, a little frustrated.

"Your age?" I wondered. Why was I talking to this girl?

"Ten," she replied.

"How long have you been ten?" I asked, just 'cause.

"I can't tell you that," she shrugged.

"That's a condition for a ride."

"Later," she smiled.

"Where do you live?" I asked a real question so we'd know where to drop her off.

"I can't tell you that exactly, but if you drop me off at Billy Baroos, I can find my way from there."

"How far away?" I questioned.

"I live in the forest behind it," she answered.

"Fine, that will work. One more..." I trailed off, thinking of something.

"Of course," she shrugged like she'd known me for years instead of minutes.

"I barely know you. You can't be saying 'of course'. That's against the rules," I said, and slit my eyes to look at her.

"Rules are meant to be broken," she said flawlessly, more in a singing voice.

"Amy, don't talk to her. She's a creep," Scout whispered, making sure the strange girl couldn't hear her. I hadn't even realized she was there.

"I have to go," the girl said and walked away.

"She's weird," I said, sighing and scratching my head.

"She might be mental," Scout whispered and turned around.

"Girls, the crying has stopped. Come in here," Mom leaned out of the small door.

"'Kay," I sighed. We slowly walked into the room.

One of the doctors began to talk. "Hello. I'm Dr. Salt," she said.

"Where's your brother? Dr. Pepper? I want a refill," I teased.

"Amelia!" Terence snapped.

"We are going to need to do some testing overnight. Is that okay? Actually, it might take more than a few nights," Dr. Salt said, ignoring my rude joke.

"Yes, that's just fine," Terence said.

"No, it's not! I want to see my child!" Mom disagreed, but you could tell she was fine with it.

"You aren't going to see your child ever again if you don't agree to the tests. You know why? She'll be dead!" Terence snapped.

"Okay, let's not fight here," Dr. Salt said, trying to calm them. "The tests are to see if there is any permanent damage, anything we didn't catch when she was born," Dr. Salt explained.

"Fine," Mom mumbled. "We'll back tomorrow at 11 o'clock sharp," Mom warned.

"She'll be ready by then. I think," Dr. Salt confirmed.

"Mom, we could stay here with Nina if you like. Just to make sure she's safe," I said.

"No, Anastasia's aunt and uncle might not allow that," Mom said, sighing.

"We can just call them. They said all they need is a heads up and it's okay. Right, Anastasia?" I said in a light tone. She nodded.

"Fine, here's my phone, sweetie," Mom handed her phone to Scout. "Do you know the number?" Mom asked.

When Scout was done with the done, Mom asked, "What time do you need to be back?"

"When you pick me up," Scout muttered.

"Okay. Bye!" Mom said and practically ran out of the hospital with Terence.

"You guys need to sleep in the kids' room, one floor up, the second door on your left," Dr. Salt said.

"We know. We were here before," Scout muttered and rolled her eyes like it was something obvious.

"Good night. Wake up at the latest 10 in the morning," Dr. Salt said and shooed us off.

"Okay. Good night," Scout said.

We got into bed and just like the last time, next thing I knew it was 10 in the morning.

"Ugh. I'm so tired," I complained.

"Hey Amy, we need to go to the testing room. The news is here," Scout said.

"Oh. Give me five minutes," I wailed.

"No, c'mon," Scout dragged me out of the bed.

"You're stubborn, aren't you?" I asked Scout. She ignored me.

"Ah, you are finally awake," Dr. Salt said. "You slept for a long, long time,"

"I know. I'm not a morning person," I growled.

"Let's get on with the news. I wanted you to be the first person to hear this. So, your little sister has cancer," Dr. Salt said.

"From falling down the stairs? Wow, that was a hard fall," I said.

"No, she's had cancer her whole life," Dr. Salt explained.

"What? No, no, no," I tried to correct her, but I dropped it.

It was silent. "Wait a second, this doesn't make any sense. How could she just..." Dr. Salt said to herself. "Amy, it says here that she got cancer right before the tests, when she was crying. There was an error the first time. That is so strange. That was right when you walked out of the room," she babbled on.

"I told you that girl was a creep," Scout whispered in my ear.

"That was a coincidence," I said.

"No, child, there is no such thing as a coincidence. I'm just joking. She's doesn't have cancer. I don't really like your parents, so tell them that," Dr. Salt said.

"Yes, I will," I agreed. I didn't think Dr. Salt was a real doctor. After all, we'd need to pay for all these medical bills and Mom and Terence would have no money. That would be good.

"Take your baby sister and call your mother. I don't want to see your face around here for a long time, missy," Dr. Salt said.

I walked to the front desk and it was the same man who was there before. "Hello, little one." Then he saw me. "Oh, um, I mean Miss. I'm so sorry about that. How can I help you?" I yawned.

"I need to use the phone," I said sleepily.

"I'm sorry. I can't let you do that," he said.

"Now," I snarled with my teeth clenched.

"Just kidding, here you go." He turned the phone around so I could dial. I punched in the number. It rang twice before Terence picked up.

"Hello? Is this Dr. Salt?" he asked.

"No, it's Amy," I said.

"Why are you calling?" he snapped.

"Number one: I got kicked out."

"Of course, what did you do?" he growled and I could almost hear him rolling his eyes.

"I talked back to Dr. Salt and told her to shut her pie hole," I lied.

"Number two?"

"They have the test results," I said.

"What are they? You need to speed up. I'm busy."

"Nina has cancer,"

"Stop playing games. They would have told us that when she was born. Or did it happen when she fell down the stairs?" Terence asked. He seemed a little more concerned with Nina's health than Mom.

"Neither, it happened when she was crying and I walked out, that's when. Dr. Salt didn't know why. It just, happened," I shrugged.

"What is it?" I heard Mom ask Terence. He ignored her.

"Put Dr. Salt on the phone," Terence ordered.

"She won't talk to me," I said sadly. I was just too lazy.

"Great Amelia, that's just great," he growled.

"I'm sorry," I whined. "You need to pick me up."

"Call Jay." He hung up.

"Love you too, Terence," I said into the phone sarcastically.

"What's the story?" the man asked.

"None of your beeswax. Stop getting in other people's business, mister," I said.

I dialed Jay's number and he picked up in one ring. "Hello?" he asked coolly.

"Jay's picking us up in a few minutes," I told Scout after my short call with him.

"What about Terence?" Scout asked.

"I don't know. He won't do anything for me because he doesn't like me," I said.

"Your mom?"

"Locked up under Terence's supervision, as normal."

"Okay, let's go upstairs," Scout said. We got on the elevator and went to the second floor, into the second door on the left.

"Are you guys leaving?" Veronica asked when we got in the room.

"Yeah, why?" I asked.

"Can I come with you?" she mumbled and looked down.

"Um, are you okay with an underage driver and hiding under the seats?" I asked.

"Sure?" she wondered, with a bewildered look on her face.

"Okay, you can come," I shrugged. "We need to get my little sister, too."

"Where is your little sister?" Veronica asked.

"She's in the baby rooms. I'll go get her," I ran down the stairs into the room where Nina was.

The same strange girl was there, except with another girl. They were almost identical, except the girl she brought with her was a few tones darker. I picked up Nina and went over to them.

"What are you still doing here? And who are you?" I asked.

"I should have a right to be here. I'm sick, or was sick except no one will take me home. This is my sister," the girl looked at her sister.

"I'm guessing you won't tell me your name, too?" I asked.

"No, I'm Mary," she said. She looked at her sister.

They were the same exact height.

"Why haven't you been telling her your name? It's rude," Mary snapped.

"I don't want to give away too much information," her sister said.

"You told me where you lived and your age. Shouldn't you tell me your name?" I wondered.

"You told her where we live and not her name? What's your problem?" Mary whispered at her. "Her name is Reneta. What's yours?" Mary said for her sister.

"I'm Amy. I have to get back to my friends," I said and backed up.

"Oh, okay. I hope I see you around," she said and waved. Out of the corner of my eye, I saw Mary smack Reneta across the face. They looked identical side by side, but when Mary smacked her, she looked like the alpha.

"What took you so long?" Scout asked when I got back in the room.

"That girl was there."

"You talked to her again?"

"No,"

"Then what took you so long?" Scout asked.

"I was talking to her sister. *That's* what took me so long. We have to get downstairs. Jay's probably here."

"Okay. Are you ready, Veronica?" Scout said.

"Yep, let's go!" Veronica replied, jumping up and down, but she was coughing. Jay was waiting when we got down the stairs.

"Hey, who are they?" he asked.

"Scout and Veronica," I answered.

"Excuse me, but you can't do that," the guy said at the desk.

"Yes I can. Bye." Jay took us to the van and we drove off.

"So just like that, your brother would do that for you?" Veronica whispered from under the seat.

"Yeah, it's weird. Most people would treat all of their siblings and family, even if they aren't biological, with disrespect. It's different with Jay. It's like he knows something about me that I don't know about myself. He'd go to the end of the world to find me. He doesn't even like Mom, but I'm half of her. He doesn't like the twins at all, which is really weird even though I'm more related to him then they are and we both have the same dad," I explained.

"Wait, wait, wait, so, you have the same dad as Jay, and the same mom as the twins? If Jay isn't related to anyone in the family besides you, why does he live with you?" Veronica asked.

"Our dad died and his mom left when he was born. Not exactly when he was born, but he said he was six or seven. Mom said she left when he was born," I shrugged.

I thought I saw Jay leaning in to hear more of our conversation.

"That's weird. I'd take Jay's word for it. I think I would remember when my mom left better than someone who doesn't know her. Besides, my dad left," Scout said.

"Guys, shush. You're gonna wake up Nina," Jay said, interrupting Scout. "Ha! Like I care," he said after a few seconds. "Oh, man, I hate these twins so much. I hate Nicole too," Jay said to himself.

"Jay, if I'm half Mom and Nina's half Mom, why do you hate her so much?" I asked.

"Because..." Jay stopped himself. "I'll tell you later, when things aren't so rough." We pulled into the driveway.

"Is anyone home?" I asked.

"No, well, Cash is."

"You left Cash alone! Jay, I know you hate them but he's only a few months old!" I babbled on.

"Amy, chillax," Jay interrupted. "He's been sleeping the whole time. There's nothing to worry about. Besides, I got a babysitter for him," Jay said coolly.

"You could have told me that," I snapped.

"I just did." He laughed.

"Shut up," I growled.

"Okay, okay," he surrendered.

We went in and I put my stuff away.

"Scout, you should go and tell Clara you're here," I said. "Veronica, you can go home and say hi to your mom and dad and sisters and brothers," I suggested.

"Okay. I'll be back in a few minutes," Veronica said and walked toward the door.

"I'll be back in a minute," Scout said and shrugged, following Veronica.

"Bye, Quinn. Thanks," Jay said to the babysitter.

"Amy, come here. I need to talk to you," Jay said when everybody was gone.

"What? Is something wrong?" I asked.

"Actually, yes, I want you to know the truth. I want you to know all your options. You don't need to stay here with all these farts," he said but his eyes were serious. I giggled. "I'm serious. You need to know the truth," he sighed. "Amy, Nicole isn't your mom." He was quiet.

"Yeah, she is," I said matter of fact.

"No, she's not. She's holding me, you, and Dad hostage with Terence. Amy, we've been kidnapped."

Chapter Three - The Escape

I couldn't believe what Jay had just said. "So, you're saying, we were kidnapped?" I asked.

"Yes, Amy. Nicole is a cheater. She said she was your mom so you wouldn't want to leave. Our mom didn't leave. Nicole forced her out. I have no clue where she is now. And Dad isn't really dead. He escaped. I was going to grab you, but Nicole caught me. Dad still thinks I'm just a few hours behind him. That's why he keeps going. Don't listen to Nicole.

"I want to take you and the dogs tonight. I want to get on a plane and fly back out to New York and live with Mom and Dad. Just like the old days. With you, well, you were six months old.

"That's why I like you, because you aren't half Nicole. I hate *them*," he looked at the twins, "'cause they're half her. You aren't. Haven't you ever noticed you don't look anything like

Nicole? She's tan skin, brown hair, brown eyes. You're light, black hair, green eyes. You look exactly like Mom." He looked down and I could tell a tear spilled over. "You're the closest thing I have to her. Trust me; I know you don't like Nicole that much. I've seen you guys fight and it's nasty. You'd love Mom."

Just then, Scout knocked on the door. Jay walked away and I ran to the door and opened it.

"Hey Scout?" I said, shaking, my voice thick.

"Yeah?" She wondered.

"I'm actually kinda busy right now, so..." I hugged her.

"Whoa, is everything all right?" she asked, expecting me to say, *"Oh, yes. I'm perfectly fine. It's just that you are my best friend and I want you to stay with me forever."*

"No, it's not," I whispered.

"What?"

I looked at her face.

"Scout," I sniffled, "I'm leaving."

"You're going to come back, aren't you?" she asked, spinning the basketball she had in her hands.

"No," I shook my head.

"Why? You just moved here."

"I know, but I also just learned something."

"What?" she asked. I knew she would ask, but I had that twinge of hope that she'd not.

"My mom, she isn't really my mom. We're leaving right now because she isn't here." A lump began to swell up in my throat.

"Why are you leaving Ms. Shea?" Scout asked.

"Nicole," I gulped. "Scout, listen, I was kidnapped and my dad never died. Nicole held my dad, Jay and me hostage and chased my mom away. Jay and I are going to find our parents," I said, fighting to hold back the tears. Why hadn't anyone told me this?

"You're leaving this second?" she asked, and I could see her eyes getting red.

I nodded. I could tell Scout held back the tears.

"Bye." She hugged me.

"Tell Veronica I said bye," I sniffled.

"I have to pack," I said and ran up the stairs. I started shoving everything I could find into my suitcase and backpack. "Jay! I'm ready!" I yelled, wiping my eyes so no wetness showed.

"Okay! Do you have the dogs in their kennels?" he yelled from his room down the hall.

"Not yet!" I quickly and carefully put the dogs in their carriers. "Ready!" I yelled. We met at the bottom of the stairs.

"Do you have a light load?" Jay asked. I nodded.

"Okay, yeah, pretty light. Let's go."

We hopped in the van and drove off. I waved at Scout and she waved back. I wiped away one of the tears spilling onto my cheek.

"It's gonna be okay, Amy," Jay said. He was happy to be leaving Mom and Terence.

"Will we ever come back here again?" I asked.

"No." He was strict.

We quietly drove to the airport and sold the car to some guy who offered a lot of money for it. We bought one-way tickets for the next trip to New York City.

"Holy crap! Small world here in Washington," Jay muttered and swiftly moved with me to hide in a magazine shop.

"What? What's wrong?" I asked.

"Blend in," he ordered.

I saw what he was talking about. There was Nicole, waiting in line for her trip to Virginia. What was she going to do in *Virginia*?

We quickly got our bags checked. Luckily we were a little late for our plane so we could get on right away. I got the window seat and slept most of the way.

"Amy!" Jay exclaimed, shaking me. "Wake up! We're here!"

I opened my eyes and I was back home, in New York. "Are you sad?" Jay asked.

"No," I lied.

"You were crying in your sleep. You can go back to Nicole if you want. She is kinda your mom," he shrugged, but I saw the fear in his eyes if I said yes.

I shook my head. "I'm not sad about that," I said.

"Then what's there to be sad about?" He simply shrugged.

"I miss Scout," I started to sob. Jay hugged me.

"Remember you didn't want to go to Tukwila?" he asked, sitting up, getting the carry-on bags.

"Yeah, but that's when I didn't know Scout," I cried and wiped some more tears.

"C'mon. We have to get off the plane," Jay said and we got our stuff.

"From here on out, we're traveling by foot, bus, train and car. Now, we're going to walk up to the bus stop and ride it to our old apartment," Jay directed. "Really, Amy, why are you so sad?" he asked again.

"I dunno. I guess I'm just kinda freaked out that Nicole isn't really my mom," I shrugged. I was still trying to take everything in, all that'd happened in the last ten hours.

"Oh Amy, we're all surprised," Jay said.

"But the divorce? How did they plan that out?"

"Well, the government found out and helped us get away free. Dad got away and Nicole said he was dead. She told that to the government and she got to keep us. She acted like she was cheating on Dad, but that was just for show."

"Why did she hold us hostage in the first place?" I asked.

Jay shrugged. "It's just what some people do, like the guy who kidnapped Jaycee Duguard. They just are evil people." We had reached the bus stop.

"You know, when I was little, this was what Mom taught me to always remind me of her," Jay pulled a piece of paper out of his backpack. He wrote down the words: "good" and "evil."

"What is that supposed to mean?" I asked.

"God is good, without the extra 'o'," he said and crossed out an 'o'. "The devil is evil, with a 'd' in front of it." He wrote a 'd' in front of the "evil."

"I always remember Mom as the 'good' because she taught me the good first. Nicole is always the evil. It wasn't even two seconds after Mom showed me this, that Nicole came in and held us hostage," Jay said.

"Why didn't Nicole take our mom? Just us and Poch?" I wondered.

Jay didn't answer for a while. "Nicole knew that Mom was... cleverer. She knew that Mom could outsmart her and we would easily get away. Nicole just wanted someone to torture, to lie to, to betray. She wanted to be the stronger person. I have no clue why, but, that's just how it is. God made everything happen for a reason. You don't change it. Everybody knows that you can't change fate." *You can't change fate, that's a good tip.*

"Jay, I heard Nicole saying she got beat up and tortured by one of her old husbands. She was trying to get back at everyone for that treatment," I said. The bus had come and we stepped on.

"How do you know this? I've been spying on her from dusk to dawn for years," Jay said and handed the bus driver five bucks.

"Have you ever tried spying on her dawn to dusk?" I asked. "It works a lot better when she isn't sleeping."

Jay glared at me. "That's nice, Amy. That's real nice. Ha, ha. You got me. We're just falling out of our chairs," Jay said sarcastically.

I punched him in the shoulder. "Cheer up. Why are you so sad?" I said, trying to cheer him up.

"So now you're happy?" Jay asked.

"Not *completely.* But kind of," I shrugged.

It was an unusually quiet bus ride. Once we got to Coney Island, we got off.

"Now what?" I asked.

"We're walking to our old apartments so we can call Dad," Jay said.

"Can't you just use your cell phone?" I wondered.

"No, that's too dangerous. Nicole knows my number and could track it down. She'd easily come back and get us," Jay said. "Oh, but that lady, oh, what's her face, from the old apartment."

"Faith!"

"Yeah, can't we use her phone? We'll just say we were going to meet somebody somewhere around here and no one else would let us use a phone. Easy as that!"

"She'll ask if you could just use your cell," I said.

"Yes, that's true. But I can say I ran out of minutes," Jay shrugged. It seemed like he had an answer to every question.

"True that. Okay, let's go." We walked through the amusement park and all around until we found our apartment building. I walked into the familiar small room, with a greenish wall and the paint peeling off.

"Oh! You two came back!" Faith squealed. She had tan skin, light red hair, and was heavyset with brown-rimmed eyeglasses. She came over and squeezed me. She held out her arms for Jay but he stayed still. "Oh, just because you're old doesn't mean you don't get hugs," she laughed and squeezed him too. "What are guys doing? Are you moving back?" she asked excitedly.

"No. We need to use the phone," Jay said. He never had liked Faith.

"Why couldn't you use your cell?" she asked.

"I ran out of minutes," Jay said, just the right pace. In that situation, I would have said too many things, too fast.

"Why did you choose this place?" Faith asked.

"We were around here and no one else would let us use their phone. Please?" I said sweetly.

"What is the phone call for?" She asked.

"We're supposed to meet someone at the amusement park except they aren't there. We need to call and see if it's the right place," Jay lied.

"Who are you meeting?" Faith asked. Why so many questions? Jeeze Louise, woman.

"My Aunt Gloria," Jay answered.

"Oh alright, but just this once," Faith warned.

We went behind the desk.

"Um, some privacy?" I asked. She rolled her eyes and walked away. I dialed the number and it rang once.

"Hello?" I was so relieved to hear Poch's voice again.

"Poch, it's Amy," I sighed into the phone.

"Amy! So where are you? Dublin?" he asked.

"No," I answered. "We're in New York at the old apartment. We're using Faith's phone. She thinks you're dead so Jay told her we were calling his Aunt Gloria."

"Well, sweetheart, Aunt Gloria's got to go now," Poch said in our Gloria's voice. I giggled. "But you're a bit off track. Why aren't you in Dublin? I thought you were supposed to be always one state behind me."

"Yeah, but there was an error. We didn't get a chance to leave until a few hours ago," I explained.

"So, let's see, do you know about Nicole?" he asked, very cautious.

"Yeah, we left right after Jay told me."

"I'm sorry about that. I never got a chance alone with you without someone hearing every word I said," Poch apologized.

"Can you meet us in Dublin in what, I don't know, a couple of days?" I wondered.

"Sure, Ames. Any news on what's happened lately with Nicole?"

"Um, well, she had twins with Terence. This guy who broke my arm. And, um, one of the twins has cancer, so that was a surprise 'cause we didn't find out until a few nights ago," I whispered the words about the guy who broke my arm so Poch wouldn't freak out.

"Oh. The dogs?"

"They're right here with me. Do you know any place that will hold dogs for a couple of weeks?" I wondered.

"Actually, I do. It's right down the street and, um, take a left at Thirty-fourth. Look for a sorta' blue building. There's a sign with a gray dog and a painting of an orange cat on the wall. You can't miss it."

"Thanks! Gotta' go, see ya' in Dublin!" I said and hung up. "We're goin' to Dublin!" I exclaimed.

"Okay, do you have the money?" Jay asked, but it seemed like he knew the answer.

"Yep, right here!" I pulled ten 100-dollar bills that I had stolen from Nicole.

"Good. We're taking the train to the international airport," Jay said and we walked away without a backward glance.

"What train do we take?" I asked.

"Wait a minute. Let me look," Jay said and looked at all the times for the trains and what places. "We're going to the amusement park for a few hours, Amy. There isn't a train that goes there until ten."

"What time is it now?" I wondered.

"Um," Jay looked at the huge clock in the train station. "Around eight," he sighed.

"Yippee!" I shrieked. "We get to go to the amusement park!" I squealed.

"Calm down. Only for two hours."

"Fine," I grumbled. "Let's go!"

"Hi! How can I help you today?" asked the clown selling tickets.

Reaching in my pocket I exclaimed, "Oh my gosh! I forgot something in the car. Can you hold this place in line."

"Well, no, I'm sorry." He frowned.

"Why can't you hold her place in line? She's just a little girl," Jay said.

"Well, if you can stand here, you can hold her place in line. But you'll have to let people go in front of you until she gets back."

I turned to Jay. "I forgot my money, *'Uncle Michael.'* I won't find the car without you."

"Wait a second," said the clown. "*You* are looking after *her*?"

"Yeah, have a problem?" Jay asked.

"No. Actually, yes. You seem way too young to have full custody of a little girl."

"I'm nine. It isn't that little," I snapped brat-like.

"You're nine? Oh, I thought you were six or seven. I'm sorry. What's your name, little one?" he said.

I turned my head sideways. "Do I know you?" I asked.

"Hold on, lift up your right arm," he ordered me. I lifted up my right wrist with the purple cast. He put his face in his hands.

"I can never get away from you, can I? I ran away from that crazy hospital and took this job across the country and you find me," he said to himself.

"I still can't place you. Nothing is ringing a bell but you look familiar," I said and snapped my fingers. "That's it! You're that guy who was a nurse!" I yelled.

"Shh!" he leaned over to shut me up.

I started to crack up. I ran over to the stage and took the microphone off of the hook.

"Hey people!" I said. Everybody turned their heads toward me. "That guy over there in the clown costume is a nurse! That dude is a nurse!" I threw the microphone on somebody's head and ran away.

A crowd started to form around the booth.

"Are you really a nurse? Isn't that what girls do?" I heard some little kids say.

"Run, Amy! That guy with the microphone is mad!" Jay screamed. We ran toward the stairs and went to the train station.

"Hurry, act like you're reading the newspaper," Jay said and handed me a newspaper piece. We sat down on a bench and pretended to read.

"Where are they? That microphone is worth a lot of money plus the concussion! This has to be millions of dollars," one guy said.

"I know!" another one said. I heard them run past us.

"Sweet," I whispered and fist-bumped Jay.

"Let's go to the city and do stuff there for a few hours," Jay whispered.

"Okey dokey." I peeked up from the paper. "It's clear."

We got on a train and went to Broadway.

"Amy, go into that store around the corner," Jay whispered harshly.

"How do you know there's a store there?" I asked.

"It's New York. Everywhere you look there's a store," Jay pointed out.

"Why should we go into a store?" I wondered.

"Terence is right there in that shop," Jay pointed across the street.

"Holy crap! Are they after us?" I asked.

"Apparently. Hurry!" Jay said quickly and gave me a shove towards the small shop. We walked normally paced to the store.

"Now, look at those key chains in the back and flip pages through the journals," Jay ordered.

"Gross, I hate key chains and journals," I scowled.

"Exactly, Terence won't look in a shop for us if it's something we hate," Jay pointed out.

"True, true, okay, where are you going to be?"

"Looking at men's perfume," Jay answered.

"You mean cologne?" I asked.

"Yeah, sure, same thing," I could hear Jay rolling his eyes.

"Hello, how can I help you today?" a Spanish man asked Jay.

"I'm looking for guy perfume," Jay said, looking around with a lack of interest.

"You mean cologne?" I heard the man correct him.

"Whatever, same thing. And, uh, where are the key chains and journals?"

"Jay," I elbowed him.

"What?"

"I think he sees us," I whispered.

"Are you hiding from someone?" the man asked.

"If we were, it wouldn't be any of your business," I snapped.

"Well, well, well. You have a little attitude, don't you, missy?" the man with the accent said matter of factly.

"My name isn't Missy," I growled.

"Missy, missy, missy," he taunted.

Jay grabbed his shoulder. "Don't get on her nerves. I really don't want to put up with it."

"Yes, sir. Now, about the hiding," the man began like he knew all about it.

"We really don't need your help right now. But thanks anyway," Jay shrugged.

"Please can I help you? If you don't get out of here fast, people will start to recognize you," he said in a low, harsh voice.

"Why would they recognize us?" I asked.

"You are on the, well, Jeanie Banlisa is on the 'America's most wanted' list," the man said.

"You mean Nicole Shea?" Jay asked, thinking she was the only really bad person we knew besides Terence.

"No, Jeanie Banlisa. Here's a picture." He pulled out his smart phone and put on a news report.

"Hello folks, today we will be talking about Jeanie Banlisa. She has been on 'America's most wanted' list for years now. Currently, she and her agency just kidnapped David Jeremy Johnson and his children, baby Amelia Trinity Johnson and seven-year-old Jason Benjamin Johnson. She's roaming around the streets of New York City, dressed up as a casual person. Please call the number below if you find her, David or his children. Thank you. Now, let's see what's happening in West Virginia right now. Jim?"

The man stopped the show when it showed the real picture of Jeanie Banlisa. She had blonde hair pulled back into a pony tail and black leather clothes.

"Do you happen to know what she looks like now?" the man asked.

"Yes, she has brown hair, light brown eyes, um, is always wearing skinny jeans, and looks about 40 but really is 30," I said.

"Do you have a picture?" the man asked.

"I do," Jay said. He pulled out his wallet and gave him a picture.

"Okay. Follow me," he said and we followed him to his car.

"Do not talk to anyone but me. Also, where is your father?" the man asked.

"Well, he's supposed to be dead but really he is just going to meet us in Dublin by noon tomorrow," Jay said.

"Okay, we need to get you on a plane then. Will I have to pay?" he asked.

"Not unless you want to come with us," I said.

"Tell me, where do you live? I mean with Jeanie?"

I sighed.

"What's wrong, child?" the man asked.

"First it's 'Mom', then it's 'Nicole' now it's 'Jeanie'. Will her name stop changing?"

"I'm afraid this is very serious business. You cannot trust anyone besides each other. I'm going to drive you to a secret agency and will be here if you need anything. Please, contact me as soon as possible," the man said, ignoring my dramatic scene.

"Why do we need to...?" I snapped.

"Amy!" Jay glared.

"I need to know if you're okay. Then you can go back to your mother and father. You'll never have to see the state of Washington again."

"But I," I started.

"Shh, Amy. We don't want to go back to Washington." Jay hit me with the back of this hand.

"Yes, I do," I stated stubbornly.

"If that's a problem, I will take you back," the man said.

"What's your name?" I asked.

"Gustavo Diaz," Gustavo said.

"Ah, Gustavo, I hope you don't mind dogs." I pulled the dogs into the tiny car.

"Oh, no." He put a hand on his forehead. "I'll order you a limousine. It will be here in fifteen minutes. Stay in the back of the store."

The store was really small. I didn't think it had a back room.

"Yes, it's very small but it's there. Now, get inside. Meet at the headquarters," Gustavo said, obviously reading my expression. He kicked us out of his little car and drove off.

"Well, that settles everything," Jay sighed.

"Jay, I never knew your name was Jason," I began.

"Yeah, well it is. When we were held hostage, we all had to change our names a little bit. Dad was called Dave, I was called Jay, and you were called Amy."

Gustavo had said the back room was *small*. This place had at least three stories of dust, boxes and crap.

"Whoa! This place is huge! I'm gonna go look at the spy stuff! You know, to hide from Terence and Nicole. Or Jeanie. Or whatever her name is," I said and began to wander.

"Yeah, okay. I'm gonna look at the knives, ropes and that stuff," Jay said. We both wandered off in different directions.

I headed to the secret gadgets part of the store. There were phone watches, trackers, and some small thing I had no idea what it would do. I got lost in thought when I heard Jay screaming my name.

"Amy! Help!" I ran to find him. Then I stopped and realized that wasn't Jay's voice.

"Hello?" I asked.

"Amy, come here," a deeper voice said.

Instantly, I ran. “Jay! Get out of here! Now! Terence is in the building!” I screamed.

Jay ran over to me. “Amy, calm down. No one is here besides us,” Jay whispered.

“Amy, help!” I heard the voice again.

“Tell me you heard that, Jay. Please tell me you heard that,” I whispered.

“I did,” Jay whispered back. “C’mon. Grab the stuff. We’re getting out of here.” We crept through the aisles quietly.

I froze.

“Amy! What’s wrong?” Jay asked shaking me.

“I, I, I saw him,” I stuttered.

“Saw who?” Jay asked.

“I saw,” I paused. “I saw Terence. He is in the building right now: just an aisle ahead. Jay, he might get the dogs. I’m scared,” I whispered.

“Okay, let’s get out of here,” he whispered, running with me to the door. When we finally got to the door, which seemed like forever, the dogs were still there and all of our stuff. “We need to get out of here. Gustavo should be here by now,” Jay said.

Once I walked out, I almost walked back into the storage space.

“Oh my, gosh! I can’t go anywhere without them following me,” I grumbled.

“Who are they?” Jay asked.

“Those people, August and May,” I said glancing over at my old friends who had walked into the shop.

“You’re friends with *months*?” Jay asked, confused.

“I’m *not* friends with them. Not!” I whispered loudly.

“Jeeze, I’ll be waiting outside if you need me,” Jay said and strolled over to the door.

“Okay, I’ll be in the storage room,” I replied.

Terence had to have left by now. He knew we were out of the storage room, so wouldn’t he sneak out back or something? He surely wouldn’t wait there for one of us to come back in. I wondered idly around the storage room, thinking Terence had left.

"Amelia," someone said real slowly. "Come here," it said again.

"No," I said firmly, biting my lip and walking forward, hoping that I could find another exit. Terence walked out. When I tried to run away, it felt like every step made me slower, like I was stepping in mud... or tar. Of course, he caught up to me and grabbed me.

"Let me go!" I screamed.

"There's no one to save you now," he said sleekly and smiled so big like Jeanie, I couldn't tell if it was a smile or a frown.

"Jay! Help! Terence got me!" I shrieked as loud as I could.

"He's gone. He got in the car and drove away already," Terence's deep, low bellowing voice boomed.

"No he didn't! He wouldn't leave unless I was there," I shrieked, fighting back tears. Terrence is going to hurt me. Why?

"I wouldn't get your hopes up," he snickered like an evil villain.

I kicked Terence in the jaw and hopped down.

"Come here, you little twit!" he yelled, trying to snatch me with his monster hands.

I ran out to the street to look for Jay.

"Jay!" I screamed over and over again.

He really had left. I couldn't believe it. Terence grabbed me and pushed me into the car.

"Jay!" I screamed again, even though I knew Jay wouldn't come. "Somebody help! He's kidnapping me!" I screamed. I banged on the windows and tried to roll them down.

"Would you shut up? The windows are soundproof and tinted. No one can see or hear you," Terence grunted. I ignored him. He drove me to the airport, and made people watch me the whole way, making sure I got off at the right stop.

I was sat down in the front of the plane and two people stared at me the whole way, wide eyed.

"Okay! I get it! You're watching me. Can you stop doing that?" I yelled right in their faces.

"I'm sorry, but this is what we're paid to do," one of them said. I put my hand on my forehead.

"Oh, really?" I asked, looking up.

"Yep!" the other one said.

I pulled out the thousand dollars in my pocket for my ride back with Jay. Well, not back, but, somewhere. They both gasped.

"How did you get that money?" they asked.

"Easy, Dad makes me lunch every day, and Mom gives me money to buy lunch. It really pays off. I will give you this money on one condition," I said, smiling.

"What's that condition?" one asked, looking much too desperate.

"You let me get off at the stop I want," I shrugged.

"No, we can't do that. We were ordered to do this," one of them said, regretting it.

"Are you getting paid to do this?" I asked, trying to sneak my way out of it. One looked down.

"No," he mumbled.

"Then why are you doing it? You only do stuff when you get money. That's it," I shrugged.

"Well, okay. But you can't tell anyone that we did this," they ordered, looking me seriously in the eye.

"Your secret is safe with me," I promised, but crossed my fingers behind my back, just in case. "Oh, and also," I said, "If I don't get where I want to, you have to pay me back a thousand bucks," I smiled.

"Okay, Tom, we need to keep this girl in our sight at all times. We don't get the money if we don't," the one on my right said.

"But Jerry, how are we supposed to take money from a little girl?" Tom asked.

"Ha! You're Tom and you're Jerry. What're your last names?" I teased.

"I'm flight attendant number six, Tom Feline," the guy on the left said, proudly, but at the same time embarrassed. I giggled.

"And I'm flight attendant number twenty-three, Jerry Mouse." Jerry looked sad.

"Oh my gosh! Your parents named you after cartoons! Are their last names Mouse and Feline?"

"No," they both said, looking at each other. While I was cracking up, they started to whisper. I knew they thought I couldn't hear.

"Tom, we should keep the money and make her get off at Sea-Tac airport," Jerry whispered. I looked at him, still pretending to laugh, and glared. He had black skin, big ears, black eyes and was quite hairy. He looked petite like me, too.

Tom, on the other hand, looked lean, with hair that was almost gray and very white skin. His eyes were blue, but the part that was supposed be white looked yellowish. They actually looked like their cartoons. What mean parents, naming their kids completely off of cartoon characters.

Once I finally gave up on the fake laughing, they both looked at me.

"We would like our 500 dollars please," Jerry said, very rudely.

"Actually, I changed my mind. I don't want to give you the money," I shrugged.

"Well," they looked shocked. "We're going to tell that you got off at the wrong stop. And you'll be in big trouble."

"What? Why? If you let me off, they will blame it all on you, so, you didn't really plan that out that great, boys," I said.

"You won't give us the money," Tom said.

Now that I looked at him, he looked kind of like Steve Martin.

"No, if I give you the money, you're gonna make me get off at Sea-Tac," I said like I'd known it before they thought of it.

"No, no we aren't. Why would we do that? Where would you get that idea?" they said too fast, and too high-pitched.

"Um, I just heard you talking. You didn't realize that was fake laughing?" I snapped.

"We were joking," Tom started.

I started to cry. "Why would you do that? I'm just a little girl, trying to escape from, Jean-..." I stopped there, realizing I almost said too much, and acted like I couldn't stop breathing heavily.

Just then, one of the other flight attendants came out to check on everybody and she saw me crying.

"Oh, move out of the way you two. Look what you've done, she's crying," the lady snapped.

She had blonde hair, blue eyes, tan skin and was wearing a blue uniform.

"Honey, are you okay? What did they say?" she asked. I whipped up a lie fast.

"They said I was fat and ugly," I sobbed.

"No we didn't! I swear to God, Emily, we didn't. I love her. See?" Jerry said trying to hug me.

"Get off of me!" I screamed. Jerry sounded like he had a crush on this Emily girl.

"Move, Jerry. You aren't good with kids. I don't know why you ever volunteered. Come here, sweetie. You can ride up front with me and the captain," Emily said. I sniffled.

"Okay," I slowly followed her to the front of the plane.

"Now, you don't listen to those farts, okay?" Emily patted my leg. I faked a smile.

"Okay," I sniffled.

"They're just mean, mean people. Tom and Jerry, whew, I'll be glad if I ever get a job that pays this much money but has a lot better workers," she sighed, talking to herself now.

"Emily, did you say that they volunteered?"

"Yes, honey, why?"

"They said that the captain picked them and they hate their jobs and I should pay them 500 dollars,"I lied.

"Did you agree?" she asked.

"I had to! They were scaring me," I wailed.

"Wait, wait, wait; $500 each or $500 altogether?" she asked.

"Five hundred dollars apiece. They have the money right now," I lied.

"You had a thousand dollars with you?" Emily asked.

"Yes, let me explain ... I was supposed to meet my father, in Dublin, Ireland, with my brother Jay," I began.

"Why were you going there?" Emily asked.

"To escape from my mother. She's a very bad person and kidnapped me and my brother, well, my half-brother, because he has a different mother. My mom was doing very bad things, so we went to live with my dad, after she made him go away. We had a stop in New York, by our old apartment, for a place to sleep," I said, carefully, not letting out too much information.

"How would you sleep there if you already moved out?" Emily asked.

"Faith, the lady at the desk always said we could sleep in her room if we needed to. Anyway, my soon-to-be stepdad, Toby, caught me, but Jay got away. I ended up here. The money is so that Jay and I could get to Dublin," I explained.

"I'm so sorry about that. We will get you to Dublin as soon as possible," Emily said and started to stand up.

"But you can't let Toby see me. He's tall and is black. He will do anything to make me live with them and be a maid," I said in a sweet voice.

"Oh dear, let me call the captain and you can fly on a private jet to Dublin," Emily said.

Emily left and I followed when she wasn't looking. I knew I shouldn't have, but I did. Poch always said, "Never eavesdrop on anybody. If it was you, you wouldn't want people in your business." But who cared what anyone thought. I can do whatever I want to do.

"Captain, there's a little girl on the plane who was put on the wrong flight. She needs to be in Dublin, Ireland by tomorrow morning, sir."

"Well, who told you that?" a man's rough voice snapped.

"The little girl, sir," Emily replied.

"She might just not want to go where she needs to. Now, get outta here! Can't you see I'm tryin' to fly a plane?" he yelled.

"Very well, sir. Very well," Emily sulked and I ran back to my spot.

"Honey, I'm sorry but the captain won't let you," she sighed.

"Okay, Emily, can you keep a secret?" I asked with all the sadness out of my voice.

"Wait, was this a trick? Are you playing me? Are you trying to get off and blame it on me?" Emily asked, hearing the tone of my voice change.

"No! I'm not at all. But can you keep a secret and not go nuts?" I growled, rolling my eyes rudely.

"Yes," she grumbled.

"Will you?" I made sure.

"That depends!" she snapped.

"Okay, why don't we go into another room because you are going to go nuts," I muttered.

"I'm not! I'm a full-grown woman!" Emily snapped and straightened the wrinkles off her blue suit.

"Who still calls dorks she doesn't like 'farts'? How old are you?" I asked, much too rudely to a stranger.

"Nineteen," she replied glumly. "I look really old for my age," she admitted.

"Alright, now, come here," I whispered. I put my hand over her mouth.

"Get your filthy hand off my mouth!" she whispered loudly, but it was muffled.

"Fine, then..." I took my skinny black coat and tied it around her mouth.

"Hmmhemhmhm!" she screamed, but it was quiet. "Lemikomlitergl!" She screamed again.

"I have no clue what you're saying, so moving on..." I took a deep breath. "My name is Amelia Trinity Johnson, my brother, Jason Benjamin Johnson, and my dad is David Jeremy Johnson. We are trying to get away from Jeanie Banlisa," I whispered.

"Ahhhhhhh! Hmei!" her muffled voice yelled again.

"Calm down, you said you wouldn't go nuts," I said. She gave up. I went behind her and untied my coat.

"You are Amelia Trinity Johnson? Wow! I never thought I would meet you!" her surprised voice almost yelled, enthusiastically.

"Keep your voice down!" I said with clenched teeth.

"Oops," she whispered.

"So can you help me?" I asked.

"Yes, I've wanted to do this case," she squealed, jumping up in down in her seat.

"Wait, you're in the agency?" I asked, getting ready to defend myself if she wasn't.

"Of course. My dad's the lead of the headquarters. I started when I was seven," she said.

"Dang," I muttered to myself.

"What's the story? Any fake names, what does she look like?" Emily pulled out a pad and a pencil.

"Her name, Nicole Johnson, switched back to Shea, and I think Garnett now. I don't know if she's gotten married yet," I babbled.

"More info," Emily ordered.

"Um, brown hair, huge brown eyes, tan skin, um, her boyfriend is Terence Garnett but I'm not so sure if that's his real name. She has two more kids, twins, Cash and Nina," I explained, trying to remember things about her.

"No, she doesn't have any kids. Number one, she was one of those women who wasn't able to have kids. Were the kids born in a hospital?" Emily kept questioning and started scrawling on the paper as quick as she could.

"Yes," I replied.

"Those kids are in huge danger. Do they look half black?"

"Yeah," I replied, not getting the big deal.

"OK, this is confidential. You are coming off the plane with me," Emily ordered and stuffed the notepad and pen in her pockets. I sat down in a random chair. "What are you doing?" she asked.

"Uh, waiting for the flight to land, obviously," I said.

"No way, we're parachuting," Emily said and grabbed my hand to help me up.

"Really?" I asked.

"Yeah, don't let the captain know. Come on." She guided me.

I followed her to a little compartment.

"Hold this." She handed me a blue, red and yellow square. "Are you ready?" she asked.

"I guess," I sighed, jumping up and down, shaking.

"Good." She grabbed me and put me in something.

"Is this your first time?" she asked, shoving the thing over me as hard and as fast as she could.

"Yeah," I replied.

"Put this on." She gave something that looked like a yellow cup with a bag attached to it, tied to a string.

"What is this?" I wondered, holding it up.

"Just put it on!" Emily ordered loudly.

"Jeeze Louise. Okay," I put it on my face.

She threw something on me and we went into the bathroom. "You're gonna flush us down the toilet?" I asked.

"No! Here." She lifted the floor board off and it was clear sky below us.

"Wait, I can't do this!" I screamed right before I fell in the tight space. She pushed me out the floor and I went, down, down, down. I was about to hit the ground and all I heard was screaming. Then I saw a light.

Chapter Four - The Truth is a Lie

When I woke up, I was in a hospital room, with tubes in my nose. I tried to pull them out.

"No, don't do that," a familiar voice said. But I didn't recognize it.

"Poch?" I asked, blinking my eyes open.

"Yes, sweetie?" his rough voice replied.

"Where are we?" I asked, not exactly conscious.

"Utah," he replied.

That was shocking. But I couldn't move or show any sign of feelings. I was too tired, and a little weak. "What happened?" I asked, closing my eyes again.

"You were parachuting out of an airliner. Luckily the plane was only about sixty feet up in the air and you landed on a lot of grass but you broke two ribs, sprained your left ankle, and broke your right wrist," he said.

The wrist was a lie. My wrist was still broken in lavender cast. I remembered that, for some reason. I tried to sit up but it hurt. "Ugh, not again," I said, pretending to play along with me breaking my wrist "again".

"What do you mean 'not again'?" Poch asked.

"Terence," I began.

"Who's Terence?" Poch asked, alert as ever.

"Jeanie's boyfriend or agent, or whatever you want to call him. He broke my wrist by twisting it," I mumbled, trying to roll over. It still hurt.

"Oh, that guy is gonna get it," Poch grumbled.

"Poch, just ignore it. If he finds you, he's going to find out where I am. Then, he is going to gladly give me a slow and painful death," I sighed like it didn't matter.

"What kind of man does that?" Poch asked, in his *unbelievable, why someone would do that* voice.

"Um, Terence, apparently," I shrugged, still rude but in a sweet voice.

A nurse came in to give me some medicine. "Hi, honey. How are you? I've never seen you awake. I love your eyes," she said. The woman had short blondish red hair and freckles all over her face. She was also really short.

"Thanks," I mumbled.

"You're welcome. Can you take pills?" she asked, pulling out a clipboard with a pen, getting ready to check something off. I nodded. "Good, these are just tiny ones. When do you want your medicine?" she asked, like I knew everything that was going on.

"Uh, I don't know," I mumbled, trying to fall asleep again.

"Well, here you go."

She gave me two itsy bitsy red pills.

"What are these?" I asked, looking up at her.

"Sleeping pills, you will need a lot of sleep in order to get back up and running," she answered, getting ready to leave the room.

I studied the girl's face. "Do I know you?" I wondered aloud, curious.

"I don't know. Do you?" she grinned sheepishly.

"Hmmm," I tried to remember everyone I knew. "Hmmm," I said again. "You look really familiar, but I don't know who you are," I said, still thinking.

"Take the pills, hon'," Poch said. He was so quiet I hadn't realized he was there. I swallowed them and thought.

"Amy," the nurse said. How did she know my name?

"How do you know my name?" I repeated my thoughts.

"Amy, I know this is really hard to believe, but, I'm your mother," the nurse said.

My mother? Wait, if this was my mother, this was also Jay's mother. She was the woman who supposedly left when Jay was born and wasn't to be seen again. I was about to burst into questions, but the pill started to kick in and I quickly drifted off.

In the middle of the night I woke and couldn't go back to sleep. I decided to wait for Scout to come and take me through the hospital, and we would see Mack, and Veronica and the sassy nurses. Then I realized Scout wasn't going to come. I would never go back and see her ever again. Never. I didn't know what to do now. I decided I would call the nurse for more sleep stuff. I took the phone and dialed the number 1, since it said it dialed the main office.

"Hello?" a female's voice asked.

"Hi, this is Amy Johnson, in room... actually I don't know," I said, looking around for the number of the room.

"Oh, one second," I heard her put down the phone and called for Dr. Rae.

"Hello, this is Dr. Rae," I heard the woman's voice who had been in my room yesterday.

"Hi, er, I'm Amy. Can I get more sleep stuff?" I mumbled, trying to remember the foggy thoughts of her.

"Oh! Amy, of course, I'll be right up!" she said enthusiastically.

"And, I'd like some explanations," I reminded her, not exactly remembering myself, but she had already set the phone down. "Bye," I muttered sarcastically into the receiver.

A couple minutes later she appeared with the pills.

"So, Amy, how are you doing?" she asked, stepping up to my bed.

"Alright," I shrugged.

"What's wrong?" she asked, reading my expressions and completely ignoring my words.

"I want explanations. Now," I said harshly.

"What kind of explanations?" Dr. Rae asked in a sweet, innocent voice. It sounded like she already knew what the question was.

"You said you were my mom earlier. What's up with that?" I wondered rudely. She gulped. "Well?" I glared at her after a long moment of silence.

"You were kidnapped," Dr. Rae said and began to back towards the door.

"I kinda figured that out," I snapped.

"And I'm your real mother," she whispered, getting in the position to bolt.

"So why am I calling you 'doctor'?" I asked, making up a question so I didn't look stupid.

"Because I am a doctor," she whispered so quietly she sounded like a little baby mouse, scared of a cat.

"Shouldn't I call you 'Mom'?" I asked rudely.

"I don't know. You can call me Daphne while you're still warming up to me," she still whispered, shrugging.

"You seem like you're new at this. You already have Jay," I said, more like a threat than a statement.

"Who's Jay?" she asked, her eyes narrowing like she really didn't know who he was.

"Um, your son. You know, Jason Benjamin Johnson," I asked.

"Yes, he's my son. But we don't call him Jay, ever," she said, shaking her head a little no.

"Well, he could have a nickname if his last name was Rae," I asked. I had no clue where this conversation was taking us.

"What?" she asked seeming to be thinking the same thing.

"Jay Rae?" I asked, thinking that's how he got his nickname.

"No, that would just be his name. *Your* name is Amy Rae," she said. This was so confusing. I'd rather talk about why a cow moos.

"No it's not. I'm Amy Johnson," I say, not very confidently.

"No, your father and I agreed, since I kept my maiden name, that if we had a girl, her name would have my last name and the boy would have David's last name," Daphne said, sinking her body down to match her eyes with my eyes.

"Holy crap! I haven't known my name for nine years. That's a first. You?" I nearly yelled. Then I remembered it was still night time by the way Daphne looked at me.

"Yeah, go to sleep, I need to go home. Please sleep in tomorrow; it's Saturday and I'm supposed to take care of you. Bye, Ames." She kissed me on the forehead and walked away. I took my medicine and quickly fell asleep again.

It was eight o'clock in the morning when I woke up. I dialed the number 1. "Hello, this is Dr. Shea, how can I help you?" the woman asked, sounding exactly, exactly, no difference, like her. I froze.

Dr. *Shea*, that's the name Jeanie used in disguise. "Hello? Who is this?" she asked with an impatient voice.

"Oh, um, I need Dr. Rae: I need to talk to her," I finally said.

"Sorry, she's not here yet. Can I help you?" she asked.

"No," I said too quickly.

"Why?" she asked, surprised by my rudeness. *I don't want to see you*. I thought; *that's why.*

I thought of a quick lie. "Oh, she was giving me something last night and we had a fight. I want to apologize to her," I hesitated.

"I can tell her, what were you guys fighting about?" Dr. *Shea* asked like she just wanted to come up here, no matter what it took.

"That's none of your business, is it?" I snapped.

"Well, I want to apologize for you," Dr. "Shea" said, way, way too quickly.

"No, I can do it myself. What's her phone number?" I asked, opening the night table. I found a notepad and a pen.

"I can't tell you that. It's confidential," she said, sounding like I was annoying her.

"If it's confidential, how do you know?" I decided to out-dumb her.

"Because I am a doctor," Dr. Shea said.

"Are you sure?" I asked.

"Yes."

"Can you send me your diploma saying you graduated to become a doctor in Utah?" I asked.

"No," the answer was firm.

"Why not?" I asked, trying not to sound like a snoop.

"Because I'm not really a doctor," she said.

"HA! You admitted it!" I yelled, but quieted down, thinking of the people in the other rooms around me.

"No, I didn't. Even if I did, no one will know because no one is in your room and no one is here with me." An evil, cruel voice was inching up her throat.

"Yes, but I recorded it," I lied smoothly.

"I was just joking; of course I have my diploma," she said quickly.

"Um, Dr. Shea, can you tell me your whole name?" I asked. I pulled out my camera and pushed record.

"Jeanie Banlisa, no, I mean, um, er, Nicole Shea."

I dropped the phone, already knowing it was her, but shocked that she admitted it, that it was official.

"Hello? Hello? Is anyone there? Hello?" she asked, almost shrieking into the receiver. Then, the phone went dead.

I took the miniature phone book and looked for Dr. Rae's number. After a lot of page flipping, I found it. "Number 86," I muttered. I pressed the eight and the six. There were four rings before someone picked up.

"This is Dr. Rae. How can I help you?" There was a loud yawn. I sighed.

"This is Amy, Daphne. The person who kidnapped me before is in this building. Go to the front desk and ask someone if you can talk to Nicole Shea. She's really Jeanie Banlisa," I said, gulping, trying to slow my breathing. I'd never been this scared of someone I loved. Well, I still thought of her as my mom, so I would still love her. How could someone that anybody loved act like this?

"Whoa, Amy, slow down. What happened?" Daphne sighed and I heard something, a bag, being put down and loud keys dangling.

"Jeanie Banlisa is downstairs in the lobby," I whispered, still breathing heavily.

"How do you know that?" Daphne asked, sounding more confident that I had just gone nuts.

"I just called for you and I out-dumbed her and she said she was Jeanie Banlisa by accident. Just ask for Nicole Shea," All the words rushed out of my mouth like they were on their own.

"OK, see you later," Daphne sighed and hung up.

I hung up harshly, hoping not to break the phone. Poch walked into the room.

"Hey, Amy, you don't look so well. Are you alright?"

"Yeah, Poch, Jeanie is in the building. Go downstairs and kill her or something!" my voice was on a high octave and sounded like a wheeze.

"Calm down. I can't leave you alone. Your mother isn't in her room and I don't know where to find her," Poch whispered so nobody else could hear us.

"She's in the lobby. I told her to go down there," I breathed.

"Well, what if Jeanie found out what room you are in and came here to take you back. I won't let that happen. So I have to stay here," Poch said and sat down in a metal fold-out chair.

"Fine," I managed to grumble/wheeze.

A couple minutes later, Daphne walked in the room with Jeanie. I hid under the covers.

"You little brat, come here right now!" Jeanie screamed and kicked her legs.

"Jeanie, calm down! The only reason Amy did this was because she was scared," Poch ran over to her and held her on the shoulders.

"Shut up David! I don't care! I'm going to kill you, little girl. *Kill you*! And no one is ever going to find out! I'm gonna beat you to death, and it's going to hurt! And you know who's going to get blamed? Them! Your parents. I'm going to be completely out of the picture. Your parents are going to be in jail, and Jay, he's gonna die too! And all your little friends back in Washington!" Jeanie shrieked.

"When is the institution going to be here?" I muttered so quietly I couldn't even hear.

Daphne grabbed the phone and dial 911 while she gave Poch Jeanie's hands. I already heard the sirens coming. A few minutes later, a policeman walked in.

"This isn't Jeanie Banlisa. She's a blonde," the officer grumbled, obviously not seeing she was wearing a wig.

Poch pulled off the wig.

"Nope, I was wrong. C'mon, Jeanie, your time is up," he grumbled and handcuffed her.

"I'll get you, you little twerp!" Jeanie yelled. "Don't worry! Even if it's the last thing I do, you're going to be at the grave before you turn 16!" she shouted and kicked and bit and did everything a maniac would do.

A couple days later, I was out of the hospital. We lived on a little farm; we had chickens, horses, cows, and even a little lake to play in. One day, I went to the cow we called Vanilla Face because she was all white and yellow. Then, something I never expected happened. I saw somebody in the bushes.

"Hello?" I asked. "Who's there?" I asked again and walked closer to the bushes.

"Amy! Amy, help me!" I heard a familiar voice.

"Scout?" I asked like an idiot, when she desperately needed help.

"Yes, I'm Scout. Amy, help!"

I ran to the bushes, taking out my pocket knife just in case. When I looked over, Terence was holding Scout, while she was screaming. I froze. I couldn't think straight, and Terence grabbed my knife.

"Amy!"

I heard one last scream from Scout, and she fell dead, bleeding.

I snapped open my eyes. "Amy! Wake up! Someone is here for you," Daphne yelled, waking me from my nightmare.

"Okay, okay. Let me get dressed." I hopped out of bed and took off my big t-shirt. I changed into a green tank top and cutoff jeans. I pulled on some socks and slipped my vans on.

"Wow, Ames, you look horrible," Poch said as he sipped his coffee.

"Thanks. I had a bad dream," I said, pulling back my short messy hair, trying to flatten it out.

"What happened?" Poch asked.

"Nothing, Daphne said someone was here for me. Who is it?" I asked.

"Oh, some funky lookin' girl. Black hair, uneven. Says the name's Scout," he shrugged and took another sip of his coffee.

"Scout!" I yelled and ran out of the yellow kitchen.

"You know this girl?" Poch asked. I ran out of our big white house.

"Scout!" I squealed.

"Hi Amy!" she stepped up to me from a car.

"How did you know where I was?" I asked and walked over to her, pushing my hair out of the way.

"Listen, I need to talk to you," Scout whispered.

"What is it?" I went over to the chicken coup.

"Your mom has been missing for a long time, and Mr. Garnett wanted to talk to you about where she was. I flew over here with him and he wants you to go back with him to find her. He really misses you," Scout said, completely forgetting I had told her my mom isn't really my mom.

"No, no, no, no, no. Scout, he kidnapped me. Jeanie is going to kill me if she gets the chance. I can't go back there. Besides, why would I want to leave my dad and my mom for some freak? I will not go back there, Scout. No way. Would you stay with your parents if you could?" My mouth and words could barely keep a pace with each other.

"Yes," she mumbled.

"See, that's what I'm doing," I shrugged and collected the eggs.

"No, Amy, he really, really misses you. He was crying on the way," Scout said.

"Scout, no!" I screamed. "I hate him! And you need to stay away from him. He'll do the same exact thing he did to me to you," I warned.

I picked up six eggs and went back to the house. Scout followed angrily.

"Amy, he's right out front in the car. He wants to talk to you," Scout said, jogging to keep up with my pace. I paused, and then kept going.

"Not without my dad being there," I put the eggs in a little basket on the porch. I went to my cow, Vanilla Face. I had obviously won that fight.

"So, what's that cow's name?" Scout asked, changing the subject so we both wouldn't get angry.

"She's Vanilla Face," I muttered and took a rusty pail and put it under Vanilla Face's stomach.

"Why did you name her that?" she wondered.

"She's the lightest cow here and her face is as white as vanilla ice cream. Jason's cow is Music, because she's always mooing and it sounds like music. Daphne's cow's name is Pearly because she is the fanciest cow. Pearly doesn't play in mud and she loves being washed. My dad's cow is Keyboard because she always looks like she's typing and looking at the computer screen," I babbled.

After I milked all of the cows, I brought a huge, gray pail of milk to the house. I set it down in the kitchen.

"Hey kiddos! Nice job on the milk, Ames. Did you already go to the chicken coup?" Daphne asked.

"Yes. Can Scout ride one of the horses with me?" I asked.

"Not now. Just brush your horse and you two can ride him together," Daphne said, leaning against the kitchen counter, stirring up some yogurt.

"Okay. C'mon Scout," I said. I ran over to the barn and took my horse into the middle with all of our grooming supplies.

"What's his name?" Scout asked.

"Dark Spirit," I replied and brushed his mane.

"Why did you choose this horse? He seems so, you know, odd," Scout said, and sat down on a stool.

"He's special. He's the only horse that looks like me. Green eyes, black hair, and pale white skin." Dark Spirit had green eyes, his head was black as ebony, and his stomach and back were chalky white.

"He doesn't seem like an ordinary horse, that's all," Scout shrugged.

"Because he's not. He's the best horse anyone could have," I snapped rudely. It came out harsher than I wanted it to. But it sounded like she was picking on my horse, so I had to defend him.

"Hey, what happened to the dogs?" Scout wondered, again changing the subject so we both wouldn't get mad.

"They're in the fields. See?" I walked out of the barn and pointed to all the trees that were a couple of acres down the hill. Then a black blur went in between the trees. "Phoenix goes the fastest, but Tracker is a lot stronger," I explained. Scout nodded. I think she forgot about Terence.

"So, wanna' have breakfast?" I asked, forgetting to groom the rest of Dark Spirit.

"Oh, er, sure. What are we having?" Scout mumbled shyly.

"I don't know what do you want ... cereal, eggs, pancakes, waffles, toast, bacon, sausage? We have tons. So?" I babbled on about food.

"I'll have toast and eggs," Scout interrupted me.

"Bacon or sausage?" I asked, being very rude by talking so much.

"Um, bacon," Scout replied with a strange tone and a look that made me look weird.

"Do you want milk, apple juice or orange juice?" I asked.

I didn't even need to know this information. Daphne was the one making breakfast but I didn't want any silent moments or else my thoughts might drift off, to something that would probably scare me.

"Milk," said Scout interrupting my thoughts.

"Okie dokey. We'll start after I finish grooming him," I chirped and walked back to the barn to groom Dark Spirit.

We went inside and sat down after I was done. "So what do you ladies want for breakfast?" Daphne asked.

"Um, can we have toast and eggs?" I asked, tracing my finger against the table.

"Yup! Bacon?" she asked, getting the pan ready on the stove.

"Yes, ma'am," Scout mumbled.

"Oh, you don't need to say that stuff around here. You're family," Daphne said and began humming a made-up tune.

"Already?" Scout asked, bewildered.

"Yes! Everybody who enters this house with permission is family," Daphne said. I tried to focus on their boring conversation so I wouldn't think about... her.

"Oh, there is somebody outside," I mumbled.

"Really? Who?" Daphne asked and shot straight up like a bullet.

"Terence," I looked down. I said the name so quietly, I couldn't hear it myself.

"Who's that?" Daphne dried her hands after doing the dishes.

"One of the people who kidnapped me. He was Jeanie's partner," I muttered and put my head down on the table.

"He needs to leave, now. Get him out," Daphne said seriously and whacked the rag she was using for the dishes down on the kitchen counter.

"I can't. He wants to see me. That's what Scout said. She rode up with him," my little voice said. Normally, I was a whole lot braver than this. I wasn't scared of him at all, even when he was attacking me, six months ago.

"Scout, you aren't going back with him. No way. You're staying here until your parents come and pick you up. I'll go get him out," Daphne murmured and stomped out of the house.

"No! Daphne, let Poch. Terence will do bad things," I warned, jumping up.

"I'm a big girl. I can handle stuff," Daphne marched out.

"Poch!" I screamed and ran to the stairs. "Get down here! Daphne's in trouble!"

Poch ran down the stairs, out the front door. He snatched part of her flannel shirt, and it nearly slipped off her shoulders. Her white tank top under it had water from the sink on it.

"Daphne, don't do this!" he yelled.

"Let go of me! Terence hurt Amy, I hurt Terence," she threatened. She stomped off in her muddy boots. I ran out and Scout followed.

"No! He's really nice once you meet him. He just needs to explain himself," Scout pleaded. "Please, don't do that. Please, I'm begging you. You need to meet him. Let him talk!" Scout shrieked. Both of my parents ignored her.

A familiar face stepped out of the faded blue truck and I hid behind Poch.

"Amy, I'm so sorry. Let me explain myself," Terence began.

"You're not touching her," Daphne looked up at his tall six-foot-four height.

"Hello. Let me introduce myself," Terence said to Daphne with a rough, soothing voice.

"Not a chance. You are going to give me some explanations. Why did you break Amy's wrist? Why would you lie to her? What kind of hideous person are you?" Daphne babbled.

"Listen, I'm sorry for what I did to Amy. I regret it and I miss her. I won't touch her again; I won't even talk to her. Just let her know straight, I can never change what I did. That's reality. But, if there is any chance she could forgive me, I know I don't deserve this. Amy, I'm really sorry," he said, with a fake tear welling up in his eye.

"You're right, you don't deserve this. Daddy, get him out of here," I fake talked.

"Terence, it's time to go. You said your goodbyes. Leave, now," Poch ordered.

"Okay, but I'm always..." Terence began.

"Yes, I know, you're always going to be there if I need you. Bye!" I interrupted him in a sarcastic voice and turned around.

"Wait, Amy! Can you, by any chance, come with me?" he asked.

Now what kind of question was that? I hated him. I had learned to shudder at his name, voice, look, and everything. I had rebelled against him. If I was strong enough, I would rip him to shreds or just put him in a paper shredder, or a Terence shredder.

"No," I snapped and marched back up the steps very confidently. I heard Daphne, Poch and Terence fighting over me. Scout slowly walked in and slammed the screen door. She clicked the regular door shut.

"Wanna' ride Dark Spirit?" Scout asked. I sighed and ran up to my room and locked the door. I hid under my black quilt, the one my Grandma Effie and Grandma Bobby made for me before they died.

Scout tried opening the door and hit her fists with it. "Amy, can I talk to you?"

"Go away," I grumbled.

"No, I'm sorry. I shouldn't have brought him here. Can I stay while I wait for Claire and Paul to get here?"

I didn't answer. I heard her stomp down the stairs. I expected she got a key from where all the keys were because she opened the door.

"I'm sorry. I didn't mean to, to, cause all of this. I ruined everything," she hesitated.

I groaned. "Just go away. Leave me alone," I grumbled.

She ran outside. I looked out my window and she was headed toward the barn. Uh, oh. She was going to get on a horse.

"Scout!" I yelled. I ran outside into the barn. It was too late. She was off down the hill on Poch's horse, Can-can. All of his animals moved a lot and Can-can looked like she was doing the can-cans.

I hopped on Dark Spirit, bareback. I kicked his sides and he took off. Suddenly, I heard a scream.

"Great," I muttered. I pulled on Dark Spirit's mane. "Go!" I yelled. He struggled to go faster. When I nearly fell off of him, I yelled "Haw!" to make him stop.

I quickly slid off and ran over to where I thought she had fallen.

"Scout?" I yelled. "Where are you?"

I hopped back on Dark Spirit and took off.

"Crap, Scout. Why did you have to go in there?" I murmured to myself. "Go!" I said again and he ran faster.

I saw Can-can trotting along and I figured Scout was close.

Hiding behind a tree, Scout lay there. It looked like she had a broken leg.

"C'mon, get up here," I said. I struggled with her weight to get her on Dark Spirit. I whistled and Can-can came running over to me. I jumped on him and said to Dark Spirit, "Trot to barn, slowly."

"Why can't I ride him?" Scout asked as she folded her arms, but she sniffled because of the pain in her leg.

"Can-can is really hard to control. He looks like a sweet little Appaloosa, but he's a crazy little horse that's uncontrollable. Dark Spirit is well trained, probably because I train him the most," I explained.

"But I want to ride him," Scout wailed.

"That's too bad. Can you hold on to Dark Spirit when he goes fast?" I asked, not believing her answer, even if it was a no.

"Yeah," she answered.

"Okay," I sighed. "Dark Spirit, go! Can-can, giddy up!" I yelled and both horses took off.

"Dark Spirit, slow!" I yelled. He galloped slowly, Scout on his back. "Good boy. Now, go back to barn and wait there for me," I ordered. It looked like he nodded his head a little yes.

"He'll do that?" Scout asked.

"Yes. Go," I whispered. Dark Spirit walked slowly to the barn and waited. "If you get hot, tell him 'in'," I yelled out to Scout. "I'll be right back."

I kicked Can-can's thigh and led him to the house. We stopped by the window and I knocked on it.

"Hey, Amy! What's up?" Jason asked, still a little tired from waking up.

"Scout got hurt. Can you call the doctor?" I asked, breathing heavily from all the warm wind blowing in my face.

"Who's Scout?" he asked.

"Remember with Jeanie? She lived across the street from us in Tukwila," I explained.

"Oh, why do you need a doctor?" he asked.

"She fell off Can-can."

"But you're riding Can-can," Jason said, blinking at me. I rolled my eyes at his idiocy.

"She fell off him when she was on him. No details. Call the doctor," I ordered.

"Whatever," he grumbled and dialed the doctor's phone number on our wall phone in the living room. When I got back to the barn, Scout wasn't outside.

"Scout, the doctor's on his way," I said walking into the barn. Nobody was there but the horses. "Where are you Scout?" I looked into Dark Spirit's fearful eyes. I threw a saddle on him and jumped on. "Go to Scout! Run!" I yelled. He took off out of the barn and into the meadow. I jumped off him and there was a rustle in the bushes. Oh, crap.

Stab Terence. He will take the knife. Don't freeze up, I said to myself. Then I smiled.

"Dark Spirit, we're still working on this one. Do it as best as you can," I patted him on the side of his stomach and climbed up on him. He trotted over to the bushes quietly and I took out my pocket knife, just in case. "Okay, Dark Spirit, this is it," I murmured and delicately stroked his mane. We snuck up behind the bushes.

"Amy! Help! Amy!" Scout screamed.

Don't let her die, I thought. No, she was too good to lose. Terence was choking her when I looked over. I put my finger to my mouth, telling Scout not to change her expression.

"Dark Spirit, attack!" I yelled.

Terence looked up, and then he was on the ground, bleeding out. Scout was bewildered.

"Scout, come on! Get on the horse," I pulled her up, using Terence's body as a boost.

"Dark Spirit, walk to barn," I ordered. He did as he was told, and I finished Terence off when they were gone.

My pocket knife was covered in blood. I needed to get rid of it. "Fantastic. That's just what I need, to get rid of my knife," I grumbled. I dragged Terence's body back to the house, making sure nobody could see.

My family would understand. He was about to kill Scout, so I told Dark Spirit to attack. I dropped my knife on him a little too hard. It wasn't like I purposely killed him, I thought.

"Accidental, who am I kidding?" I muttered. I ran back to the house with the knife in my hand.

The doctor was there when I got there.

"Hello. My name is Dr. Chong. I take care of humans and creatures. I would like to help you. You have broken your leg?" he looked at me staring at my legs.

"No, my friend Scout: she's out in the barn," I said.

"Thank you. You will not regret this. I am the choice, and I am honored to do this for you," he babbled on.

"Shut up and go to the barn!" I yelled.

"Yes." He looked down, probably hoping Daphne or Poch would scold me. He was out of luck.

"Guys," I began when he was gone. "Terence was about to kill Scout." They started interrupting. "Wait, wait, wait, let me finish. I did what any normal person would do: I told Dark Spirit to attack. He did attack, but my pocket knife fell into him too. We need to get his body out, before the police come," I burst into explanation.

"Great, Amy. That's just great. You killed him and now the po-po is after us. You just think of the greatest ideas," Jason snapped.

"What would you do in that situation?" I asked.

"Kill him," Jason looked down.

"That's what I thought. So, can anybody help me or do you want me to do it myself?" I asked. Daphne looked like she was in pain. "What?" I asked.

"Wow, you just did something I could never do in my life. I can't believe a nine-year-old girl outdid me."

"So will you help?" I asked, hoping Daphne would just cut to the chase.

"Yes," Daphne said and looked down, ashamed probably because of me.

"Whatever," Jason agreed.

"Ames, this is a big deal," Poch said.

"Do you want the police to come after us?" I asked. He sighed and hesitated.

"Is that a yes or a no?" I asked.

"A yes," he grumbled.

"Great!" I grinned. "Come on, let's go," I said, beginning to walk out of the room.

"After Dr. Chong leaves," Daphne said, remembering someone was here.

"I can make him leave," I said confidently.

"I doubt that very much," Jason grumbled and rolled his eyes.

"Shut up and let me do it. Daphne, you go and say he needs to leave and there is a family crisis. You say that he can come back later. Jason, Poch and I will pretend to harvest and plant plants out there," I explained my plan.

"Not bad, let's go," Daphne said.

We all went out there and I 'planted' seeds closest to the barn so I could overhear them.

"Hey, uh, Dr. Chong, there is something going on and we need you to leave," Daphne said and dug a small hole.

"What's going on?" he asked.

"Er... personal things. You need to go," Daphne says.

"I cannot leave a patient helpless," he said sounding like with any excuse he would go away.

"Go away!" she screamed and started punching him in the stomach to get rid of him. "Get out, get out, get out!" Dr. Chong ran away to his car.

"He's gone, we're clear," I yelled. We went over to the body and dragged it to a tree.

"So, what are we going to do with it?" Poch asked, standing up, the cool breeze tangling his short black hair.

"We dig as deep as we can until we reach hell and Satan will take it from there," I said, in an exaggerated tone.

"Like that will happen," Jason said sarcastically and rolled his eyes. I stuck my tongue out at him.

"No, I think we should put him in the road by the neighbors' house when they aren't looking," Daphne suggested.

"Not bad. All we need to do is make him look like he got hit by a car. Whoever he's closest to, they will have to answer the questions from the police," Jason said, shrugging.

"For now, we'll hide him under the floor boards in the barn, near the chicken coop area," Poch said.

"Okay, let's go," I jumped up and walked out from under the tree. We lifted up the gray-brown boards, digging up dirt, making sure the blood wouldn't stain anything.

"What are you doing?" Scout asked.

"Hiding the body, the last thing we need is the cops chasing us," I said as I got down on my knees.

"Around what, one o'clock tomorrow or the next night, we're gonna take the body and make it look like he got hit by a car. The neighbors will get blamed. I'm going to take Dark Spirit and act like a little girl, taking some milk to the neighbors, to make it back by tomorrow," I suggested.

"Why don't you just take the truck?" Jason asked, thinking of why I didn't need to ride the horse to make the story sound real.

"Uh, er... it broke down," I shrugged.

"Sounds good enough. But why wouldn't your parents take the milk there?" Daphne asked. Good thing I had them. I never would have thought of these questions if I happened to see someone.

"Hmmm, do you or Poch look younger?" I asked. "I think Daphne does, she is going to be my older sister who takes care of the family, and Jason is going to be her twin. He is clumsy and doesn't do anything. Poch will be working on the fields all day, and my sister, Scout, broke her leg, and Daphne had to look after her. That's why I had to bring the milk to the neighbors.

"Our doors will be locked while Jason and Poch take the body to the street. Scout will be indoors, sleeping, and, Daphne, you will be too. We'll say that Poch has gone out, working on harvesting someone else's yard. He had to leave early to get there on time. Jason, you're out, doing something and won't come back for a while," I explained for the story.

"That sounds like a pretty good idea. Let's do it," Jason said.

"'Kay, we'll start tomorrow night," Daphne said. "And, um, David, take Scout into the house, she can sleep on the guest bed," Daphne smiled and walked back to the house.

"Wait! We need to practice," I said.

"Amy, not tonight, tomorrow, we," Poch grumbled and yawned.

"No, practice, it's the real deal tomorrow night, not a practice. Let's go! Let's go! We need to do this thing!" I yelled.

"Okay, fine!" Poch shrieked, to make me shut up. "Let me go tell Daphne first, though. We need to be back kinda early. You know, to get our sleep so we can do this tomorrow," he explained.

"I know why we need to get back, Poch, I'm almost ten. I understand things," I grumbled. He didn't answer.

Poch went into the house to tell Daphne. I ran back up to the house, dragging Scout behind.

Later that night, I sat up in my bed while Scout was asleep.

"It's okay. It's fine. No one will catch you. Why would someone be looking for someone out on the streets at one in the morning?" I muttered to myself and changed into my jeans and pulled on an overcoat.

Thoughts of everybody in my life ran through my head. I laid down on my bed and rubbed my temples. I began to drift into memories of the past:

Me being snatched when I was a baby, I was crying, crying so hard like it was a rainstorm that never ended. I saw the fright in Jason's eyes. He was panicked and didn't know what to do. He held me in his arms and whispered in my ear that everything was fine and we'd be back with Momma in no time at all.

In Jeanie's arms, laughing, playing with her necklace. I saw the worry in Jason's eyes when he was only a year older than I was now. Poch looked into Jason's eyes and saw the fear. They had some type of connection. Then Poch snatched me up and I stopped laughing. "I want Momma!" I cried. Jeanie shrugged and grinned. "No Ames, it's time to have a nap," Poch grumbled and glared at Jeanie.

"Amy, it's time to go," Jason whispered in my little room.

"Where are you going?" I heard a booming voice say. It was Terence.

"Nowhere," Jason mumbled. "Get out!" he yelled.

The rest of life was a blur, but then something happened. It went past present moment, into the future. There was Jeanie with a whole gang with her trying to come after us.

"Okay, she's in Maine, get ready," I heard Jeanie say. As I was walking down the street I saw someone following me. Then she began fast walking. I decided to let her past, but she came directly behind me. I thought she was just an early morning jogger.

But she wasn't. She was running now. And she was running towards me.

Chapter Five - The Agency

"It's going to be okay, Amy. Everything is going to go smoothly. The police won't catch you," Jason kept telling me.

"But what if it doesn't work out? What if we get caught? It'll be because of me. All of us will be in jail because of me," I said, shaking.

"No, it won't be because of you. It will be because we agreed to your idea. It was just an idea, and we agreed to do it.

We have Scout, too. She can say that Terence nearly killed her and Dark Spirit attacked him."

"What if they blame it on Dark Spirit? Then they will kill him," I said panicky.

"You worry too much. Let's finish the practice, and everything will work out," he said coolly.

"Alright, let's get this thing started," Poch said when he got back. "Amy, you take Dark Spirit, I'll take Can-can, and Jason, take Donny," he said.

Donny was Jason's horse; he named him that because he was obsessed with the Donny Darko movies and Donny was a Morgan, so she was dark.

"What about Goosebumps?" I asked.

That was Daphne's horse. Why we named her that was that Goosebumps would always give you goosebumps when you looked at her. She is one of those giant, brown furry horses.

"She'll have to stay here," Jason said, saddling Donny up.

"We need to leave right now. We aren't going to be able to bring the body with us this time," Poch said. "Saddle up, and Amy, get into your girly clothes. Don't forget to bring a basket of milk bottles with you," Poch reminded us.

I ran up to my room and put on some cowboy pants and a red flannel shirt with cowboy boots and a cowboy hat. When I got back, I braided my hair.

"Put the pink blanket on Dark Spirit," Jason said. He threw me the pink blanket and I put it on Dark Spirit's back. This was normally Goosebumps' blanket and mine was the green one.

I saddled him up with the pearl-embroidered saddle. "Good, get the pink reins," Poch ordered. I quietly put the hook in Dark Spirit's mouth, and did the rest of the grooming.

"Are you ready?" Jason asked.

"Yup, I need the milk basket with like, muffins or something," I said, stroking Dark Spirit's neck.

"Oh yeah, right. Dad, get the basket with the food in it," Jason ordered.

"Okay. Be right there!" Poch yelled and ran inside.

"I'll see you later tonight, Jason. Bye," I said and took a deep breath.

"It will be alright. Don't worry about it," Jason said and gave me a side hug.

"Yeah, it will be alright," I repeated.

"Trot till I tell you to stop," I ordered Dark Spirit.

We walked to the street with a tiny but long forest by the side of our farm, and about a mile down, a cop pulled me over to stop.

"Why ain't you in bed, little girl?" he asked. He spit out some tobacco he was chewing.

"Oh, I need to deliver some milk to the neighbors," I began and kept a straight face. *Don't talk too fast, and don't hesitate. Don't look to the left, up, blink or pause. He probably knows how to tell if you're lying.*

"Why didn't your parents just drive down there themselves?" he asked.

"Our truck broke down," I explained.

"Alright, you're coming back home with me," he grumbled and got closer to me and Dark Spirit.

"What about my horse?" I asked a little too quickly.

"He's going to have to go," the policeman shrugged.

"No, he's not leaving," I said stubbornly and grabbed on tighter.

"Why didn't an older sibling bring the milk?" he asked after a long pause.

"I have a sister, who broke her leg, and my oldest sister has to take care of her while my dad went to harvest someone's plants. He needed to leave early tonight to get there on time," I explained, pacing my words.

"Any other siblings?" he asked.

"My older brother, but he's really clumsy and comes and goes as he pleases. Right now he's gone," I explained. He huffed.

"Well, you're going to have to give the milk to me, and I will deliver it. You go home and get some sleep," he smiled, finally figuring out how to get me back home.

"No, it's their birthday and I need to give it to them," I lied. Good thing I thought of that really quickly.

"What's your name? I will tell them you sent it," the officer finally said.

"No, I'm not supposed to tell anybody my name. I need to get going. It's late," I said and Dark Spirit began to trot.

"You're coming back with me," he said, not changing his mind.

"No I'm not. Go!" I yelled and Dark Spirit ran as fast as he could.

"Oh my god, that little liar," I heard him grumble.

"Hurry up!" I whispered. Dark Spirit went faster. The policeman got in his car and turned on his sirens. I kicked Dark Spirit's right side so he turned left into the forest.

"Go!" I whispered. He struggled to go faster. I nearly fell off when I saw Donny step in front of me.

"Jason, you nearly killed me!" I whispered harshly.

"Sorry, I didn't see you," he said in a normal leveled voice.

"Shush! I've got a cop chasing me!" We heard sirens whiz by.

"Dang, you got him mad, Amy." Jason straightened his back and looked at me, surprised.

"I know. I tried to lose him before he knew where I was going," I explained.

Can-can and Poch walked up to us. "Hey, Ames, what are you doing here? I thought you were supposed to be on the road," Poch said.

"I was, but," I stopped because Jason interrupted me.

"A cop is after us," he said.

Poch cursed at me. "Amy, that's just great. C'mon, we're going home." The horses trotted home quickly. "Giddy up!" Poch said.

"Go!" I whispered.

"Kill!" Jason said. Donny took off and went straight ahead.

We put the horses in the barn and went back to the house.

"We have to get it right tomorrow, Amy. Try to blend in," Poch ordered. "What time is it?" he asked.

I looked at my analog, slap-on watch. "It's 2:15. We need to go to bed," I said.

"Yeah, see ya' in the morning." Poch walked us back to the house.

I climbed into my bed and when I was about to fall asleep, my tiny red cell phone rang. I looked at the number, I didn't recognize it. I flipped it open anyways. "Hello?" I asked.

"May I please speak to Amelia Trinity Kay Johnson?" a male voice asked.

"It's Rae, actually. Anyway, speaking. Who is this?" I grumbled, mad at him for waking me up.

"Amy, you might not remember me, but my name is Gustavo Diaz. I helped you escape from Terence in New York City a couple of months ago. Sorry I am calling so late."

"Yeah, I remember. Of course, and that's okay, I was just going to sleep so you caught me just in time," I muttered and sat back down on my bed.

"Amy, listen, you need to go into hiding. Terence has found you and he is coming, if he hasn't already," Gustavo warned.

"He did. We killed him." I hesitated.

"Oh! Well, that is a surprise. He brought a girl with him named Anastasia Hacker. Did you find her?"

"Yes, she broke her leg; she's asleep right now."

"Ah, you need to be very careful around her. She met Terence; she might have agreed to stay on his side."

"No, he was about to kill her. She isn't on his side," I said, assuring him.

"You cannot be sure of that. Partners will do that for each other. They act like they're killing another, but they really die for them and the second partner lives on and keeps the secret and makes the worst mistake in their life," he said.

I heard Jason walking down the hall. "Wait one second! Someone's coming," I whispered. Jason knocked on my door.

"Amy, I need to talk to you. Can I come in?" Jason whispered.

"Yes," I answered. He walked in.

"Is someone else here? I heard you talking to someone," Jason looked around the room.

"No, I was talking to myself," I slid my phone under my pillow.

"We need to talk. I'm leaving, and I need you not to tell anybody anything. Can you do that?" he whispered and sat down on my bed.

"That depends," I said. "You can't leave right when we might be blamed for everything!" I said.

"That's why I'm leaving. You can come too. It would all be blamed on Mom and Dad," he offered.

"But, we're a happy family, you can't leave. This is what we wanted for years and we finally got it! I mean really, Jason!" I said and took a long, deep look in his eyes.

"Hey, I saw you slide the phone under your pillow. Who's on the phone?" he asked.

"No one. No one at all. Why would you think that? I mean pshht. Of course not," I lied; it was so noticeable.

"Amy, who is it?" Jason asked and tried to snatch the phone from under the pillow.

"Okay, even if there was someone on the phone, it wouldn't be any of your business," I snapped and lay down on the pillow, making sure he couldn't get to my phone.

"Amy. Who's on the phone?" he asked, his teeth clenched.

I gave up. "Gustavo Diaz," I sighed.

"No, Amy, don't talk to someone you barely know. I don't even know him," Jason said and grabbed the cell phone from under my pillow.

"Yes you do, in New York, a couple of months ago. Don't you remember?" I asked. He thought for a moment.

"Oh, yeah, why is he on the phone?" Jason asked, being a lot less mean.

"I don't know, just, let me talk to him," I said and put the phone to my ear. "What is it?" I asked Gustavo.

"Where are you this moment?" Gustavo wondered.

"Utah," I answered, surprised at his question.

"Okay, you need to get out of Utah and go to Maine. Right when you get out of the airport, look for a white van. In the van, a woman named Emily will take you from there. Do you know her?" he asked.

"Yes," I replied.

"The money will be in your barn, on the big white horse with the black head," Gustavo said quietly and very calmly, but very fast.

"Okay, when I am supposed to leave?" I asked.

"Please try to make it by next week. Until then, you need to do your best to hide. Call me at this number once you have reached Maine. When will you be leaving?" he wondered, like I had a clue what was going on.

"Uh, er, I don't know. It's going to be later than tomorrow, at least."

"I will see you soon. Goodbye."

"Bye," I said, but he had already hung up.

"What's going to happen?" Jason asked.

"We need to go to Maine by next week. Do you think that we should tell Poch and Daphne?" I asked.

"Why do we need to go to Maine?"

"I don't know. I think he said we need to hide. We'll take Scout back to Washington on the way," I said and tucked myself back into my bed.

"How are we going to get all of the money?" he wondered.

"I know, just be very, very quiet," I said. "I'll get the money. Pretend like its wabbit season," I teased.

"Okay," Jason whispered, not laughing at my joke.

I snuck into the barn and looked on Dark Spirit. There was a handmade, brown leather pouch around his neck. I looked inside and there had to be at least ten thousand dollars. I took off the pouch and there was a little note. It said:

Dear Amy,

This is for the plane tickets so you can all go, drop off the girl, and then go to Maine. Please, make it there by this Monday. You will need to miss the first couple of weeks of school to do this. We will excuse you.

A blonde woman, Emily, will be in a white van that says 'PUBLIC STORAGE' on it. Explain to your parents that this is very dangerous and there is a chance of death. If you will do this for me, each of you can choose to have one item in the world. It will be completely free. If you do not agree you need to fly back to either New York or Washington.

Gustavo Diaz

I brought the little pouch back to the house.

"How are you going to tell them that you need to go to Maine?" Jason asked. I breathed in threw my nose and exhaled deeply. I looked up at him.

"I don't know. I guess I'll tell them we need to hide and go on the thingy or fly back to New York or Washington," I shrugged.

"I have an idea!" Jason said enthusiastically.

"What?" I asked.

"I'll say I'm running away, and you say that you want to follow me. You tell them to come and that I got on a plane to Maine. You guys will follow and everything will work out smoothly."

"I'll call my friend Lisa. She lives in Maine and can take care of the cows and horses for us. We can give her some money too," I suggested.

"Okay, we might need some of Great-Grandma May's jewelry," Jason said, just before Daphne came out of the house.

"Hey, what are you guys doing out here?" she asked, blinking so her eyes could adjust to the little light in the barn.

"Oh, uh, er, I heard one of the horses jumping up and down," I lied. It didn't make any sense, but Daphne was half asleep, so I guessed she would believe me.

"Okay," she mumbled. "Just go back to bed," and walked sleepily back to the house.

"Okay, hurry up and bring it back," Jason said.

"Alright, just gimmie a sec," I said. I stuffed all of the money into the little pouch.

"Where am I supposed to hide this?" I asked, tucking my straight hair behind my ear.

"I don't know. Under your bed?" Jason suggested.

"No, they check there all the time," I said, yawning.

"Okay, um, stuff it in one of your pillows," he guessed, thinking I'd say no.

"They'd find that," I said again.

"You aren't making any progress with me, Amy. We need to go to sleep. Where do you want to hide it?" Jason grumbled.

"How about, um, on my dresser. I can make it blend in with the stuff," I shrugged.

"Okay, you could have said that earlier. Now go to bed," Jason ordered.

I went back to my room and turned on my little lamp. I walked over to my wooden dresser and put the pouch under the moose head hanging out of the wall. I barely got enough sleep, partly because I fell asleep at four AM.

"Amy, get up!" Jason was shaking me. I opened my blue curtains when I was still in bed. The sun was just rising.

"What do you want?" I asked. I looked at the clock. It was six o'clock in the morning.

"Where did you put the pouch?" Jason asked.

"It's on my dresser," I grumbled and rolled over.

"No, Amy, it's not. Someone must have stolen it," Jason said.

I got up and dragged my feet over to my dresser to see if someone actually did steal it.

"It's right here, you moron," I snapped. He snatched it out of my hands.

"Hey, what are you doing?" I asked.

"I need $200 dollars to get out. Remember our plan?"

"Oh yeah, bye," I said and went back to my bed.

The dogs came into my room and sat on my bed. Phoenix looked sick. "Move!" I yelled. They wouldn't budge. I pushed them out of the way but they moved back to their spots. "Great, we need to call the vet. She probably got some kind of ticks," I grumbled.

"We're out of money right now. We will call the vet later," Jason said. "I'll see you in Maine."

He went to his room and took his suitcase downstairs. I heard the door slam and he was gone. About an hour later, I took my cell phone from my night stand. I had one text message from Jason. It said,

Hey amy. Im in the arport right now. Wat is lisa's address? C u in mane. Jason

I sighed and texted him back,

Um, I kinda forgot. Ill txt u back wen I find out. amy

I went through my contact list and at the end was Lisa. I pressed call. It rang three times until someone answered.

"Hello?" Lisa asked with heavy breathing.

"Hey Lisa, it's Amy," I began.

"Who are you?" Lisa asked.

"You lived next to me in New York. I have two dobermans and, um, an older brother Jay. My dad's name is Dave and my mom is um, Nicole," I said, remembering the lies.

"Oh, yeah, yeah, yeah. What's up?" she asked.

"Well, this is a lot to ask, but do you still live in Maine?" I wondered, already knowing the answer.

"Yes," she answered.

"Do you have a couple extra stalls I can use?" I asked.

"I think?" she guessed, wondering why I would need a stall.

"We have four horses and need a place to stay. Do you think that will work?" I heard her smile.

"Yup, of course it will. I mean, our families are friends." She had a huge grin on her face, I knew it.

"Thanks, I'll see you in a couple of days. What's your address?" I asked.

"It's right outside the airport in a blue house. I live by the beach. Okay, bye!" Lisa was about to hang up.

"Wait! We might come without the horses," I said, just in case.

"That's fine. Just, show up kind of unexpectedly," Lisa said mysteriously. I had a feeling that we weren't allowed to go over there. "Okey dokey, see ya' later," Lisa chirped and hung up.

I hung up, got dressed and went out to the stalls. I took my phone out to the stalls and started to comb Dark Spirit. I called the vet, Dr. Chong.

"Hello. This is Dr. Chong and I take care of humans and creatures," he said. I rudely interrupted him.

"Shut up. I'm Amy Rae and I need you to come to my farm in Utah. You know where I live. Be here by eleven." I hung up.

I put my phone on a shelf and saddled Dark Spirit. I jumped on him and started to ride around. It must have already been an hour because Daphne ran out screaming, "Jason! Amy, do you know where Jason is?"

"Um, yes," I said and there was an awkward silence.

"Well where is he?" she snapped.

"He went to Maine," I said calmly.

"He what?" she almost whispered.

"He went, to Maine," I repeated.

"I heard what you said!" she screamed. "But why?"

"He wanted to get away. I don't exactly know but he told me a little bit," I shrugged.

"We're going after him," she said with clenched teeth.

"Um, we still need to put the body on the road. We forgot to last night," I said, lying so I wouldn't have to explain that last night was a practice.

"Alright, the sun is still rising. I'll go wake up David," she said and walked away to the house. A couple minutes later, they both walked out.

"Daphne, you'll need to stay here with Scout. Amy, we're going into the forest to do this," Poch said.

We got the body and the horses trotted into the forest. We walked about three quarters of a mile, and dropped him by the road. We ran back to the house quickly, making sure nobody would catch us.

"That's done, now, where is Jason?" Poch asked.

"Um, honey, he went to Maine. That's what Amy told me," Daphne sighed.

"Well, where are we going to get the money to go there, get Scout on the plane back to Washington, go to Maine and fly back here?" Poch asked.

"Uh, I have a little bit of money," I offered.

"No, this will take about a thousand dollars, Amy. Not just a couple bucks," Daphne said to me.

"I know. But I have a lot of money. I'll explain it later," I said and put Dark Spirit in the stalls.

I ran up to my room and grabbed the brown leather pouch. All the money was still in it. I brought it down to the kitchen table and shook the bag so all the money would fall out.

"Amy, where did you get all of this money? Did you steal it?" Daphne asked, amazed.

"No, I didn't steal it and I said I would explain later. We have enough money and no extra treats, even though we have an extra five thousand. We drop Scout off and we'll meet Jason in

Maine. I'll tell you everything, I promise. Just wait a little bit until we get to Maine," I explained.

"What about the horses?" Poch asked.

"My friend Lisa will take care of them. We will put the horses on the plane, and I think I have enough money for that. Or we will get someone to take care of them at the farm. We need to go back to either Washington or New York after we finish this. The agency will make sure we get our school work and still learn. As I said, let me explain later," I said right before they burst into questions about the agency.

We took Scout to the airport with us, pushing her in a wheelchair we found in our closet.

"Why is this so sudden? Why do you need to take me back right away?" Scout asked.

"That's confidential. I'm sorry but we cannot tell you," I said.

She pouted. "What is it, seriously? Daphne, David?" she looked up at them hopefully. Daphne gave a meaningful look, but Poch ignored her. "Okay, fine. Don't tell me."

We were the last ones to board the plane. The flight was very short, considering that Scout fell asleep and didn't ask any questions and that it was a nice view and I got window seat. I walked onto the platform when the plane landed. I remembered the first time I had come to Sea-Tac Airport. I was with Jeanie, thinking Poch was dead. Now, I was here again, thinking that Scout was doing something behind my back.

We got in a taxi, Daphne, me and Scout squished in the back while Poch got the roomy front. I told the man Scout's address and we were off to my old neighborhood. When we finally got there, we got Scout out and took her to the doorstep. I rang the doorbell. Clara opened the door.

"Scout! You're in huge trouble, young lady! Where the heck were you? I was worried sick. We put up signs everywhere! What happened to your leg? Get in here right now! You have a lot of explaining to do, Miss Hacker," Clara yelled.

Paul walked out. "Scout, where were you? You're grounded for three months!" he said in a husky voice.

"I know I'm in trouble, okay! So just shut up!" Scout yelled and stomped back to her room, limping.

"What's with her?" I asked.

"She's been acting like this ever since you left. All the attitude and all that. I'm scared she'll leave forever; I think she found out we aren't her real parents, or real aunt and uncle, and that her dad left and her mom died. I don't want her to know she's a foster child," Clara said, ashamed.

"Well, you guys should be heading on your way. Scout is going to do a lot of talking," Paul said.

We walked out to the cab and I told him to come back later. He quickly drove off.

"Amy! What the heck did you do that for? Now we have to wait for a couple of hours to get back to the airport and we might lose Jason, he could get away," Daphne complained.

I pointed at the house Jeanie had bought.

"C'mon, let me show you something," I said. I led them to the door; it was unlocked. I walked in; the floors creaked. The broken wine bottle still lay there, staining the floor.

"Let me show you my room," I said. I guided them up the creaking stairs, and down the creaking hall way. I walked into the gray room. Some girls about my age were standing over the bed. I froze. I didn't know that someone already had moved in. They both turned their heads slowly at the exact same pace.

"I'm sorry, I didn't know someone had moved in. I was just showing my parents my old room," I said.

"You better be sorry," the lighter one said. They were both half black, but one of them was a couple shades darker.

The one who said the threatening words was obviously much prettier and wore a black button-up dress. She had short black heels and a black hat with a little net over her face. A red rose was attached to the black hat. She wore sparkly earrings with her blondish brownish hair in a tight bun.

"Reneta!" the darker girl scolded.

She was wearing a strapless white dress and she had white flat shoes with little red bows on the toes. Her darker hair was almost to her waist and she had long, dangling earrings.

"But Mary, we lived here before!" I heard Reneta whisper. Then I remembered them from the hospital.

"You know what Katrina said. No one is allowed but us. They are not us," Reneta snapped.

"Well, maybe we will get rewarded for being nice," Mary said. "I'm sorry about her. She has an anger issue," Mary said to us.

"No, I don't! I'm just following the rules."

Mary clamped her hand over Reneta's mouth.

"You should take a look at the house and be on your way. Our uh, mom, yeah, our mom doesn't want anybody coming into the house while we're redesigning it. I mean, we aren't supposed to be here. Come on, Reneta. We better get out before Mom finds us." Mary took Reneta's hand and walked out of the house.

"That was weird. Okay, here was Jason's room and Jeanie and Terence's room, and this was the twins' room," I said, gesturing towards them.

A little thought popped up in my head when I showed Daphne and Poch the twins' room downstairs. Where were the twins? I decided not to worry about it.

"Um, that was the house. So we better get going now," I said.

"Okay, sweetheart. You look worried. What is it?" Daphne asked.

"I, uh, just want to make sure they don't get in trouble with their mom. That's all," I lied.

"No, what is it, really?" she asked. I sighed.

"The twins were kidnapped, too, and I don't know where they are now. I don't know if they're dead or alive," I said.

"It'll be alright. Now we do seriously need to get out of here," Poch said, not caring at all about the twins, probably because he or Daphne knew who they were.

The cabbie drove to the door and we hopped in. "Sea-Tac Airport," I said.

"Um, Daphne, I need to tell you something," I said and gulped.

"What is it?" she asked with that tone in movies that parents have.

"Well, we need to go to either Washington or New York when we're done. It's not safe in Utah," I whispered so the cab driver couldn't hear.

"Well, what are we gonna do with the horses? We can't sell them, I love them too much. And the cows, what are we going to do with them?" Daphne wondered.

"Well, um, er, we can put them in a horse ranch or on the farm. Besides, we don't even pay attention to the cows. We just had them for free milk," I say.

"But we won't see them every day," Daphne complained.

"I know, but like, every other weekend we could go out there," I said, like I was the responsible adult.

"What are you guys talking about?" Poch asked, eavesdropping. So much for his lesson about never listening to people when they don't want to be heard.

"David, Amy says we need to go back to Washington or New York because Utah isn't safe. We will have to get rid of the cows but the horses will need to go to a ranch," Daphne wailed like a young child.

"Amy, let me see the note that says that," Poch ordered. I knew he was being sarcastic, but I pulled out my brown leather pouch and took out the note. I gave it to him and he read it silently.

"Amy, you know I was being sarcastic," He said. It wasn't a question.

"Really?" I played dumb.

"Yeah, but, if we want to keep the horses, why don't we move to Washington? It has that little field and all the little trees we could tie them up to. Although there isn't enough room for them, we will need to take them out every single day and ride around for two hours. Can you do that?" Poch offered.

"Yes," Daphne and I both said at the same time.

About ten hours later, we landed in the Maine airport. When the dogs came up with the luggage, they were barking like crazy, trying to get out of the carriers. We got a rental car and drove to Lisa's house. I tried to lead the way, trying to remember where her house was. I called her up, just in case we got lost.

"Hi this is Lisa," she said.

"Hey Lisa, it's Amy Johnson," I said and looked out the window at the sunset.

"Oh, hey, Amy what's up?" she asked.

"Um, how do you get to your house from the airport?" I asked.

"Oh, you take a right out of the airport and keep going until Fifty-seventh Street. Take a left there, and go straight for about half an hour. You'll start to see beach signs. Follow them until you find the beach with a row of houses in front of it. I live in a blue house and I'll be in the front," she instructed. I listened to her annoying voice, trying to keep focused.

"Okay, thanks!" I said trying to sound happy but my tone was way off.

"Poch, go back to Fifty-seventh Street. It's only a couple of minutes away, right?" I said and looked up at the signs to see if I was correct, even though I wouldn't find my answer there.

I gave him directions to Lisa's house.

"Alright, thanks. Now, where do you think Jason is?" he asked, looking around to find him, as if he could.

"I don't know. He just told me he was leaving. Let me call him," I pulled out my phone and flipped it open.

"Hey Amy," Jason gasped for breath.

"What's wrong?" I wondered.

"I think one of Jeanie's partners got on my track. This one guy keeps following me. Can I call you back?" he asked, his breath accelerating.

"Wait, just where are you?"

"I'm on the beach, next to Lisa's place. I think, wait! I just saw her. Does she have blonde hair and blue eyes? Kind of tan?" he wondered, still gasping for breath.

"Er, yeah," I guessed, not really understanding him.

"Okay, where are you?" he breathed.

"We're about 15 minutes away from Lisa's," I said.

"Gotta' go," said Jason. I heard him cuss before he hung up the phone.

"Jason's by Lisa's house. He thinks he's being followed. Drive fast," I ordered.

"Why the heck is he being followed?" Daphne yelled.

"Jeanie, she might have told one of her spies to follow him. We need to hurry," I said.

"David! Drive faster!" Daphne screamed.

"If I go any faster a cop is going to pull us over!" Poch shrieked.

"Hold on! We can go back and get there faster! Drive back to the airport and someone will be waiting there!" I said.

"It's too late, Amy. You should have said that earlier," Poch said with clenched teeth.

I pulled out my phone again and looked at the recently contacted list. I dialed Gustavo's number. I rang a few times until he picked up.

"Hello? This is Gustavo," He said.

"Hey, it's Amelia Rae, I'm sorry but we missed Emily. I kinda forgot about her. Sorry about that," I said.

"That's fine; I knew you wouldn't go. She wasn't even planning on going there. No, I'm joking. I believe Jason rode with her."

"Okay, that's all I needed to call for. Where do I meet you in Maine?" I wondered.

"Do you know the beach about thirty minutes away from the airport?"

"Yes, I'm headed there right now."

"Perfect. I'm waiting at the front of the west entrance. I will see you very soon." He hung up before I could say goodbye.

"Okay, we need to go the west entrance," I told Poch.

"Okay, why? Who are you meeting?" he wondered and the speedometer inched towards eighty.

"A man who is in the agency," I answered.

"Agency? What agency? I'm not letting you do this! No way you're working in this agency!" he yelled, annoyed.

I was about to start a fight, but I ignored him instead. I must have fallen asleep because Daphne was shaking me to wake up. I looked out the window and Gustavo was standing there with sunglasses on. I hopped out of the darkly tinted car and rubbed my eyes, tired from my nap.

"Ah, Amy, you have come, I saw you brother a couple of blocks that way." Gustavo pointed to the east. "Quick! He is being followed by one of Jeanie's agents, the worst one yet. Her name is Maggie Ages. She looks Spanish, with dark skin. Maybe Italian. Hurry! We can talk later." He pushed me into the car and signaled go to Poch.

We drove way too fast to be going on the small neighborly road and finally spotted Jason. The car squealed to a stop and I flew open the door before it completely parked.

"Get in!" I yelled. Jason hopped in and we drove to Lisa's house.

"Whoa, that was a close one," Jason said. "She was about to come up and talk to me. I was running like crazy," he panted.

"Stop! I see Lisa!" I yelled even though everybody was right next to me. I flung opened the door to the big car and hopped out. "Hey Lisa!" I yelled.

"Amy? Is that really *Amy Johnson*?" she asked.

"No, actually, it's Amy Rae, but, close enough. The horses couldn't fit on the plane. Can we come in?" I said and ran over to her.

"Oh! Come in? I was thinking more that you guys would stay on the shore. You never mentioned going into the house! Whew, um, that is going to be a little problem. Uh, how about you wait right here and I'll be back," she babbled.

She ran into her house and there was a lot of screaming and yelling. Finally, a little old lady with a big gray poof ball of hair on her head walked out.

"But Nannin! They need a place to stay. Look at them!" she said. Nannin had a little maid outfit on with a duster in her hand.

"No!" she grouched. She sounded like a troll.

"Um, excuse me, but, Lisa's mother said we could stay here," I said to the little old lady.

"Her *mother* told you that? When?" she asked, amazed.

"I called her up a couple of weeks ago and she answered the phone. Lisa was calling her Mom so she must have been her mother," I said.

"No," she grouched at me. "I think you're making this all up. Her mother won't even talk to me when she's here. I'm sent to the grocery store or something. I just get paid a lot of money to do this job. I don't like the kids or Maine," she snapped.

Lisa gasped and ran inside. When she walked out, she had a cell phone in her hand and a video camera. She tapped the phone and pressed the screen a lot. My phone started to beep and I looked at it.

Message from Lisa. It said. I read it.

Plz ask Nannin to say she dosnt lik the kidz she had this job just 2 get a lot of $$$ lisa

"Um, can you say that one more time?" I asked her.

"What? That I don't like the kids here and they're little parasites? And the only reason I got this job is to get paid a lot of money." Her voice was cracked and rumbling.

"Oh, well, where else can we stay?" I asked.

"I don't give a crap. Go to some rotten motel," she grumbled. My phone beeped again. It was another message.

Is ur dad w/ u? if he is tell him 2 cum out & act al important. Thnx lisa.

I texted back,

kk

I went to grab Poch out of the car. When I opened the door, thank god he was wearing a suit and sunglasses.

"Poch, act like you're really important and work for, um, the lady of this household," I said.

"Alright." He stepped out and walked slowly to the old lady.

"Ma'am, I need to speak with the lady of this household," he said sternly.

"Oh, a man like you needs to talk to her. Of course, Lisa, go call your mother right now," she snapped.

"What's your name sweetheart?" she asked Poch. "Wanna' take a walk on the beach?" she said blinking.

"Oh, uh, Dad, I think Mom is going to be a little disappointed in you," I said. Then Daphne walked out.

"There you are, what are you guys talking about?" she said.

"Nothing, now. The lady of this house must be very busy! This is extremely important," he said. Lisa walked out again.

"You can stay! Oh, and, um, Miriam," Lisa started.

"Do not call me that! I am Mrs. Ramer!" Lisa's Nannin yelled.

"Not any more. I recorded your little speech about not liking us, and Mom said you're fired, she's on the phone right now," Lisa said and grinned. Miriam snatched the phone away from her and started yelling.

We stayed at Lisa's house for one night, and then had to leave. Gustavo called at 6:00 in the morning and said we had a meeting. We went to Augusta to meet him in a super-secret agency that looked nothing like an agency. I was expecting some type of little compartment you'd have to squeeze into. When we got there, Gustavo called.

"Hello?" I asked as I flipped open the phone.

"Hello, this is Gustavo; I can see you right now. I'm in a flower shop across the street. You'll need to go through an alley to get to the door. Right now it looks like old brick apartment building," he told me.

"Okay, I'll see you then, bye!" I said.

"Wait, Emily will be at the front desk," he said. I was about to say something but he already hung up.

"Okay, c'mon guys, this way," I said. I led them through a dark alley, and on the other side, there was an ice cream shop, and candies, and little kids, and all sorts of stuff for babies. There was a sign that said 'MICK'S FLOWER SHOP' on it.

"In here!" I said. They followed me into the little shop.

"Hi, I'm Miranda! How can I help you today?" Emily asked. I walked up to her.

"Emily, where is the agency?" I asked.

"What agency?" she asked.

"Wait, do you know Gustavo?" I whispered.

"Gustavo who? I'm just trying to get by and dress up as a clown to get money," Emily chirped.

"Is there another Emily?" I asked.

"No," she said. "I'm just joking. It's in the staff room in a closet. There's a lot of stuff in the closet so you'll have to move it out of the way and the door is on the floor. Gustavo is waiting there for you. It's really awesome down there! Oops, customer!" she said.

I led my family into the staff room. There was a closet, like any other, and I opened it. There were dirt and flower seeds scattered all over the floor. I moved everything out of the way. The only way I could see the door was because Emily told me. I easily climbed through, but Poch and Jason had a hard time.

"You have some explaining to do, mister," Daphne told Jason.

"Not now," he grumbled.

Gustavo interrupted them.

"Ah, you've come. Come look at this view, over here," he said. We walked to where he was. "You can see the whole street, but they can't see you," Gustavo said.

"Wow, this is so beautiful," Daphne said.

"Now," Gustavo clapped his hands officially. "Let's talk."

Chapter Six - The Plan

"What do we need to do?" Daphne asked.

"You guys need to go to Washington or New York. We will do the rest. I will warn you: There will be drills, and there will be the panic alarm. We will send some of our agents to your home, for a practice. The real thing, when Jeanie's real agents come to get you, we won't help. We won't know at the time, I'm almost sure of it. And we're definitely not going to get up in the middle of the night to protect you. All we know is that Jeanie has people that will attack you. There will be back-up. I've heard you have some horses and cows. Am I correct?" Gustavo asked.

I nodded like I was the boss of the family. "Alright, the cows will have to go. You can sell them at a good price on the Internet. The horses, you can only keep if you move to Washington. I found the perfect place, it's eh, kind of creepy but it will work. It's on 133rd street, and there are lots of kids in the neighborhood. The Green River runs right by it, Billy Barooes is just across the street and you'll love it!" he exclaimed.

"Oh, we went there, actually. I used to live there, and someone has already bought the house. There are two little girls who live there with their mom," I explained.

"No, there were two little girls who lived with their mother only about a hundred years ago. You're the first ones since!" he explained, narrowing his eyes like he knew I was lying. But I wasn't.

"Never mind, we'll move back in. How will we pay to get back? We're struggling to get ourselves fed. How can we afford a plane ticket?" Daphne asked.

"I will pay. It's my gift to you since you are taking such a risk," Gustavo did a small bow.

"No, I'm not going to let you do that," Daphne said. Everybody had settled into the uncomfortable chairs.

"Well, I will take it out of the agency's bank then," Gustavo shrugged.

"No, I want to pay for it by myself," Daphne protested.

"Hmm," he said and put his index finger to his chin. "Ah, you may do a job for me, it's a lot of work, but you get will get a big pay. Can you do a little of spring cleaning for me? I want to get a head start," he suggested.

Daphne sighed. "Alright, you can pay for us or the agency can," She sighed. I knew the cleaning idea would change her mind. She absolutely *hated* cleaning.

"Great, then I will see you again in three months! I will meet you at Applebee's restaurant. Goodbye and thank you for working with me," Gustavo said. We got practically picked up and shot out of the room by the guards. After that, we got on a plane and took a long flight back to Washington.

I would miss the fields, and my room. I would miss the chickens and cows. I would especially miss waking up in the morning, and getting the eggs from the coup. I'd miss the beating hot sun on my back when I would work, but now I was going back to Washington, back to where all my good friends were. This would be good, going back to meet new people, and have our house back... I was pretty sure.

The plane ride was long and I slept most of the time, because I hadn't gotten my full ten hours of sleep a night for about a month. I needed to rest, to know everything would be alright and I wouldn't get slaughtered when I went to sleep. I didn't want to worry about the monsters under my bed, like I did when I was little, not the fat, green, furry ones who had sharp teeth; the ones with guns who chewed tobacco and killed innocent people. These were the *real* monsters; the ones that scared every single soul who thought about them.

Again, Daphne was shaking me to wake up. "Daphne, I don't want the men with guns coming, I want to go to another continent. I don't want to stay here," I wailed.

"Keep your voice down. We can talk about it later," She shushed me.

That was the only thing that I could think about, guns, mean men and women, Jeanie, monsters, my family, my life, my family's life. I wasn't going to chicken out and worry. I was going to be strong. I was going to show that I wasn't scared. I knew we all were, we all knew it too, deep inside, we all knew. We knew what would happened if this went wrong.

We drove to the old house in a small Toyota Prius. I got out and smelled the fresh air. It was just as I remembered: flowers, gasoline, and rich soil. The birds were chirping and the river was slithering loudly through.

"Wow, this place is beautiful," Daphne said, looking out of the car, her eyes wondering.

"This is a lot like my neighborhood when I was a kid. David, can you get the dogs?" Daphne said.

"Yeah, sure," I saw Poch roll his eyes.

"I'll go get the horses with Jason," I suggested quietly and slipped away.

We hopped in a huge car that Poch bought and went to the horse airport, a couple hours away. We led all of the horses into the back and paid the men thousands of dollars.

It was quiet for a long time. "Are you scared? You know, of Jeanie's agents?" I asked.

Jason sighed. "Amy, you know the answer to that."

"You just don't want to admit you're scared," I said in a matter-of-fact voice.

"Alright, Amy, I'm scared of Jeanie's agents and her. Now, if you tell anyone I said that, your face is going to be as flat as a pancake and a huge hole in the wall," he threatened.

"Okay, cross my heart, swear to die stick a needle in my eye, hand to God, even if he doesn't want to see my hand," I promised.

"Good," Jason snapped.

When we got back and took the horses from the horse trailer, some men were already there, building a little barn with dark red wood.

"How much money are we going to spend?" I asked. I opened the trailer and led the horses out.

"Over a million at least," Jason estimated. I sighed.

All of a sudden, all the kids in the neighborhood came running to the house. "Holy crap, Amy, are these all friends of yours?" Jason asked.

"Um, I guess?" I turned around towards them. Scout was the last one there, rolling in her wheelchair with a snarling look on her face.

"Move it!" she yelled. Everybody moved out of the way, acting like she was going to eat them if they don't obey. She rolled over to where I was standing. "Amy, what are you doing here?" she asked rudely. She was wearing black eye liner and bright red lipstick.

"We had to move back. What happened to you?"

"Shut up!" she shrieked.

Daphne walked out to see what was going on. "Whoa, is that you, Scout?" she asked.

"Yes," Scout grumbled.

"What's wrong? You used to be all happy all the time. Remember? You'd always make everyone smile, Scout. You were the reason I'm not suicidal. You need to clean up," I said.

"Nobody cares about me, so I don't care about anyone," She grumbled.

"Scout, I care about you. Why can't you care about everyone like the old days?" I froze. "Are, y-you Jeanie's?" I couldn't finish the sentence.

"No, I'm not, but after my leg gets better I'm running away to find her. Andrew left so now there are no stories, nothing. Clara and Paul didn't think I was listening and I overheard everything. I'm not loved, my parents gave me up," she snapped.

"Yes, Scout, but you were adopted. Somebody has to love you," I pointed out.

"Well my mom and dad left me. So who does?" Scout grouched.

She still had an ugly expression on her face, slitting her eyes.

"Clara and Paul, your dad left because he was afraid he would do something wrong, trust me on this, at first my mom left, but she came back because we found her. Your mom died, she couldn't help that. Your dad left because he wanted the best for you. Not the worst," I explained, thinking that was a complete lie. "Come here," I ordered.

She rolled herself over to me. "Do you still think you're hated?" I asked. She nodded, considering it. "Well get some sense into yourself, woman!" I yelled. I slapped her across the face.

"Ow, that hurt, Amy. I wouldn't do that to you," she complained and touched her stinging cheek.

"Why wouldn't you do that to me?" I challenged.

"Because I care about you," she blurted out. "I mean, it's rude, duh," She corrected herself.

"Think about it, woman!" I smacked her again. "Do you like me doing this to you?" I yelled.

"No," she said and started to hide her face.

"That's what you're doing to us. Are you cared about?" I screamed.

"No, I mean yes," she whimpered.

"Good. Who's next?" I asked. There were a lot more kids than before. They all ran away, though, probably scared of me. "Why did you turn out like that?" I asked Scout.

She wiped all of her makeup off, it smearing all over her face. "Katrina and Reneta. They are, well, the meanest people I ever met. They tell you to do all of the junk to be their friend. And they're really pretty. If you're their friends, you are like, awesome," she explained.

"Why don't you want to be friends with Mary?" I asked.

"You know these people?" Scout wondered, still holding her sore face.

"Yes, Scout, let's go way back to the beginning," I said moving my hand left to right. "When we were at the hospital, Mary was that girl who you kept calling a creep. Remember when Dr. Salt said that Nina had *cancer*." I said putting air quotation marks around cancer.

"Oh, yeah, right. Now I remember, but not Katrina, she wasn't there," Scout said, remembering.

"No, she wasn't there. So what's this Katrina girl like?" I said.

"Well, she has light brown wavy hair to the middle of her back, she's really pale, like, not tan at all, um, she has gray eyes, and always wears a gray button- down dress with black gloves and gray heels that are about six inches high and she can actually walk in them. She has a strong French accent and talks in French with Reneta a lot. Have you seen her and Reneta together? They look like child super-models. Mary is a lot nicer but not as pretty, I mean, of course she isn't ugly, just not as amazing as them."

Just then a beautiful girl walked up. I knew it must be Katrina before she said, "Bonjour, I'm Katrina, who are you?"

"I'm Amy," I said and put my hands in my pocket. She held out her right hand.

I was about to shake her hand when she looked at my filthy blob with fingers attached to it.

"Oh, I'm sorry, my family is proper and clean and we don't deal with klutzes like you," she announced rudely.

"Boy, you got a bit of a 'tude, don't you?" I challenged.

Oh, little girl, you don't want to go there, do you?" she asked rhetorically.

"Yes I do, pretty girl," I snapped.

"Amy!" Scout whispered. "Sorry Katrina, she is competitive," Scout apologized.

"No, if she wants to fight, she can fight," Katrina said stepping closer to me.

I clapped my hands and Phoenix and Tracker walked up behind me. "Oh, so you have a back-up? I should have one too... girls!" She narrowed her eyes.

Reneta and Mary walked up behind her. Mary started to talk in French to her. Whatever Katrina spit out at Mary, wasn't good. They both gasped and Mary flicked Katrina off. Katrina pushed her around calling her ugly in English. I started to crack up.

"What's so funny?" Katrina snapped. I struggled to stop laughing. "You are such a-" I stopped. "Never mind, I shouldn't say anything."

"You want to go there, don't you?"

"Yup I certainly do!" I said.

Then, quicker than I could see, I punched her in the jaw, but it seemed too light to be real. She froze.

"Okay, ladies, let's get going," she ordered, not at all bruised.

"Oh, no. You can't chicken out like that," I said.

"Bah-cock!" she responded. I laughed. She screeched. The sound hurt your ears. She charged toward me. I kicked her in the stomach and she flew back. All of the kids had come back outside and their jaws dropped.

All of a sudden, I got the best idea ever. I ran to my backyard. Everyone was starting to go home, thinking I ditched, or chickened out, but I came back on Can-can.

"That horse broke my leg!" Scout warned. Everybody jumped back.

"Giddy up!" I yelled. The horse was about to attack Katrina when Poch came out.

"Stop!" He screamed. "Stop, stop, stop!" He ran out and pushed Can-can away. Katrina was laying on the ground, fake-crying. He picked her up. "Are you alright?" She sniffled and nodded. "Amy, go to your room right now. You know not to attack people, for crying out loud, her parents could sue us! Get in your room," he scolded.

I ran up to my room and stayed there for a long time. I probably missed dinner. In the morning, I woke up at nine o'clock and went downstairs.

"So, sweetie, guess what!" Daphne squealed.

"What?" I asked grumpily. She poured cold water on my head so I'd wake up. "What the heck's your problem?" I yelled. I was for sure awake now. I went to the bathroom to dry my hair with a towel. When I went downstairs, she took me into the kitchen. "What?"

"Okay, get into your best mood, okay?"

"Why do you keep on saying 'okay'?" I asked. She slapped me.

"Get in a good mood or else you're going to ruin this."

"Alright," I sighed. "Pretty ponies and rainbow butterflies!" I squealed sarcastically.

"Better. Now, try to guess," she said.

"Um, you got a new job as a football player?" I asked, already knowing the answer.

"No," she glared at me.

"What's better than that?" I asked and slammed the fridge door.

"Okay," she sighed. "Here's the news."

Chapter Seven – Demons

"Amy, you're going to have a baby brother or sister," Poch said as he walked into the kitchen.

"I don't see how that's better than a female football player but um, uh, er, yay?" I said grumpily.

"Now, you young lady, are officially grounded," Daphne snapped.

"Why? What did I do?" I asked.

"You beat up that poor girl, first of all," Poch began.

"I did not beat her up! She's a little brat/twerp/barf bag who thinks she's too pretty for everybody and she scares everyone! I wanted her to get a taste of her medicine!" I yelled. "She's a big, big, giant booger that dresses all fancy!" I yelled again.

"Okay, if that's the absolute truth, then you aren't grounded, but you need to be a little more excited. Actually, get ready to be mad. Amy, I've been pregnant for three months," Daphne said.

"Three months and you haven't told me? Wow, that's just great! What's her name? Cinderella?" I asked.

"Why would you think of that name?" Poch asked.

"Because she's such a princess you only care about her and didn't plan on even telling me!" I yelled. "No way, you are not naming it Cinderella. I will be suicidal, I swear!" I shrieked.

"No, I wasn't thinking that. In the Philippines Cinderella is called Abadeha. It's beautiful," Daphne said.

"Whatever. Do you even know this is a girl?" I asked.

"Not entirely. What do you want to name the baby if it's a boy?" Daphne wondered.

"Well, Abadeha is from the Philippines, so why don't we name him Phil?" I shrugged.

"No way! I will not name my son Phil. That's an old-man name, no offence to all of the Phils in the world," Daphne said.

"Okay, um Pizza?" I teased. "Pinecone?"

"No! Who would name their son Pinecone, Amy, really?" Daphne asked.

"No, I'm serious I think it's a pretty good name," I joked.

"And you think Cinderella is embarrassing," Poch rolled his eyes.

"Well, Phil is a normal name," I protested.

"Whatever, her name is Abadeha, so tough nuts to you," Daphne said. "Do you like that name?" she asked Poch.

"It's beautiful," he said.

Great, my little sister's name is going to be Cinderella… in the Philippines.

I was almost 10 years old.

In the fourth grade, my teacher was Ms. Chaplin, one of the nicest teachers in the school. Scout got Mrs. Galway, she was nice, but strict, and Benny, Herbert and Julie got Mr. Camp. He was the meanest teacher of all times. He would spit at you if you got a question wrong, and if you didn't raise your hand when he asked a question, he would smack you silly, except for Katrina and Reneta. They were his favorites, in their button-down dresses and fancy hats with nets around their faces.

I went to Tukwila Elementary, home of the Tigers, and they would tell you what teacher you had a couple of weeks before school. Ms. Chapin was only 23, at least according to her teacher's license.

One day, I decided to take Phoenix and Tracker for a walk around the neighborhood. Katrina was walking along the dirty street, her high heels clicking. "Amy, come here," she ordered. I was about to argue, but what was it worth? I would get in trouble anyways.

"What do you want?" I snapped.

"I want you to stay away from Scout. This is for your own protection. Terence is still alive," she said.

"How do you know about Terence? He's not alive. My horse, or dad's horse, killed him," I blurted out, but covered my mouth because that was a little too much info for some random girl.

"Amy, I'm not in the agency, but obviously I will not help you," Katrina said.

"How did you know about this?" I asked.

"Oh, Scout has a lot of... adventures, in this journal of hers." She waved around a red leather book, with a lock on it.

"Give that back!" I yelled.

"To who? It's not your journal, why should you read it?" Katrina asked sleekly.

"I wouldn't, but you would, you did!" I yelled.

"Do me a favor, and don't talk to her. She is very dangerous," Katrina warned. What was she talking about and how did she know about this?

"What does that have to do with anything?" I asked.

"She will murder you if talk to anybody about this."

"You're confusing me. What are you talking about?"

"Nothing, nothing at all. I'm just joking with you, I mean who thought I was real?"

"Katrina, where do you live?" I asked.

"That's none of your business. So why don't you just go finish your walk, and we won't talk to each other ever again. Deal?" Katrina said quickly and began to start walking.

I walked back into the house. "Hey, you okay? You seem kind of sad," Jason said.

"The brat Katrina keeps messing with me. She is so weird," I muttered.

"I know, I saw her walking around the neighborhood with a little Yorkie. She had the bow and everything. Where does she live?" Jason asked.

"She won't tell me. It's weird, it's like, she doesn't have a house, but she's all fancy and stuff."

"Strange, maybe she just doesn't want people to rob her," Jason shrugged and bit into an apple.

"Why would she worry about that? She's only like 10."

"I don't know. Go to sleep," Jason said and flopped down on the living room couch.

"But it's only 4:30," I complained.

"So? I need to talk with Mom and Dad, privately." He looked up at me.

"Fine, what do you need to talk about?" I asked, startin' to get nosy.

"It's called private, Amy. Have you ever heard of it?"

I stomped up to my room and flopped down on my bed. It turns out, I was tired, I fell asleep by 5:00. I woke up at 8:00 the next day. It was freezing downstairs, so I cranked up the heat to 80, when normally it's at 68. I lay down on the couch and turned on Sponge Bob Square Pants. I sat there for an hour then went back to the kitchen. The heat was back to 68 again. I stared at it for a couple of minutes.

I noticed it started to go down even more every couple minutes. "That's strange," I said to myself. It was too early to wake up anybody in the house so I tried lighting a fire in the fireplace. It wouldn't light. "Hmm, there must be something wrong with the heat sources," I muttered.

Daphne came into the room. "Hey honey, watcha' doin' up so early?" she asked.

"I woke up and couldn't fall back asleep. Did you know that all of the heat sources are down?" I said.

"No, how did you figure that out?" she yawned.

"I turned up the heater to 80 when it was on 68. An hour later, it went back to 68," I explained.

"Was someone else in here?" she wondered.

"No," I answered.

"Why didn't you light a fire? You're almost ten. You know how to do that." She narrowed her eyes.

"I did, but it wouldn't light. I tried the matches and the lighter. Nothing would work," I explained.

"Hmm, I'll get it checked out by David. *You,* missy, need to go take care of your pony," she ordered.

"Whatever, let me get dressed." I stomped upstairs to my room and put on some blue skinny jeans, a black sweatshirt, and my black converse shoes. I took the dogs out, they needed to get out anyway. The men were already there. "Hi, I'm Amy. Can I get that horse over there, the white one with the black head?" I asked.

"Sure, I'm Darrel. Come here, boy," the dirty man said and snapped his fingers. Dark Spirit trotted over.

"This your horsy?" he asked.

"Yeah, we needed to take the horses from Utah," I explained.

"It must be strange moving from a farm to a big city," he said.

"No, not really. We had to go-" I paused and made a quick lie. "-live with my Aunt Florence. We moved from New York, New York," I sleekly lied.

"Oh, you're a city girl. Always wanted to go to the Big Apple. What's it like there?" he asked.

"Nothin' much different than here. Sometimes a few celebrities came around our penthouse,"

"Who'd you see?" he asked, eagerly.

"Yeah, um, I think one time Anne Hathaway. I was gone when she was there but it was all over. All the kids were super excited that an actual celeb came."

"Ah, I'd be like that too. I've never moved away from Seattle. I love it here. I've never even left the state."

"You've never been anywhere but Seattle? That must be tough," I said.

"Nope, I love here and always will. Well, I better get back to the little ponies' barn. I like your horses. Not that big one though, she scares the holy lord out of me. Thanks for talking to me," Darrel said.

"You're welcome. You too." I jumped on Dark Spirit, bareback, and we walked across the street. It was probably illegal to have horses in this small neighborhood.

I saw little Mary walking along the road with her ugly, beat-up pit bull. "Hey Mary! Why you so sad?" I asked.

"Reneta and Katrina are being brats. They think they're all pretty and beautiful with their pretty little doggies while they drink tea. Little Popeye here is a cute little puppy, just a little beat up, that's all," she said to a little more to herself than to me.

"Mary, do you know anything about Katrina knowing my personal business?" I asked. She sighed.

"She's been all over your case since you've been here. I'm sorry that I couldn't tell you," she apologized. I exhaled through my nose.

"Why the heck is she all over me?" I asked.

"You lived there, in that house, right?" Mary glanced over at my house.

"Yeah, why?" I wondered.

"Well, she got kicked out, and the fake story is that she couldn't pay the rent, but who would believe that? She's filthy rich,"

"What's the real reason?" I asked.

She paused. "I can't tell you that, I'm sorry. We live alone, and Katrina makes the rules. If we disobey her, she makes us, um, well, I don't really know." I could tell she was trying to hide something.

"Like, does she make you be her maids?" I asked.

"We already are," She looked glum. "Oh, um, sorry, I have to go," she said quickly, trying to get an excuse to leave.

"Wait!" I called but she didn't listen and ran swiftly to the back road. "Unbelievable," I said to myself. Now how was I supposed to find out any information when the person who knew the most who would actually be nice to me said it was against the rules?

After I went back to the almost finished barn, Darrel was about to leave. "Hey, Amy, who's that pretty girl you talkin' to?" he asked.

"Oh, that's my friend Mary."

"You looked like you were fighting 'bout somethin'" he said.

"No, her friend Katrina and her sister Reneta won't let her tell me something. Katrina's been stalking me too. They're going to do something to her if she tells anyone."

"Well, I don't want to get involved with your petty lil' girly stuff, but if it's a secret, it needs to be kept and I would threaten to do something bad, too. You have to stop snoopin' around in their personal business," he said.

"Yeah, but they're doing it to me," I pointed out.

"Amy, hon, you choose what you do. Revenge isn't the best thing in the world. In my case, it was the worst. I better get going," he said.

"Will you be working here tomorrow?" I asked.

"Yup, I'll work for you every day you want me to." He smiled.

I tied Dark Spirit to a tree and heard Darrel's loud engine growl to a start.

It was my birthday. August 28. The worst day of the year. I had too much attention, and I don't like attention... at all. If I wanted attention, I would go up to somebody and ask for attention. On birthdays, whether you ask for it or not, you get tons of attention. I also get a whole bunch of crap like Scottish dresses, horse models, and big, giant books. People say that if you don't like presents, why not just ask for money. Poch is a lawyer and made tons of money a month. He's good too. He will not stop until he is proven right. He's never lost, and always wins. My allowance is about ten bucks a week.

On my birthday. I woke up to my alarm; somebody probably set it. I looked at the clock. Eleven o'clock in the morning. I had slept long enough. My holey sweats were stained badly. I brushed my hair, and went downstairs. Almost everybody in the neighborhood was there. "Great," I whispered to myself.

"Happy birthday, Amy!" they all yelled. There were presents everywhere. The one that caught my eye was the one in a box, almost as tall as me. "Who's this from?" I asked.

"Me!" Scout yelled.

"What? This is huge!" I opened it and it was a big cardboard box that said: POSTAL SERVICE TO CLARA HACKER.

"Um, Scout, this is addressed to Clara," I reminded her.

"We just used that box. Look inside of it!" I read more of the box ... PLASMA TV. She got me a TV for my birthday?

"You really didn't need to get me a TV for my birthday," I said.

"Look inside of the box! It's not a TV," she yelled.

"Okay, okay, I'm going to." I rolled my eyes. Inside the box was a barely touched, white grand piano. "Are you serious? You're giving me a piano? This looks like you just bought it," I said. I didn't want her spending $5,000 on me.

"I know, it was the one Clara had but we didn't know how to play. When she saw you play that one song on it, she immediately wanted to give it to you."

"We, tell her thanks. Thanks to you, too," I said.

The next one was a small present, about two inches wide, and half an inch tall. I read who it was from: Julie Sanchez. She was the girl who had ADHD. Did she even come? I looked around. A short, skinny woman with blondish reddish hair and green eyes came over to me. “Hi Amy, I’m Mrs. Sanchez, Julie’s mom. Do you remember me?” she asked.

“Um, yeah?” I guessed.

“Oh, it’s okay if you don’t. That was a long time ago. Your mom was really excited about your birthday and told everybody in the neighborhood.” I sighed. “Julie couldn’t make it because she had to go to a doctor’s appointment. I don’t know what she got you. She wanted it to be a secret,” Mrs. Sanchez said. I faked a smile. When I opened it, it was a piece of a square bark with words carved into it. Then I noticed there was also blood stains. Did she carve this with her nails? I read the note:

Amy, I need to tell you something. Katrina and Reneta are very dangerous. Stay away from them. They will harm you. Happy Birthday. Julie~

At the end was a staring eye, made with blood. “So what did she get you?” Mrs. Sanchez asked.

“Oh, just a block of bark with a little note scratched into it,” I said. That was true enough, right?

“Oh, that was sweet. Well, I better be on my way, then,” she said and took off.

After I went through all the presents I had breakfast.

“So, honey, you looked scared when you read what Julie gave you. What did it say?” Daphne asked.

“Oh, um, that she liked that I was back, but that some people fell in the river, so be careful,” I lied.

The day went quickly by. When I went under my covers, I decided I would talk to Julie tomorrow, whether she liked it or not.

First thing in the morning, I gobbled down a granola bar and headed out to Julie’s place.

I pressed the call button on the phone.

"Hi, this is Gunner Sanchez," I think Julie's dad said.

"Hi, I'm here to talk to Julie," I said.

"Oh, Julie isn't here right now," He said.

"Well, can I talk to Mrs. Sanchez?" I asked.

"She's not home either. Oh! Look at that, lucky you! They just walked through the back door. Let me put Julie on the phone." He coughed and the phone rattled.

"Hello?" Julie asked.

"Hi Julie, this is Amy. You gave me a birthday present yesterday, well, your mom did, but, why did you write that note?" I asked. "There are blood stains all over it too."

"Stay away from Katrina and Reneta," She said in a very creepy voice. The phone went dead.

"Great," I muttered. I wanted to know more about my house. I *needed* to know more about my house. When I got back, the house was completely quiet. All the workers were gone, all the cars were gone, and it looked like no one was home. I went inside.

"Hello? Hello? Is anybody home?" I yelled. There was a note on the dining room table. It said everyone had gone up to Maggie and Peter's house. They would be back in three hours. "Okay, I have some time to look some stuff up without any questions." I grabbed Poch's slow laptop and plugged it in.

I went to Google, and typed in 5611 South 133rd Street, Tukwila, Washington 98178. A whole bunch of pictures and biographies popped up. The one picture I did notice was a white man, and a black woman. There were three little girls about my age standing in front of the house. The photo was all scratched up and black and white but I could clearly see who it was. One girl was chalky white, the one who stood by the tall white man. The girl in the middle was a dark tan or light black. The last girl was the darkest, but not as dark as the woman. I couldn't believe it, but it was Katrina, Reneta, and Mary. Lightest to darkest, they stood in a perfectly straight line.

Behind them, in between the man and the woman, was a teenager. He was a white boy, and had the same features as Katrina. I knew that they had a whole lot of explaining to do. I sat there and stared at the picture. It only seemed like a couple of minutes, but when I look at the clock, it was already 11:30. I hopped on my bike and went to the Foster Library. I had to go up this huge hill to get there. Finally, I reached my goal and went in.

An old, frail woman with gray hair was sitting at the desk. "Hi, how can I help you today?" her crippled voice asked me.

"Yeah, hi, I'm looking for information about the house I just moved into. Can you help me?" I asked. "It's for a project in school. My teacher last year said that I needed to do this and I haven't done anything but move into a house. I think he'll finally be happy that I finished a project," I lied quickly.

But when I told her which house, she said, "Oh, that one, you'll need to go someplace else. We don't have records on that one." She opened a thick volume she was reading.

"Okay, well, how do you get to Tukwila City Hall from here?" I asked.

After she gave me directions, she said,"Tell me if you find anything. I've been curious about that house for a really long time. I moved here 20 years ago and no one will tell me anything. Maybe they'll tell you because you are a little girl, you live in the house, and you need to do a project." She sighed. "I'll be waiting here all day for you."

I pedaled over to the Tukwila City Hall. I'm glad I brought my cell phone with me, because I probably wouldn't make it back before two. I hit nine and held it down until it said calling Poch. It rang three times.

"Hey Amy, what's up?" he asked.

"I'm probably not going to be back before two o'clock, is that okay?" I asked.

"What? Where are you?" he asked.

"Where are you, in that case?" I asked, passing the Lover's building.

"I'm at Maggie and Peter's house," he said.

"Why did you leave me? You knew I was going to be back any minute," I accused him.

"I know, but they called, wanting us to be there in less than half an hour,"

"A couple minutes late wouldn't have hurt. Bye!" I yelled over the rushing wind. I hung up the phone and ran into the building.

An officer was sitting at the desk doing some paper work.

"Hi, I'm Amy Rae and I wanted to find some history on my house for a project in school. My teacher last year told me to do it over summer and I moved into a new house so I had to start over. I haven't started working on this one yet," I said.

"Hello, I'm Officer Schutt. Where do you live?" he asked.

"5611 south 133rd Street Tukwila, 98178," I said.

"Oh, the 5611 case, that we don't do, ma'am. That file is permanently closed," he apologized.

"Where can I get information about that?"

"Nowhere. No town, state, country, continent, or whatever you want to say doesn't do that," He said.

"Well do *you* know anything about that house?" I asked. I did my puppy dog eyes.

"Okay fine," he sighed. He looked to the left and then right. He handed me a notepad and a pencil. "In 1789 through 1798, there was a white family that lived in that house. They hired maids that were black. Their names were Mary Whitmore, Angelina Whitmore, and Reneta Whitmore. The children, Reneta and Mary, are half black; their father, is the man that owned the house. There was also a set of twins." He pulled up the picture on the computer that I remembered from looking it up at home. "Before he met his wife, the twins' mother, he was married to the most beautiful woman anyone could ever imagine.

"She had long, light brown hair, and blue eyes with a grayish tint in them, her skin was chalky white. She never cared about anything more than her children, well, her husband. She gave birth to Jebadiah Jr. first. He had straight, light brown hair and some freckles. Her second child looked just like her mother. She was selfish and self-centered.

"The mother, Horizon, was murdered. She was shot then stabbed when poor Katrina was only three. Angelina Whitmore wasn't very pretty, quite ugly, in fact. But she wanted to be married so badly and have children. Then, she met Jebadiah Sr., the father. She agreed to be the maid and do everything he asked her to do. No, not asked, told her to do.

He refused to have any more children, and just loved his one and only Horizon. But, that was part of the agreement, so he made do. He was very handsome, too. He had sleek brown hair, and light brown eyes, white skin, and always had time for his family. Well, not the second one. They gave birth to twins, one, very beautiful, named Reneta. The darker one, Mary, looked like her mother, but had a little of her father.

"Jebadiah Sr. said that since Reneta was much more beautiful and whiter, she would not do chores. Only Mary would have to do them with her mother." I scrawled all of the notes down on the notepad. "The three girls looked very much alike at the same age. When Reneta and Mary were six years old, he slaughtered their mother, his white children laughing the whole time.

"When the twins were nine and Katrina was 12, all three of them died. When they were having a picnic in their backyard Reneta and Katrina were eating and Mary was in a corner of the yard eating an apple. They were all found them dead in those positions, but no one knew how they died... maybe from and apple falling on their head, or maybe choking.

"Now, run along, I've told you too much," he said.

"Thank you, really, this'll help me a lot," I said.

"No problem, just don't tell anyone!" he whispered.

"I won't," I promised. I hopped on my bike and rode off. It was almost four o'clock when I got back to the library. Thank God that lady was gone. I hurried home and opened the door.

"Amy, we were worried sick about you! Where did you go?" Daphne scolded me.

"I told Poch that I would be back later than two, didn't I?" I asked.

"No, I didn't get any calls," He shrugged.

"Yes you did. You said that you were at Maggie and Peter's house. There was even a note on the table," I said, proving myself right.

"No, we went to the mall to get some school supplies. There was no note on the table, I sent you a text," Daphne said.

"Well then who wrote the note?" I asked.

"Amy, did you tell anyone our address?" Jason asked. "Um, uh, er..." I hesitated. "Yes, to the librarian and police officer so I could find out more about this house," I said. My phone rang, thankfully, and I answered it.

"Amy, this is Gustavo, we're tracking Jeanie's agents and one is after you. You need to get out of the house now! They're only minutes away! Hurry up! Get your stuff ready, and be quick, as fast as you can. These people will kill you and are a lot more dangerous then they seem." The phone went dead quickly.

"What is it?" Poch asked, panicked.

"Jeanie's agents are after us. Gustavo said they're only minutes away. We have to hurry!" I yelled. I put the dogs in their kennels and we put them in the van quickly. Everybody packed some of their clothes in our suit cases and we drove off. Everybody rolled up their tinted windows so no one could see us. Normally, full grown adults in the CSI would do this, not a ten year old girl.

I called Gustavo, wondering what do to do next.

He said, "Let's see, you need to go to Maine, and we will be waiting for you here."

"Not unless we're flying or taking a week to drive," I said.

"Alright, put me on speaker, I'll do the same for you," He said. I pressed the speaker button.

"Okay, can everybody hear me?" he asked.

"Yup," "Yes," "Yeah," "Sure," we all said.

"You guys will need to follow our plan. Now, are any of you unable to do some things?" he asked.

"Yes, Daphne is like four months pregnant," I said.

"Alright, I'm sorry Daphne, but you will need to stay with the agency in Seattle. It's a little art shop on 37th Avenue," he said

"Okay," she grumbled but I think she was actually happily surprised.

"Everybody else needs to go there too, but they can't stay here like she is. Does everybody understand that?" he asked.

"Yes, we all do. Where do we go?" Jason asked.

"You need to go to the agency, and we will explain there," Gustavo said. "All of the case members know how to handle this. Goodbye," he said and the phone went dead almost before he finished talking.

"Well, we're going to Seattle!" I hollered.

"Shut up! Only for a little bit, though," Jason snapped.

"Well, okay, I'm just trying to bring out the spirit," I joked.

"Amelia, this is no time for joking," Daphne ordered. She put a dark red layer of lipstick on and some mascara.

"You know, Daphne, you don't need to look pretty while we go to the agency. It's just going to be us and some agents, of course. It's not like a crowd of paparazzi is going to come or one of the presidents," I said.

"Amy, shut up. Nobody wants to hear you right now. I'm sorry, but I'm just sayin' the truth," Daphne snapped. I shut up right away.

When we got there, I ran to the art shop and, as always, Emily was at the front desk. I turned around and looked at the window.

Why was my life so hard? Why was it me? Why did it have to be me, out of eight billion people in the world, why did it have to be me? Was I some bad luck charm?

We stepped up in line. “Hi, I’m Alagra, how can I help you today?” she asked.

“Hey Emily, can we go into the back room?” I whispered.

“I’m sorry, what was that?” she asked. I knew she was faking it.

“Oh, can I see the rarest art you have here?” I winked at her.

“Of course, come right this way,” She said and led us to the back room when nobody was looking. “Go right there, just take off that huge picture frame,” she said. We took off Leonardo DeVinci’s”Mona Lisa” and walked through a huge cardboard hole. There was a door that said Confidential Room. Talk to guide if you have any interests.

I walked in but nothing was there but a brick wall.

“That’s stupid. Where else are we suppose to find a door?” Jason said. But he missed what I saw. A tiny little door handle. I opened it and Gustavo was waiting there in a black suit.

“Hello, you have come faster than I imagined. Take a seat. Wait! I’m getting a call,” Gustavo said. He flipped open a phone. “Oopsie, looks like that was one of the agents here, I forgot. Sorry about that, really,” he said. “Wow, that’s just great,” Jason muttered.

We drove back and for some reason, we all fell asleep right when we got home.

On the first day of school, I found out Katrina was in my class. She was elected the favorite student in the whole fourth grade and she was the teacher’s pet. She got straight As and was never late. Plus, she only hung out with the popular kids, like Vanessa Campbell. Vanessa was the prettiest girl in school, (or was until Katrina and Reneta moved) and all of the boys had a crush on her. No way would she let a dump like me talk to her.

How I knew this was that the school newspapers were all over how Katrina and Reneta were the prettiest. Like I'd ever read them but everywhere there was a sign that said, Katrina and Reneta Whitmore are prettier than Vanessa Campbell! I was sick of it. Katrina had to be the most beautifu. I never was anyway, but wished I knew the feeling of it.

It turns out that Ms. Chaplin was a complete fake and hated all of the kids but Katrina and Reneta. I never liked that old lady. Being 23 was like being an old fart. You never got to live. You're old and frail.

I sat in the back row of the classroom, with all of the stinky boys like Jaws (that was his nickname and nobody knew his real name), and Victor who sat there picking his nose all day. I had to sit next to *them*.

Why Jaws irritated me was that he thought he was so cool. I got a ride up for showing him what he earned. I punched him in the nose, but my parents didn't find out because I wouldn't tell the staff my phone number.

"Amy, please tell us your phone number," Ms. Mia begged. She was a stinky lady who was really skinny and had obviously dyed hair which was hot pink, green, fire red, sea blue and purple. I sighed. "Okay, the truth is, is that I don't know my phone number," I lied.

"Oh, here's one that I know!" I said excitedly.

"What is it? Tell us, Amy, please!" they begged.

"Okay, I know that my dad's speed dial on my mom's phone is the number six," I said.

"Yes, but that's on your mother's phone and that's a speed dial. What is a real one?"

A real phone number? Well, I know my friend Ashley's phone number. But she lived in New York and I think she died," I shrugged happily.

"Okay, this is really annoying. We'll just have to wait until your parents pick you up," Ms. Mia said. Most kids in the school had their parents pick them up. I wasn't one of those kids. Only one-third of the kids actually rode the bus. Almost everybody in my class had their parents pick them up.

"Alright Amy, you won, you don't need to tell your parents. But, I want you to give them this note," Mr. Hater pulled out an orange slip. Nobody knew his real last name; he was just so mean that became his permanent name. Even the teachers didn't know his name. "Can I read it?" I asked. "No!" he said a little too quickly.

"I mean, no, it's not for children. You know those stores with the signs that say adults only?" he asked. "No," I said. "Well, kids aren't allowed to read this. Do you understand?" he asked. "No, I mean yes, yes sir, I do," I said quickly.

"Well, you'll need to stay in here for the rest of class," Ms. Mia said. "No recess?" I asked. "Nope, if you punch other children, you'll get in trouble. Now, have you learned your lesson?" she asked. "Yes," I said.

It was a complete lie. I didn't give a crap about what teachers said. You actually *pay real money* for people to scream at you. Who would want that?

Scout, was one of the few people who rode the bus. We always sat next to each other. "Amy, you weren't at recess or class today. Everybody noticed. And, Jaws got punched in the face while you were gone. You know the big scary one that sits next to you?" she said. "Yeah, I know. I was the one that punched him. I got sent to the office for that." I pulled out the orange envelope.

"What's that?" Scout asked.

"A note that I'm not supposed to read," I said. I opened it up.

"Hey, I thought you said you weren't supposed to read it," Scout said and looked me in the eyes.

"So? I don't follow the directions," I snapped. I opened it up. It said:

Dear Mr. and Mrs. Rae,

Your daughter Amy has been acting up and punched another child. Will you sign here and put the date? Please call the number below. There is also a meeting about naughty children like your own. It's November third at six. We will talk about all of the children and what they do. I want you to come and talk about what (s)he does at home. We can talk smack about your child if you like. Sign here if you want us to talk bad, even if you aren't there to embarrass them.

Forever yours,

Mr. Hater

Nice. He would go and talk bad about kids for fun. Now I know how he got his name.

"Hey Scout! Wanna' come to this conference with me and listen to the adults talk? The kids are supposed to go somewhere fun," I said.

"Oh, I would but I'm in a wheelchair, remember?"

"But you'll be out by..." I looked at the date. "November third, right?"

"Yeah, but why do you want me to come?" she wondered.

"Because, it would be fun to listen to them," I said.

"Whatever, it's our stop," Scout interjected.

I hadn't even been paying attention to the bus ride.

I hopped off the bus and wheeled her back to the house. Dainty little Reneta and Katrina were the last ones to walk off the bus. Mary came running after them, her white dress filthy with dust. I felt so sorry for her. Bu I needed to get on their case and Mary wasn't any help so I had to ignore her.

I walked to Scout's house, and instead of staying there like I normally do before Poch and Daphne get off of work, I decided to follow Katrina, Reneta and Mary.

"Hey Scout, I'll be right back, I saw this lost dog sign and I wanted to check it out more. I saw it somewhere along the back road," I lied.

"Okay, but be back before 3:45. There was a TV show I wanted to show you," she said as she wheeled herself over to the kitchen table.

When I got out of the house and knew that Scout couldn't see me, I ran as fast as I could to follow the girls. I saw little footprints, fading away by the second. I quickly followed them and when I looked behind me, the fooprints were gone. "Okay, I only have a little bit of time," I whispered. I quickly followed, and when it looked like they were in sight, I stopped and saw their backs, quickly running behind the trees.

I hid, afraid they might see me. When I could barely see them at all, I went forward; then again, I could barely see the footprints. I followed them, and heard Katrina talking in French, probably telling Mary to shut up, because even I could hear Mary talking a lot.

I kept walking. Then, I realized the things were getting familiar. When they looked behind them, I almost turned around and walked straight back. Instead, I jumped into the trees quietly.

They walked on and I kept following. They turned and made a loop. I stopped when I saw them walking down the street of Julie's house. I watched and watched.

When they finally got to my house, they paused and looked all around to make sure nobody was watching.

I hid behind the cement block but peeked over just enough so they wouldn't see me. They opened the front door. I was about to run over and ask them what was going on. But, I kept my cool and stayed hidden. I crept forward a little bit.

When I finally reached my window, I looked up into it. Katrina was staring down at me with black eyes, there was no white at all. I was panic stricken. I was about to fall over when she opened her mouth. She let out the most piercing scream ever and her mouth got all black and wide. Her eyes opened up so they looked like black holes. She punched the window and pieces of sharp glass came right at me, about to hit me in the eye. I fell flat to the ground and covered up my face.

When I looked up, she was only inches away from my face, still screaming that piercing scream. I squeezed my eyes shut and said a prayer to myself in my head. *As I lay me down to sleep, I pray the Lord my soul to keep. If I die before I wake, I pray the Lord, my soul to take. Amen.*

I repeated that continuously in my head. Katrina kept shaking me so hard my brain rattled. Then, her piercing scream stopped, but turned into a low growling sound that was much, much more terrifying. Suddenly, that stopped too, no more shaking or growling. It was finished. But it was real and I had evidence: the window was shattered and I was all scraped up and bleeding. I also had bruises from the shakings on my arms.

I stumbled back to Scout's house, limping. I opened the door, not bothering to be polite. Clara gasped and ran over to me.

"What happened? Amy, Amy, honey, can you hear me?" Clara asked bewildered, shaking me.

"Katrina," I whispered. Clara looked at my house and saw the broken window. "Katrina what? What did she do?" she asked.

"She's a... a... a..." I tried to say the word but couldn't.

"She's a what?" Clara asked.

"A demon," I mumbled and got dizzy. Nobody would believe me. Nobody would think Katrina had black holes for eyes and rattled my brain or gave me these cuts and bruises. Nobody would even think she cut glass with her bare hands and made it into thousands of tiny sharp crystals that aimed right for me. Not even Jason would believe this.

"Amy, you need to go lay down. I'll take you to Scout's bed," Clara said and walked me over. I couldn't believe what I just saw. I bet Clara thought I was having a nervous breakdown. "Okay, dear, just stay there and I'll call your parents," she said. "And the mental doctor," I heard her mutter under her breath. I didn't think I was supposed to hear that.

About half an hour later, I heard Clara open the front door. They said their hellos and they walked back to Scout's room. "Amy, are you awake?" Poch asked since my eyes were closed. I opened my eyes and blinked a few times.

"What happened? Tell me everything," Daphne demanded.

"You won't believe me," I mumbled.

"Yes, I will, tell me anything and I'll believe you," Daphne said.

"No, you won't. I know that for a fact," I mumbled.

"What happened?" Poch asked sternly.

"Katrina," I managed to say.

"Katrina couldn't have anything to do with this. Not at all, she's a sweet little girl and wouldn't harm a fly," Daphne said in a scolding voice.

"Exactly, I told you that you wouldn't believe me," I snapped.

"I mean, um, yeah, Katrina's so mean, roar," Daphne said sarcastically.

"Daphne, shut up. Just go into the house unexpectedly," I ordered.

"Well, we're going to have to call Jason to do that," Poch said. He dialed a number on his tiny blue cell phone. Poch walked out of the room to talk privately.

"I need to go to the bathroom, I'll be right back." Daphne said. She lifted her fancy Coach purse up and walked to the bathroom with her gray, high-heel boots clicking on the hard wood floor.

"I need to go make some dinner. I'll be back in a bit," Clara said and walked to the kitchen.

Okay, now I was alone I could think... until Katrina was staring at me in the window. Her vicious black eyes had gone to their normal gray, and she was all pretty again. She put her index finger to her lips to motion me to be quiet. She disappeared quickly.

"Poch! Daphne! Come here! Now!" I shrieked, sounding like Reagan McNeil from the movie *The Exorcist*. I was shrieking, scared of Katrina coming back.

In a flash, she was standing over me. She had a smug smile on her face. "Ah, ah, ah, we don't want to make Mommy and Daddy worried, do we?" she asked. "It will be quick, don't worry. And, if you don't die now, your final destination will come." She smiled again.

"W-what does that mean?" I stuttered.

"It means that death will strike back. Now, I'm going to write a little note, and if the note disappears, I will leave forever and never come back. I'll move, and nothing will happen," she explained.

"What are you doing to me? What's going to happen?" I asked in a tiny little mouse voice.

"Oh, it's a little game I like to play. My mother tagged me, I tagged Mary, and she tagged her sister. I honestly wanted her sister to be, but, there are no redoes. So, I'll just write on this little notepad that I brought with me," she said. She pulled out a notepad from her dress pocket. She wrote in her delicate hand writing:

Dear Mother,

This will be my one hundredth kill. I hope I will see you soon. When will you come visit me? Can you make this note disappear if you won't write back? And if you make it disappear, the person will live. It's a little game I like to play. Remember that I haven't missed one person of the kill! And, this time, can you actually write back? I miss you very much.

Love,

Your daughter Katrina Baggin

I was scared to death. I hoped her mother wouldn't write back. I heard Daphne walking back to Scout's room.

"I'll come back for you and I'll always be watching. You, your friends, especially that little Julie who I have completely taken control of. Ha! She'll do anything for me. Maybe I should keep her like I kept Mary," Katrina said and smiled an evil smile... like Jeanie.

In a flash, she was gone.

The note was still sitting on the desk, but it blended in with all of the other stuff.

"Hey, Amy, why were you screaming?" Daphne asked like she didn't have a clue.

"Katrina was here. She left that note over there," I said, shaking in fear.

"Where?" she asked.

"It's on the table, let me show you," I said and tried to get up.

"No, you need to stay in bed."

"But I can show you and prove that it's Katrina," I said.

"Nope, you need to stay in here. I'll be back; I need to take a business call," she said.

"NO! Don't leave!" I sobbed and fastened a grip on her arm.

"C'mon Amy, just for a couple minutes," Daphne said and walked out, shaking her limp arm.

"Back to my plan," said Katrina as she sat on the bed, playing with a snagged piece of blanket. "So, where were we?" she asked.

"Don't do this to me. How many people have you done this to?" I asked, trying to distract her until somebody came into the room.

"Oh, I lost count a while ago. But once people find out my secret, they have to die immediately. I wouldn't want the whole town to die, so I would just kill that one person, so they wouldn't tell anybody," Katrina shrugged.

"But I won't. I promise, I'll do anything if you just let me live," I begged.

"Amy, Amy, Amy, you shouldn't be saying anything. But, I will let you live, on one condition," she said. She smiled a huge smile.

"Not a condition, I hate conditions," I groaned.

"Well then, you need to die," she blinked very slowly.

"Just tell me the condition first," I insisted.

"Okay, fair enough. I'll tell you the condition later tonight. Don't worry; I'll be in your bedroom by nine o'clock," she said.

"How will my parents not notice you?" I quietly asked.

"Shut up and let me be there by nine. If you aren't there I'm going to kill you," she yelled and disappeared.

"Beaver dam, I hate her!" I whispered harshly.

She popped back up on the bed and scowled at me. "You know, I heard that," she snapped.

"You were supposed to!" I snapped back even though she wasn't.

"I doubt that very highly," she growled and disappeared again.

Poch walked back into the room. "Amy was someone else in here?" he asked.

I decided to play dumb. "What? No, nobody else in here. I was just talking to myself," I lied casually.

"Okay, 'cause I heard another little girl in here who sounded like Katrina. She said if you weren't in your room by nine she would kill you," he said like he'd been putting his ear to the door.

Maybe he had been.

"No, that was you making stuff up. Katrina, like, took a vacation to France or something. All I heard was that she wasn't in the neighborhood and on a vacation," I lied, saying a little too much.

"Alright, but, Amy, do you lie to me?" he asked.

"No! No way! I wouldn't lie to you in a million years!" I said crossing my fingers behind my back.

"Good, because there's this killer in Seattle and they're going around in other people's houses if they find out their personal business and slaughter them. They threatened them that if they tell anybody, they'll kill them in their sleep. It sounded like they were in here," he said.

I got a tingly feeling inside.

"Are you okay?" he asked.

"Yeah, just a little cold," I lied.

"Well here." He handed me a sewn quilt and laid it on top of me.

"Do you want to stay here or at the house?" Poch asked me.

"The house," I said a little too quickly.

"Okay, I'll take you over there. But there's a window that's been broken so be really careful," he warned.

"Really?" I asked, even though I already knew it. It didn't sound like I didn't know about it at all.

"Yup, it's all over. But it looks like someone broke it from the inside. Do you know anybody that would sneak into our house and do that?"

"No, not at all. People around here are nice," I told him.

"Well, I'm going to take you back to the house. Come here," he said as he struggled with my 65 pounds.

He laid me in my bed and turned the light out. "Get some sleep; you're probably very tired from all that went on today," he ordered. He walked out of the room and downstairs.

Okay, everybody was gone, now I had to wait. I looked at my digital clock. It was only five. What was I supposed to do for four hours?

I soon fell asleep and slept and slept.

Thank God Tracker came over and licked me on the nose so I woke up at nine. I pulled the curtain next to my bed aside. There were little stars in the sky.

Most people from here probably couldn't see them, but I certainly could. In New York, there wasn't a single star, ever.

Well, not that the human eye could see. It was all covered by the flashing signs and huge lights.

While I was looking out my window, I saw a little girl, but it wasn't Katrina. I leaned farther to see who it was. Then another girl popped up behind her and mouthed the words, "Close your window." I did what I think was told and shut my window.

When I turned around, Katrina was in a position to push me out. I screamed. "Shut up!" she said with her heavy French accent.

"Why should I? You just tried to push me out the window!" I whispered harshly.

"Be quiet, now do want to know the condition?" she asked.

"Yes," I sighed. "Well, then, you have to promise though," she said.

"No, you said it was alright if I heard it first," I pointed out.

"Whatever. So, here it is:"

What is it?" I snapped.

"Amy, you have to be nice to know the condition," she said politely.

"Okay," I sighed. "What is it?" I asked sarcastically, but politely.

She rolled her eyes. "You either need to die, or your mother or father does. Which one is it?" she asked. I couldn't believe she was making me choose this.

"I can't," I wailed.

"Then, your death is waiting," she said and raised an eyebrow.

"Can it be someone else?" I asked.

"Hmm, maybe," she answered. "Let's go with this. You can choose Scout, Herbert, Benny, Julie, Emily or your precious helper Gustavo," she said.

"Well, it can't be Scout, Gustavo, or Emily, definitely," I said.

"Alright, then Herbert, Benny, Julie, or your parents? Which one is it?" she asked.

"How long do I have?" I asked.

"Maybe, just maybe, you'll have a week," she said.

"A week!? That's nothing! What can I decide in a week?" I shrieked.

She slapped me with ice cold fingers. "Shut up! A week is plenty of time. It's a lot more time than I had," she snapped.

"How much time did you have?" I asked.

"Amy, you have to realize how lucky you are. You can actually choose someone else's death. I didn't have any time. It happened to me and I didn't like it. I bet you won't either. I've killed tons of people. Someone has to die every time to feel what I had to feel. But it's even worse with me. It was my own mother that killed me! Now she won't even talk to me anymore. At least you have someone that can love you. I just have Mary and Reneta," she said glumly.

"Where are you from?" I blurted out.

"I'm from Russia," she whispered, not bothering to look up.

Russia? I could have sworn she was French. "I thought you were French," I said.

"Do we really have to talk about where I'm from right now?" she snapped. I shut up.

"So who's it going to be? You, your parents, Benny, Herbert, or Julie?" Katrina asked.

"I don't know. I'll tell you once I figure it out. How can I get to you?" I said.

"Oh, I'll know when you want me to come. I'll be right here. All you need to do is wonder aloud and I'll come,"

"How will you hear me?" I asked. She disappeared.

I woke up, wondering if last night was real. I walked downstairs and looked at my scraped-up arm. I went into the bathroom and looked in the mirror. There was a small red line above my left eyebrow and part of my lip was cut. My chin had huge scratch marks. On my arms, there were scrapes all along them. These marks looked ugly. Nothing like you'd see in the movies where they're all perfect and you look all cool. I looked like a booger-eating troll! I ran downstairs to get my cereal and head out to school.

"Hey, what are you doing? You need to get back in bed," Daphne said. I looked at her. How could Katrina kill somebody like that? She was even carrying a baby. "We excused you from school, you know, since you had that accident yesterday. You might be feeling overwhelmed."

"Yeah, I am," I said but it wasn't about what happened yesterday. How could I choose to kill somebody? I lay down on the couch and turned on the TV. Daphne went upstairs and Poch came down.

"Hey, Amy, can you keep a secret?" he asked.

"Yeah, what is it?"

"I'm going to take you out to do anything you want today, but you can't tell Daphne," he whispered.

"How much money will you spend on me?" I whispered back.

"It has to be less than 300 dollars," he said.

"Can I get a piercing?" I asked. I really needed to get my mind off all this surreal stuff. Get into a silly problem that was just jibber jabber.

"Only on the ears, your mom would kill me if it was anywhere else," he said.

"Okay, can I get a quad piercing?" I asked. "That's where I have eight earrings, four on one side and four on another," I said.

"No, but you can have two more since you already got your ears pierced."

"So, triple?" I asked.

"Yes, now, shush," he shushed me.

"Where is Daphne going?" I asked.

"She's going to Grandma's house. She's telling her mom that she's pregnant and her mother hates me!" he whispered harshly. "Wait! Here she comes," he said and stood up straight.

"Hey, honey, so what are you going to do with Amy today?" Daphne asked.

"Oh, I'm just gonna hang around the house. Maybe watch some TV. But I have to get some work done at the office, so I'll need Amy to come with me. Martha will watch her, trust me."

"Who's Martha?" Daphne asked. "I don't want this Martha girl watching Amy." She acted like there was something suspicious going on.

"No, she's a good friend of mine and when she found out that I was alive, she moved to the office down here to work with me," Poch explained.

"Don't leave Amy with her for more than two hours," Daphne ordered.

When Daphne left and was out of sight, we had breakfast. "So, why do you want your ears pierced so badly? Don't most little girls want ponies or puppies?" Poch asked.

"Yes, but I'm not *like* most girls. I don't wear pink and dress in skirts and dresses all day and put my hair in bows," I said.

"That's true. Only the creeps do that," Poch said.

"What time will we leave?" I asked, trying to avoid the word creeps.

"How about, hmm, maybe around 11 o'clock? That's a good time to go. But you have to make sure Daphne doesn't know about it," he said. "I don't want her to know that I pierced your ears."

"Well, okay, but I'm just saying that I also want a haircut. That's only like 30 bucks, right? It'll be around a hundred dollars to get my ears pierced, 'cause one ear is about $15," I said shaking my hand.

"Alright, if I'm spending 130 bucks on you, it better be worth it. And don't tell your mother!"

"I won't, I won't," I promised.

"Good, because if she finds out about this," Poch started to say.

"I know, Poch, I know that she'll kill you and take us away forever," I said.

"Yeah, right. So, I'll be upstairs. You need to take a shower too," he said.

I groaned. "Yeah, bye,"

He ran upstairs. I went upstairs to turn on the water and went to walk back out, but the door slammed shut. "Ha, ha, very funny Poch," I said and rolled my eyes. I tried to open the door but it wouldn't budge. "C'mon, let me out. I'm serious," I said. The door still wouldn't open. I banged on the door. "Poch! Let me out! This isn't funny!" I yelled.

I decided to give up and wait for him to open the door. While waiting, I played around with a brush and some of Daphne's beauty products. I felt the water in the shower. It should have been warm by now. It had been ten minutes. It wasn't warm at all. It was ice cold. "Katrina," I whispered. Nothing happened. She said she would be here if I said her name aloud. Well, that was a lie. I turned around and she was inches away from my face. I let out a piercing scream.

"What?" she snapped.

"W-w-well, did you make the water cold?" I stuttered.

"No, if I did I didn't mean to. I was taking a shower, like my father told me to. He shut the door and locked it so he could have privacy time with his new girlfriend, Rosalie. She isn't anything. They just love each other so much, that he doesn't have any time for me anymore," she said. I felt a twinge of regret for her. She'd been the center of attention and then popped out like popcorn.

"Now I can't get out. I'm stuck here while he takes her out and buys her jewelry," she said.

"I thought your father died of old age, and, didn't he die like, a long time ago?" I asked.

"Yes, but he never pays attention to me. He wanders in the ghost world with his beautiful girlfriend. She's prettier than even *my* mother. And she's the most beautiful woman I've ever seen." Katrina was starting to drift off in her thoughts. I squeezed my eyes shut and tried to distract myself from death.

"How did your dad die?" I asked.

"He got hit in the head with a hammer. One of his enemies got back at him," she explained.

"Oh," was all I could say. "Can you take me to the ghost world sometime?"

"Maybe, but have you made up your mind?" she asked, completely ruining my plan of distraction.

"About what?" I played dumb.

"Who I'm going to kill?" she said.

"Oh, well, I'll have to say, um, er, uh..." I tried to think. It was either Benny or Daphne. Who was it going to be? Then the door opened and the water turned to steam.

"Amy, why wouldn't you open the door?" Poch asked.

"I couldn't. It was bolted shut," I explained. I looked around for Katrina but she was nowhere to be seen.

"I thought you were going to drown or something," he said.

"In the shower?" I asked.

He sighed and ignored me. "It's almost eleven. You're going to have to skip the shower for now. Come on, hurry up and get your clothes on," he rushed me.

I walked into my gray room and opened my drawers. I got on a short sleeve shirt with a picture of a wolf on it and a furry vest. I put on black jeans and a pair of white Converse. I ran downstairs.

"What about a coat?" he asked.

"It's in the living room," I said. I put on a blue puffy jacket and we walked out the door. When I looked behind me, Katrina had her black eyes again, looking out the window. I shuddered.

"What's wrong?" Poch asked.

"Nothing," I said and looked back again. He followed my gaze but by the time his eyes met the window, Katrina was gone.

"Whatcha' lookin' at?" he asked.

"Oh, nothing, I just saw the dogs looking at me," I lied.

"Well, if you're not feelin' well enough to go out, you just tell me, 'kay?" he said.

"Okay, I will," I promised, but I needed a distraction.

We hopped in the car and we drove to Westfield Mall. "Oh, great, this is something I hadn't thought about," Poch muttered.

"What is it?" I asked.

"Parking, the parking is horrible here. You can't find a parking spot in a million years here," he growled.

"I see one," I said.

"It's going to be taken by the time we get there," he said.

"Poch, you're right in front of it. Look over there," I pointed to the empty spots.

"Jeeze, Ames, you're good. I'd never have seen that."

"Poch, there's a whole bunch of them. There's barely anybody at the mall, here. Look, compared to New York, this is great," I said.

He sighed. "Why do you always have to be the one who sees the brighter side of things? I never do that," he said enviously.

When we got into the mall, there were a lot more people than cars in the parking lot. "This place is crowded," he complained.

"Now you know why Jeanie did the shopping. Wow, you can't handle anything, can you?" I asked.

"Hey, don't make fun of me. I'm a dad, not a Mr. Mom."

"True, true," I agreed. I looked at the mall map, and followed the directions to get to Claire's, since the man at the jewelry counter told us to go there to get my ears pierced.

"How do you know this place so well?" Poch asked.

"Poch, have you ever heard of something called maps? They're very handy," I teased. He ignored that.

I walked into the shop and it was bright purple. "Hi, can I help you with anything?" a heavyset woman asked me.

"Yeah, actually, um, I'm here to get my ears pierced," I said.

"We're going to need the signature of someone over 18 years old," she said.

"I know," I said, nodding my head.

"So, where are your parents?" she asked.

"You said I needed them, but you didn't say right now," I said.

"Oh, so you're one of *those* kids," she snapped. I started to fake cry. "Daddy, that girl is being mean to me!" I said running out to Poch.

He walked in. "I heard there was a problem in here. Which girl was being mean to you?" he asked.

"That one!" I said, pointing to the fat woman.

"No, no, no, sir, I'm not being mean to anybody. Nope, not at all. Your little girl here was being mean to me, if you want to play real," she said quickly. "By the way, do you have any plans on Friday?" she asked.

"I'm married," he snapped.

"But I'm asking; do have any plans on Friday?" she wondered. I listened carefully to their conversation, trying to distract myself. But if I distract myself too much, I'm not going to have enough time to make up my mind about who gets killed.

"I'm not cheating on my wife," he snapped again.

"Okay, this conversation is over. Now, where were we?" she said, getting closer to him.

"Okay, honey, let's go," Poch said to me.

"Oh, well, okay, I didn't know you wanted to go so fast," the woman said, flattered.

"I was talking to my daughter," he growled.

"Oh, yeah, yes, of course, I mean, did you think that I thought that you were talking to me? Pshed! That's stupid," she said.

"Are you calling me stupid?" he asked.

"No, no, no, no, no way, not at all, I mean, like, I totally look up to you. You are like my number one role model," she said, searching for words.

"I don't know you," Poch said after a long pause. We walked out.

"She was weird," I said.

"Tell me about it. Do you think she liked me?" Poch wondered.

"Of course, did you hear her flirting with you?" I asked, shocked that he didn't notice.

"Let's go to another shop," he suggested. We walked to another shop, which seemed like it would pierce ears. When we were done with that, we walked to a hair salon to cut my hair. We couldn't go in because Daphne called and wanted us home. When we got home I went to my room. Katrina was sitting on the edge of the bed.

"Hey, what are you doing in here?" I asked.

"I've decided," she said calmly, staring into the nothingness.

"You've decided what?" I asked.

"I'm going to," she started. *Please don't say that said you've decided to kill me*. "I'm going to take you to the ghost world," she finished. *Whew, at least she wasn't going to kill me*.

"When are you taking me?" I asked.

"Now, grab your stuff. I'm going to figure out what that Rosalie does to make Daddy love her more than he loves me," she said confidently.

"Well, how do we get into the ghost world?" I wondered, not caring about her dad loving his girlfriend more than her.

"You go under water for three minutes, and come back up. I'll tell you the rest of the story when you get out of the water," she said blankly.

"I'll die if I do that," I said after a long moment.

"Que, pourquoi personnes devront être intelligentes ces jours?" she asked herself in disgust. I had no clue what she meant, but whatever it was it wasn't nice.

"So, where is it?" I asked.

"It's on the back road. I can only take you there, if you can get out of the house. Can you do that?" she said.

"Probably, but I need a story. What should I say?" I said.

"You should say you need to get out and go to the ghost world," she said simply.

"No, something that my parents might actually believe me," I said.

"Okay, easy, say you need to take your dogs on a walk," she shrugged.

"But I'm not going to bring my dogs," I pointed out. "How would I go on a walk with my dogs if they aren't even with us?" I asked.

"You take them with you when we go into the ghost world."

"Dogs are allowed in the ghost world?" I asked.

"Yeah, dogs are allowed on earth, so they would be allowed in the ghost world," she shrugged.

"What's it like in the ghost world?" I asked.

"It's exactly the same, but there's a lot of old people, there're some babies, sometimes children," Katrina was still staring at nothingness.

"Well, how does it not get overpopulated? I mean, if there're people coming in every second, and nobody's dying, how do you, well, get less people?" I wondered.

"We alive them," said Katrina.

"You what?" I asked.

"We alive them. If people die here, that's like being born in the ghost world. People stay the same age as when they died, but they live that much longer until they really do die. If they die of old age, they turn into a baby. Does that make sense?" she asked, thinking that it probably didn't make any sense at all.

"Technically, but," I began.

"No questions, we need to go. I'll explain later," she said and was gone.

"Hey, Poch, I'm going to take the dogs on a walk, 'kay?" I asked, trying not to overdo it.

"You'll need to talk with your mother about that. She's in the kitchen," he said and sat down on the living room couch. I sighed. When I got in the kitchen, Daphne was on the phone.

"Can I take the dogs for a long walk? Not long, but I wanted to walk kind of slow," I said to her.

"Sure, be back in less than 25 minutes. We have to go to the doctors in one hour," she said.

I took the dogs' leashes and called them. When Tracker came running down and Phoenix didn't I decided to leave her behind. Why had she been acting so odd lately? For over a couple months now, she's been in pain or something.

I followed Katrina once I was outside. "Where is this ghost world?" I asked, adjusting Tracker's harness. "And, if people keep aging in it, why haven't you aged?" I asked.

"Number one: around the corner. Number two: because I stay on earth," she replied.

"That doesn't make any sense," I told her. Before she launched into a whole story, I stopped her. "Make it quick, I have to be back in 25 minutes," I said. She sighed.

"Ghosts don't age on earth, like human beings don't age in the ghost world," she said shortly.

"So it's like Peter Pan in Neverland?" I asked. She nodded, not knowing what I meant. Obviously she hadn't seen Peter Pan in her eighteenth century. "It's a cartoon," I explained.

We walked into a small ditch on a dirt wall that I wouldn't have seen by myself on the back road. "Wow, everything is so faded here," I said when we got into the ghost world.

"No, actually, you are the faded one. The way I see earth is the way you see the ghost world. So I'm at the same exact place you are, but in the olden days," she said.

"Oh, can we go to Cork, Ireland?" I asked.

"It must be quick because you can snap out of places," she said. She read my expression. "No, that's only on earth. You can here, but I can't," she explained.

"Sweet! Now how do I do that?" I asked.

"Well, you want to go to Cork, so think about what it's like," she said. I closed my eyes and thought. All of a sudden, her voice stopped and I opened my eyes. I was in Ireland. Well, ghost Ireland.

What if I got lost and never found my way back? I quickly thought of my street again and I was there in an instant. "How do you not get scared?" I asked.

"You get used to it," she said.

"But it's like if you get lost in another world. It literally *is* getting lost in another world," I said, bewildered that she never got scared.

"All you have to do is think of a place again," she shrugged.

"But what if you forget about it?" I wondered, thinking up excuses.

"Just think the name of it. It's really easy and fun to do. You just need to have no one that cares about you," Katrina said.

"I wouldn't do that. Why don't you just go back to your family and stop traveling?"

"Because," she paused. "I don't want to talk about it," she snapped.

I walked down the streets of the old Tukwila. Everything was pretty much the same. Some of the houses were different colors, though. One house stood out. "Wow, this house looks like it's recent," I said, amazed.

"You're correct. Don't you see how this is getting more faded by the second? For me it's getting more seeable, but this house is burning down right now." Katrina sounded calm.

"Are you kidding me? This is Herbert's house! He's in it right now! We need to get out, now! C'mon, we need to go," I said, running towards the portal door. I was there is a second. Katrina was running after me.

"Wait! You haven't chosen yet, so I decided for you!" she yelled. I ran out of the ghost world with Tracker and ran so hard I felt like my lungs were going to burst. When I got to Herbert's house, only a little smoke was coming on to the deck but everybody was downstairs. I ran to the door and banged on it.

"Okay, okay, I'm comin'! Hold your horses!" I heard a woman say.

A little girl opened the door. She was dark, dark black with thick short braids in her hair. Her dark eyes twinkled.

"Who are you?" she asked.

"I'm Amy, I need to tell you something, there's a fire in the house and I need all of your brothers and sisters and family to get out of the house or else something bad will happen," I said.

"Hi, I'm Maple. I have a new baby sister on the way!" she said excitedly.

"Maple, can I talk to Herbert?" I asked.

"Okay." She skipped to Herbert and he ran over to me.

"Well, hell*o* Amy!" he said.

"Herbert, there's a fire in your house. I can see smoke coming out of the windows. Come here," I said. I grabbed his wrist and showed him the smoke. It had gotten thicker.

"Holy crap!" he yelled. "Mama, there's a fire in the house! Get everybody out!" he yelled. Nobody ran out except Maple, his older sister Lee, his brother Drew. All the little kids got carried out with the older kids. I ran into the house to get everybody out.

"Who are you and what are you doing in my house? I'm expecting!" Herbert's mom said.

"I'm Herbert's friend and there's a fire upstairs," I said.

"No there isn't. Stop fooling around and get out of my house!" she yelled.

"But ma'am, there is a fire in your house!" I screamed back.

"Get out! I want all of my children back in here, it's soaking out there. Get them in," she ordered.

"No, I want them to come over to my house. I need to show all of them something," I lied quickly.

"Well, have them be back in less than two hours," She yelled. The smoke had gotten downstairs and was rolling across the ceiling.

"You're going to be dead in two hours," I muttered.

"Get out!" she shooed me.

"I need to get everybody else out of the house. Your mom is coming out and no offense, but she's mean," I said to Maple.

"Momma ain't mean! You da mean one!" Maple sassed me. I ignored her.

"You guys need to come over to my house. And, Herbert, why aren't you in school?" I asked.

"Um, why aren't you in school?" he asked. I didn't say anything. We walked to my house and I told Daphne what was going on. I had to stay at the house by myself with all of Herbert's family. I looked out the window at his small green house. I felt bad for him. We watched as the fire got redder and it burned the roof. We all sat behind the window and watched silently as their house went up in flames.

"I want to see Momma," Maple said.

"Momma's gone, Maple. She wouldn't come out of the house like I told her to," I whispered.

"Oh, you mean that lady in the house that was fat? That's Mrs. Wig. She claims she is a Mrs., but I think she's lying," Lee said.

"Where's your parents?" I asked. "

"Mom is at her boyfriend's and Dad's on a business trip," Lee explained.

"You're parents are divorced?" I asked. "I thought they were married."

"No, my mom is cheating on our dad. Since he's gone she's been dating this one guy named Terence Garnett. He's bald and dark black. His teeth are shiny white and he smiles too much. He already has two kids, twins, named Nina and Cash. I can tell their momma was white, or at least half white. They're very, very, light," she babbled.

I thought that we killed Terence in Utah. I was about to say that my kidnapper mother used him and they had been partners. But I didn't. "I think I might know that guy. If you see him with his kids, ask the kids if they know who Amy Johnson is," I said.

"Okay, but he is really mean and always bringing us down when we say something and he thinks he's the big boss and all," she grumbled.

"Was anybody else in the house?" I changed the subject.

"Spot! Lee, we need to get Spot!" Maple cried.

"Who's Spot?" I asked.

"He's our puppy. Lee, c'mon, he's going to die!" Maple wailed and grabbed Lee's hand.

"No, you are going to die. We can get another puppy soon," Lee promised.

"No, Spot can't be replaced. Maple's right," Herbert protested.

"No, you aren't going in there," she snapped.

"I'm going to save Spot!" Maple said.

"I said, no," Lee said sternly.

"But, Lee-e!" Maple protested, making Lee two syllables. Lee ignored her. A couple minutes later, everybody started to clear out and do their own thing. I went to check on everybody. When I was done, I realized not everybody was there. Oh, no. Maple had left.

I ran outside. "Maple!" I yelled. I saw her going into the flaming house and rushed after her. "Maple, come here!" I yelled.

"I'm not leaving Spot!" she yelled back. I picked her up and held her in my arms. I started to leave. "No!" she shrieked in my ear.

"Spot! Come here boy! Come on!" Maple yelled. The puppy cautiously walked to us but stopped half way there and lay down. I searched my pocket for a piece of string. Once I found it, I tied it around Spot's collar really tightly and tugged on it to make him move. He moved easily and we were out.

I put Maple down and took out my cell phone. I dialed 911.

"911, what's the emergency?" a lady asked.

"My neighbor's house is on fire!" I yelled over the rushing flames.

"Is anybody in the house?" she asked calmly.

"I think there is a lady in there. The kids all came over to my house," I informed her.

"We will need to talk to whoever is inside of the house, please," the lady said.

"I'm not going in there! I'm ten and the lady might already be dead," I yelled.

"Well then, we can't send a fire fighter to your location," she sighed.

I snapped my phone shut. "Crap, crap, crap," I grumbled. Luckily, a police car drove down the road. They didn't stop to look at the house, or stop at all. That was it. Herbert's house was too far back and nobody could see it. That's why the car didn't stop.

"Stay here," I ordered Maple. "Don't go back in no matter what happens," I said and ran to the cops. I knocked on the window and one of them rolled it down.

"What do you wan, little girl?" the fat guy asked.

"There's a house fire over there," I said and pointed to the direction it was in.

"I don't see notin'," the guy said.

"Wait, Steve, look! There are flames," a black woman said. She looked sort of faded, like Katrina.

"Where is it?" she asked. I ran over and pointed. She followed and went in. "Wait! You're going to burn yourself!" I yelled. She didn't listen. When she came back out, she was perfectly fine.

"How did you do that?" I asked.

"Do what?" she asked.

"Go into the house and not get burned. That's not possible," I narrowed my eyes.

"I have a little secret. I'm not meaning to make you stay up all night and wonder, but you wouldn't believe me," she said after a long time.

"Yes I would," I protested. "I think you're trying to hide the fact that you're a ghost," I said. It sounded a lot stupider than I thought it would.

"Pshed, I ain't no ghost, little girl. There's no such thing as ghosts," she spit out in my face, laughing.

"Well, I'm going to test you," I announced. "Come here," I ordered.

"Ma'am, I need to stay at work, there's been an emergency." She tried to excuse herself.

"No, I just want you to see something. By the way, is your name Rosalie?" I asked, just making sure.

"Why, yes it is. How did you guess?" she asked.

"Does your boyfriend have a daughter named Katrina?" I wondered.

"Silly little girl, I'm married. He's in Idaho right now, on business."

"How old are you?" I asked.

"I'm 27, why? And that's a little personal."

"Well, shoot," I muttered.

"Never mind, go away," I said and ran off. That was embarrassing. When I got back to the house with Maple, everybody had their fingers crossed, praying. Daphne walked into the house back from her doctor's appointment.

"So, Amy, I need to talk to you privately," she muttered as she put her bag down on the kitchen counter. I followed her into the kitchen.

"What is it?" I asked.

"Okay, you can't tell David, can you do that?" she asked. I nodded.

"Why can't I tell him?" I asked. "Because it's going to break his heart." She sighed and wiped her eyes with her jacket.

"Oh, great, here comes the mushy stuff," I grumbled.

"No, once I have this baby..." she looked down and decided to change this subject. "I think he really wanted a boy, but we're having a baby girl," she said, sniffling.

"No, I think he really wanted a girl."

"I even thought of a name for a girl so it isn't Cinderella," I said. Daphne looked up at me,surprised I "bought" her baby being a girl and Poch would get mad. "What about the name Esther?" I asked.

"That's a good name. You should tell your father, he'd like it. Abadeha isn't that good of a name anyway," Daphne walked away. What was she really hiding? I knew she had chickened out telling me.

"What is it really? I know it's not that Poch is going to be sad that it's a boy," I promised.

"No, never mind. I'm not going to tell you," she put her head in her arms. She sat down on the kitchen counter and sobbed.

"When is the baby due?" I asked, changing the subject.

"Oh, in February, not for a while," she said, changing the subject once again. "So, what's going on in school? Are you getting good grades?" I just nodded and walked out of the kitchen.

"What was she saying?" Herbert asked quickly when I got into my room. He was sitting on my bed.

"Why are you in here?" I snapped.

"I got bored, sI decided to see what was in your room." He looked sheepish. "I've been looking around in the bathroom a little, in the closet, a little in your dresser," he said, ashamed.

"Why have you been looking in my stuff?" I asked.

"It's interesting. What was really interesting was that there was a lot of money in your dresser. There was a little over a thousand dollars," he said and traced his fingers on the wrinkled blanket.

"Don't snoop around in my stuff!" I shrieked. I slapped him on the face. "What else did you see?" I asked.

"Well, I looked at your cell phone and I listened to your messages," he said. "And read your texts." He looked down.

"What did you hear?" I snapped.

"On one voice message a man named Gustavo said that Jeanie got bailed out. He also said you guys need to go to the Westfield Mall. You need to go to Claire's." He looked subdued.

"Ugh," I groaned.

"Why do we keep on having to do this? She got bailed out, now she's after us," I said out loud.

"What are you talking about?" he asked.

"Nothing, nothing at all," I panicked.

"Daphne!" I yelled and ran downstairs. I saw Herbert go back into my room to snoop around. I didn't do anything.

"What is it?" she asked.

"We need to go to the mall. Gustavo needs us to go to Claire's," I whispered.

"Okay, we'll leave in a bit. Go back to your room. I need to think about something, privately." I ran back upstairs. Of course, Herbert was looking at something I got in a contest when I was little. He dropped it immediately.

"Take your brothers and sisters to the neighbor's house or stay here. We'll be back in a minute, and get out of my room," I snapped. Luckily, I had the keys to my room so I locked it. The only way he could get in now was the dog door. I locked that too. When I saw him eyeing the window on my door, I opened my room back up, locked all of the windows, walked back out and locked my door again.

"Jeeze, you're like, superprotective, Amy," Herbert said. I unlocked the dog door, remembering Phoenix and Tracker were still in there. I glared at him. They would keep him out.

I hopped in the car and Daphne drove to the Westfield Mall. I tried to bring up the conversation again. "What were you trying to say, really, not that you are having a baby girl?" I asked.

"Nothing, Amy. That was it; I wasn't going to say anything else."

"Are you going to like, leave once Esther is born?" I asked. She didn't say anything. I decided not to taunt her, but I knew she was leaving and I wasn't allowed to tell Poch, that was for sure. It would break his heart, as she said.

We saw Gustavo at Claire's and I ran up to him.

"Amy, you got my message. Five months from now, your mother here," he paused. I looked at Daphne and I could tell she was signaling him to shut up. "Is going to have a gorgeous baby," he finished. "What is the name of the child?" he asked.

"Esther. I picked the name out," I bragged.

"It's a very beautiful name. I expect a young lady named Esther should have a thick accent," he daydreamed.

"Maybe we'll just make her talk like my friend Katrina does," I teased.

"Where did you get that name, Esther, anyway?" Daphne asked.

"The movie *Orphan*. She's the killer," I replied.

"No, I'm not naming my daughter that," Daphne said.

"You're leaving anyway, why would you care?" I snapped. She didn't say anything.

"Well, you guys will need to get prepared for Jeanie. This time, anything that will happen is real. No more drills," Gustavo said.

"You called us over just for that?" Daphne asked.

"Everything is better if it is in person, that's what I believe. I'm sorry if I'm wasting your money on gasoline. My bad," he apologized.

We drove back in silence. When I got into the house, Poch came running up to us. "Where the heck have you guys been? I've been calling you both and Amy, your door was locked, so I thought you were in there but you wouldn't answer me," Poch panted.

"Sorry, Gustavo called," I said. I glared at Daphne.

"Whoa, did you guys get in a little fight here?" Poch asked. I ignored him and walked off to my room.

I wanted to go to the ghost world again. Tomorrow, I decided. I needed to see what was going to happen. I fell asleep with my door locked and woke up at 6:30 a.m. Great, I was alone, nobody was awake. I had time to go into the ghost world. Just in case somebody woke up and didn't find me, I scrawled on a piece of paper:

I'm on a long walk. Be back in a bit. Don't worry if I'm gone a long time.

Amy

I ran to the little dirt wall and stepped inside it. I thought of where Katrina might be. I forgot, and I was suddenly in my house, with old music playing. Katrina was sitting at the table with a blank face. "Hey, Katrina, I need to ask you something," I said.

"Shut up and get out of here. You don't belong in the ghost world," she whispered harshly.

"Whoa, I'm just asking if somebody is going to die. Can you tell me?" I asked. She didn't answer.

"Why won't you tell me? I didn't do anything," I promised. Still no answer. She was as still as stone. "Please, Katrina, why won't you tell me?" I pleaded. I saw a corner of her mouth twitch.

Then, she moved her head to face me. She let out a piercing scream and her pretty blue gray eyes turned into black holes again. Her mouth opened wide to an even bigger black hole. "Get out of here before I kill you," she growled. Her voice was deep and rumbling, and could belong only to a big, buff, man.

"You can't hurt me. I'm in the ghost world, you aren't on earth," I yelled over the commotion, still very frightened. She stopped and went back to her blank face, staring ahead.

"Okay, fine, what is it?" Katrina snapped after a long pause. I sighed.

"Does Daphne Rae die any time soon?" I asked. For some reason, I had that feeling that she would. I didn't know how I got it, I just kind of did.

"Follow me," she ordered. She led me through the house and out the back door. We walked in silence. She took me a long way. I heard her heels click against the pavement. Everything was going slowly. I wasn't aging at all. I was staying the same. Nothing was changing.

Katrina led me up a hill, and we waited. A train came and whirled to a stop. "Can I get a ride to Mindaloni's Mansion?" Katrina asked.

"Yeah, two tickets?" the man asked.

"Yes, two, please. Thank you very much," she said.

I followed her on the train and we took a seat. "I have to be back before ten, you do know that, right?" I asked. She nodded but still didn't say anything. We stopped at the third stop and I saw a huge purple thing bigger than the whole town. "That's so far away," I complained.

"Think about what's inside it," Katrina ordered. She touched my arm as I thought. We were there in a split second. An old woman, skin and bones, was sitting behind a desk.

"What do you want to know?" the old woman asked. Her voice was very crackly and shaky.

"Um, I have a human friend, named Daphne Rae. Can you tell me when she is going to die?" I asked.

"Where does she live?" the old lady asked.

"Tukwila, Washington," I replied.

"Oh, ah, ah, ah, Mindaloni does not see anything good in this. Daphne is going to die, murdered, while she is running away. She just gave birth to a beautiful baby girl, Abadeha Esther Rae Johnson.

"The killer is on the loose. Daphne gets thrown in the river and her foot gets caught and pulls her under. It's so terrible," she said with her face in her hand.

"Thanks," I whispered. I walked down the purple hallway and Katrina touched my hand. I was back at the dirt wall. I walked out without saying good bye. When I got back to the house, Daphne ran up to the door.

"Where have you been? I was worried sick," she exclaimed.

"Wait, I put a note on the table. How could you not see it?" I asked.

"Nothing was at any table. What are you talking about?" She was confused.

"C'mon, let me show you." I took her hand and led her through the door. The house smelled like coffee and hash browns. I looked on the table and nothing was there. "What? This doesn't make any sense. I left it right here," I put my index finger down on the table top. "You threw it away. You had to, Daphne. Why would you do that? I was just taking a walk. Now you're going to tell Poch and he'll like, just be freaking out," I snapped.

"I didn't see anything, young lady. Now, you don't talk like that to me," she scolded. "Hey, is this whole attitude thing about me leaving?" Daphne asked. I shrugged.

"I don't know, is it?" I asked.

"Look, this is for your own good. I don't want to leave," she said quietly.

"What is it? Why are you leaving? Is it another guy? Do you have another family somewhere? Do you work for Jeanie?" I guessed. I immediately regretted it. Daphne shot a glare.

"I can't tell you exactly, but it's one thing that you guessed," Daphne looked down. "Don't tell Dave, please, don't," she begged.

"Okay, I won't tell him if you do this," I started.

"Do what? What should I do?" she asked.

"Don't go," I whispered.

"Okay, you can tell him. Tell him in February at the earliest," she insisted.

"February, that's way too soon!" I yelled.

"Shut up!" she whispered.

Poch marched down the stairs and poured himself some coffee. "Hey kiddo, why are you all dressed and ready to go?" Poch asked.

"I um," I started.

"Amy went out today and didn't even leave a note. I thought she was dead or had been kidnapped," Daphne interrupted.

"Thanks," I mouthed and rolled my eyes. "I can explain," I began.

"Yes, I hope you can, 'cause you definitely couldn't explain it to me," Daphne lied.

"Amy?" Poch looked at me.

"Look, I went on a walk, I left a note, but, let me finish, Daphne threw it out so she could blame me," I said quickly, trying to get everything in before they interrupted me.

"Daphne! You can't do this! If you fight with Amy, you can't just get her in trouble,"

"I-I didn't. I promise, Dave," Daphne said, her eyes reddening.

"No, one more chance, that's it," Poch snapped. He marched back upstairs.

"Amy," Daphne growled. She stomped off and got in the car. She drove off. I looked out the window and waited for her to come back. Ten minutes past. She wasn't back. Fifteen minutes. She still wasn't back. Twenty minutes, fifty minutes, an hour. It was past three hours. She still hadn't come back yet.

"Where's Daphne?" Poch asked. He was the first one to speak.

"I don't know. She got in the car three hours ago. I don't think she's coming back," I whispered, tears welling up in my eyes.

"She is. I'll just call her. Wait here," he ordered and went to the wall phone.

"Hey, it's me. I'm just calling to see where you are and wondering when you're going to be back. Um, call me when you get this. Bye," he said. He looked at me.

Days went by. Weeks. Months fled by. I'd even missed the council where the teachers talk bad about the students. Finally, it was February. The baby was due in February, right? Maybe she was late. Yeah, the baby had to be late. Daphne wouldn't keep the baby. She didn't know how to take care of a kid without anybody's help. Absolutely not. On March 12, I decided she had kept the baby and met another guy, maybe gotten another family.

Two days later, as I was staring out the window, a black car pulled into the driveway. It was dark outside so I couldn't tell who it was. The man got out of the driver's side and got a basket out of the passenger seat. He carried it to the door and rang the doorbell, ran back to the car and shut the door, but the car didn't move. I heard yelling and screaming. I went to get the box from the doorstep.

"Amy!" was all I heard. Oh no. That was Daphne. That guy dropped a basket off at our door and he was going to drive Daphne into the river.

"Poch! Come here, now, Daphne is stuck in the car out there and somebody is going to drive her into the river!" I yelled. Poch came running over.

"What's happening?" he asked but was too late. The car was in the river and had gone under.

"Daphne, she's gone. She's dead, Poch," I said, shaking.

"No, no, no way, she can't be dead. How would you know?" Poch asked.

"That day she left, when I was gone that morning, I took a train and I saw a psychic. They said that Daphne Rae would die." We were both standing out in the cold hugging ourselves to keep warm. I looked in the basket. There was a baby with a little note attached to it.

Abadeha Esther Rae Johnson. Born: March 14, 2012, 5:03 a.m. Parents: Daphne Rae and David Johnson Born at Highline Medical Center weight: 6. 01 lbs.

This was the baby, the baby whose mother was murdered right after delivery. "Poch, you should look at this," I said. He came over to me.

"What the heck is a baby doing here?" he asked.

"It's her. This is Abadeha. Look at this," I said. He was bewildered.

When I looked up, the yard was empty. Like nothing ever happened. The car driver had gotten away. "I'll be right back. I need to call the police," Poch remembered. He ran back inside. A couple minutes later the cops came into our yard.

I picked Esther up from the basket with all of her blankets. She looked at the car in the water. She had little red brown hairs sticking out from the top of her head. Her lips were a faded pink color like mine and skinny. She grabbed the necklace I was wearing and pulled on it.

Then, Esther stared up at me with shocking green eyes and blinked. I stared back at her. Jason walked out into the front yard. "Why are you carrying a baby?" he asked.

"It's Esther, our sister. Remember? Daphne was pregnant. She just died. Somebody drove her into the river but he got away," I explained.

"We need to get her inside, asleep. Let me take her," Jason said. He picked her up out of my arms and walked back into the house. I followed him in. "Amy, make a crate or something big enough for Esther," he demanded. I got the basket from outside.

"Okay, that works. Go get a pillow," he ordered.

"A pillow is the size of Esther, not something her head should rest on," I pointed out.

"Exactly, you idiot. We put the pillow in the basket and then put Esther in the basket," Jason snapped.

"Okay, okay, where will she sleep?" I asked.

"In the basket, idiot, like I said."

"No, what *room*," I snapped back.

"In Dad's room, of course. Who else would she sleep with?" he asked.

"I don't know. I was just wondering," I looked down.

A police officer walked into the house. "So, kids, do you know anything about this murder?" he asked. He was tall with a red beard and mustache. He had freckles all over his face.

"Um, no," I lied.

"I don't know. I just live in my room and sleep all day. I don't care what goes on in the outside world," Jason shrugged.

"Do you know the lady that got murdered at all?" he asked.

"Yes, she was our mom," I said.

"I'm sorry for your loss, but I heard about her dropping a baby off at the doorstep. Is that true?" he questioned us. I nodded and burst into an explanation.

"She was pregnant and she ran away because we got in a fight over me going for a walk. We waited and waited for months but she didn't come back and tonight she dropped off her baby and then the killer drove her into the river," I said quickly.

"Alright, well, you kids better get some shut eye. It's gettin' late," the cop said.

Poch walked into the house with an angry look on his face. "Go to bed," he snapped.

"But it's only 9:30," I began.

"I don't care. Go to bed," he said.

"Why are you so mad at us?" I wondered aloud.

"I'm not mad at you. It's just that Daphne left and she died. That's all. I'm trying to get over the fact that..." he couldn't finish his sentence.

"Get over the fact that what?" I asked.

"Don't push it, Amy," Jason whispered.

I went up to my room and thought. I thought for hours. Poch came in to see if I was asleep at three in the morning so I pretended I had fallen asleep, but I was still thinking.

I knew why Katrina was now ignoring me. I didn't choose the week I was supposed to. She decided who would die and since she didn't have a mom, she didn't want me to have Daphne. I knew it. She said she'd go away if she got to kill someone and never come back. She had decided to kill Daphne. That had to be it. It just had to be. There was no other explanation.

Chapter Eight - Run Away

I was going to have a talk with Katrina. I didn't care if she liked it or not. I was going to talk to her in the ghost world so *I* would be the strong one. I could go to any place I wanted to. That's what I was going to do.

The next morning, I hopped downstairs and skipped breakfast.

I went out the door and ran and ran. Beads of sweat dropped down my neck. When I finally got to the dirt door, I opened it, not bothering to close it. I had some strange feeling about it. I ran into the house and saw Katrina. She was sitting there blankly in the same spot as last time.

"Hey, why haven't you been on Earth for a long time?" I blurted out. She didn't answer. "Okay, well, did you kill Daphne or not?" I asked. A strange twisted smile appeared on her face. I looked at her straight in the eye. I could already tell she was growing. She was a little taller and her hair was a little longer. Her face had narrowed a little bit, too.

"So? Did you?" I snapped. She paused.

"Technically," Katrina's voice said as soft as feathers.

"How?" I wondered.

"I asked someone," she declared.

"Well, you didn't answer my question about not coming to Earth anymore. Why not?" I questioned, my panting slowing down. She sighed.

"Amy, remember when we went to that psychic here?" she asked.

"Yes," I answered. "She said that Daphne would die," I remembered.

"But do you remember that I have to touch your hand to go with you?" she asked.

"Yeah," I shrugged but I hadn't known that.

"Well, one thing that I didn't know was that if I touch somebody's hand to travel, my rings go to them," Katrina sounded sad.

"Your *rings*?" I asked, wondering what in the world her rings were.

"Yes, look at your hands," She ordered. I looked down at my hands. There were two rings. One was a sapphire on my left thumb and the other one was a round oval with little designs in it on my right pinkie.

"I never noticed these," I said, trying to not make her accuse me.

"Look at your wrists too. The bracelets," she whispered. I looked at my hands. There were two bracelets on my left and one bracelet on my right hand. The bracelet on my left hand was a thin gold band with a black cross and golden skull and rubies. On my right hand, there was a big sliver bracelet that was made of foam.

"What do they mean?" I asked.

"Those are the portals to the ghost world and the Earth world. And the necklace, that's a portal too," she said, ashamed that she had gotten her portal keys taken away.

I looked at my necklace. It was a rusty key with a square emerald, a ruby heart and a diamond sapphire. "Why don't I just take them off and give them to you?" I asked, thinking it was as easy as that.

"They won't come off," Katrina said blankly. I tried to take the necklace off. It fell back on me.

"Okay, you're right. But you can't come back to Earth because you don't have the keys?" I asked.

"Yes," she smiled. "But there is something you don't know and it's growing by the second," she said accusingly.

"Why are you telling me this?" I asked.

"Because it's all your fault," she grinned.

I pushed myself away from the dining room table and ran. I went as fast as I could to get away from the ghost world. Again, I didn't bother to close the door. Katrina's words echoed in my head. *All your fault.* How would something be my fault if I didn't even know what it was? I ran back into the house, panting.

"Hey, I thought you were going slowly. Why are you panting?" Poch asked.

"I decided to run at the very end of it," I explained.

"Okay, but we need to go to Maggie and Peter's house to drop off the horses. I can't believe we still have them," Poch said, not caring a bit about my panting.

"Yeah, really," I agreed. "I'll go check on them."

"Yeah, that's a good idea. I don't think they're that healthy so be careful with them," he warned. I nodded my head thankfully.

I went out to the yard and got some food for the horses. I looked at Dark Spirit. He had sorrow in his eyes. All of the horses' looks were filled with sorrow, especially Goosebumps, Daphne's horse. She had seen her owner die with her own eyes. I felt so sorry for her. I dumped some hay in each one of their stalls and rode them around a little. I could see some of the sadness going away.

"Good," I said and patted Dark Spirit on his thigh.

When I looked around the street, there were more people than normal and a lot of oldies. They had strange looks on their faces. I couldn't explain it; it was like they were thanking me, but not in words. I didn't even know them. Why would they thank me? I shuddered and went back inside.

"Okay, I guess I'll go to Maggie and Peter's house now. And, Amy, don't go anywhere. Just stay in the house," Poch shrugged, unhappily.

"Can I come with you?" I blurted out.

"Oh, well, sure, but, I'm just saying you normally stay here," Poch narrowed his eyes, trying to figure me out.

"I know, I haven't seen Maggie in a while and I wanted to see her," I lied. I needed to run away, far away and Maggie's house would do the job.

"But you hate Maggie, you know what? Never mind. Can you grab Esther? She's been up half the night," He grumbled.

"Sure," I mumbled. I ran upstairs. She was sleeping in Poch's room in the basket on the floor. I picked her up and walked down stairs.

An hour later, we came to a huge gray house with birds cawing, dogs barking, cats meowing, hamsters squealing and horses neighing. There must have been more than a million pets in that house. I sighed.

"I told you that you wouldn't want to come," Poch said.

"No, I do," I lied.

"Yeah, right," Poch said sarcastically and rolled his eyes. I was glad he had his first words of humor for the day.

"Whatever. I'm being *nice.* Have you heard about it?" I asked.

"Yeah, yeah, get inside," he grumbled.

I carried Esther to the door and knocked once. Maggie came running to the door and squeezed me really tight.

"Amy, Amy, Amy!" she yelled. "Guess what? I have everything planned out for what we're going to do. Do you want to know?" she asked excitedly.

"Not really," I admitted, backing away from her grip, trying to keep Esther safe.

"Okay, so first we're going to color with all of my new colorful pens. I have 48 of them!" Her bright curly red hair flew everywhere. Maggie's circular glasses were crooked.

"How about you let Esther do that," I suggested.

"Who's Esther?" she asked.

"My new sister, she was born yesterday morning," I said.

"Oh, it's too bad that I hate babies. They're superdeeduper annoying."

"Yeah, like they're so much more annoying than you," I muttered under my breath. I was glad she didn't hear that.

"So, we have to take care of Kibbles, the dog first. And then Fizbee, Champ, Dixie, Squirmy, Horizon, Raisons, Froggy, Kitty, Mr. Licorice, Trash Bag, Grouchy," she continued.

"Wait. Are these all of your pets?" I interrupted her.

"Yes, why?" she asked. "I want a chinchilla named Fuzzball and a green parakeet name Pickles." Her eyes shone with delight.

"You don't have enough?" I asked.

"No, I also wanted some new horses," Maggie sighed.

"That's good because I've got four new horses for you," I mumbled.

"Really? Yay, yay, yay, did you hear that Peter? We're getting a new pony! In fact, *four* ponies!" Maggie yelled. Peter came running down.

"Really? I want a big one!" he yelled.

"Yes, yes! There're four whole ponies! Did you hear that?" she screamed.

"I'm going to go get them," I said and ran outside and saw all the horses in the trailer.

"Hey, I'm just getting the horses out. The kids look pretty excited," Poch said.

"Yeah, they wanted horses and when I told them we were giving them the horses, they went crazy," I explained.

Peter came up to us and looked in the trailer. "Aw, I want the big one. What's its name?" he asked.

"Oh, buddy, we might keep that one. Sorry," Poch apologized.

"Why?" Peter asked.

"Because, they're our horses, so scram," I said more harshly than I meant.

He ran off crying, "Mommy, Daddy, Mommy, Daddy, Amy is being mean to me."

"Amy you need to be nicer to your cousins. Do you understand?" Poch asked, showing no concern.

"No," I muttered.

Unlike Maggie, Peter's hair was jet black like his mom's, Poch's and mine.

Maggie got her hair from her smart-alecky dad, Berry. I thought he had a funny name, Berry. You could eat him! But his hair was a sharp orange. He had a lot of freckles, too. Maggie also got her eyesight from her dad. Maggie was like Berry, and Peter was like Aunt Pat.

Soon, Aunt Pat came running outside. Her hair was a mess and she still looked like she was in pajamas. "Hey, you guys," she greeted us. "*Dave*," she glared.

"Patr*icia*," Poch glared back.

Obviously Poch didn't like the name David and Aunt Pat didn't like the name Patricia. They reminded me of young children.

"Hey Amy, I've missed you," Pat gave me an awkward one armed hug.

"Hi, Aunt Pat. Maggie and Peter are excited to get *three* horses. Not four. Three, even though we brought four," I babbled quickly.

"Okay, so, let's see the horses," Pat said and pulled down part of the trailer.

"Holy crap! What did you do to these horses? They look horrible," she yelled, jumping back. "So what's been going on, Amy?" Pat continued.

"Well, um, uh, Daphne just died," I said and gulped. I went on like I hadn't said anything important. "And, well, before she got murdered, she had Esther," I went on. Pat stopped and stared at me.

"Daphne died?" she asked. "Wow, that's too bad. I liked that girl definitely more than than your dad," she said and shot a glare at Poch. "And what a cute little baby, what did you say her name was again?" she asked, tickling Esther's chin until she giggled.

"Esther. She was born yesterday," I explained.

"Oh, so she's a March baby, huh?" she asked and took Esther out of my arms. "What a cute little baby! I think someone more professional," Pat looked at Poch. "should take care of this baby," she finished.

"Yeah, someone more professional who doesn't have a billion pets in their house just because they're kids wanted them," Poch snapped.

"Well, at least someone that doesn't let somebody kill their wife, for crying out loud! Like Amy, perhaps," she said and smiled at me.

"Yes, someone like Amy who lives with me," he snapped.

"Oh, Amy, would you like to move in with me?" Pat pleaded.

"No, she's my daughter and she lives with me," Poch disagreed.

While I pretended to wander off, I was really running away. I would find a way to live on my own in the forest. I ran and ran. I wasn't looking where I was going. I fell down a couple of times, but when I was sure I was at least more than ten miles into the forest, I ran into a cold, hard wall.

What the heck was a wall doing in the middle of the forest? Then, I realized that I was moving. I was being sucked into a hole. “Help! Somebody! Help!” I shrieked. I screamed and screamed, but no one could hear me.

Soon, I landed in what looked like the other side of the forest. That was stupid. It was just a door that sucked and popped you out the other end. But when I looked back, the door was gone.

“Crap, that was stupid,” I muttered and kept running.

I saw a hole to a mainland. Whew, I thought I was lost for sure. But right before I got out to the mainland, a dark hand shot out in front of me. I screamed. A girl, a little older than me, motioned to close my mouth in a weird way. It’s like she grabbed her lips and pulled them together. I nodded. She firmly grabbed my arm and led me to a house. It was a little ways away, but it was definitely worth the walk.

A huge bamboo house had bee built by hand, and there weren’t any doors. It only had one floor, but it was amazing. “Did you build this?” I asked.

“Cluke boji juba hoog daut?” I guess she asked. It was obviously a foreign language. I decided to motion it out. I pointed to her and pretended to build things. She nodded her head.

“This is so cool!” I said. She looked confused.

Then, two girls came out of the house. “Bogna hib?” the leanest girl said. They were all very skinny, but she seemed to be the skinniest.

“M fana kofg hoog gi daoo,” said the girl who brought me here. She pointed to herself and said, “Beta.” I’m expecting that was her name.

I waved and said, “Beta.” She pointed to me.

“Amy?” I guessed. She nodded.

“Alfalfa,” the biggest one said.

“Cecelia,” the skinny one said.

“Hib shuj, Amy,” Beta said.

They all had tan skin and straight hair but it looked uneven. Beta had long silky brown-black hair. Alfalfa had short hair, very uneven, and Cecelia had wavy regular brown hair. She didn't look so messed up and her hair was even. She had white teeth, unlike the others' mucky brown, and she was wearing fresh, modern clothes unlike the rags made out of animal skins. Cecelia came over to me.

"Hello, I'm Cecelia," she said in English.

"Is this place kind of strange? I'm sorry if I bothered you, I need to get back to my house now," I said.

"Where do you live?" she asked.

"Tukwila, Washington. Why?" I wondered.

"What year were you born in?" Cecelia ignored me.

"2001. Why are you asking me these questions?" I asked.

"You don't have a clue where you are, do you?" she said.

"No, not really," I admitted.

"Well, let's just say you went through a portal. Now, I think you're in the Philippines in about the 1600s. Don't freak out or anything, but you can't go back unless you find the portal. I ran into it when I was 5 years old. I never found it again, but, hey, you might be lucky. Alfalfa and Beta here don't know any English so I'll be your helper. It's hardest when you don't know any of their language and they don't know any of yours," Cecelia said.

Then, a huge, gray wolf stepped out of the house with little puppies. I shrieked.

"Stay calm, they don't know you, just hold out your hand like this," Cecelia said and showed me how to hold out my hand up to their nose with the back side of the palm facing them.

"Why are there wolves in the house?" I asked.

"They're like family here. They rescued Alfalfa and Beta. When they were babies, and their parents found out that they were girls, they threw them in this forest. Their friend, Ricala, was here too, but she went into the mainland and got shot by a bow and arrow," Cecelia explained.

"Is that why Beta pulled me out of the way before I went into the mainland?" I asked.

"Yes, Beta is the nice one around here, so, if you have a problem and I'm not around ask her, not Alfalfa, she warned. I nodded.

"Well, I'm kind of hungry, what do you have to eat?" I asked.

"Beta was going hunting when she found you, so we're kind of short on food. But let me show you all the wolves. This one is Trevor, he's the alpha so don't bother him. Only Alfalfa relates to the alphas, so that's why we called her Alfalfa. I named the girls because they are stupid. Trust me on that. They don't take it as an offense, so you can call them stupid heads if you want," she explained.

"Okay, but I'm really starving. Do have any hamburgers?" I asked. Cecelia was kind of boring me but I didn't say anything.

I learned most of Beta and Alfalfa's language, but a couple of words didn't make sense. "M'j cio," I complained. *I'm hungry*. "M'kk foo," Alfalfa said. *I'll go*.

I became part of the beta group with the wolves, the second most important. There were seven wolves. Trevor and She-she were the alphas. Trevor was a light gray and She-she was pitch black.

The betas (the ones I was with) were Jugi,(Joo-Jee), a small brown malewolf; Iguo (Igoo) (my favorite) had shiny white hair with black specks which made me like her the most; and Oozuki,(Oozookee) a black wolf with a brownish back (who was Beta's favorite).

There was only two regulars, Haroo, a crispy white wolf, and Secraty (Sek-ra-tie) which meant secret in their language. Secraty really kept to herself. Secraty was a calico wolf with brown, black and white.

The pups were my favorite, to be honest. Trevor and She-she's puppies were Fifo (Fee-foo) and Yukee (You-key). Iguo and Oozuki's pups were Wasanlin (Wa-son-len) and Biksby (Bikspee). Haroo and Secraty only had one puppy because their other ones died at birth or got lost. Linsalia (Lin-sa-lee-a) was their only puppy.

I fell asleep on Iguo's stomach that night. In the morning, I decided I was going to go back to the modern day.

That was the same day Beta was teaching me how to hunt. I was going to miss the wolves and Beta, Alfalfa, and Cecelia. But I missed my own family even more. I needed to find them before the portal closed.

"Hey, Cecelia, how many days does it take for the portal to close forever?" I asked.

"Only ten days, but some people get unlucky and it takes longer. It's only in one spot for ten seconds, and it leaves to show up on another continent, maybe another world. But, hey, where would it go and not burn up?" she teased. I knew. The ghost world. I wanted to see the ghost world too. I even missed, I didn't want to admit it, but I missed Katrina. I nodded, not exactly knowing what she meant.

"Igsh oona," Beta said. *Watch me*. She crept up behind a rabbit and crouched. I watched her make a noise then crept to the other side of the rabbit. When the rabbit was looking the other way, she walked quickly over and stopped when she was about to make a noise, like move a rock or something. She stomped on the rabbit's tail and then did the most disgusting thing ever. She bit the rabbit's neck with her bare teeth.

"Ew!" I yelled.

The rabbit looked at me with fear. He turned his head around and bit Beta. She didn't seem to notice and snapped his neck. She continued snapping every bone in his body.

"Hib shuj pligw," I said. *This is gross*.

"Juba kio hiop deshz ople hiop pokl," Beta said. *You need to get used to it*.

We ran home as quickly as we could. Beta was carrying the rabbit.

"Cluke qufl juba lerpauq hib xule?" Alfalfa asked. *What did you catch this time*?

"Hijxv," I said. *Rabbit*.

"M'j tervl yalup g klobwed," I announced. *I'm going for a walk*. I didn't know where to start, so I took off where Beta had brought me a couple of weeks ago. I walked and walked and walked. When I was near the place where the portal was, I decided to go back. When I walked a little further, I turned around and gasped.

Part Two:

The Short Side of Beta Wiltserin

Chapter Nine - Alpha

I've always wondered about my before life. Who were my mother and father? Did they really love me? Would I get to see them, ever? I wondered every night and every day. I patted Jugi lightly on the head. "Good boy," I whispered. I tried not to wake up Alfalfa and Cecelia.

I was starving. I wanted a chicken this time, not just a rodent. My stomach growled. "Sh," I told it. I didn't want anybody to wake up, even the wolves, especially the alphas.

That made me think that I wished I was Alfalfa; I could get along well with the leaders. Even though I panicked whenever something scary happened, I wanted to be an alpha, a leader. Poor Cecelia, she could only relate to Secraty, Haroo and the pup, Linsalia. They didn't know what to do even if something normal happened.

I needed food to go to sleep. I had the second most food; the alphas were always fed their fill first, then the betas, then the regulars. Cecelia taught us that. The alphas were the most important, then the betas, then the regulars.

I wanted to be smart like Cecelia. She had told us she went to a place called kindergarten which was some type of learning school. I don't know all of the fancy math, as she calls it. She says we're stupid heads in some language, but I don't know what that means. Alfalfa thought right away it was something mean, but I think she's calling us smart in a fancy math word way. I think.

It was hard to sleep with the world's light shining so brightly into the door of our house. I was thinking of going to our cold-holder, which Cecelia called a refrigerator. We kept all of our left-over food in the cold-holder. But only the alphas could give permission to pick something out of it.

I knew I was a good person, but, if a good person does a bad thing, they turn into a bad person. I didn't want to be a bad person, but I was so hungry, I could eat one of the wolves, even though I would never in my whole life do that. I shivered and snuggled closer to Oozuki, my favorite wolf.

I barely slept that night, but in the morning I was fine. "Beta, your stomach was growling the whole night, I couldn't sleep at all," Alfalfa said meanly to me when I woke.

"I'm sorry. I didn't mean to. I was starving. Can I get some food out of the cold-holder?" I asked.

"It's called the refrigerator," Cecelia corrected me.

"But that word is so big, I can't speak it," I argued.

"Stop arguing! It's making me go crazy!" Alfalfa snapped.

"I'm sorry," I apologized.

"Me too," Cecelia agreed.

"You can have a little bit of food out of the fridge," Alfalfa ordered, with what Cecelia calls a chin held high.

Cecelia told us that if we couldn't pronounce, whatever that meant, refrigerator, say fridge. I still said cold-holder, secretly.

I walked over to the cold-holder. "No, you can't eat anything anymore. You're being rude," Alfalfa said.

"I'm sorry. What can I do to be polite?" I asked.

"You need to say thank you," Alfalfa demanded.

"Thank you for letting me eat this yummy food," I thanked her.

I missed Ricala. Alfalfa was mean because she could boss us around. Now, anyone I saw who went onto the mainland I must stop before it was too late.

I took out a plucked chicken. I gave it to Cecelia who said she had to do something to make it healthy. I didn't know what healthy meant, but I agreed. She rubbed two sticks together until they made a bright red light, dancing over the wood. Cecelia called this a fire. We threw pine cones and leaves into the fire. It made big popping sounds like when I hunt for my food and bend the rodent backwards and forwards.

"Why can't I just eat it?" I asked.

"Because you will get sick and die," Cecelia answered.

"No I won't. I've eaten it before without putting it over the dancing red popping things," I said quietly, but it was in a mean voice.

"Fire, Beta, it's called a fire. If it's raw, you can get sick." I never had gotten sick before. Cecelia said it's when your throat is scratching and you make weird noises with your mouth or you can't stop rubbing your eyes. When it was finally done, I gobbled it down in almost one bite.

Today was the day Cecelia was going to show us something glorious that was sweet but sometimes gross. We had to get on our rags, as Cecelia called them. She made us green fancy dresses made out of rose petals. They were tied together by flower stems. Our rags were made out of deerskin and shaped to our bodies. They could get stains on them and we could wash them off in the river, put them back on and they'd be good as new. I put on my rags and walked out under the trees. The rough ground scraped up my feet.

"Come here and climb up this tree like me," Cecelia ordered. I walked to the tree and followed her up. "Grab these yellow things called bananas," she ordered. "They don't look yellow. They look green and brown," Alfalfa complained.

"They're good; now get down from the tree," Cecelia ordered.

I jumped off while Cecelia slowly climbed down. "Follow me," she said and walked and walked. We finally reached what she was looking for. It was a little bush with small red things. "These are called strawberries. Don't eat them; just pick them out of the bushes," Cecelia said. I reached down to pick one up and I heard the plant screaming in pain.

"No! We can't do this, it's hurting the little plant," I exclaimed.

"No it's not; they want us to eat them. That's what they're for," Cecelia said softly. I kept picking them and hearing them scream.

After what seemed like forever, we stopped and moved on to the next activity. "Go into the water and catch a fish, but they can be slippery so be careful," she said. I walked into the water but it was too strong and pulled me away.

"Beta!" I heard Cecelia and Alfalfa scream. But I could get out of the stream when I want to. When I knew it was time to get out, I swayed to a side and rolled onto the rough ground. Cecelia was right when she said to wear the deerskin. I didn't feel anything but if I had been wearing my dress, I would have been covered in warm, red water which Cecelia calls blood.

I walked back into the house and tried to find some sticks to make the dancing red stuff. I rubbed and rubbed on the sticks and a little red dot flew up. That wasn't enough. I rubbed harder and harder. It didn't take Cecelia this long. I rubbed as hard and as fast as I could and then, red flames started to dance. I smiled. I had done it. But my hands started to burn and I dropped it. Oh no. I had dropped it and now it would go out. But it didn't. It stayed. I smiled again.

Cecelia came running back. "Beta, how did you get back here?" she asked.

"I stopped at the stream when I knew I was next to the house," I said. I tried to touch the dancing red stuff, but my hand got really hot.

"Did you make this?" Cecelia asked.

"Yes, is it good?" I asked.

"It's perfect! How did you get it so big?" she asked.

"I just rubbed and rubbed, then I held it for a couple seconds, then it got hot and I dropped it," I said.

"You didn't put it down right when you saw the flame?" she asked.

"Of course not," I laughed.

"Here, we finished picking our nuts, berries and fruits. Try them," Cecelia encouraged.

"Okay," I agreed. There was a round purple thing. "What's this?" I asked and picked it up.

"That's called a grape. You can peel off the skin if you want to," she said and showed me how. I ate it whole. It was a thick juicy fruit with seeds in it.

"Do I eat the seeds?" I asked.

"No, spit them out," Alfalfa snapped. "You're a stupid head," Alfalfa snapped again.

"Alf," Cecelia said and gave a warning look at Alfalfa. Maybe stupid head wasn't a nice name.

Next, I tried the nuts. They were little brown things and they were really crunchy. "Mm, this is good," I said.

"I know. We'll keep this in the refrigerator," Cecelia said.

"Okay, so I can take this whenever I want?" I asked.

"Whenever you want," Cecelia confirmed. Alfalfa was about to say no, but Cecelia didn't let her.

I slept well that night. I dreamt of the dancing red stuff filling the forest. At first, I sat and watched the beauty of it take over the lands. Then, I realized it wasn't any dream. It was a nightmare. It was blazing hot and I couldn't breathe. I screamed for help but nobody could hear me. My eyes snapped open. I was just breathing in Oozuki's soft, warm hair. I coughed and got up to eat some nuts.

Alfalfa was awake and she stared at me. Her eyes looked yellow. "Alfalfa, I can eat this. Cecelia said so," I whispered.

"Cecelia isn't the boss, is she? Now, I want you to get back in bed and go to sleep. You aren't allowed up," Alfalfa ordered. She-she growled and said I was allowed to have some berries.

"Shut up, She-she," Alfalfa ordered.

"No, listen to the real alpha, she will tell me what to do," I said, scared Alfalfa would get me in trouble.

"No, I tell you what to do. She picked me, so I choose," Alfalfa said. She-she barked this time. I went over to the cold-holder and opened it up.

"Don't move another inch," Alfalfa snarled like Trevor when he was protecting us from a stranger.

"No," I finally said. I put my arm into the cold-holder and I picked up some berries.

Alfalfa stood up to make me sit back down. I didn't budge. "Move," she snapped. I didn't say anything. I ate my berries and then went back to bed.

I fell back asleep quickly, but still filled with fear of Alfalfa. In the morning, Alfalfa wouldn't speak to me or look at me.

"Okay, we're going to get some fish today," Cecelia said.

"No, I think I'll just wait here," Alfalfa said. "I wanted to talk to She-she about something."

"What did you want to talk about?" Cecelia asked.

"Nothing, I mean, it's personal," Alfalfa said quickly.

"Well, okay, but we'll be back soon," Cecelia warned.

"That's okay; it will be a short talk."

Cecelia and I went outside after we ate some blueberries, strawberries and blackberries. We walked into the river and Cecelia showed me how to catch fish. I got ten of them and she caught seven. Cecelia said that, in all, we had 17 fish. That was big math and I don't know how to do fancy stuff like that.

I heard Alfalfa hit She-she and She-she screamed. I couldn't bear to leave She-she in pain, so I ran into the bamboo house. Trevor was growling at Alfalfa now. Before she could hurt him, he wacked his paw on her face. Four warm, watery red lines scarred her face. She didn't give up.

I ran over to She-she. She had the warm, watery red stuff behind her ears and on her legs. I grabbed a towel which we had woven out of leaves from the counter. I ran to the river and dipped it in. I ran back swiftly and wrapped it around She-she's cut-up leg. I half carried her back to the spot where all of the other wolves were. Cecelia was already there, comforting the pups.

I watched silently as Trevor and Alfalfa fought. I knew what would happen. This had happened before with Lingush. She was one of the alphas; she also had been an abandoned little girl. She thought she had all of the control, so, the wolves pushed her out into the mainland while she slept fast.

Alfalfa was next in line. She would be brought out to the mainland in her fast sleep, then she would be shot and forced to marry an older man. It's what always happened. Ricala even sent me a postcard of what happened. Lingush sent me another one right after. Soon it will be Alfalfa sending me the card.

I hoped we would get more people in our pack; I didn't want to be the only human. I wouldn't mind, but I would much rather have a human friend to talk to.

I decided not to watch the fight anymore. I dug my face in Oozuki's chest. When the fight was over, I knew who had won, and who would always win, the alpha male, Trevor. He smiled when Alfalfa was lying on the floor, half dead. She'd wait. She'd wait until the time was right. Some ask how they know the time. When it's time, you'll know. I know I did the first time I got sent out onto the mainland.

It was the time when I was only a young child. The wolves didn't know us, Ricala, Lingush, Alfalfa, and I, so we were still getting to know each other. That also meant we didn't know the boundaries. We thought we could do whatever we wanted, as infants do, and I went too far. That's why I always behave now.

Iguo had just gone out hunting and unluckily found nothing. I said that was stupid, that anybody could catch food. That's why I'm always the one who hunts now.

Trevor got mad, and he yelled at me. I got scared and ran off. They said before I left that if I caught something, they would let me hunt all the time. I came back the next day, scared and without anything.

They saw I was empty handed so they scolded me for being mean to Iguo. I apologized, and they accepted, except I did it once again when Iguo still hadn't caught anything. I was sent out again, came back empty handed, and Trevor put his paw down.

"You will go into the mainland, at once. You have been nothing but a naughty little child. Take her away," Trevor had ordered. They had named Ricala and Lingush, but not me or Alfalfa.

When I was in a deep sleep, I knew something bad was going to happen to me. I was lifted and put out in the mainland. It was scary, very scary. A young man, about my age was going to help me escape back to the wolves, but his older brother caught him and told on me. I ran back to the forest, not knowing which way was home. Lingush found me and helped me back.

I apologized to the wolves and swore to never say anything mean again. They accepted, thinking it must have been hard to find my way back into the forest. That hour I vowed to myself that I would always listen to the wolves, no matter what they say, and I would be the one to hunt.

And now, it was Alfalfa's turn.

Chapter Ten - Strange Girl

The next day, I wanted to go hunt so I could think of some things without being bothered. I felt so much like Secraty right now. I wanted to keep to myself. I went hunting close to the mainland. I was there with my deerskin and a leather pouch to store food. I almost caught a rabbit, squirrel and a rat. I'd much rather have had a chicken, but I hadn't caught any food yet.

While I was walking with my bare feet crunching against the ground, a girl was about to go straight into the mainland. What was she thinking? I ran in front of her and held out a hand to stop her. I motioned her to close her mouth and she nodded in a weird way. I brought her back to the bamboo house.

"Qufl juba yuik hib?" she asked. I looked at her. What was she saying?

"What are you talking about?" I asked. She just acted like I spoke in a silly language.

"Who's this?" Cecelia asked.

"I found her in the forest," I said. I pointed to myself and said, "Beta." I pointed to her.

"Amy?" she sounded like she didn't know her own name. I pointed to Alfalfa who had come out too.

"Alfalfa," I said. Then I looked at Cecelia. "Cecelia." Then, I said to Alfalfa and Cecelia, "This is Amy."

Cecelia walked up to Amy and talked in a strange language. All I heard was blah, blah, blah. I couldn't understand anything.

Amy was one of the betas, like me. Her favorite wolf was Iguo, but she loved the pups. I thought she was going to fit in just fine, but her clothes would have to go. They were ugly rags.

She wore a red shirt with buttons in the middle and funny-looking squares on it. She had some things that covered her legs, too. I thought there were only dresses. Her clothes covering her legs were the color of a very clean ocean and she had boots: wonderful boots that only the most fantastic person could weave. They were a glorious bright color of the leaves. There was wolf fur on the top rim of them. Her hair was very short and very black. Her skin was as white as fresh snow and her eyes were the colors of the river in the fall, dark, dark green.

In a couple of hours, she had learned how to speak some reasonable language, but she kept talking to Cecelia in the strange language.

The next day, she wanted to go for a walk. Amy didn't seem to know where to go, so I was about to show her. She left quickly, though. She didn't come back.

I guess she had decided to leave and go back on her own. Amy wasn't smart enough to live on her own. She would go onto the mainland for sure. Days passed, but she still wasn't back from her walk yet.

"Cecelia, do you think Amy didn't want to live with us anymore?" I asked.

"No, I think she just wanted to see her family again. Maybe she found a way back home," she replied.

"But why would she leave without telling us?" I asked.

"Sometimes people find a way back unexpectedly, Beta. I bet someone will be back soon. I *want* her to go; you should too. That way she can thank us for not getting mad at her for seeing her family," Cecelia said.

"Oh," was all I could say. I thought it was rude leaving and not telling anybody. I mean, how was family important anyway if they just left you behind? Animals will stay with you, that's for sure. The wolves had stayed with me and taken care of me since I was an itsy, bitsy baby.

"I'm kind of hungry," I announced. "We're going to need to get some meat tomorrow and we need some more fruits. Also, I'm going to show you something called a vegetable," Cecelia said.

"A vegetable, what is a vegetable like?" I asked.

"Oh, sometimes they're good, sometimes they're bad," she said.

"What are the good ones?"

"Well, let's see: carrots, they are good. So are corn and green beans. Tomatoes are icky, unless you like mushy stuff, and celery, those are good, especially with peanut butter and blackberries on it," She said.

"How do you make peanut butter?" I asked.

"You crunch peanuts into butter, stupid head," Cecelia said. I nodded my head, not knowing what peanuts were.

"What are the bad ones?" I wondered, trying not to say anything that would make me look like a stupid head.

"There are plenty of those. There's cauliflower, brussel sprouts, broccoli, and tons of other things I don't even want to say. But, they're all very healthy," she said.

"What's not healthy?" I asked.

"Oh, if you could just go into the future, Beta, it's so amazing."

"What's the future?" I blurted out.

"Oh, it takes place ahead of time. Like, five minutes from now, is the future. But if it's six minutes from now, the five minutes will be the past," she explained. I nodded, not really knowing what she was talking about.

Weeks went by, and things were the same as always. No visitors. No Amy. No anybody. It was really windy, the day that someone finally visited. Bamboo trees were swinging everywhere, the earth screaming. That's when, finally, Amy came by.

"Amy!" I yelled in joy, over the wind. She was with somebody. She was with another girl, like us. She walked in with a whole bunch of stuff in her hands. She had bags and bags of stuff. Her friend was carrying two big boards with more bags on her arms.

They set all the stuff down and lifted the boards onto the empty space to get in and out. She was trapping us in, that's what she was doing. Then she'd run off again.

"No!" I yelled, but no one could hear me. Cecelia was helping them, too. She was part of this. "No, please don't do this!" I said. I heard a clink, the boards locked, and the wind almost completely stopped.

"This is Scout," Amy said and pulled off her head sweater. It was attached to her real sweater. "Scout, juba gfd qmjf," Cecelia said.

"What are you talking about?" I asked.

"She's telling her where to sleep, don't worry, Beta," said Amy.

"Why are you locking us in the house?" I whispered.

"We're not, we're putting doors on it so you can stay warm and evil things don't come in at night," she said.

"Well, what if the evil things come in during the day and are locked in?" I asked.

"The doors will be closed the whole time," she said.

"What about the wolves? How will they come and go as they please?" I asked.

"They can't. We have to open the door for them. In the day, if it's really nice outside, we might open the doors," she said.

"Where did you make up these things called doors?" I asked.

"I didn't make them up. I copied them from the future, I mean, um, the year 2000. It has very interesting things," she said.

"I want to go there. I never get to go to this place called the future and Cecelia talks about it all the time," I groaned. Amy glanced at Cecelia.

"I brought some beds for you," Amy changed the subject. "They're very comfortable. You just need a lot of breath. It's called an air mattress," she explained.

"Shouldn't it be called a breath mattress if you fill it with your breath?" I asked. Amy laughed. "Sure, you can call it that," she said.

Amy, Cecelia, and Scout dumped all the bags on the floor. There were strange words on everything and they were all in jars or boxes. Then, Amy took out a red thing. She opened it up and it had buttons all over it. On the top, there was a picture.

"What's that?" I asked.

"It's a cell phone, stupid head," Cecelia answered. Why hadn't I gotten one of these cell phone things?

"What's it for?" I asked. "You can call people on it," Amy said, interrupting Cecelia's explanation.

"Why don't you just use your voice?" I asked.

"Because, what if someone was really far away and couldn't hear you?" Amy said after a moment.

"Then walk over to them," I answered.

"No, what if it was really, really, far away and it took days to get there?" she said.

"If you wanted to talk to them so badly, they must be your friend and someone that you like. If they like you, shouldn't you live close together?" I asked, shrugging my shoulders.

"You have a point, but it's easier," Amy said, giving excuses for her cell phone thing. I gave up on that conversation. I walked over to the wolves and sat down. Scout gasped when she saw the wolves. Amy soothed her in another language.

"They won't hurt you, I promise," I said. Scout didn't hear me. She looked at me crazily and backed away. "I said: they won't hurt you. Why don't you understand me?" I snapped. She still didn't do anything.

I stood up. "I said, they won't hurt you," I snapped again. I walked quickly over to her. Scout looked at the wolves strangely. She said something that sounded like she was making fun of something. I pushed her over. "I said that they won't hurt you, so stop picking on them," I snapped. Amy and Cecelia had gone outside to set up some more things. Alfalfa was the only one left who was smiling pleasantly and sitting by the wolves.

Scout looked horrified. "Why were you doing that? What? Were you a stupid head when you were back home?" I asked.

"Cluke boji juba hoog daut?" she said.

"Huh? Why were you doing that?" I asked. She tried to run to the door, but her sluggish feet were too slow. I easily beat her to the door. She pushed me, a weak push. I pushed her back, a much, much, stronger one. She hit her head on the door. Scout put her hand on her head and when she brought it down, wet, warm, red stuff was on her hand.

"I'm sorry," I apologized, but my tone wasn't right. It sounded more like a threat. Scout opened the door and ran out.

"Amy, Amy," she shouted. She would tell on me and I would get in trouble. I would have to sleep outside tonight, like always. Sometimes I felt like Cecelia was the alpha. She always told us what to do. Cecelia stomped back into the house.

"Beta, no! Look what you did! You sleep outside tonight," Cecelia yelled. I looked down.

"I'm sorry. She was picking on the wolves. If you ask me, it was really Alfalfa," I lied. I had never lied in my life. I wondered how it would turn out.

Cecelia stomped over to Alfalfa. "No, no, no! You can't do things like that!" she yelled. Alfalfa was confused.

"What are you talking about? It was Beta! I swear to God!" Cecelia had taught us all about God and if you swear to him and you're lying, you go to Satan. I was perfectly fine before I was swearing to God.

"Whatever, but whichever one of you did this, you know it and the guilt will live with you for the rest of your life, unless you get punished," said Cecelia.

No, guilt wouldn't live with me. I could make it go away. All I had to do is ignore it. I didn't need to get punished for letting someone know that it's not nice to make fun of wolves.

In a few weeks, Scout was speaking reasonably in our language, but she was still afraid to talk to me. She would only speak to Amy, Cecelia and Alfalfa. Scout also kept complaining to Amy and cried every night. Even the wolves were getting annoyed.

One day, I went out to hunt for chickens. I craved one so badly. I ran a long, long way. Once I was finally on farmland, I crouched down and crawled. I found a white chicken flecked with black spots. I broke a twig and the chicken turned its head toward the place I was in. I quietly ran to his other side. In a flash, I was grabbing the chicken's neck. I snapped everything until it was for sure dead.

When I got back to the bamboo house, everybody was on the top of it. "What are you doing?" I asked.

"We're building a second story to your house. There'll be a lot more room," said Amy. I didn't know what she meant, so I went back into the house. I started to pluck the chicken and eat it raw. Then I remembered that Cecelia would get mad at me so I got two sticks and made a fire.

There was a cold, smooth material under rocks. Cecelia had showed it to me before and said it was clay. She also had said that if you fire it, it will turn smooth and feel like glass. I shaped it to a large bowl and began. I put it in the fire and waited.

Cecelia realized what I was doing and jumped off from the house. "Here, Beta, let me help you," She looked at the bowl and took a floppy thing from the things that Amy brought. She flapped it around and the fire died.

"No, why'd you do that?" I asked. She didn't answer me. She got thick logs and placed them where the twigs once were. Cecelia got a long metal thing and pressed a button. A red little fire started.

When the red dancing flame touched one of the logs, it blew up with fire. She dropped the bowl in it. "When do we take it out?" I asked.

"In a week, if the fire stays up. Maybe we could do a little less," she said. I sat down next to the dancing red flames.

Weeks passed, then months, Scout still sometimes cried in her sleep. I wondered why. Was it about her family? What was family to me? I didn't care. Why should anybody else?

"I want to eat," I complained.

"Okay, just hold on for a little bit. I need to let the pop tarts pop and the toast pop," Cecelia said. Amy and Scout brought strange foods with them when they came.

I got back hunting one day, and there were colorful circles tied to rope and the rope was tied to the house.

"What are those?" I asked.

"They're balloons. What else?" Scout snapped.

"Why do we have them?" I wondered. To myself, I wasn't sounding very smart, as Cecelia calls it.

"It's Amy's birthday today," Cecelia said.

"How do you keep track of when your birthday is? I want one," I complained.

"You have one; we just don't know what it is. A birthday is the day you were born, and you get presents to celebrate it," Alfalfa said, a lot more kindly than Scout.

"How do you know this?" I asked.

"Because I'm not a stupid head like you, right, Cecelia?" she asked, being meaner.

"No, you both are. You're just less of one," Amy corrected.

"What's today?" Scout asked.

"It's August twenty-eighth, what else?" Amy snapped.

"Oh yeah, remember last year I got you a piano?" Scout asked. What the heck was a piano?

"Yeah, too bad I can't play it anymore," she said sadly.

Seriously, had people gone insane these days? What was a piano? "What's a piano?" I asked.

"Ha! You don't know what a piano is; you're such an idiot, Beta. Can you believe that, guys? She doesn't know what a piano is!" Alfalfa made fun of me.

"Hey, shut up Alfalfa. You didn't, you still don't know what a piano is," Amy said, standing up for me.

"Yes I do," she said in a brattish voice.

"Then what is it?" Amy challenged.

"It's, um, well, if you know the answer, why are you asking me?" Alfalfa stuttered.

"No, I know the answer, I'm just seeing if you know. That's all," she shrugged her shoulders.

"Yeah, well, it's an um, uh, er, something, that, uh, um, does, um, something. Yeah, it's something that does something," Alfalfa said like she knew everything in the world.

"Let's be a little more specific," Amy suggested.

"Nah, no thanks," Alfalfa said like she could.

While they argued, I went into the house. I laid down on the new thing that Amy and Scout brought. When I finally decided that I liked sleeping with the wolves better, I rolled off the bed and landed on Oozuki. He growled and went back to sleeping.

I got bored so I got up and went to eat something. Cecelia would have snapped at me if I told the truth, so I said I was hungry. She always said, *'If you aren't hungry, why would you waste food? What if we're starving, and since you were bored, we will die.'*

I ate and ate. When I couldn't eat another crumb, I sat back. Scout asked Amy something in their silly language. She answered back a soothing answer. Scout nodded and went back to work on the top of the house.

Our food was almost gone by the next day.

"Beta, I'm starving. Go get a rabbit or something," Alfalfa ordered.

"I am too, and when you don't have any food in you, it's hard to concentrate," I protested.

"Yeah, well, we wouldn't be hungry if you hadn't eaten all the food yesterday."

"I was hungry!" I exclaimed, although I wasn't.

"Mm, hmm, sure you were," Alfalfa rolled her eyes.

I gave up and went hunting. I tried to shoot a rabbit with a bow and arrow Amy gave me, but he ran away. There were a couple squirrels in the trees, and I could see them. I ran around for hours, trying to find food, but it was getting dark and all the animals were going to sleep.

When I came back empty handed, Alfalfa slapped me and Cecelia scolded me. "I'm sorry, they were all up in the trees," I apologized.

"First thing tomorrow, I'm going to wake you up and you are going to go hunting," Alfalfa said.

"Yes," I nodded my head sadly.

The next day, nothing was out in the woods again. I stayed out there all day until dark. It was getting colder, and the fruits weren't growing on their bushes. Some of the fish were swimming in the river, but it was much too cold to go in. Our only hope was meat, and we couldn't find it.

I came home again, empty handed. I got yelled at and complained at, but deep in their eyes, I could tell they had a twinge of sadness for me. I was starving too, and I was the one who hunted for it.

The next day, I sat in bed, not bothering to go hunt. "Come on, Beta. You need to go hunt," Amy said. We were all still in bed. My stomach hurt so much from hunger, I could barely move. I dragged my feet to the door and then went outside. It was cold, and little pieces of water came falling down. It dampened my clothes.

Later, I saw a nut tree. I climbed it, but there were only five nuts. We could all have one, or I could eat them all so I wouldn't be hungry. Should I get myself full, or should we all get something to bring our hopes up? I decided to bring all the nuts back. I smiled gratefully and ran home.

"I found something!" I yelled. Everybody's head turned a little.

"What is it?" Scout asked.

"I found five nuts, but that was it," I said. They grumbled, but took a nut. Alfalfa and I ate very quickly, but Amy, Cecelia and Scout nibbled on theirs to make it last.

I had found something, that wasn't a lie. But it was a lie that it filled us up. It helped only a little and within fifteen minutes, we were all hungry again. That night, I was starved. Why couldn't help come to us? My eyes shut, and I felt like I had had my last day as I slowly drifted into a dark sleep.

Part Three:

Until Then

Chapter Eleven – Starving

My stomach growled and I rolled over. This was going to be a long, long night. I missed Daphne's comfort, her voice, Poch's voice. My stomach growled again. Beta hadn't found food in three days. It's been hard, building the upstairs of the house. I was scorching for something to drink. If it was always this hard living in the 1600s, I would go back as soon as I found that portal again.

I had gotten lucky, finding it again with Scout. We even had all of the supplies. Even though we had extra food, we didn't tell anybody. I saved that food for when I was absolutely about to die. Should I eat it? This felt like death. I would have to get everybody to the place where I found the portal so we could go back into our time. I thought about other things besides food to get hunger off my mind.

When I woke up, I had won. I had lived through another night. I blinked.

"Amy," Scout whispered.

"What?" I whispered back.

"Do you think we could live through another day of no food?" she asked.

"I think so but we definitely need water. This is our third day without it," I said. Patches on my tongue refused to get moistened.

I dragged my feet out of bed and grabbed a ladder. Then, it hit me. I was reading in school a few years ago that there was a time in the 1600s when all of the town people took all the food in the forest and nothing remained. I wasn't sure that it was real, but I decided to tell people that I believed it.

"Scout," I whispered, trying not to wake anybody up. "I read a couple of years ago that some people from town in the 1600s hunted all the food and there wasn't any left. I think that's just happened," I said, bewildered.

"Yeah, that or the girls aren't finding the boys that attractive," she joked. I partly smiled at her joke that I didn't understand.

I walked to the top of the house on the ladder. So far we had a floor on the flat bottom part of the house, all the sides up, and part of a roof. I collected the bamboo and shredded it with a pocket knife. The glue gun was on a little table we had built upstairs. I grabbed it and got to work. A couple minutes later, Scout came up.

"Hey, can you grab some…" I stopped to cough. A speck of blood came out of my mouth.

"Bamboo," I finished.

"Yeah," she coughed back. We worked silently until Cecelia came up.

"Hi," I greeted her when she got into the top part of the house.

"Hi," she said with a scratchy voice.

We worked slowly, and finally, I collapsed. I threw up blood, and I don't know why. They ran over to me as quickly as they could, nearly collapsing themselves.

"Amy, Amy, are you okay?" Cecelia asked, but she didn't have much of a voice.

Her brown hair sparkled in the dim light and her eyes were as alarmed as I felt. "Amy, what happened?" Scout asked.

"She fell over, I don't know why," Cecelia replied, answering for me. I tried to tell them everything was going to be okay, and I was fine, but that would be a horrible, nasty, lie anyone could see.

Soon, I had enough strength to get up. They ran over when they saw me stand up.

"Amy, what happened?" they asked.

"Um, I'm not sure," I said and coughed. I went back to work, supergluing the shredded bamboo. "Hey, why don't we just catch fish in the river?" I asked. Why hadn't we just gone fishing?

"Beta complains it's too cold," Cecelia said, rolling her eyes.

"Why doesn't she just use the fishing poles?" I asked.

"I don't know. Ask her," Cecelia shrugged.

So I did. I hopped down the ladder, walked inside and asked Beta, "Why don't you go fishing?"

"Because, the water is so cold," she replied. I had used this foreign language so much; it was almost like English to me.

"Then, why don't you," –cough- "use the fishing poles?" I asked.

"I don't know how to use them," she admitted.

"That's okay. I can teach you," I said.

That afternoon, we grabbed the fishing poles and went to the fishing hole. Luckily, for some reason, I brought fish food. I stabbed a pebble on the pole, and Beta did the same. I put mine in the water, and so did she.

"Now what?" she asked.

"We wait until you feel a pull," I replied.

"Then what?"

"You take the fishing pole out of the water and we take it home," I said. "Easy as that."

We stayed for forty-five minutes.

"I'm getting bored," Beta declared.

"Well, do you want food or not?" I asked. We continued waiting. A couple of minutes later, a large tug almost pulled me into the water. I rolled the line out quickly. I walked backwards holding the pole so the fish wouldn't get away. "Beta, come help pull!" I yelled. She dropped her pole and ran over to me.

She pulled hard and the fish went flying over us. I ran over to the fish, slowly, compared with Beta. We were both slow but she was faster.

"What do we do with it?" she asked.

"Well, it's about a fifty-pound fish, so, I'll carry the poles, and you carry the fish," I said. She nodded and did what she was told. We wouldn't starve, after all. Because of me, we lived. I smiled to myself.

"We have a present!" I said as we walked back to the house. Alfalfa's, Scout's, and Cecelia's heads shot up. They all gasped.

"Oh my gosh! How did you find this?" Cecelia asked, bewildered and weak.

"Well, first we put a little kibble on the pole. Then, we..."

Cecelia cut me off. "I know how, I'm just amazed," she said and glared at me. We were all speaking in the foreign language so Alfalfa and Beta wouldn't wonder what we were saying.

Cecelia started a fire and put a big, smooth, flat stone with rusty wires connected to it over the fire. The stone was held up by two, sturdy, small logs.

"Wow, this will keep us fed for days," Scout said.

"Not at the rate we've been eating, or not eating. It will likely be gone in a day. Four hungry girls, one fifty-pound fish, hmm, I think it will be gone by tomorrow. Don't eat until you're full. Only eat until you're not hungry anymore. And, don't eat everything until we have more fish!" Cecelia cried. My mouth watered as I watched the fish sizzle.

After what seemed like a million years, the fish was ready, a brownish color. All the pink was gone.

"I'm alpha; I eat all I want first!" Alfalfa said and stepped towards the fish.

"No, you don't. If you're the alpha, you make sure everybody is well-fed first, and then you eat," Cecelia snapped. She-she looked like she almost nodded her head. Oh, yes, the fish would have to fill seven hungry wolves too and about five pups.

We cut off the head and tail, then the fins which had pretty much burned off. I took the middle torso part, but it was only about two inches. Everybody else got about two inches, and the rest went to the wolves.

"Mm, what kind of fish is this?" Scout asked.

"It's halibut," Cecelia replied. I scraped off the brown parts and ate the soft, chewy white parts. Everybody enjoyed it, and we went to sleep with what felt like full stomachs.

I took Beta and Alfalfa out fishing every day after that. Soon we had fish that lasted for a couple of days before we had to go back to fishing.

Then one day, Scout came up to me. "Amy, I want something besides fish," she ordered, being a little snappy.

"Well, I'm sorry, but that's all we can afford right now. We can't be specialists right now," I said and continued gluing bamboo to the walls.

"But I'm sick of fish. Please, can we have something else?" she pleaded.

"I'll try," I promised.

The next morning, I went out on my own before anybody woke up. I looked at a tree and studied it for a long time. I finally peeled a piece of bark from it.

What caught my eye was a bug eating the inside the bark that had been on the tree. I peeled off another piece and peeled the next layer. I chewed on it. It wasn't the best thing ever, but it was food, alright.

This is going to make them so happy, well, at least Scout, something besides fish. I walked home quickly, and woke everybody up to taste the new food I found. They all tried it and shrugged, except for Scout.

"This doesn't taste good," she complained.

"Scout! You ask for different food besides fish. I find it, and all you can do is complain! Can you be just a little generous? We actually have food and we aren't starving like we were. If you want something different, find it yourself!" I yelled.

I ran outside and up the ladder. I sat down in the chair. I heard mumbles down below. I couldn't hear them that well, and I really wanted to. My pocket knife had a sharp nub on it so I stabbed in into the floor but nobody could tell.

"Really, I ask for something besides fish and she finds what? Tree bark, that's *so* appetizing," I heard Scout say harshly.

"Well, Scout, you did ask for something besides fish. If you wanted something in particular, you should have asked," Cecelia said, standing up for me.

"Yeah, but if you wanted something different to eat would you want really tree bark, really?" Scout asked.

"Well, I would definitely appreciate it," Beta said quietly.

"No, tree bark isn't food; it's something that bugs eat. Scout's right," Alfalfa said, siding with her.

"Exactly! Someone gets my point," Scout exclaimed.

Cecelia came up the ladder. "Hey," she said. I forced myself off the ground even though I wanted to hear more. I put my foot on the hole, just in case.

"Hey," I said back. We were talking in English now.

"Sorry that Scout's not being appreciative," she apologized.

"No, it's not your fault. She can just not eat if she doesn't like what she's served," I shrugged.

"Yeah, I had a little brother that did that. He wouldn't eat anything you put down for him. If he didn't choose it himself, he said it was gross."

"You had a little brother?" I asked.

"Well, yeah. Don't we all have siblings, one time or another? But I only remember him vaguely. He was a baby when I got lost in the portal," she said.

"Wow, I'm so sorry. I had to leave my little sister and older brother when I came here," I said, not really caring about my life.

"Don't you miss your mom and dad? You got away, but you came back. Why? If I ever got away, I wouldn't hesitate. I would never come back, even though I'd have no clue where I was," she said.

"Well, I miss my dad," I admitted, trying not to talk about Daphne.

"Don't you like your mom, too?" Cecelia wondered.

"Yeah, I do, but she died a year ago or something like that. I'm pretty sure she died March 14, the same day my little sister was born," I shrugged like it didn't matter, and tried not to make it matter.

"Oh, did she die giving birth?" she guessed.

"No, she got mad and left while she was pregnant. She got captured by this guy, dropped Esther off at the door and got driven into the river," I mumbled. Did Cecelia not understand how hard it was for me to talk about my dead mom?

"Oh, I'm sorry," she apologized.

We went back to work on the house. It was almost finished.

"What was your life like? I mean, before you came here, and when you were little," Cecelia asked.

"It's a long story," I said, slowly gluing bamboo.

"I think I can handle it," she said.

"Oh, I'm sorry. Did I say it's a long story? I meant I didn't want to talk about it," I snapped.

"I was just wondering," she said shyly.

"Okay, fine. I was kidnapped and then moved to Utah, fell off a plane, thought my dad died, found he really wasn't dead, found my mom, she died, came here to sell my horses. End of story, happy?" I snapped.

"You were kidnapped?" she asked amazed.

"Yes, I was held hostage." I was angry.

"By whom?" she asked.

"Jeanie Banlisa," I gulped. I shuddered at the name.

"Wait a second! Did you just say Jeanie Banlisa?" she wondered, obviously knowing what I just said.

"Yeah, of course I did. Why?" I grumbled.

"Jeanie Banlisa is my older sister, but she has a different mom. Our dad's name is Banlisa," she said. I dropped the glue.

"Your sister kidnapped me?" I asked, but it wasn't for her to answer.

"Yes, well, that's what I think. She's really old, though. She was like, thirty or something. My dad was really young when he had her and kinda old when he had me," Cecelia babbled.

"Oh my gosh. Is she a brunette?" I asked.

"No, she's a natural blonde but dyes her hair brown. Come to think of it, she kind of looks like Nikki Reed," she said.

"Yep, that's her. She sometimes goes by the name Nicole Shea?" I asked.

"Of course, she uses it all the time. But don't worry; we're two completely different people. My dad used to say I was the white dog and she was the black cat. Whenever she was around, something would go wrong."

Exactly, that was her. I stomped downstairs. "Wait! Amy, are you mad at me?" she yelled after me. I got a pail for some reason and ran. I ran far enough to say it was at least a half a mile.

Why did Cecelia have to be Jeanie's sister? I thought I could trust Cecelia but later in life, she would turn out just like Jeanie. I knew it, I knew it, I knew it. I ran so fast, I couldn't tell what was going on around me. Then, I ran, face first, into a cow.

Chapter Twelve – Town

What the heck was a cow doing out in the middle of nowhere? I looked up and realized this wasn't the middle of nowhere. I had run into the mainland. I tried to run back, but somebody caught me.

"Little girl! Why are you so close to the forest? Where shall your husband be?" a townsman asked.

"Oh, um, yeah, uh, my husband and I got in a fight," I tried to whip up a lie. "And I got mad, so I was trying to run away. Can you keep a secret?" I asked.

"No, absolutely not! Do you think women should be able to just do whatever they want?" he asked like the answer was obvious.

"Um, duh, yeah, pretty much," I said and realized that was a mistake.

"What did you say?"

"That women have a right to do things they want," I replied.

"No! No, no, no! Women are stupid! They are less than half as smart as men. All they do is stay home, take care of the kids, and cook! That's all women are for," he said.

"No! Of course not, you moron!" I yelled.

"Oh, so you're a fighter, eh? Haven't gotten me one of those for a long time," he said. "And why, child, why aren't you wearing your dress?"

"Haven't you heard of Coco Chanel?" I asked.

"No, actually I haven't," he admitted.

"Well, that proves one thing that I can do is smarter than you!" I said. Now I remembered. Back a long time ago, there was an argument that women were dumber the men. This makes a lot more sense.

"Who's this Coco Chanel? Is this another woman? Because, if it shall be, I don't keep track of woman. They are wasteful," he said.

This was the Philippines, but for some reason he was white as snow with a British accent. "Dude!" I yelled.

"What in my golly world does 'dude' mean?" he asked.

"There you have it! You're a moron."

"What is a moron?" he wondered.

"Oh my God! I can't believe it! You don't know anything!" I shrieked.

"Why, you talk quite unprofessional," he said, narrowing his eyes.

"Okay, now, here's the easiest quiz in the world. Ready?" I asked, so I could make him see the stupidity of his idea of women being stupid. He nodded.

"What's arithmetic?" I asked. He hesitated. I pretended I had a watch on my hand.

"I'm waiting," I snapped.

"You have yourself a little behavior problem, don't you?" he tried to change the subject.

"It's call a 'tude.' Now, what's the answer?" I snapped.

"By golly! You're making that question up!" he yelled.

"No, I'm not. It's called math," I said in a smart-alecky voice.

"Math, arithmetic isn't called math," he said bewildered.

"Yeah, well, here," I said. I handed him my cell phone. He was so going to be embarrassed.

"What's this?" he asked.

"It's a cell phone. This hasn't even come out yet, not for another four hundred years. See? I know some things you don't know. Like, who's the first president?" I asked. Oops, there wasn't such thing as a president yet.

"What's a president?" he asked.

"Exactly, smarty pants. It's George Washington. So, what's your name?" I asked.

"It's Harold O'Farrell," he answered.

"Well, Harold," I began. He looked shocked.

"What the heck is your problem, man?" I asked.

"No one has called me Harold before," he said, blinking his eyes.

"Well, you did say your name is Harold.What else am I going to call you?"

"People around here call me Sir O'Farrell," he answered.

"That name sounds like some moron..." I stopped. "Never mind, but what's the difference between boys and girls? Think long and hard before answering. Have you ever given girls a chance, at anything?" I asked. "Really? Do you think if you gave a girl a chance and a good education, they could make it? Really, it doesn't matter what it looks like on the outside, what's important is on the inside. For example, do you have slaves?" I asked.

"Of course, they don't say a word. They're so polite."

"Yes, but how about this: I want you to pinkie promise me this," I said and held up my pinkie. He looked confused but held up his pinkie too. I hooked it with his. His hand was soft like plush. It felt like it hadn't touched anything his whole life.

"Now, you can't break this promise, okay?" I confirmed.

"Okay," he agreed.

"I want you to let your slaves take your place for a day. It's still morning, go home, and I'll come with you. You are going to do everything they do without a complaint, and then tell me if you still want them to do those jobs. And remember, they feel the exact same way as you but worse. You took them from their home and made them work. Harold, they had a life, a family, friends, pets, love. To be honest, they hate the living guts out of you. If they had a chance to run away or kill you, they would take it. Trust me," I said.

"No, I can't do that. They have jobs," he said quickly.

"Yes, well, you promised. You said you wouldn't break it," I told him. He nodded sadly and led me back to his huge house.

I walked in and a little, skinny, black lady walked up to me. "You got yourself a new wife, huh?" she asked. She moved on to me.

"I am so sorry, child. Take these coins and you can sneak to the market for some food," she whispered.

"No, I can't," I said and pushed her hand away.

"Yes, you can. You're acting like you have equal rights to the colored," she said.

"Because I do. Now, moving on," I declared in a loud voice. "Harold here is going to be your slave for the day. I'm making him take a little test. You order him around, as in a lot, please," I explained.

"No, that's against the law," the old bony woman said.

"Not in my time. Who cares if you break the law? Now, Harold, get to work," I ordered.

"But I don't want to," he started to complain. The lady looked like she was going to do something for him or else she'd get scolded. Instead, I kicked him in the shin.

"Oh my heavens, child! Don't ever do that! He will tear you to pieces and eat you raw," the skinny slave said.

"No he won't. I'm very mad at you. Why haven't you taken control of this pervert?" I asked. Back at home, I would have been grounded for saying that.

"I can't," she wailed.

"Yes you can. Come on, kick him in the jaw," I encouraged. She did what she was told.

"I'm sorry, Sir O'Farrell," she said.

"Don't apologize!" I screamed. She seemed shocked.

"Be tough! Come on! Harold, clean all the toilets in this house!" I spit in his face. I stomped on his foot while he got up.

"I'm going to court," he said.

"Like that will matter!" I said.

"Oh! You'll be there! Show up at nine o'clock tonight!" he yelled.

I stared at him for a very long time.

"What?" he said annoyed. I was going to do the annoying trick on him. I would stare at him for a long time and stalk him. I did that for about half an hour and he lost it. "Go away, little girl!" he yelled.

I started to laugh.

"What's so funny?" he said.

"You have some really, really, really, gigantic, black-hole big ears," I said and laughed. He tried to grab me but I was too fast for him. I ran all around the house, telling the slaves to follow me. Since I was white, they did. I ran out the door and looked back. The little old lady wouldn't follow.

"Hurry!" I yelled and pointed towards the woods.

"Wait in there for a while until I come back," I said to the other slaves. "Come on!" I yelled to the old lady.

"I was born a slave, lived a slave and now I shall die a slave. Sweetheart, some of us are lucky, and others aren't. I was one of the unlucky ones and I have to deal with that. I'll be alright, don't worry about me," her crippled voice said, shaking.

"I don't care if you want to be unlucky. If you want me to, I'll make you *my* slave. Hurry!" I encouraged, doing anything to get her out of the house.

She nodded and tried to run unsuccessfully. I ran over to help her. Since she was almost lighter than I was, I half dragged, half carried her. Once she got into the forest, I looked back at Harold.

He smiled in a grateful way, like I had proven a point to him.

I wasn't that far away so I went back to his house and lifted up a hand for a high five. That scared the crap out of him and he ran away. Oops, still four hundred years too early.

Chapter Thirteen – Home

I tried to count all the slaves I had set free, unsuccessfully. "Wait! Stop!" I yelled. It looked like they had slammed on the brakes hard and they all stopped at once. "How many of you are here?" I asked.

"Five," one replied.

"Okay, what are your names?" I asked. The old, bony woman spoke first.

"I'm Henrietta and this is Ronsie," she said. She pointed to a little black girl with dark braids and long hair. "She's my little granddaughter," Henrietta said and went on.

"This is Erlonie, my daughter, and this is her, well, we aren't allowed to be married but it was a secret, so her husband, Fasolino. Fasolino here had another son before he met Erlonie, so there's also Plonka. We have funny names around here, don't you think?" she asked. I nodded and smiled.

Ronsie looked about six and Plonka looked around my age. "Now, what's your name?" Henrietta asked. "Oh, um, uh," I stuttered. I couldn't look away from Plonka and Ronsie's stare.

Ronsie reminded me of Maple, one of Herbert's little sisters. That made me determined to find that portal again.

"Well, do you have a name?" Henrietta asked, interrupting my thoughts. I gulped and tore my eyes away from theirs.

"Yeah, um, Amy," I said.

"Oh, why that's a beautiful name," she said like it really was.

"Thank you," I barely whispered. "I hope you like our house," I said.

"What do you mean, 'our'?" Plonka asked.

"I live with some of my friends, Scout, Alfalfa, Beta, Cecelia and the wolves," I said.

"I thought you got in a fight with your husband. I couldn't help overhearing you and Sir O'Farrell," Plonka said.

"I was lying. I'm way too young to have a husband, at least in my time. Most people get husbands when they're around twenty-five years old," I said.

He gasped. "That's very old. Can people even live that long?"

"Yeah, all the time, most people die around seventy or eighty," I said.

"That's sure old. Henrietta has learned how to live, so she's still alive. She's the oldest person in town," Ronsie whispered. I could tell she was very shy.

Soon enough, we were back at the bamboo house. "M gatou pora ipoler kp nar cuxaloj," I said. *I found some people on the mainland.* "M quof eruse g lifo," I said in our secret language. *I almost became a wife*. The slaves looked confused, but they hid it pretty well.

"Really?" Scout asked in English and walked out on the second story. "Where did you get them?" she asked and turned to the slaves.

"On the mainland. I almost became a wife!" I explained.

"Did you almost get caught like Ricala and Lingiush?" Beta asked. We were all talking in our language.

"I think," I answered.

"Who are these?" Alfalfa asked.

"Oh, um, Henrietta, Ronsie, Erlonie, Fasolino and Plonka," I said and pointed to each one when I said their names.

"Oh, hello," Cecelia said in English.

"Hello, I hope you don't mind us being here. We will clean and get food, I promise," Henrietta said and bowed her head.

"No, what are you talking about? All you need to do is sleep on the floor, that's all. Now, um, oh! You can also help us build the upper story of the house," Cecelia said.

"Thank you very much," Henrietta said.

"That's not fair! With Sir O'Farrell, we didn't have to sleep on the floor. We got plush beds," Plonka complained. Erlonie whispered something to him and then spanked him.

When the wolves came out, they gasped. "Don't worry. These are Trevor, She-she, Fifo, Oozuki, Secraty, Linsalia, Iguo, Jugi, Wasanlin, Biksby, and Yukee. They won't hurt you," I soothed them. Erlonie ran away screaming, with Fasolino running after her.

"It's okay," I told Henrietta. She nodded. She took one step forward and Trevor growled at her. Henrietta was obviously well connected with animals.

She bowed her head while Trevor met her eyes.

Her eyes were warm. Finally, he back off from her and moved on to Ronsie. “Gamma!” she wailed.

“Now, now, Ronsie, bow your head,” she ordered. Ronsie did as she was told and curtseyed.

“Don’t make eye contact unless they want you to,” she said calmly. I looked at Ronsie. She had a grim smile on her face. I watched Trevor slowly approach her. “Don’t move a muscle,” Henrietta said sternly.

“Yes, Gamma,” Ronsie replied. Her eyes were sharp. They looked threatening, not warm like Henrietta’s.

“Ronsie, your eyes are too sharp!” Henrietta said frustrated but still calm. Ronsie nodded, but didn’t let her eyes warm.

Then, I noticed something strange. Ronsie was a light black, but her eyes were ice blue, almost silver. How could her eyes be so light? They even sparkled. No one would give up, and finally Trevor backed down, but kept an eye on Ronsie. He even slept with one eye open.

One day, Wasanlin was having a little fight with Biksby.

I could tell they were both kind of scared of Ronsie. Beta somehow knew what the dogs were saying, and she told me that Wasanlin was going to try to scare Ronsie. Whoever scared her first, the other would have to give up all their dinners for three days in a row or give all their food to the other for one day.

Wasanlin was the first one up. He snarled, and he was about three times the size of Ronsie, so I have no clue why they would be scared of her.

“Ronsie, watch out!” I said when Wasanlin was just about to jump on her. She moved at incredible speed, kicking Wasanlin in the jaw. He ran away whimpering. I guess Wasanlin was the one who needed to be warned.

“Oh my gosh! Wasanlin, are you okay?” I asked as I ran over to him. Everybody soon gathered around, except for Ronsie. There was something with her that reminded me of something, someone, a place. She suddenly reminded me of Reneta.

"Um, Ronsie, can I talk with you?" I asked and grabbed her hand.

"What, why?" she asked but she followed along anyways.

"Hey," I turned around to face her once we were inside so nobody could hear us.

"What?" she asked.

"Do you know anybody named Reneta? She's a little taller than me, and um, she's dark, but she's pale, do you know what I mean?" I asked.

"I don't know. Do I?" she asked. "I believe so," she said after a long pause and then sighed.

"You believe so what? You know her, or you know what I'm talking about when I say dark but pale?" I asked.

"I mean, I believe I know what you mean by dark but pale," she snapped like it was an obvious question.

"Yeah, well, it was really weird, but you were kind of reminding me of her when you kicked Wasanlin in the jaw," I said.

"Hmm, well, how old is she?" Ronsie asked.

"Oh, I don't know. She's older than me, that's for sure," I half lied.

"Well, when was she born?" Ronsie asked.

"I don't know the exact date. I don't know how old she is, okay? Why does that even have anything to do with it?" I snapped.

"I'm just wondering," she said and pretended to cry.

I knew how much older than me she was. Like, two hundred years older. Let's just say we were working with decimals. "Reneta is two tenths older than me," I blurted out.

"I thought you didn't know how old she was," Ronsie narrowed her icy blue eyes.

"Yeah, well, it's an estimate," I said quickly.

"What's that?" she asked like she really didn't know what I meant by that word.

"Oh, it's a make-believe word," I said. I really didn't feel like explaining what estimate meant. "Okay, so, well, I guess if you meet her just tell me," I suggested.

"No, thanks. Who I meet is for me to know and you to find out," she grinned.

"Whatever," I grumbled.

We all picked up Wasanlin, except for Ronsie, and carried him to the river. We washed off the blood and wrapped his wounds in something that the slaves had used for bandages.

"Hey, where are Erlonie and Fasolino?" I asked.

"I don't know. I guess they didn't want to come back," Plonka said. I nodded.

"Do they leave a lot?" I asked.

"Don't like to talk about it," he said glumly.

Plonka was a skinny, dark kid with his ribs showing. His teeth were gleaming white with muddy brown eyes.

"Oh, I'm sorry," I said. They must have left whenever they got the chance without bothering to bring the rest of the family. Guess this was their chance and they had finally gotten their wish.

I fell asleep at a reasonable hour that night, well, at least I think so. I could barely keep track of the days going. I believed it was around September tenth.

My dream that night was at first a normal dream: a blurred one with muffled voices. Then, it turned into a memorable dream.

It started from when I was a baby, I don't even remember that. I saw Jeanie taking me and Jason away, and Poch running after us. I was just a helpless little baby, sleeping soundly, but I woke and was screaming. Jason was terrified, but destined to save me and him as soon as possible. This wasn't like any other dream. This one was crystal clear, and everybody spoke loudly and was easy to hear.

A little bit later, I saw myself in the hospital, finding Dr. Rae, finding Daphne, finding... Mom. Then, the beloved little neighborhood in Tukwila rushed past me. That's when I found out fantasy can be realism. I remembered the black-hole eyes on Katrina, riding my bike to the library and secretly finding out more things about the dark blue house.

I remembered something then. Something that was entirely my fault...my fault alone. It repeated in my head. I still had on the jewelry that would take me to the portal. All the ghosts were taking over the world. My dreams led me here. Then, I saw myself sleeping. That's when my eyes snapped open.

Wasanlin's wails woke me up. He wouldn't move. All day long, we sat there and comforted him, for that was what Henrietta told us to do. As far as we knew, She-she was the only one who could comfort him. By the end of the day, Wasanlin had closed his eyes. We tried to open them.

"Let me check his heart," Henrietta ordered. She put two fingers on his neck and gasped. "He's gone," she said.

"What would have killed him?" Plonka asked. I glared at Ronsie.

"No clue," I muttered. "No clue."

"Come on, he was going to attack me. One kick in the jaw isn't going to kill him," Ronsie protested as Henrietta shrieked at her.

"No! Ronsie, he was a pup! When they're wolves, you can do that, but that leads to a fight! You are sleeping outside tonight!" she yelled at the top of her lungs. She reminded me of Cecelia.

I was up half the night listening to their argument. Finally, I barely fell asleep. I slept during that day. But when I woke, there was another sick wolf. This time, it was Jugi.

"No, no, no, Jugi can't die. He's the best one," Scout cried.

Ronsie had a grim look the whole day and kept making cold looks at Jugi. I had a feeling he was going to die that night.

"Scout, don't be surprised if we lose a lot of wolves. I have a bad feeling about some of the slaves being here," I whispered.

That night, he nearly died, but in the morning, he was dead for sure. Scout went crazy and wouldn't eat anything. She would stare at a wall for hours. Scout wouldn't even sleep. She nibbled on some food after three days and drank a small cup of water. Then, she went back to her wall.

After a week of this, I got so tired. "Scout, listen, I know Jugi died and he was your favorite. It's hard, okay? I understand that. You need to toughen up and go back to living, not staring at a wall," I snapped. She didn't answer me and didn't even try to look at me.

Over the days, she got skinnier and skinnier. There were dark bags starting to form under her eyes. How could she be this depressed over Jugi dying? It was sad, no doubt about that, but still, there were ten more left, and if we kept them healthy, there would probably be more.

"Amy," Scout finally said. I was shocked. Her voice was scratchy and it seemed like she was really thirsty.

"What?" I snapped. I was sick of her, and I didn't care if she was sad. I had had enough of it.

"I'm sorry," she apologized.

Instead of saying "You better be," like I used to, I said, "It's okay." She nodded and went back to staring at the wall. Her clothes had become overly grown rags. They were still clean, but way too big.

Days passed. Scout's neck was just bones. On her face, the only bones you could see were the bones under her eyes. The rest of her face was sucked into her body. If she didn't eat, she would soon die and be up in heaven with Jugi.

"Listen Scout, do you want to die?" I asked.

"Well, there's nothing left to do with my life, so, yeah, pretty much," she said, her voice scratchy.

"Okay, but what if we made it fun? What if I took you out onto the mainland where they sell the best foods, and we could go play in the forest and hide in trees? Would you want to do that?" I asked.

"No," she replied. She didn't really do anything with Jugi anyways, so why was she so sad?

"Wait a second," I said. "Is this even about Jugi's death?" She didn't answer.

"It's not, is it? That's just an excuse. What's the real reason?" I asked.

"Amy," she whispered. "I want to go home. I thought we were just going to be here for a little bit and I thought I could handle it. I want to go home, please, can we?" she asked.

I sighed. All that work on the house, but she wanted to go home. And the wolves, what would they do, if all of us abandoned them? I guess the slaves would take care of them, but I didn't trust Ronsie.

"Okay guys, we're switching locations," I said after a long hour. Only Scout, Cecelia, Alfalfa and Beta heard since it was in our language.

"Are we going to where the portal is?" Cecelia whispered in my ear. I nodded. "What about the slaves, and the wolves, and all the work into the house?" Cecelia asked.

"I have a plan. This is what we're going to do: we're going to tell the slaves we're testing something out with the wolves, and we need them to watch the house. We might be gone for a while, so it's all up to them what they do with it, alright? When we find the portal, we make sure it's to our time zone. Then, the portal can't close with someone in it, so we push the wolves in and then we go in last. Okay? Can we do that?" I said. They all nodded.

"Don't worry, everything is going to go smoothly, and Beta and Alfalfa, we're going to find you a family," I said.

"What's family to me?" Beta snapped. "No one's ever cared about me; I'm just going to stay here, with the wolves, if you don't mind," she said.

"Actually, I do mind. So you're going to stay with us. We are going to let the wolves free, but we can still see them."

We switched locations that day. We told the slaves we were looking for something and they needed to stay at the house. They did as they were told, and when Plonka refused at first, I said I'd send him straight back to Sir O'Farrell.

It took a couple of weeks, and then the portal popped up.

"The portal!" I cried. Before we shoved the wolves in, we checked for our time. After the wolves, we shoved Scout in, then Beta, then Alfalfa, then Cecelia, then me. We all tumbled to the ground.

"It doesn't look any different," Beta said.

"Yes, it does. We just need to walk ten miles that way," I pointed straight ahead.

The portal was gone when we looked back.

I was relieved when we finally found Pat's house. I guess Peter and Maggie were waiting for us because they ran outside and started to jump up and down.

"Uncle David said you were missing, but we're the first ones to find you so we get a lot of money!" Maggie exclaimed.

"How long ago did Uncle David say that?" I asked.

"Oh, let's see," Peter said and quickly did the math in his head. "Six and a half months ago. The whole town has been crazy about you!" he said and sounded like a geek.

"Okay, guys, this is top secret, can you keep it?" I asked. They nodded anxiously. "Well, we're hiding, and if you tell them, we're in trouble because we'll lose the game. Can you keep that secret?" They looked confused but nodded. "Oh! And also, there are huge dogs, so you have to keep that a secret too, okay?" I assured them.

"Okay," they agreed and went back inside.

We ran to the street and kept on walking. Then, I noticed Cecelia, Alfalfa and Beta were barefoot. "Aren't your feet cold? It's like, 40 degrees out and raining," I asked. They shook their heads no. I shivered but kept walking. Once we were a safe distance from anybody else's house, I called a cab. I had a stash of about seventy-five dollars in my little bag. The cab arrived in about fifteen minutes.

"Oh, you guys are little girls, do you have your parents' permission?" the man asked.

"Yeah, do you want the signature?" I asked.

"Yes please," he said. I took out a little pad and scrawled out, *I give these girls permission to ride on the taxi. Lisa Fernando, Paul Fernando*

"Alright, hop in," he growled. Three of us sat squashed in the back, including me, Beta and Cecelia. Since it was a van, Scout and Alfalfa got special chairs.

"Where do you want to go?" he asked.

"Um, Tukwila, you can drop us off at Interurban Avenue," I said. He nodded. An hour later, we got to the bus stop next to my house. Cecelia smiled like she knew she was home already. "Thank you," I said.

"That will be fifty dollars. Just because you're little doesn't mean you don't have to pay up!" I handed him three twenties and he gave me back a ten dollar bill.

We ran home as fast as we could. Scout was the slowest because she was so skinny. She burst into her house and jumped into her aunt's arms. I ran back to my house quickly and opened the door. Poch was sitting at the round kitchen table, drinking his coffee and reading the paper. He put his face in his hands.

"Oh, Amy, why did you have to leave just when everything was going so hard?" he asked himself.

"I'm sorry, Poch. I didn't know it was that hard for you," I apologized.

"Great, now I'm hearing things again," he muttered to himself.

He turned around anyway and saw me. He blinked a couple of times. "It's just an illusion. She'll be gone in a couple of seconds," he said.

I walked forward. "No, Poch, I'm really here," I said. I went over and hugged him. He still didn't believe himself, so I backed away. Jason came running downstairs, not bothering to look at Poch.

"Jason! Wait!" I said. He slowly turned around.

"Amy?" he asked like he couldn't believe it.

"Yes, it's me and Poch doesn't believe it's really me," I said. Jason ran over and hugged me.

"How'd you find your way back?" he asked.

"I found a cab, and, uh, told him to drop me off here," I said.

"Wait, wait, wait, you see her, too?" Poch asked.

"Yeah, Dad, she's here. You've gone crazy," he said.

Poch got up and hugged me. "Welcome home," he said and kissed me on the cheek.

"Poch, I have something to tell you," I said. We had gotten lucky enough to be able to say the wolves were dogs and put them on the floor in the cab. "I brought home some dogs, and people. I found them when I was gone, and they had dogs with them. Can they stay here awhile until they find their houses?" I asked.

"How many dogs?" he asked.

"Ten," I said sheepishly.

"How many friends did you bring?"

"Four," I said.

"Whatever, but you pay for them, they eat off your plate, and the girls, well, we're going to have to give up some of our food for them. That's a commitment," he said.

"You're acting like I'm getting a dog," I said and rolled my eyes.

"May I use the phone?" Cecelia asked as she stepped out.

"Sure, it's right over there," Poch said and pointed to the wall phone. She picked it up and dialed. She started talking in a different language.

"Je crois que je peux trouver mon chemin du retour, mais j'ai besoin d'un billet d'avion. Peux-tu veuillez m'envoyer un?" she asked.

"Whoa, I didn't know she knew how to speak gibberish," I joked.

"It's called French. I used to take it. She wants her parents to mail her a plane ticket, if I'm correct," Poch said.

"Wow, I didn't know you could speak French," I said. He shrugged.

When Cecelia was done, she walked over to me. "My dad said he didn't remember having another daughter and he wouldn't mail me a plane ticket," she said glumly.

"Try your mom," I suggested.

She looked up at Poch. "Go 'head," he shrugged.

"I want to know a different language," I complained to Poch as Cecelia went over to the wall phone.

"Okay, what do you want to learn?" Poch asked.

"Um, er, uh, how about, um, uh, German?" I stuttered.

"Okay, if that's what you want. Do you know what this means: Erfahren Sie es selbst, ich bin nicht lehren Sie, es sei denn Sie mir 50 Dollar pro Lektion zahlen," he said.

"What the heck does that mean?" I asked.

"Learn by yourself. I'm not teaching you unless you give me fifty dollars a lesson," he said.

"That's so not fair!" I wailed.

"I'm just joking. You must be starving. Let's eat," he suggested.

"Can I see Esther?" I asked.

"Oh, Amy, there's something I want to tell you about Esther," Poch said.

"What is it? Please say you didn't give her up for adoption," I pleaded.

"No, it turns out Esther is deaf, so we're learning sign language. That's the only way to communicate with her," he said. "Where are your other friends?" Poch asked. I had completely forgotten about them.

"Oh, there right over here," I said. "Alfalfa, Beta, come here," I said in our language. I still needed to teach them some English. They walked out with the wolves.

"Holy crap, Amy, these aren't dogs, these are wolves," Poch said.

"No, they're dogs, they're just, half wolves," I lied.

"Well, okay, what are their names?" he asked.

"Oh, Iguo, Oozuki, She-she, Trevor, Linsalia, Biksby, Fifo, and Secraty. They won't hurt you," I said. "The girls don't know English. They have their own special language," I said, changing the subject.

"You translate, I teach," Poch suggested.

After our first lesson of English, they got it pretty well. We would practice two times a day, for half an hour. In all, we practiced seven hours a week.

Cecelia would have slept on a mini-couch in my room if the wolves hadn't taken over.

That first night back, let's just say something unexpected came up.

Chapter Fourteen – Tag

Phoenix was lying on my bed while Tracker growled. What the heck was their problem? Around 10:00 at night, Phoenix had two more puppies. Twelve mutts, I was living with twelve dogs. Could you believe that? The puppies were cute little Doberman pinschers and the girl, which we decided to name Autumn since the first orange leaves had fallen that day, was a fighter.

Clarence was the shy one who was a mama's boy. We figured that out the third week we had them.

Our legal pets got along well with our illegal pets, so that was a relief. Good thing that Poch was a lawyer and made good money, or else we would have been homeless with twelve dogs. I skipped downstairs one day and flopped onto the couch.

I had been practicing my sign language and so far I could spell the alphabet, drop the f- bomb, say I love you, the color gray, and say bull's crap, which was strictly not allowed. Esther even knew sign language and she didn't know how to talk yet! She probably never would know how to talk, but still, six months and signing.

That day, I was going for a walk to buy ten new collars, and right before I left, something horrible happened.

"Amy, this Monday you're going back to school. Fifth grade, wow, you're gettin' old," Poch said.

"What? No, don't Cecelia or Alfalfa or Beta have to go to school?"

"They do, but I need you to help them, especially Alfalfa and Beta, since they don't know much English," he said.

"Whatever," I grumbled and stomped outside in the heavy mist. I got out of the neighborhood and walked to a little shop by a gas station. It didn't look like it had dog collars, but it was worth a try.

"Excuse me, do you have any dog collars?" I asked the big man with tattoos all over.

"I don't know, let me ask the manager," he said. "Oh, wait, he's not here. He got fired," the buff man grumbled.

"Okay, well, can you check the back?" I asked. He got up, which seemed like it took forever and went into the back. A couple minutes later, he came back with a box of leather circles, spiked collars and ones with designs. "How many do you need?" he asked.

"Oh, uh, ten," I stuttered.

"The whole box is yours. It's free," he said. I nodded and took the box home.

I struggled as I put the collars on the wolves, but once it was done, I went to Poch for more German lessons.

"What are we going to learn today?" I asked.

"You've been learning words, so now you're going to be learning sentences," Poch said.

"Like what?" I asked.

"Like: *Wie geht es dir heute?*" he said.

"What does that mean?" I asked.

"'How are you today?'" he answered.

"Um, wait! I know this one. *Ich bin nicht gut,"* I answered. "Is that I'm not good?"

"I'm pretty sure; I'll have to look that up to make it official," he said.

I learned how to say, 'How are you,' *Wie geht's dir?* 'I'm doing well, *Ich bin gut*, and, 'This is my home,' *Dies ist mein Zuhause*.

On Monday I started at Tukwila Elementary again. The day before we went we took Alfalfa, Beta and Cecelia out school shopping. Cecelia was the one who loved all of it and got the most fashionable outfits.

"Alfalfa and Beta, why don't you dance around in your school clothes for a while," I said. "I need to talk to Cecelia, alone."

Cecelia looked confused but played along and walked with me out the door. "We'll be back in a little bit," I said to Poch. He nodded without looking up.

"What did you want to show me?" Cecelia asked.

"It's right around here," I answered. Then, I heard someone's feet click-clacking against the wet pavement next to us. I looked up. "Reneta?" I asked.

"What is it?" she snapped.

"What are you doing here?" I asked, excited.

"Don't let her in," she commanded, ignoring my question.

"Why not?" I snapped.

"Because she's not allowed," Reneta insisted.

"Who are you?" Cecelia asked.

"I'm Reneta. Who are you?" Reneta raised her chin.

"Cecelia. Do you live around here?" Cecelia replied. Reneta ignored her.

I opened the dirt door and Cecelia followed. "Whoa! What is this place?" she asked, bewildered.

"Oh, some place I like to hang out," I said. I walked over to my big blue house and stepped inside, not so quietly. I knocked on the wall to make sure I could come in. When there was no answer, I walked in further. Katrina was still sitting at the kitchen table, staring at a wall.

She had definitely gotten older. She was at least a foot taller and her hair was a straight, almost blond color. Katrina had little freckles on her nose and under her eyes. All of her baby fat was gone. She had hit puberty and for once, she had changed her clothes. She was now wearing a grayish t-shirt and blue jeans. Her shoes were classy flats and her light hair swept down over her gray-blue eyes.

"Amy, where have you been?" she asked and shot a dark look at me.

"I got lost," I admitted.

"No, you didn't. You ran away. You have the portals and all the people are getting out. The world's overpopulating," she snapped.

"I'm sorry," I apologized.

"You better be," she warned. She got up and ran outside. I ran after her but she went into somebody else's house.

"C'mon!" I urged Cecelia when she slowed down.

I pounded on the door of the small white house. "Kiki, I think another one of your friends is here!" a female voice said. A skinny dark black woman opened the door. "Hello, are you looking for Kiki? She's right down the hallway in the kitchen," she said.

"Actually, I'm looking for Katrina. Is she here?"

"Why, yes she is. She'll be in the kitchen," the lady said. I rushed past her almost before she stopped talking.

"Who the heck are you?" a black girl asked me, the same height and style as Katrina.

"I'm Amy Rae," I panted.

"Can I see your death certificate?" she asked.

"Death certificate? Shouldn't it be birth certificate?" Cecelia asked.

"Shut up!" I whispered and clamped my hand over her mouth. "Actually, funny story, my parents don't let me see my death certificate, and they brought it with them when they were brought back to the normal world, so, um, I don't have it," I lied. "I need to talk to Katrina, that's the reason I'm here."

"What is it?" Katrina snapped when we got to a private space downstairs.

"What do you mean, overpopulating?" I asked.

"Nothing, just go away," she growled. Cecelia gracefully walked down the stairs and excused herself for interrupting.

"Je suis désolé, vraiment. Je ne veux pas! J'ai juste besoin de revenir à notre maison et voulait voir si c'était bien avec Amy," she said in I believe French.

"Vous parlez Français ? Qui rendrait beaucoup plus facile pour moi si vous avez parlé tout ça autour de moi tout le temps," Katrina exclaimed.

"Vraiment ? Moi aussi! C'est dommage, qu'elle ne sait pas ce que nous disons parcequ'elle va toujours se demander nous," Cecelia kind of groaned.

"Bien que vous ne devez lui dire," Katrina smiled. I had a bad feeling, like Katrina was sucking Cecelia into a plan.

"What are you talking about?" I asked. When Cecelia was about to answer, Katrina answered instead.

"Nothing. It's really none of your business anyway," Katrina snapped.

"Cecelia, what were you talking about?" She looked at Katrina for help.

"Dites-lui que nous parlons de comment Paris était si joli!" Katrina snapped. They must be commenting on Paris.

"We were just agreeing on how pretty Paris was," Cecelia said shyly.

"Are you sure?" I asked. "You can tell me the truth. Don't let Katrina scare you."

Cecelia nodded. "I think I should go back to the house now," she muttered. She turned away toward the door.

"Ich weiß, Sie Deutsches sprechen können und ich weiß, daß Sie wissen, was ich sage," Katrina snapped in German. "I know you can speak German, and I know you know what I'm saying."

"Okay, what do you want to talk about?" I asked in English.

"You need to stop coming and going into the ghost world as you please. You need to help me get all the ghosts back to the ghost world. Actually, I'm being nice helping you, because if you put them out, you need to put them back inside yourself!" she said quietly.

"What are you talking about? I didn't 'let' the ghost out," I answered.

"Yes you did, remember, you opened the portal and didn't close it. All of the ghosts went out, and it's your fault," she snapped.

It's all my fault. It repeated in my head, as I remembered the painful memory. "I'm sorry, but I don't exactly know how to capture ghosts!" I spit at her.

"It's easy, it's just like capturing real people, but it's much, much harder because they can go wherever they want, whenever they want."

I walked back to the portal, wondering how I was going to catch over hundreds of ghosts, with just me and another ghost. Or *was* it just me and another ghost? I had to get every single kid in the neighborhood.

"Cecelia, I need to talk to you for a minute," I burst into the house, back on Earth.

"Whoa, whoa, hold it there kiddo. Why do you keep needing to talk to Cecelia?" Poch asked.

I ran past him and he barely missed me as he grabbed for me.

"Cecelia, I need to tell you something!" I yelled. I ran upstairs to find her. She was in my room, but she had pulled the ladder down from the attic. I just saw her foot go up as I walked in. I ran after her but right before I got on the first step, the stairs to the attic slammed up against the ceiling and the chain locked itself.

"Katrina, stop it, I'm serious," I growled. Katrina wasn't the one who answered. Then I heard the screaming and pounding of Cecelia on the door.

"She's not good, Amy. She's a threat to the ghost world," Mary's scratchy voice whispered.

"Amy! Help me, please!" Cecelia cried. "Let me out. This isn't funny!" she sobbed.

For the first time, Mary seemed mean. "Mary," I began but she interrupted me.

"Shh! She can hear you. Come with me, I will show you the wonders of being in the afterlife," she said.

"No, I know there're no re-do's, now, let Cecelia out, now," I said sternly. She smiled and vanished.

"Hold on, Cecelia!" I yelled. I could tell she was on the ground, banging on the door now. Then, the lock opened up. "Get off the ground, Cecelia, now!" I screamed.

"What?" she asked. It was too late; the stairs had slammed down on the ground.

"Are you okay?" I asked as I ran over to her.

"I think, but my finger really hurts," she complained.

"*Au moins je ne suis pas en France quand tout le monde s'inquiète,*" she muttered.

"What?" I asked.

"Nothing, I'm just glad nobody's paying attention," she said.

"Um, talk to my dad about that. Nothing else hurts, right?" I said, making sure she was okay.

"No, not really," she told me.

I waited until she walked down out of my room and heard her reach the first story of the house. I climbed up the little stairs and made sure nobody else was there. I looked out the little window, and there were a lot more people than normal, hanging around casually, which didn't make any sense. There were also a lot of old people.

Then, I noticed some boxes that were all dusty. I walked over to them. One said, "PRIVATE DO NOT OPEN UNDER ANY CIRCUMSTANCES!" I opened it anyway, like I always would. There were old pictures that were all covered in layers of dust.

There was a picture of a little baby that looked a lot like Katrina. I tried to blow off the dust but only a little dust came off. I rubbed it with my shirt until all of it was clean. The next picture was of a boy about ten years old, a little younger than me. He was wearing overalls and a white shirt. His hair was blond and his face was mucky. This must have been Katrina's brother, Jebadiah.

I kept on looking through pictures until Katrina popped up. "Can't you read? It says do not open!" she said harshly.

"I don't care," I snapped. She walked over to me and took the picture out of my hand. It was of a big dog that looked like a great Dane but I couldn't be sure. Katrina took one glance at it and threw it at the wall. The glass shattered and I could tell she immediately regretted doing that, but she didn't show it.

She threw all of the pictures back in the box and picked the it up. "Get out!" she growled. I did as she told me, and just for the fun of it, I closed it and tried to lock it, even though she could just think of a place and she'd be there in an instant.

I heard the pictures hit the floor and the glass shatter as a warning for me to go away. I quickly went downstairs.

"Hey, if Cecelia wouldn't talk to you, I don't know why you'd lock her in the attic," Poch snapped at me when I got back.

"It wasn't me. There's no explanation, it closed and locked," I shrugged.

"Cecelia is that true?" he asked. She hesitated and then nodded.

"Are you lying?" he asks. She shook her head no. "You can tell me if she's lying. She won't get mad at you," he confirmed.

"No, it's true, it just shut and Amy was trying to tell me not to go up there, but I did and it locked. I'm not so sure about the opening part, but it doesn't seem like anything Amy would do," she told him.

Beta and Alfalfa came downstairs. They had been sleeping in the guest room and had stayed up all night learning English. "Good morning, sleepy heads," Poch greeted them when they got to the kitchen.

"Good morning," they both yawned. They were up for the school shopping, but they must have been zonked out for staying up 'til six in the morning.

"I need to tell Cecelia something, privately, why can't I?" I asked.

"Because you broke her finger," Poch answered.

"No I didn't! I need just like, two seconds with her," I said.

"Okay, two seconds, on the clock," he grinned.

"Okay, fine then, two minutes," I grumbled.

Cecelia followed me outside. "What do we need to talk about?" she asked.

"Listen, we're going to play a game of, well, tag," I began.

"You just wanted to talk to me about playing tag? No thanks," she snapped.

"No, that's not it. We have to find every kid in this neighborhood and shove them into that little door I showed you, but I will tell you this: the people who are faded, it's weird but true, will be the hiders, and they're good. They can disappear into thin air, literally. Trust me, it's super creepy," I said. She shrugged.

I told her to tell Poch that I was just going on a walk. I rang all the doorbells in the neighborhood. Only a third of them had kids. Once I got every kid, black or white, young or old, skinny or fat, I told them the rules. I hoped Katrina was doing the same, getting all her ghost friends and telling them to get the ghosts that had gotten out. I saw a familiar white dress and braided hair rush past me.

"Mary! I need to talk to you," I yelled. She glanced back at me but kept running. She had slowed to a jog once I caught up to her, then a walk.

"What do you want?" she snapped.

"I want to see if you can help me catch ghosts that came out of the portal and won't go back in," I begged.

"No, then I would be catching myself, wouldn't I?" she grinned.

"I guess so," I muttered. Why did she have to turn into the mean one? I thought she was the one you could keep all of your promises to, like Scout.

Scout! I forgot to get all of my casual friends, Scout, Benny, Veronica, Herbert and Julie. I ran to their houses and got them with all of the kids waiting by the river. They agreed, awkwardly, and joined the others. I went back inside.

"Hey, Ames, looks like you got a crowd, doesn't it?" Poch asked.

"Yeah, we're playing a game," I muttered and ran past him. "Beta, Alfalfa and Cecelia, you need to play a game of tag with us," I ordered and pushed them out the door.

"You guys stay here, and Scout you come with me. Herber, tell Maple I said 'hi'. And Beta and Alfalfa come with me. Cecelia too," I ordered. They did as they were told and started to play a mini-game of tag. I ran to the portal with the others following.

I ran to Katrina's house and burst throughthe door. A man wearing a suit and a dark-haired woman were sitting on the couch. "Oh my! What are you doing in our house, young dear?" the woman asked.

"I'm looking for Katrina, is she here?" I panted.

"Yes, she's right upstairs," the woman's whispery voice told me. I ran upstairs before she finished her sentence.

"We didn't say you could go up there!" said the man.

I ignored them and kept running. I looked in each room, and on the last one, Katrina was sitting on the window seat, looking silently out the window. When I opened the door, she didn't bother to look.

"I got a whole bunch of kids to help put the ghosts back here," I told her.

"Humans won't help with anything. We need more ghosts. Not people," she said quietly.

"Well, get your friends to help. I said that we're playing a game of tag," I said.

"How are we supposed to get through the portal?" Katrina asked.

"You open the door and walk out," I answered

"Yes, but the door is closed, only the person with the keys can open it." Katrina rolled her eyes like it was obvious and everybody should know that. I smiled and held up a hand.

"Whatever. Go back to the human world and I'll be there in a little bit," she grumbled.

I ran back downstairs, and I didn't want to face her parents, so I just thought of the front of the house and I zapped there. The girls were waiting silently at the doorstep. "Just think of the portal and we'll be there quickly," I said.

"What portal?" Scout asked.

"Yeah, what portal?" Cecelia agreed.

"I mean the door. We sometimes call it a portal," I lied.

"Who's 'we'?" Scout asked.

"Just me and Katrina, Mary and Reneta," I said.

"So you hang out with them privately?" Scout wondered.

"Shut up! Alright? I have enough things on my mind already and it can't get any worse!" I yelled. I thought of the portal and zipped away.

I opened the door and left it opened a crack so they could get out. I ran as fast as I could back to the river, and soon after, all of the girls arrived. I didn't mean to make Beta and Alfalfa mad, just Scout and Cecelia.

"Okay, they're starting to come," I warned everybody. "They don't know we're playing tag with them, and it's more like we have to drag them back than just touch them, alright?" I told everyone. They all nodded.

"Hey, but I have asthma. I can't play," a short brunette girl said.

"OK, you just go back to your house then," I snapped. "If you're going to slow us down, please leave right now!" I called out. A quarter of the kids left. "Alright, that makes, well, uh, ten now." Herbert, Julie, Scout, Benny, Veronica, Cecelia, Beta, Alfalfa and two other boys in the neighborhood who I think were named Jonathon and Mason.

"Okay, so, what do we do? Just play tag?" Mason mumbled.

He had on a baseball cap and a chilled expression. He was olive color and had dark brown eyes.

"No, absolutely not," I snapped at him.

"Jeeze, okay? I didn't mean to do anything," he said backing away.

"She has a short temper," Scout warned.

"Shut it, Scout, or I'll shut it for you," I snapped at her.

"Told you," Scout smiled.

I gave directions. "We chase around the faded people, like, uh, that person!" I said and pointed to a kid playing basketball, just shooting hoops at Scout's house.

"That's it? You just tag them?" Mason asked.

"No, you bring them back to a door, which one of these people will show you, and you shut the door once they're in.

Strict rule, do not leave the door open. It loses the whole concept of the game," I explained. Mason nodded.

I looked at Jonathon, who looked exactly like Mason, but a shorter version.

"Oh, is your name Jonathon?" I asked. He shook his head no. "What is it?" I asked and I kneeled down.

"My name is Pizza!" he yelled.

"Sh, sh," I shushed him and smacked my hand over his mouth.

"Is his name Jonathon?" I asked Mason.

"Yes, but he calls himself the Pizza Guy," he informed me.

"Okay, Pizza Guy," I said. "You are going to have to go back home and play video games!"

Jonathon turned to Mason. "I want to play video games! Please, please, please, with a pretty cherry?" he begged.

"No, Grandpop said no electronic devices until the end of the week until you're off your punishment," he told him. "You can't hang out with us, okay? Go play with your little toys," Mason grumbled.

"They aren't toys!" Jonathon said and stomped off.

"So, we, um, just start to catch them without us looking and they're going to pretend they don't know we're playing a game, so, yeah," I said and went after the basketball-playing boy. We all got at least one part of him and dragged him to the door. I made sure he was a ghost by checking the coolness of his skin.

"Hey, what are you doing? I was just at my house playing basketball. What did I do to you?" he asked.

"Which house?" I answered with a question.

"The green one where I was playing basketball," he answered.

"Nice try, that's my house," Scout grumbled. We tossed him into the door and closed it tight.

"All right, one down, about hundred more to go," I muttered so no one could hear me. An old lady who was fragile and faded, just like the other ghosts, was walking down the street with a cane. "Her!" I yelled and pointed.

"Amy, that's an old woman," Veronica whispered.

"I don't care; she's part of the game," I snapped. I ran up to her.

"Ma'am, I'm doing testing for free. I'm doing a thing where I tell you where you want to go and lead you there. Do you want to try it?"

She looked at my cute face, and rolled her eyes. "Well, alright. But just this once," her smoky voice said.

"Okay, you need to close your eyes and take my hand," I instructed her. She held out her hand and closed her eyes. The fragile old lady's hands were icy. Definitely, she was a ghost.

"Now, Ma'am, where do you want to go?" I asked and led her closer to the dirt wall.

"I want to go to the Virgin Islands and I want a dark tan, so I'm all crisp and even my bones are a shiny copper," she said and smiled. Wrinkles spread out across her face.

"Now, Ma'am," I began.

"Please, call me Miriam," she insisted.

"Now, Miriam, where's the place you absolutely don't want to go?" I asked. I led her further toward the door.

"Oh, my old home, it was somewhere along here, and, boy oh boy, I left it as soon as I got the chance because, well, you see here," she began.

The other kids opened the portal. "Too late," I said and she opened her eyes. We shoved her into the portal and she landed on her hands and knees. She tried to get up but she was too old. I shut the door tight and gave an extra pull to make sure.

"Who else do we tag?" Herbert asked.

"Oh, just let me look," I told him. I walked down the road and back into our neighborhood.

Then, I saw a middle-aged man wearing a suit walking his dog. "Excuse me sir, do you know where the beginning of the train tracks are?" I asked.

"Yeah," he murmured and kept walking.

"Can I politely take your hand and lead you there? You look like you're in a hurry, and I know a short way," I lied.

"Actually, I have to get back to my house. I'm throwing a little get-together," he said, trying to dodge me.

"Ooh! I'd love to go to a get-together. Can I come?" I asked with a twinkle in my eye.

"I'm sorry, but it's for adults only. We're going out to an adult place," he lied.

"But I thought you said it was at your house!" I said.

"It is," he answered.

"Well then, why can't I come?" I cried.

"Because I don't like kids, okay? Can you please get away from me now?" He pulled away.

I started to fake cry, and he tried to move on but couldn't. Katrina walked out from behind some bushes. "So, Walter, why are you making this girl cry?" she asked.

"Oh! Ha, ha, ha, it's such a relief to have you here, Katrina!" he said with a smile and jumped up surprisingly.

"You didn't answer my question," she growled.

"Sorry, I'll let her come to my house," he muttered, not looking her in the eye.

"Amy, take him where you want him to go," Katrina ordered me.

"You know her?" Walter asked.

"Yes, she lives in the neighborhood. I see her walking by sometimes. Now, Amy, take him where you want him to go. In fact, I'll come with you," she said and guided him toward the dirt wall. He followed.

"Where are you taking me?" he asked.

"Close your eyes and then I'll tell you!" I squealed.

He did as he was told. "Now where are you taking me?" he asked.

"One second! Let's just get a little closer," I suggested.

I walked so close to the door, if I lifted a pinkie I could touch it. I tried to open it silently, but the big whoosh couldn't help itself. "You're going to hell," I yelled and tossed him in.

"What?" he asked but it was too late and the door had been pulled shut, hard.

"Let me out of here!" he begged and banged against the door.

"Was he one of them?" I whispered to Katrina. She nodded.

"What about everybody else? Were they ones?" I asked. She nodded again.

"Okay, that's enough for the day. We can go home now," I said and everyone went back to their houses.

I looked up at the sky when we got back, and I don't know how many hours had passed but it was dark out and the stars twinkled. I sat on the little picnic bench and a mist started to form. Soon, it started to pour down rain.

"Wow, you are soaking wet! What are you doing out there?" Poch asked.

"Oh, I just was looking up at the stars," I answered. He nodded.

"You four go off to bed. It's almost ten and it's a school night," he said. It was Sunday night and my first day of school in months. I laid down on my bed after I changed into pajamas and gotten all dried. I hadn't realized how tired I was and quickly drifted to sleep.

My alarm woke me up the next morning at 7:45. I rolled out of bed and headed for the shower. Everybody else was up and since Cecelia was the first one up, she was ready to go. Today was going to be a bad day, I could tell.

First thing, I ran out of hot water when I was taking the shower. Then, Poch had poured my cereal into a bowl and already poured the milk, so my cereal was all mushy. And since we didn't have any more cereal left or anything left to eat, I walked toward the bus stop so I could eat breakfast at school.

Of course, I was late for the bus, so we tried to get the car started. It wouldn't work, so we had to walk in the pouring-down rain. I grabbed my green backpack and headed out the door. I was late for school, and that caused me to miss breakfast.

My teacher was Ms. Rangolia, an Italian lady who was pretty and, best of all, nice. That was the best thing of the day. I got a nice teacher.

Cecelia got Ms. Dana, who was one of those teachers that would give you all A's no matter what, which got on Cecelia's nerves. Why would she want a strict teacher?

Beta was in the same class I was, and Alfalfa was with Cecelia.

"Okay, class, let's welcome *back* Amy Johnson!" Ms. Rangolia squealed.

I went up to her and said my name was changed to Amy *Rae, not* Johnson.

"Amy Rae, sorry about that, and welcome to our school, Beta Wiltserin," she smiled. Beta looked down and refused to come up and introduce herself.

"Beta, it's okay. Just go up and smile. They'll like you," I confirmed. She shook her head no.

"Sorry, Ms. Rangolia, she's kind of shy," I apologize.

"Oh, no, don't apologize. I was shy too! You don't need to worry about that," she smiled.

"Now, Amy, you are going to sit by Adrian, okay?" she asked. I nodded.

"And Beta, you're going to sit next to Jaws and that little girl, Fran-Jessica, alright? She's going to be really nice to you and help you with all of your problems, okay?" Ms. Rangolia whispered. Beta nodded and walked over to her seat. I walked to my seat as well and slumped down. Jaws had to be in my class. Great. That was just great.

"Boys and girls, today we're going to learn how to multiply three numbers by three numbers!" Ms. Rangolia said excitedly.

I wasn't paying any attention, just thinking about how to get the ghosts back into the ghost world which I recently found out was called Gloma. How many were left to go? Would I get them all before they repopulated again?

Unfortunately, Ms. Rangolia interrupted my thoughts by asking me the answer to the word problem on the board. "What's the answer?" she repeated.

"Um, uh, seven," I guessed.

"Are you sure?" she asked, looking me in the eye.

"Um, yes Ms. Rangolia, I'm sure my answer is correct," I lied.

I looked up at the board, and of course, it wasn't seven. It was *forty*-seven.

"Alright, moving on, even though the correct answer is forty-seven, we'll forget that since it's Amy's first day back," she beamed and went on to the next problem. This was too much, to go back to school while chasing the ghosts. I needed a break.

I wanted to see how Emily was doing and Gustavo. I hadn't seen them in forever. Just while I was thinking about Gustavo and Emily, my cell phone started to ring its little *'You Make Me Smile'* song. I'd forgotten it was in my backpack.

"Whose phone is that?" Ms. Rangolia asked. I slowly stood up and walked over to my cubby. I unzipped my backpack and slowly got out my little red cell phone. I flipped it open.

"Hello?" I asked. The whole class was staring at me.

"Amy, you need to get down to the agency quick! We just saw Jeanie's agents tracking down your house!" Gustavo exclaimed.

"Can you call my dad and tell him? I'm in school right now," I muttered.

"Yes, I can," he said.

"And by the way, I'm probably going to get in a whole lot of trouble for you calling," I gave him a heads up.

"That's okay. I can tell them not to get you in trouble," he said and I heard him dialing other numbers on a phone. The classroom's phone started to ring.

A very familiar kid raised her hand to get the phone. "Veronica, you can get it," Ms. Rangolia excused her. But it wasn't the Veronica in my class.

"Ms. Rangolia's class, this is Veronica," she murmured.

"Ms. Rangolia, it's for you!" Veronica said and put the phone down.

"This is Amanda," Ms. Rangolia greeted.

"Hello?" I whispered into my cell phone.

"One second, Amy!" Gustavo hushed me. I could hear a faint voice on the other end, and whenever Gustavo stopped to talk, Ms. Rangolia started to talk. Did he call her? How would he know the number?

"Okay, thank you, b-bye," Ms. Rangolia said and hung up. So did Gustavo.

"Alright, Louie, your mom is waiting in the office. Grab your things and go," Ms. Rangolia said. So it wasn't Gustavo.

"Who were you talking to?" I asked Gustavo.

"Oh, yeah, the pizza delivery place. I was starting to get really hungry," he said. I rolled my eyes.

"Call me back at 3:45," I said and hung up. I strolled back to my seat.

"Now, Amy, you know you need to put your phone in the office and pick it up at the end of the day. What you just did was not acceptable," Ms. Rangolia softly scolded me. I nodded and looked at my work.

The rest of the day went by in a breeze. Actually, it was 2:30 when Gustavo called so it was only ten minutes until we packed up.

"Did you have a good day back?" Ms. Rangolia asked me when we were in line waiting for the final bell of the day to ring. I nodded.

"And Beta, I hope you like being at our school! We can get you back up to seventh grade where you belong in no time," Ms. Rangolia said. Beta smiled. That was right. Beta was thirteen years old.

When the final bell rang, I ran out the door, even though Ms. Rangolia strictly told us not to, and ran to Ms. Dana's classroom.

Cecelia and Alfalfa walked out casually and pretended to be like the rest of the kids, chatting about stupid things.

"Hey, what is your teacher like?" I asked.

"I love her!" Alfalfa squealed. "She gives me little brown things she calls tootsie rolls!" she exclaimed and chewed on one she showed to me.

"You?" I asked Cecelia.

"Horrible, that teacher is absolutely horrible. She gives you candies whenever you raise your hand to say 'I need to go to the bathroom' or something like that," she grumbled.

I looked at Alfalfa's incredibly long, silky black hair, which was now turning reddish, since I showed her how to take a shower and take all the dirt out of it.

I flipped open my phone and pressed down six, the speed dial to Poch's work phone. "Hello, this is lawyer Mr. Johnson. How can I help?" he asked in a stern voice.

"Poch, we need to go to the barber shop!" I complained.

"Amy! You know you can't call me when I'm working. That's a strict rule!" he snapped. I was quiet.

"The money's under the paper in my little box on my dresser," he gave up. "Be back before 7:00!" he ordered.

"Love you, Poch!" I said and hung up.

I ran to the buses and the three girls followed. I was just about to hop on bus ten when the fat blond bus driver stopped me. "Hold it! Where's your form?" Ms. Ally's grumbly voice asked.

"Crap," I muttered. "Sorry, I need to get one, actually, not one, four," I said. She handed me four cream-colored papers that said, "SIGN HERE IF YOU EXPECT YOUR CHILD(REN) TO RIDE ON BUS #10. UP TO 2 CHILDREN PER FORM"

"Wait! I only need two, my mistake," I said and threw two on the ground.

"Hey, little girl, pick those up!" she yelled and stumbled forward to pick the papers up.

I ran home as fast as I could, while Alfalfa, Beta and Cecelia followed. I ran down the big swirly hill and past all the casinos. I got to the little bridge that led to my neighborhood. When I finally got to the house with the others dragging behind, I got out my little rusty key and unlocked the door.

"'Sup Amy, why're you in a hurry?" Jason asked coolly.

"Can you drive us to the barber shop, the High-def cuts?" I asked.

"Yeah, but I'm not paying for anything," he said.

"Don't have to!" I yelled and ran upstairs into Poch's room.

There was a cardboard box and in it was $100 in cash. I ran to Jason's big Jeep Cherokee and hopped in. His car was a mess and smelled like cigarette smoke. I coughed and Alfalfa and Beta squeezed in the back with me. Cecelia sat in the front seat, which wasn't fair.

"Hey! Why does she get to sit in the front seat?" I asked.

"Because she was patient enough to wait until the back seat was crammed and there was no room," Jason snapped. I rolled my eyes.

"Hey! I'm turning 18; I'm the smart one now," he said.

"No, just because you're an adult doesn't mean you're smart!" I snapped.

Then a painful memory hit me for no reason at all. I remembered getting out of the bath water and rubbing my burning eyes. I walked to my room while the radio played Green Day's song, *Holiday,* and the phone rang. It rang in my head over and over again.

"Amy, Amy, you're going to be all right, sweetie," a voice in my mind said. It wasn't a good voice. It was Nicole Shea-

Johnson's voice. A little voice pretending to be nice and soft, but with a harsh, devilish flow to it.

"This is Martha Jones, I'm sorry, but, hold on a second. Don't you remember me? I work with your father," the voices repeated in my head. The last thing I saw was a little girl, standing in front of the house, with black-hole eyes, and then my dreams took me away.

I dreamt that there were two little babies, a girl and a boy. They were both half black (or at least one of their parents was) and they reminded me of Cash and Nina, sort of.

But they were different, they were completely different. The girl had extraordinarily beautiful brown eyes with little specks of red and blue and green in them. They all called her Tatum.

The boy wasn't a beauty. He had little blood red scars on his face. He looked a bit older than Tatum, but still pretty much the same. He wasn't a chubby baby, like most, but he floated by with everybody calling him Harley. I always thought of it as a girl name, but I shrugged and more pictures floated by.

"Amy, Amy! It's going to be alright. Where did you go?" I heard Poch's soothing voice.

"I'm right here," I tried to say, but all that came out was a muffled noise that even I couldn't understand. I fluttered opened my eyes and blinked a couple of times.

I was in a hospital again.

"What happened?" I wondered aloud.

"Amy!" Poch beamed and ran over to me.

"You were driving to the barber shop and Jason said you hit your head on the dashboard or something. You wouldn't wake up and it's been almost a whole five days!" he exclaimed.

"But what about Harley?" I asked. I didn't think I said it aloud, but apparently I did.

"Who the heck is Harley?" Poch asked.

"What? Nobody. Who's Harley?" I lied.

"What did you see when you were asleep?" Poch asked.

"Nothing much," I lied. It was full of colors and excitement, much more than nothing.

"Okay, fine, Harley was a little baby in my dreams who was all beaten up on the face. He didn't look so good, and he had a little sister, I think, named Tatum," I said. He hadn't heard me, that was good, but then I realized I said it in my head.

"Why won't you tell me?" he asked.

"Because, there isn't much to it," I lied.

"I want to know, why you can't tell me?" he demanded.

Thankfully a nurse came up to me and asked if I was alright and what I saw last before I fell asleep. "Um, I think it was my house. No, actually, it was a girl," I admitted.

"What did she look like?" the nurse pretended to act interested.

"Uh," I rubbed my temples. "I don't remember. But she wasn't a normal girl. She was, like, dressed in..." I remembered the ghosts and how mad Katrina would be. "Like, sweats, and she was wearing, uh, pajamas or something," I lied. The nurse nodded.

"Okay, well, do you remember anything else?" she asked.

"I don't know. What do you mean?" I asked.

"Okay, what's your name?" she asked.

"Amelia Trinity Kay Johnson Rae," I answered.

"No, it's Alicia Yuseem," she answered.

"What? No it's not," I looked at her. I studied her for a long time.

She looked vaguely familiar. "Emily!" I yelled. She walked up to me and hugged me.

"I was wondering when you were going to remember!" she laughed and pulled her black wig off. She smiled at me. "You need to go into hiding again, and we're having you switch locations," she told me.

"But what does Alicia Yuseem have to do with anything?" I asked.

"That's going to be your stage name. I might be able to transfer you back to New York!" she exclaimed.

"But I want to stay in Tukwila," I complained.

"I'm sorry, sweetie, but it's a hard life to live. You need to restart a lot. We'll need to change your look too. Maybe dye your hair, make you wear contacts to change your eye color, make you lose a couple pounds," she said.

I slumped back down in my bed. "Why can't I stay in Tukwila?" I whispered.

"Because, sweetheart, I told you. You know you can't form a relationship when you know you'll be moving in a couple of months." She rubbed my arm apologetically.

I rolled over and got out of the bed. I took my bag of clothes into the bathroom and stripped down. My instincts told me to just do whatever, so I turned on the shower and stepped in. I just stood there for about an hour and a half and stepped out.

When I got out of the shower and into the little hospital room, Emily was gone and Poch had his face in his hands. "What is it?" I asked and ran over to him.

"What? Oh, nothing. I was just thinking about something," he murmured and looked out the window.

"Is there something you want to tell me?" I asked.

"No," he said like it was the end of the conversation, but it wasn't. "Yes, Amy, there is," he admitted. I listened to everything he said.

He had met a new girl, and for my stage name, he picked it out. The girl's name was Alisha, too. She was thirty-five, a year younger than Poch. Alisha was single, so he asked her out on a date and blah, blah, blah, blah, blah.

But this is what hit me most of all. "Amy, I know this is weird, but Alisha and I are going to have a baby," he said. I was shocked. He went out on one date with her, and they were going to have a baby.

"We didn't even meet her and you're having a baby with her?" I asked. Now, I was mad. It had hit the limit.

"No, Jason met her and said she was fantastic and that she could live with us. She's waiting in the hall if you want to meet her," he offered. I didn't say anything, so he called her in.

She was black, with wavy black hair. Alisha was pretty, and looked nice. "Hi Amy, I'm Alisha," she said and held her hand out. I boringly shook her hand.

Another kid. We already had Esther, Cecelia, Beta and Alfalfa, wasn't that good enough? "Did you tell her everything?" she asked Poch. He shook his head. There was *more?*

"What is it?" I snapped. Please say they aren't going to get married, please say they aren't going to get married.

"Amy, we're getting married," Alisha whispered.

Chapter Fifteen - Their Return

I stomped out of the room and down the hall. Somebody about my size was walking toward the elevator and I could tell Poch and Alisha thought it was me. I turned toward the millions of stairs and opened the door. It clicked shut and I walked up the stairs, and then back down, slowly.

Another baby. We barely paid any attention to Esther and left her home alone a lot.

I heard Poch's voice echoing up the stairs. Quickly, I saw a white box that I never would have noticed if I wasn't looking for a place to hide. It matched the blank walls, and I jumped into it and looked out for them between the cracks. I saw Poch's feet walk up the stairs and I looked up at him.

Whew, he didn't see the box. Alisha followed up the stairs, her skinniness not making as much of a racket as Poch. "It'll be okay, David. You've lost her before." Alisha giggled. They started kissing, and I slowly removed the top because my legs were starting to cramp up.

They wouldn't take their eyes off one another, so I slowly got out and walked towards the downstairs. It was only a couple of feet away. I ran swiftly down the stairs, two floors of them, and they still didn't look up.

I opened the door to the thirteenth story and listened. I could still hear them kissing and I yelled out, "Come and get me, Alisha and Poch!" I still heard the sound of kissing, so I burst out of the stairs and ran over the finely carpeted floor and pressed the button on the elevator.

"C'mon, c'mon, c'mon," I muttered. Finally, the elevator bell rang and the doors slid open. I got in, thankful it was empty, and pressed all the buttons. While I was traveling up to the eighteenth story, I pressed the stop button and sank down. I burst out crying and lay down on the floor.

"Amy! Where are you?" I heard Alisha's voice yell. My ear sank down on the floor and I heard everything they were saying. Poch was cussing, and Alisha was shushing him. "David, there are children in this hospital!" she whispered.

Then, their voices sounded like they were next to me. Maybe they were riding the elevator up. I kicked the start button for the elevator and kept on hitting the lobby button. Finally, it did as it was told and I rode down to the lobby.

"Hello, little one!" the familiar man said. I still had my spike bracelet on so I lifted it up. "Oh my gosh! What? How can you still be here?" he asked.

"Don't call me little one!" I demanded. He sank under the desk and crawled away.

Memories.

The wind was painful, how it blew on my face and burned my eyes. I heard Poch and Alisha coming out of the building and

I quickly hid behind a car. My little red phone was still in my pocket.

I pulled it out and quickly went through my contact list. Finally, I found who I was looking for and called Jason. It rang two times. "Pick up, pick up." I muttered and hopped around.

"Hey, this is Jason. I probably won't call you back. Uh, bye," the receiver said and beeped.

"Hey this is Amy and you need to pick me up now!" I whispered harshly into the phone and snapped it shut.

Waiting wasn't an option. I needed to find a way home and get over my grudge with Poch and Alisha. I barely knew the girl and they were getting married and having a baby. Really, my life couldn't get any worse. Once I cooled down, I crept up to them. Poch was just smoking, and Alisha was talking on the phone.

Once they were done talking on the phone and smoking, I tiptoed up to them. They still couldn't see me, or at least I thought they couldn't see me. "I think we've got a little shadow!" Alisha whispered and smiled a little bit.

"Amy, I'm sorry about what's happened. I didn't know you'd be that upset," Poch apologized. "And by the way, we've discussed it, and we want you to call Alisha 'Mom,' okay?" Poch asked.

Really? I barely knew the woman and now she was my mom? That didn't seem right.

"Also, Alisha pointed out that you need to start calling me Dad. What's a Poch?" Poch wondered.

"Why? You were perfectly fine when I called you Poch," I pointed out.

"Honey, we're going to do things the way we want to do them from now on. You aren't the only girl in his life." Alisha said and picked up one of Poch's cigarettes. She lit it and blew it in my face. I coughed.

"Aren't you pregnant?" I managed to ask between coughs.

"That's none of your business!" she snapped and marched off towards the car.

"Sorry, honey, it's the way things go." Poch apologized and walked to the car in his official business suit.

Maybe I'll just run away. No, running away from your problems doesn't help. It either leads to new problems or the old ones follow. Hmm. Maybe, just maybe, I could manage to go to an orphanage and tell them I escaped a burning house and all my sisters and brothers died in it. Nah, I didn't want to put up with nuns. Probably I could ask to go to boarding school. Probably, but I would miss my friends.

But then, I realized a boarding school would be perfect. I didn't have any real friends.

No, Scout was just there to annoy me. I didn't care about her. She could go to hell and I wouldn't care. It seemed like a real relationship, but I lied to myself. Friends weren't my thing. No, not even Cecelia, Beta and Alfalfa. I didn't need them. I could go back to just the way things were before I knew Jeanie was a criminal.

Lonely, only the other lonely friends would hang out with me. The ones who would go to juvenile detention, they could be my friends, the bad ones. I don't need any goody two shoes to look after. I needed someone like, like... Katrina.

I quickly followed along into the car. It was already filled with smoke. I coughed.

"Don't like that, eh? Well, get used to it!" Alisha snapped at me and rolled the windows up.

Definitely a boarding school would be the solution.

The car ride home was quite the experience with Alisha. She had been an assistant for Poch, and she was planning on doing it for the rest of her life. I learned a few more interesting things about her, like her favorite color was green.

List of things to do: number one, change favorite color to orange.

Blah, blah, blah, I couldn't listen to another word she said so I rolled down the car window and stuck my head out so the wind would overtake her voice. When the car stopped I ran into the house and picked up baby Esther.

"Oh my, David didn't tell me that he had another daughter," Alisha exclaimed.

"Yeah, she's not exactly the center of attention around here, and we normally forget about her. It's embarrassing but true," Poch shrugged.

I ran up to my room with her and looked out my window. Scout was playing with all the neighborhood kids and was walking towards my house. I ran to my door and locked it. Then, I put a chair in front of it and my closet door clicked with the door to the hallway so it wouldn't open.

The doorbell rang, and Alisha introduced herself and told Scout I was in my room. "Amy, it's Scout and we're wondering if you want to come outside with us!" Scout said and knocked on my door. She tried to open it, but of course, it was locked.

"Amy, what are you mad about?" she wondered. I smacked the door and heard her jump back. "Amy, what's wrong? Can you let me in?" she asks.

"No, go away," I snapped.

"What's wrong?" she wondered, trying to help me with my problem.

"It's none of your business! Get out of here, and I don't want you coming back unless it's important, alright?" I opened the door but since the closet door was in the way, it wouldn't open very far.

"Amy, are you crying?" Scout said and stepped up to the door.

"No! Shut up!" I said and slammed the door. She jumped back, the door almost hitting her. She marched down stairs and I looked back out the window.

I was going to get back at someone, somehow. I didn't care who it was or how, I was going to get back at them.

"Hey Ames, you're going to need to pack some boxes for the move," Poch said and pounded on my door. No answer. "Amy?" he says.

I wandered into my bathroom and locked the door in there. He finally got in, but he didn't know where I was. I got under the sink, way back into the counter to blend in with all the stuff.

"Amy? Where are you?" he asked.

Suddenly, Katrina appeared in the cramped cabinet with me. "Come with me," she whispered and I considered it. I finally struggled to get out of the cupboard with her and she listened at the door. "Okay, he's gone. Let's go." she said. I followed her out into the main part of my room. "Ready?" she asked. I nodded and took her hand.

"Where are we going?" I asked.

"If you don't want your dad to marry again, it's simple what we have to do. If he will not make her leave, we'll make her go," she smiled.

"By?" I wondered.

"By ripping her insides out and killing her the same way they killed me."

I wasn't sure about this. All the ghosts were back in Gloma, which was good. Jeanie was in jail. I was back in my era. Now, we needed to kill Alisha? My life wasn't just a silly game like most eleven-year-olds'. Mine was serious and full of life-threatening conditions. I could do it, I could kill Alisha. I didn't want to, but I did. It doesn't make any sense.

Was this my life? The same story repeated in every chapter? Kill, threaten, punish and die. It was pretty much my life. I just wanted to die, but I would become a ghost, and I'd still be alive, technically. This never was going to end, was it? I sighed and followed Katrina to wherever her destination was.

She led me to the portal to Gloma and then turned around to face me. "If you don't want your father to marry Alisha, there is one simple thing you need to do," Katrina insisted.

I could do a lot of things but I couldn't kill Alisha. I barely knew the woman, and I wanted her to break up with Poch and take the baby to raise by herself. But that was out of the question, and I would have to deal with it, like always.

"Katrina, what's going to happen?" I whispered.

"We're going to Mindaloni's Mansion and see," she answered.

I tried to open the dirt wall with the rusty knob, but it was locked. "Katrina, it's locked," I muttered and pulled harder.

"It's not locked, idiot," she snapped and tugged on it.

"It's not working. I guess we can try again later," I shrugged and started to turn.

"No, Amy! It's not like that. What if you got stuck in Gloma? It's not like I don't sleep!" she yelled.

Then sleep on the ground here. Nobody will find you, I thought. "Whatever," I snapped and turned away. The tears that had welled up in her eyes were swept away.

"Go home, Amy," she snapped.

"I can't get back into my room if you don't come," I muttered and turned away. Katrina dug her nails into my skin. "Ow!" I complained, but she ignored me. In a split second, I was in my room and Katrina's gone.

Days went by, and every now and then I checked the portal, but it was locked. Why wasn't it unlocking? My door remained shut and locked at all hours, and only the dogs slept with me, all twelve of them.

One day, Poch came banging on the door. "Amy, I need to talk," he said. I managed to say yes and I unlocked the door.

"Amy, it's about time to shorten down to just our family," he sighed.

"You're breaking up with Alisha?" I asked hopefully.

"No, I'm sorry, but you wouldn't let me talk to you, so I couldn't tell you, but the rest of the girls are gone," he sighed and patted my knee.

"What do you mean, they're gone?" I asked.

"We took them to the orphanage, and Cecelia is going back home with her family," he said.

You mean they're gone forever, and I didn't get to say goodbye? I so badly wanted to ask, but I didn't. Stay strong, Amy. No pain, no gain.

"They're gone and they aren't coming back. Tomorrow we're going to the pound, and it's enough to have two dogs, right? Also, I really want you to call me 'Dad,' okay?" Poch said.

"Dad, no, this whole mess. Beta and Alfalfa, they didn't know English because they were abandoned in the forest when they were little and they grew up with the wolves and had their own language..." I speed talked.

"Wait, wolves? What wolves are you talking about?" he covered my mouth and then let me talk.

"The dogs we brought here aren't dogs, they're wolves. And I know you'll think I'm crazy, but will you honestly believe me if I say something that sounds stupid?" I ask.

"Yes, I will. Even if you say you time-traveled and met the girls and then you met slaves or something, I'd believe you," he said.

"Well, that's actually what happened," I whispered so quietly, not even the dogs could hear it perfectly.

"Pshed, Amy, you know that stuff isn't real. Go to sleep. Next week there's going to be a very, very big day!" he cheered.

I brought Esther in my room and asked her in sign language, "Do you want to go on a trip with me, forever?"

Amazingly, she signed back, "Yes."

"There's going to be a new baby," I said and cradled my arms. She started to clap but I snagged her hands hard so it would kind of hurt her.

"No, that's a bad thing," I signed and got into bed.

She stood up and stumbled over to my bed. "Can I sleep with you?" she said.

I nodded and picked her up into my bed. It's surprising how much babies can say in sign language, because they don't need to use their vocal cords.

"Amy, where do you go after you die?" Esther wondered.

"You go to a place called heaven, but that's only if you're a good girl. If you act badly, you go to a bad place," I told her.

"What's that bad place?" she asked.

"I can't tell you that, it's a bad word and it'll give you nightmares," I signed.

"Well, what's heaven like?" she asked.

"I don't know, and no one ever will know. But it's supposed to be like paradise, somewhere where everything will go smoothly, and nobody does anything wrong," I said.

"How do you know, if no one's ever been there?" Esther asked.

"I don't know, it's a myth, where you've heard about it, and it's been there so long, some people truly with all their hearts believe in it," I explained.

Esther asked a couple more questions, and then I told her to go to sleep. The next morning Esther was still sleeping soundly when I woke up. I walked down the stairs and ate my breakfast.

"Do you know what happened to your sister last night? I couldn't find her anywhere," Alisha asked.

"Yeah, she slept with me," I answered and took a bite of some toast.

"She scared me to death, and obviously yelling for her wouldn't work. Do you know why she doesn't answer?" she wondered. I started laughing, nearly choking on my toast.

"What?" she asked embarrassed.

"You do know that Esther is deaf, right?" I laughed.

"Yes, I certainly do," Alisha lied. I walked out the door to school and decided to meet somebody new, just one friend who would stay the same, in my class, but after a while I gave up and at the end of the day, the bus took me home. I ran back to my house. "Where's Esther?" I asked.

"You're looking for your little sister? Weird, but she's upstairs taking a nap," Jason shrugged and went back to his phone.

My feet dragged to the kitchen counter, and I pulled out my homework. Each equation was very long, or at least it felt like it. Finally, I got it done and I ran upstairs. Esther was sleepily stumbling towards me. She signed *Amy* and smiled. Esther ran over to me, sort of, and jumped up in my arms. I looked into her light green eyes and smiled back.

"Can we talk more about heaven?" Esther signed with her tiny fingers.

"Well, what do you want to know?" I asked.

"Can we go on a trip to one of them?" she asked.

"No, Esther, I'm afraid not, and hopefully youwon't see it for a long time. Let's talk about something more like ponies, okay?" I suggested.

"Amy, ready to go?" Poch asked me as he burst into my room.

"Where?" I wondered.

"It's time to narrow down on the pets, Ames. We're going to have to give up all the dogs except for Tracker and Phoenix. Okay?" Poch said.

"No! Autumn and Clarence are Tracker and Phoenix's puppies. You can't just take their kids away. What if somebody you loved and trusted took me, Jason and Esther away just like that and you never saw us again? Hmm, how would you feel?" I yelled.

"Amy, look, they're used to this kind of stuff, so it'll be alright." Poch grumbled, mad at my outburst.

"Poch, I mean, Dad, the puppies are only a month old and they aren't ready to leave yet," I begged.

"That's it; we keep the puppies until they're a couple months old. Alright?" he said sternly. I nodded.

Instead of going to the pound and taking a chance of just killing the dogs and we don't get a profit, I told Poch to make a sign that said, *'Dogs for Sale! $30 each!'* We only sold one of the dogs that day, and the day after that we sold two. We sold them all until only two of the wolves were left.

The only ones left were Iguo and Oozuki. I begged over and over again to keep just Iguo, but Poch specifically sold him cheaper than the others so that he would go away and I would stop complaining.

"Goodbye, Iguo. I won't see you again after this, so I want to make this count," I whispered in the secret language. He licked my face. My arms wrapped around him and refused to let go.

"Amy, the people want their dog, let go," Poch ordered and told them the details: renaming them was okay, just make sure it wasn't completely different, and all the other stuff. Later that day, Oozuki was sold to Mason's parents.

"Okay, that's enough of dog selling. So, um, I'll give all the money to Alisha and we can form a college fund for the baby," Poch muttered.

"No way! You sold my dogs, and it was my idea to get money. That money is all mine!" I screamed at him.

"No, Amy, you don't understand money." Poch rolled his eyes and went up to bed. After 11:00, I went into Poch's and Alisha's room and took all the money. Then, I ran back to my room and put it in the little brown pouch that Gustavo had given me, $140 in all.

After that, I quickly fell asleep. Early the next morning, I woke up and almost went to school but realized it was a Saturday. Esther crawled into bed with me and tried to wake me after I fell back asleep, but it wouldn't work. "Ama!" she yelled, trying to say Amy, but she couldn't hear herself. Then she screamed, "Lama!" I opened my eyes and sat up. Esther clapped and tried to lead me downstairs.

I gobbled down my breakfast and looked at the refrigerator. It was covered in multiple pictures of swans, obviously drawn by Esther. "Esther, did you draw these?" I signed. She nodded her head and I walked closer to the pictures to get another look. I remembered Tierney, my piano teacher back in New York, teaching me Swan Lake.

When I turned around, Esther was gone and had crawled off to another place. As I looked for her, I heard the piano playing. Esther was sitting at the huge grand piano playing Swan Lake in the simple way, finger picking.

"Esther, what do you mean by all of the swans?" I asked.

"Devils take over swans, and if you are not nice to them, they will do bad things to you," she signed.

"No, don't think like that, swans can be very nice," I said and she went back to playing her song. "Esther, I'm not joking! You don't joke around like that," I snapped Then I realized I had no clue what time it was. It was already 5:00 at night. "Crap, I've wasted my whole day," I muttered.

Around 11:00, I fell asleep again. My dreams were vivid, and they had the devil possessing the swans, and in the background Esther's finger picking played.

Katrina was one of the swans and she was dressed in this funky swan outfit, shrunk down to a normal swan size, but still had her bluish-grey eyes.

All of a sudden, I looked at my arm, and then I had the pretty but weird swan outfit. I shrunk down into a little swan, and then the Katrina swan rose up and turned reddish, she grew more and more, and then she turned out to be the devil.

Esther woke me again, shaking me. My eyes fluttered opened, and she signaled me to be quiet and stop shaking. Esther looked out the window and there was a swan flying around the window. Then, the bird stopped and stared us right in the eye, with pitch-black eyes. Suddenly, there was a crash and all the glass on the window hit me and Esther.

My eyes suddenly opened, for real. "Amy, you were screaming. Why?" Esther asked.

"I had bad dreams," I explained and rubbed my eyes.

"What were they?" she wondered.

"It doesn't matter, what are you waking me up for?" I signed.

"I wanted you to hear my music," she smiled and ran downstairs.

Sluggishly, I followed her down the stairs. The piano played the real thing, the real Swan Lake.

"Esther, how are you playing the piano so well?" I signed.

"The birdies taught me," she said and went back to her playing.

I couldn't play that song until I was nine years old. Somehow, I felt a twinge of jealousness. I leaned back on the wall and heard her play the furious part. Esther turned around to look at me. "What's wrong?" she asked.

"Nothing," I signed and stumbled away. Then I realized that wasn't... normal. But I ignored it.

All day, I just sat there and didn't do anything, except try to beat Esther at playing the piano. Doo-doo, doo-doo-doo-doo-doo-doo, I still couldn't get it exactly right.

"Sorry I played. I'll stop," Esther apologized.

"No, keep playing," I urged but I didn't want her to.

"You don't want me to," she signed and I looked down. How could a one-year-old outdo me? Why would Esther give up piano for me? I would never give up playing piano for anyone. Not even for Esther.

"You don't give up like that; you fight until you have what you want!" I demanded and sat down at the piano again, realizing I had stood up. I went back to the melody and by midnight, I had the song memorized, but I still couldn't get it as well as Esther. How could the birds teach her?

Every night after that, my dreams were about swans. In the middle of the night, Poch came running to me and woke me up. "Go away," I grumbled.

"Amy, no, Jeanie is here," he whispered.

That woke me right up. "What is she doing here?" I screamed.

"Shh, shh, shh, Amy, you need to get dressed and get your sister right now. Esther is downstairs, and you're the smallest. It will be easier for you to sneak in and get her," he whispered. I agreed and tiptoed downstairs.

Esther was sleeping on a little bed, right next to the piano in our mini music room, close to the back door. Then, I saw Jeanie. I saw her similarities to Cecelia. She was with somebody, but I couldn't tell who.

"Shut up, Terence! They already know we're here, and that little brat is probably listening to every word I say!" I heard Jeanie's harsh voice whisper.

"No, Jeanie, trust me, I can knock that girl out in a second. She's so little, I can barely see her," Terence's deep voice soothed.

I could have sworn I'd killed him, or Dark Spirit or someone had. Maybe the Terence in the room was just a robot replica.

An amazing thing hit me, just then. Poch's gun was in a cupboard just beside me. I was hiding in another one and heard every word they said. My shaking hand lifted the dark pistol up. I was only eleven years old, but I could do it. I could kill them, like I killed the doctor's eye in the hospital.

Suddenly, bam! The bullet flew out of the cupboard and shot Terence in the leg.

"Show yourself, Amelia!" Jeanie screamed.

Finally, I got enough courage to talk. "So, Jeanie, how's life?" I asked, carefully not letting my voice crack. I heard she had a gun too and she was reloading it.

"That doesn't matter! Now where are you?" she snapped.

"I saw Cecelia a couple weeks ago. She said she misses you," I babbled on.

"How the hell do you know about Cecelia?" she snapped. That was one of the first times I had heard Jeanie swear.

"She came over. Don't you care about her at all?" I asked. Jeanie paused.

"No, not at all," she snapped.

"Why not? You haven't seen her since she was five, if then, I suppose," I guessed. "If you even bothered to go back home she'd be delighted, but I guess you're so focused on killing me that you don't want to make her day, or your dad's either. Only if you put the gun down, I could tell you where they are, and maybe where your mother is too," I gulped.

"No, get your filthy self out here so I can kill you," she snapped. There had to be some type of internet in this cabinet. Finally, I found a rusty old laptop and went to my favorite search engine.

"What's your mother's name?" I asked.

"Lassette Banlisa," she blurted out. Lassette Banlisa. I typed it out. A picture of a woman around fifty popped up with blonde hair and a whole family tree website.

Jeanie Banlisa was her daughter. Not much luck for both of them, really. Who would want a daughter like Jeanie, and Jeanie, she was just plain out dumped. Nowhere in life would she find a comfortable place. Then it said Lassette lived in Dublin, Ireland.

"Your mother lives in Ireland," I said and sneaked my way to the piano room without Jeanie noticing. Quietly, I grabbed Esther and went outside. "Katrina, please, I'll pay you back a million if you take me up to my room," I whisper.

"This one time," Katrina appeared and took me up. I thought I was safe in my room, but Jeanie kicked down the door.

"Oh, so, little Amelia, how have you been? Have you missed me?" Jeanie asked.

Why did I ever ask to go up?

"No one will help you now, but you've tried to kill me. As my mother always said, *'Un peu non meurs.'*" Jeanie quoted and sauntered forward to kill me. Katrina was right behind her with a butcher knife.

"You're right, but some of the dead ones kill the living," Katrina whispered and Jeanie was shocked there was another person there. Katrina slit open Jeanie's neck, and Jeanie fell to the ground.

Terence came up behind Katrina and grabbed her by the neck. Katrina acted like she couldn't breathe. "Well, well, well, Amelia, we meet again." Terence's white teeth shone as Katrina continued to "struggle."

"Your little friend here is going to go bye-bye in a second if you don't volunteer to let me kill you and your family," he said, thinking I'd say not to kill her.

"Fine, go ahead and kill her," I suggested.

"Are you serious? You're just going to let her die like that?" he curiously wondered.

"Yeah, um, bye!" I said and waved to her.

"Wow, sorry kid," he apologized to Katrina. She easily broke out of his grip.

"You don't mess with the undead!" she screamed and held Terence up with her single hand.

He fell unconscious and Katrina started to eat his body.

"What are you doing?" I asked.

"I have to eat something, Amy. It's either this or a brick," she said and blood got all over her face. She was gone in a flash. Ew. That was the most disgusting thing I had seen in my life.

"Amy, how did you get in here?" Poch asked, running towards me, squeezing me.

"I... don't know. I guess I climbed," I lied.

"I'm just glad you're safe. Now, I want you to stay home from school tomorrow. After what you just did you need a day to stay home," he sighed. "Go watch a movie or something. Is your sister still asleep?" he asked and took her from my arms.

"Yeah, sleeping like a baby," I joked. Downstairs, I turned on a movie to help me relax. I was still shaking.

Katrina appeared on the couch next to me. "Can I sleep in your room tonight?" she asked.

"Sure," I whispered and she was gone. Soon, I fell asleep with the swans dancing in the moonlight.

In the morning, Esther shook me awake because she wanted to show me a new swan. "Cool, Esther, why don't you name them?" I signed.

"I do. This one's name is Jeanie," she said. "She grants all your wishes but if you are mean to her, she will eat you," Esther explained. She went on to the next one. "This is called Hurri-Kat because she's named after a hurricane and her name it Katrina.

"My favorite is the one that is like a girl named Mary. She's not like the others, though. She's a black swan in all the places she's supposed to be white and she's red in the places she's supposed to be black," Esther explained happily.

"That's it, Esther! No more swans, I don't want to hear about it!" I screamed at her and made my expression harsh.

Esther burst out crying and crawled to Poch.

"Amy, don't tell her she can't draw her birds," Poch complained. "Of course you can draw whatever you want," he signed to Esther.

"But Poch, I mean Dad, you need to look at these swans. They each represent someone who I know is dead, Dad. She said the devil takes people's souls or something and turns them into swans to be slaves. And then, she says that the birds taught her how to play the piano and she's playing Tchaikovsky!" I yelled.

"Honey, a one-year-old can't play professional music, and you know that," he said.

"No, she can. Trust me," I begged.

"No, Amy," he replied, and the conversation was over.

When the clocked ticked 3:30 I ran over to Scout's house. She should be home from school by now. Scout opened the door and nearly shut it again.

"Scout, wait!" I pleaded.

"Wow, so look who's crawling back? What do you want, Amy? I thought you hated me," she snapped.

"Scout, I'm sorry. I was depressed, my dad was getting married again and having another kid, so I just was ignoring everybody and going into my shell and I thought that would make everything better, but it didn't," I gushed out.

"I don't care. You don't do things like that," she grumbled. Scout had gotten a lot skinnier and taller. She was almost six inches taller than me now, unlike her stocky old self.

"If there's any way I can pay you back, tell me. I really need to talk to you," I begged.

"Go spout that crap to someone else. Did you know how bad I felt that day you locked me out of your room? I thought you would just completely hate me forever. Who's going to be hated forever now? That's right, you," she snapped and slammed the door.

"Scout, please," I begged and pounded on the door.

Clara opened the door after a moment. "Oh, Amy, I'm sorry, but we've made a rule in the house. I can't let you talk to Scout," Clara apologized like she didn't care and almost shut the door again.

"Well, what's the rule?" I ask.

"You can't come into our house. You broke Scout's heart, and I'm afraid I don't want you in my home and neither does my husband," Clara said and clicked the door shut. Great.

I walked over to Veronica's house and knocked on her door. I was expecting her mom to open the door. "Is Veronica here?" I asked.

"Ronny, someone's here to see you!" Mrs. Beploe yelled and Veronica came down.

"Oh, Amy, um, sorry, but, um, I'm sort of busy right now," Veronica said.

"No, you ain't little girl! Get yo' butt outta here!" Mrs. Beploe sassed her and kicked her out.

"What do you want?" Veronica snapped when we were both outside in the wind.

"Can I talk to you?" I asked.

"Why? I thought you hated everybody now," Veronica snapped.

"I'm sorry, I was just, well, my dad was getting remarried without me knowing and now he's having another kid. I thought ignoring everybody would solve the problem, but obviously it didn't," I explained. "Please, talk to me. Scout doesn't even let me in her house anymore, and I just really need to talk to someone," I begged.

"Fine," she grumbled and we walked out into the cold.

Chapter Sixteen - The End

"What do you need to talk about?" she asked.

"This sounds really, really crazy, but I think I know how the devil possesses people," I said as we walked down the street.

"What? Linda Blair?" she teased.

"No, they turn into swans. And I didn't just make this up. My little sister can see the swans and pictures of evil swans are all over the house. It's really creepy," I shivered and we walked around the neighborhood slowly.

"Why do you want to tell me this?" Veronica asked.

"Because I really needed to tell someone who would have a slight chance of believing me. You need to come to my house and you can tell who the swans represent," I said.

We walked back to my house and immediately Veronica saw who the swans were. "This is so weird. How can a one-year-old know this?" she asked.

I shrugged. "They have such good imaginations, it brings things to life." After that, we talked a little more and Veronica knew everything about the Gloma. She really believed it, too, I could tell.

That night, I dreamt about the swans again. But this time it was everybody I knew who turned into a swan. Did that mean we were all going to die?

Alisha woke me up saying we needed to get ready for the wedding because it was next week and we were having it in our back yard. I had to wear a stupid white dress that went down to my knees with "pretty" little straps for shoulders.

"Oh, Amy! You're going to just be in love with these shoes I got you!" Alisha squealed.

"Yippee," I said sarcastically in a glum voice.

"Cheer up," Alisha ordered.

In the back yard, there were chairs all over and a big white sheet of clear cloth was thrown over the trees for decoration. The bridesmaids were Alisha's sisters Holly, Sierra and Anne. The groomsmen were Jason, Poch's cousin Hernandez, who was a little Mexican, and Poch's best friend Uncle Jay, (who Jason was named after).

There was a whole bunch of photographers and blah, I didn't like it at all. Alisha chose me to be one of the flower girls which wasn't fair. I hated helping in weddings. When the music started to play I was supposed to throw the flowers on the ground and make a mess, but I just stood there.

"Go, Amy," one of the bridesmaids urged.

"Shut up. I don't even know who you are," I snapped.

Slowly, I started throwing the flower pedals. Behind me, Alisha cried in happiness. Suddenly, I felt if anything went wrong in this wedding, it would be my fault. While I was thinking this, I tripped over some twigs. Everybody was looking at me like I was an idiot. Then, I started shaking uncontrollably. There was somebody who was going to kill Poch. Was it Jeanie? No.

"Somebody get her inside!" I heard somebody yell. Who were they talking about? Poch came and picked me up.

"It's okay, Amy, it's going to be okay," he kept murmuring in my ear. For some reason, I suddenly got into my bed. There was a glass of water on my night table and pictures of swans all over the floor.

"Amy, you're awake!" Poch sighed relief.

"Yeah, what happened to the wedding? Why am I in my bed?" I asked.

"You had a blackout, Amy. It's where you've been so overwhelmed, it just comes out of you and you black out," he whispered.

"How do you know that?" I asked, sitting up.

"Alisha told me," Poch answered.

"Poch, I mean Dad, it wasn't being stressed that made me black out," I began.

"Yes it was. Now go back to sleep," he ordered like he knew the truth. Poch stomped out of the room.

My phone rang. "Hello?" I asked.

"Hello, Amy, this is Emily. There's been a news breakout and one of Jeanie's agents is tracking down everybody who was on Jeanie's little list and getting really close to them. Then, she slaughters them, very harshly. Please, do not get close to anybody, and you will be transferred to somewhere besides Washington," Emily chirped.

"Wait, what agent?" I asked.

"Um, all we know is that she has dark skin," she said.

"Do you know anything else?" I asked but she had already hung up.

On the floor, I picked up one of the many pictures of swans. The one I picked up looked like a male. I got out of bed and looked for Esther. She was by the piano, finger picking part of Swan Lake with Alisha right beside her. When she was done, Alisha clapped.

"Esther, play the real thing," I signed after I tapped on her shoulder.

"You, in bed... now," Alisha ordered.

"I'm showing you something," I muttered and showed Esther what to do.

"Esther, what is she talking about?" Alisha asked. Esther had learned to lip read and she shrugged. "Amy, just go back to bed," Alisha ordered.

"What happened?" I asked.

"You started shaking at the wedding and had a blackout," she answered and cradled Esther.

"Follow me," I ordered Esther. Gratefully, Alisha didn't know what I said and Esther followed me. Once in my room, I turned around and faced her. "Who is this?" I asked and held up the swan picture that was a boy.

"That's Daddy," she answered.

"When you're a swan, what does that mean?" I signed.

"You died and came back to life. But if you are like the daddy swan, it means that you will die and never, ever come back," she answered.

"When is Daddy going to die?" I asked. She shrugged.

"How is he going to die?" I asked after a moment of quiet.

"He'll get killed by Alisha," she signed and walked away. Alisha? No, she wouldn't kill him.

I took the boxes in my room out to the car and we drove away to houses available in New Jersey. We finally found one in Princeton and we drove home from the real estate agent's office.

"Alisha, I know what you're going to do, so you can leave," I said when we were alone in the kitchen.

"What's that?" she chirped.

"You can leave, there's a door right there," I whispered.

"Hmm, you said you wanted me to leave? I can easily get you in trouble for that," she warned and showed me the knife she was cutting some chicken with, giving me clues.

"No, I don't want you to leave right now, but I do know you are going to do something horrible to us," I inferred.

"Like what?" Alisha leaned forward. I didn't answer.

"That's what I thought," she grinned and went back to cutting.

As we pulled into our new driveway, Emily gave us our new names. "Alright, Amy, your name is going to be Alicia. Alisha, your name is going to be Berry. David, your name is going to be Howard. Jason, your name will be Toby. And little baby Esther's name is going to be Delilah!"

"This will be okay," Poch promised.

"No it's not. There's something you don't know... about something." I hesitated. Alisha gave me a warning glare.

"You know what? You've been acting weird lately so I'm just going to not trust you until you get back to normal," he muttered.

There were only two rooms, so 'Toby', 'Delilah' and I had to share one room. The only extra bedroom was supposed to be 'Howard's' office. Our room was small, and I couldn't fit all my stuff on one dresser, my bed, and my part of the wall, so a lot of stuff was thrown out.

The house was smaller, too. One flight of stairs, a small kitchen, a living room about the size of a large hot tub, and a dining room the size of five horses squashed together was the downstairs. Upstairs were my room, Poch's and Alisha's room, and a small office.

Autumn and Clarence, the puppies, we had to sell.

"Don't worry, Ames, I mean Alicia. Everything will be fine, and Jeanie's agent won't come near us, I swear," Poch promised.

"Yeah," I agreed; I left out, *She's closer than you think, Poch. Alisha is going to make your insides live on your outsides.*

"Alisha, I know what you're going to do, so you can leave," I said when we were alone in the kitchen.

"What's that?" she chirped.

"You can leave, there's a door right there," I whispered.

"Hmm, you said you wanted me to leave? I can easily get you in trouble for that," she warned and showed me the knife she was cutting chicken with, giving me clues.

"No, I don't want you to leave right now, but I do know you are going to do something horrible to us," I inferred.

"Like what?" Alisha leaned forward. I didn't answer.

"That's what I thought," she grinned and went back to cutting.

A couple months later, when it was edging toward the end of April, I came home from school and saw Poch, bloody and dead on the kitchen floor. "Poch!" I yelled and sank down to him. "Wake up," I whispered, but he wouldn't. I shook him. No reply. I ran to Alisha.

"Why'd you do that to him?" I yelled and shoved Alisha down. She hit her head on the sharp part of the kitchen counter.

"Ow," she whispered and touched her head. She glared at me.

"Huh? Why'd you do that?" I screamed as tears streaked down my face and my throat got thick. I'd already thought he died once, and twice was too much.

"You knew what was going to happen, Amelia. You killed my husband, and now I'll kill you," Alisha grumbled.

"I didn't kill your husband! What are you talking about?" I sobbed.

"You killed my Terence!" she yelled.

"You were married to Terence?" I asked, bewildered.

"Yes, we both worked for Jeanie and she thought it would be good to get as close as possible to you or one of your friends. And about being pregnant, that was all a lie. My real kids are Harley and Tatum, also known as Nina and Cash," she said in a soothing voice.

My backpack fell off and I fell to the floor along with it, slamming down on the hard, cold kitchen floor. Finding this out was as shocking as being struck by lightning. I didn't think the babies were that unlucky.

Alisha walked over to me and took her shiny clean kitchen knife. Then, everything went blank, and I felt a shocking pain run through my back. I realized I was being stabbed. My eyes drifted close as I went into the darkness with swans dancing behind me.

Was this the end to all my problems? Or was it just one more? I didn't know. But slowly, I slid into more darkness, almost enough so I couldn't think.

Alisha whispered in my ear. "Rot in pain, Amelia Rae."

And that was it.

For now.

Coming Soon...

Book II: Toy Boxes

CPSIA information can be obtained
at www.ICGtesting.com
Printed in the USA
FSOW01n2047211014
3273FS

9 780982 992043